Aldeburgh Studies in M

General Editor: Paul Banl

*Volume 2*

# The Travel Diaries of Peter Pears

## 1936–1978

Peter Pears in Japan, February 1956. (Photo: Z. Kaimasu)

# The Travel Diaries
# of Peter Pears

## 1936–1978

EDITED BY

## Philip Reed

THE BOYDELL PRESS

THE BRITTEN–PEARS LIBRARY

First published 1995 by The Boydell Press, Woodbridge
in conjunction with
The Britten–Pears Library, Aldeburgh
Reprinted in paperback 1999


ISBN  0 85115 364 X hardback
ISBN  0 85115 741 6 paperback


Aldeburgh Studies in Music
ISSN 0969–3548


The Boydell Press is an imprint of Boydell & Brewer Ltd
PO Box 9, Woodbridge, Suffolk IP12 3DF, UK
and of Boydell & Brewer Inc.
PO Box 41026, Rochester, NY 14604–4126, USA
website: http://www.boydell.co.uk


A catalogue record for this title is available
from the British Library

Library of Congress Catalog Card Number: 95–3357


This publication is printed on acid-free paper

Printed and bound in Great Britain by
Athenaeum Press Ltd, Gateshead, Tyne & Wear.

# Contents

# Foreword

Peter Pears was a true patrician. He was a man of wide culture, which expressed itself in all aspects of his life: in his music-making, in his bearing, in his knowledgeable appreciation of all the arts, in his taste and sense of values. His many interests spanned cricket, good food and wine: he regarded as his greatest triumph the day that he scored 81 in a county trial test at the Oval in 1928; and he not only enjoyed fine food, but was also an inventive cook himself.

To think of him solely as one of the greatest singing artists of his time is to ignore the other many talents he possessed. His interest in early music brought to light composers who were neglected at that time: for instance, works by Schütz and Pérotin, by Dowland and the Elizabethans were championed by Pears. Through his unique performing artistry, he revealed these and other masters to the concert-going public. He commissioned new works from young composers to include in his repertory and gave many first performances of contemporary music. Quite apart from Britten works, the list of premières Pears gave is long and distinguished, encompassing over forty different composers.

As well as possessing a fine musician's ear, Pears had a remarkable eye for the visual arts. As in music, his informed enthusiasm ranged from the early and classical to the new and contemporary. He could guide one through the treasures of Venice with consummate expertise, often to places seldom frequented by tourists. On the other hand, his eye for works by young artists was keen and adventurous, spotting a talent before it had become generally recognized. Over the years he assembled a remarkable collection of paintings and pieces of sculpture which reflected his wide and eclectic taste.

His profession took him to many parts of the world where he took the opportunity to observe and absorb other cultures. Both musically and visually, the Far East was an eye- and ear-opener. It was a very different India he experienced from the one his ancestors served in as military men and civil servants. His diaries recount particularly vividly his several visits to Russia. Germany was a country to which he frequently returned, and over the years his use of the language became fluent – not always faultless, but always expressive! At the age of sixty-four he made his début at the Metropolitan Opera, singing in the U.S. première of *Death in Venice*, and four years later he appeared there as Captain Vere in *Billy Budd*; these final visits to New York were a triumphant rounding-off of his career in a country he had first toured as part of a vocal sextet some forty years earlier.

Pears enjoyed his travels and, quite apart from his professional itineraries, he visited many parts of the world for relaxation and exploration. 'I wonder as I wander', the unaccompanied song which he sang so memorably, could indeed sum up much of his character.

But he returned to base in Aldeburgh, to the home he shared with Benjamin Britten, and to the partnership which gave the world some of the greatest music of our time. There he studied the new works which the composer had written for him. There the two musicians rehearsed their recital programmes – the great Schubert and Schumann cycles, and the rest of their extensive repertoire. There they planned the Aldeburgh Festival, in which they gave so many unforgettable performances of music ranging from before Bach to Britten and after. In the last years of his life he taught at his beloved School at Snape (the Britten–Pears School for Advanced Musical Studies), handing on his musicianship and wide performing experience to a new generation of singers. There he died the day after giving a masterclass on Bach's *St Matthew Passion* – his own noble interpretation of the Evangelist being one of his most outstanding achievements.

This is not the place to enumerate Peter Pears's repertoire, nor to eulogize his artistry. The *Festschrift* published on his 75th birthday contains tributes from fellow artists and friends, and lists his performances and recordings. But let it be said, whatever he sang, whether one of Britten's great operatic roles, a Schumann song, a Mozart aria or a simple folksong, his consummate phrasing, colouring and timing and the clarity of his diction expressed the music in an inevitable way. His musical authority and imagination, his integrity and intelligence, his impeccable taste, must indeed have gratified and delighted his composers as much as it did his audiences.

Marion Thorpe
London, September 1994

# Editorial Method and Acknowledgements

*The texts of the diaries*

Those diaries which were published in Pears's lifetime and supervised by him adhere to the style of their original publication in all matters of spelling, punctuation and layout. These principles apply to Chapters 5, 9 and 10. Two further diaries were published by Pears in edited forms, *Moscow Christmas* (Chapter 6) and *The New York Death in Venice* (Chapter 11); in the case of the former, only slight editorial suppressions were made by Pears (see p. 135); the latter, however, first appeared in a substantially revised format. In both instances, I have chosen to return to Pears's manuscript drafts as the textual source.

The remaining diaries replicate throughout Pears's idiosyncratic punctuation, abbreviations and spelling; occasionally, for the sake of clarity of meaning, obvious mistakes have been silently corrected. All underlined text in diaries and letters has been denoted herein, as is usual, by italics. The Appendix faithfully adheres to Pears's German.

In Chapters 2 and 4 editorial interventions have been made to sustain the flow of Pears's narrative. The interpolated text is enclosed within square brackets [ ].

The use of a $^{\S}$ in an annotation indicates that supplementary information may be found in the Personalia (pp. 214–26).

The present volume would have been impossible without the generous cooperation and encouragement of Sir Peter Pears's executors – the late Isador Caplan, Dr Donald Mitchell, and Marion Thorpe – and their fellow trustees of the Britten–Pears Foundation. To this executorial triumvirate and to their colleagues on the board of trustees, I extend my warmest acknowledgements. Further thanks must be expressed specifically to two of Pears's executors. I am pleased to acknowledge with special gratitude the contribution made to this volume by Marion Thorpe, a long-standing friend of both Pears and Britten, who not only provided the Foreword but kindly undertook to translate the idiosyncratic German of Pears's Ansbach diary into idiomatic English. I owe a debt of gratitude to Donald Mitchell who read through, and commented on, an early draft of the book. Throughout the project, I have been mindful of our work together over the last ten years and of how much I have learned from him during our editing of the Britten letters and diaries. Much of that experience has informed the commentary in the present volume.

Throughout the course of the project I have been conscious of the invaluable assistance rendered by the Librarian, Prof. Paul Banks, and his staff at the Britten–Pears Library, Aldeburgh. To Paul Banks, General Editor of the

Aldeburgh Studies in Music series, I owe a special debt of gratitude: not only has he been a daily source of information and sound advice, but has read through and commented in detail on all the earlier drafts of the book. Many of his suggestions have been shamelessly incorporated into the final text; any outstanding errors, of course, remain my own responsibility. I am also grateful to Judith Henderson, Cataloguer (Britten–Pears Library), for the provision of the index.

A special expression of thanks should be voiced to my friend and collaborator Dr Mervyn Cooke. Without the ground-breaking work undertaken by Dr Cooke, my task in dealing with Pears's diary of the trip to the Far East (Chapter 2) would have been infinitely harder. As this book goes to press, I am pleased to be able to report that Dr Cooke's study of the relationship between Britten and the musics of the Far East will be the subject of a forthcoming volume in this series.

I am pleased to acknowledge the courteous assistance of Richard Barber and the staff of Boydell & Brewer in seeing the volume through the press. Richard Barber's belief in this project and in the series as a whole has been a welcome aspect of our discussions.

Finally, I wish to thank the following individuals and institutions for the help given me throughout the preparation of the volume: Eileen Bell; Sally Blake; Herrick Bunney; Jill Burrows; Cathy Carson (London Symphony Orchestra); Rosemary Chase; Reginald Close; Sheila Colvin (Aldeburgh Foundation); John Cornish; Jeremy Cullum; Embassy of the Federal Republic of Germany (Cultural Department); Sharon Goddard; Goethe Institute, London; Indian Institute Library, Oxford (Dr Gillian Evison); Institute of Commonwealth Studies, London (David Blake); Yukiko Kishinami (London and Tokyo); Prof. Ludmila Kovnatskaya (St Petersburg); Kara Lyttle; Mark Lyttle; Prof. Edward Mendelson (New York); Mexican Embassy (Cultural Department); National Art Library, Victoria and Albert Museum; NHK, Tokyo (M. Sakamoto, Akira Sugama); Sue Phipps; Royal Horticultural Society; Royal Institute of British Architects (Mary Nixon); Royal Scottish National Orchestra (Paul Hughes); Dr Eric Roseberry; Humphrey Stone; Janet Stone; Rosamund Strode; Syd Swan; Theodor and Jean Uppman.

Extracts from Britten's and Pears's correspondence are © 1995 the Trustees of the Britten–Pears Foundation and may not be further reproduced without written permission; they appear in the present volume by kind permission. The extracts in Chapter 2 from *Ausflug Ost* by Prince Ludwig of Hesse and the Rhine appear by kind permission of his widow, HRH Princess Margaret of Hesse and the Rhine. I am further grateful to Princess Margaret for permission to include Pears's Ansbach diary (Chapter 3 and Appendix).

Every effort has been made to trace copyright holders. I should be glad, however, to hear from those that I have been unable to locate or have inadvertently omitted, to whom I extend my apologies.

Philip Reed
Suffolk
September 1994

# List of Illustrations

Frontispiece: Peter Pears in Japan, February 1956. (Photo: Z. Kaimasu)

*Between pages 114 and 115*

1    The New English Singers, 1936. Left to right: Mary Morris, Eric Greene, Peter Pears, Dorothy Silk, Cuthbert Kelly and Nellie Carson.

2    A new English singer: Pears in the 1930s. (Photo: Polyfoto)

3    Arrival at Bombay, 13 December 1955: Pears and Britten with their hosts.

4    Britten and Pears after one of their recitals in Surabaja. (Photo: Nikola Drakulic, Surabaja)

5    Ubud, Bali, 20 January 1956. Pears, Prince Ludwig, Princess Margaret and Britten pose in traditional Balinese costume. Princess Margaret described this occasion in a letter the next day:

> Our very primitive life . . . in Ubud continued to be very colourful. [Our host] made us put on Balinese dress and be photographed. I . . . wrapped in a sarong with a lace curtain over my ample bust, beautiful gardenias in my hair (a false *black* pigtail had been added) looked too stupid for words. Ben also togged up looked like a governess at a fancy dress. Peter looked like a Rhine Maiden and Lu like a *Fasching* Rajah! We laughed so much we could hardly be photographed!

6    Macau, 4 February 1956. Britten and Pears are congratulated by the Portuguese Governor after their recital in the eighteenth-century theatre.

7    Arrival at Tokyo, 8 February 1956. (Photo: NHK, Tokyo)

8    Press conference, Tokyo, 9 February 1956. (Photo: NHK, Tokyo)

9    Tokyo, 9 February 1956. Pears's and Britten's first recital on television. (Photo: NHK, Tokyo)

# List of Abbreviations

BPL        Britten–Pears Library, Aldeburgh

CHPP     Christopher Headington, *Peter Pears: A Biography* (London: Faber and Faber, 1992)

DMPR    Donald Mitchell and Philip Reed (eds), *Letters from a Life: The Selected Letters and Diaries of Benjamin Britten 1913–1976*, Volumes 1 and 2 (London: Faber and Faber, 1991)

GV         Galina Vishnevskaya, *Galina: A Russian Story* (London: Hodder and Stoughton, 1984)

MC        Mervyn Cooke, *Oriental Influences in the Music of Benjamin Britten*, PhD diss. (King's College, Cambridge, 1988)

PFL       Donald Mitchell and John Evans, *Pictures from a Life: Benjamin Britten 1913–1976* (London: Faber and Faber, 1978)

PPT      Marion Thorpe (ed.), *Peter Pears: A Tribute on His 75th Birthday* (London: Faber Music/The Britten Estate, 1985)

TBB      Anthony Gishford (ed.), *Tribute to Benjamin Britten on His Fiftieth Birthday* (London: Faber and Faber, 1963)


*Library sigla*

GB-ALb   Britten–Pears Library, Aldeburgh

# 1 American Tour
## with the New English Singers (1936)

In 1936 Peter Pears made his first journey across the Atlantic to tour the United States and Canada as a member of the New English Singers, a vocal sextet specializing in Elizabethan madrigals and English folksongs. Their director, the English bass Cuthbert Kelly, had first formed a vocal quartet in 1917 following wartime concerts at the church of St Martin-in-the-Fields. Three years later, as the English Singers, the ensemble – now enlarged to six voices – toured the United States for the first time. In October 1932 Kelly formed a new group, the New English Singers, which Pears joined in 1936 while he was still a member of the BBC Singers 'B' (a vocal octet). Kelly's ensemble was popular with the public who enjoyed the informality of their concerts (the six singers were seated round a table in an Elizabethan manner). The personnel for the 1936 tour comprised: Dorothy Silk and Nellie Carson (sopranos); Mary Morris (contralto); Eric Greene and Pears (tenors), with Kelly (bass): see Plate 1.

Pears remained a member of the New English Singers until 1938, and made a second tour of the United States with the group between October 1937 and January 1938. He evidently enjoyed the experience of singing in a small ensemble and exploring repertoire not normally part of his work at the BBC. He subsequently formed three groups of his own on similar lines to the New English Singers: in 1939 the Round Table Singers, for whom Britten intended his Gerard Manley Hopkins settings, *A.M.D.G.*, and in 1941 the Elizabethan Singers, for whom Britten originally composed his *Hymn to St Cecilia*, Op. 27, although in fact he failed to complete the work in time for its scheduled première by them in New York (DMPR, pp. 694, 906–7). Much later, in 1967, Pears was to form the Wilbye Consort, another vocal ensemble modelled on these earlier groups (CHPP, pp. 260–61).

Pears probably began to write the diary of his first North American tour to alleviate the tedium of the Atlantic voyage. Once in the United States (they disembarked in New York on 14 November) the narrative continued for only four days before the pressures of being a busy professional singer on tour prevented Pears from continuing: there was simply not enough time. It was a pattern that he would occasionally follow in future years and in future diaries. Nevertheless, the text as the twenty-six-year-old Pears left it reflects much of his personality at this period in his life, a few months before he and Benjamin Britten were to enter more fully into each other's lives. His acute eye for observation of people and places, his opinions on colleagues and friends, his passion for art and literature, his delight in just living – all run like threads through this first diary.

The text of what Pears himself entitled *AMERICAN TOUR WITH "NEW ENGLISH SINGERS"* was never published in the singer's lifetime. Extracts appeared in Christopher Headington's 1992 biography of Pears (CHPP, pp. 55–62), but its inclusion in this volume is the first occasion the entire text has been made available. The original diary (*GB-ALb* 1-9400530) may be found in a notebook which Pears appears to have used between *c.*1934–6. Among its other contents is a list of Elizabethan madrigals (with comments) which probably relates to the New English Singers' repertory.

The diary ends on 17 November, less than a fortnight after its beginning and only a few days into the tour proper; but the tour was to continue until Christmas and the schedule given in Pears's pocket diary suggests that they gave concerts in Sackville, Nova Scotia (18 November), Winnipeg (22nd and 23rd), Saskatoon, Saskatchewan (25th), Edmonton (27th), Calgary (28th), Winona, Minnesota (1 December), Madison (2nd), Van Wert, Ohio (3rd), and New York (5th, at the Town Hall). Further engagements in New York included a broadcast on 20 December. While in New York Pears took advantage of the city's artistic life, apparently attending a performance of Kurt Weill's latest work, *Johnny Johnson*, then running at the 44th Street Theatre, and a concert given by the New York Philharmonic Orchestra conducted by John Barbirolli at Carnegie Hall on the 19th.

Pears sailed back to England on 26 December, arriving home on 3 January 1937. It was the end of his first North American tour and the longest period he had yet spent abroad. To celebrate their return to the UK, the New English Singers gave a concert at the Wigmore Hall on 19 February (see p. 15) which was enthusiastically received. Hubert Foss, writing in *The Sunday Times* (21 February 1937), described the occasion as 'one of unalloyed pleasure, for these artists have a rare understanding of liberty within the strict law operative in the period of their choice'.

*Friday November 6th 1936*

Boat should have started last night 12.0 but owing to fog at Hamburg was 12 hours late. Result: I spent last night in bed instead of in bunk. Left Waterloo 9.20 this morning. Trevor and Basil[1] got up, at, comparatively shriek of dawn and saw me off. Dear Anne[2] turned up at the platform and gave me a lovely red carnation. Eric[3] arrived at 9.17 AM but the train was still there. Cosy journey down; the country looking just as lovely as the South of England in November can – browns and greens of real quality and character – surely much more interesting for light effects than summer greenery or spring greenery-yallery. If not, why not? Constable loved this time of the year, so did Claude and Rembrandt. Why not Monet? Went on to the boat "Washington" at something before noon. One couldn't see much of her from outside (although she is truly less than half the tonnage of e.g. Queen Mary) but inside she is like a very good well run cheap Lyons hotel,[4] The Regent Palace perhaps, not quite so gaudy but very comfortable. Cabin small, but has a W.C. of its own ("Oh: That'll be useful!" said Cuthbert [Kelly]). The whole boat is obviously extremely efficiently got up, very much more so, I understand, than the Cunarders. (Poor old England!). Mr. Taylor (some official of the Cunard line?, also singer semi pro?) was helping us get on board. Nice man in an unassuming way. Stayed to lunch, which was really pretty good. There was a magnificent menu from which one could (embarrassingly enough) choose anything. Clam Chowder for me. Very good Ice Cream. Vanilla of America is not quite the same as the English variety, a bit coarser, but the ice as velvety as possible. Good stories from Cuthbert:

1. Charles Lamb,[5] crossing the channel, buttonholed by a bore who told him at length of a man who could guarantee to cure his stammering. Charles couldn't get a word until the flood stopped. Then "I kn-n-n-now th-that m-m-man," he said quietly. "He c-c-c-cured me!"

---

1    Trevor Harvey[§] (1911–1989), English conductor, and Basil Douglas[§] (1914–1992), English musical administrator, who shared a flat with Pears at 105 Charlotte Street, London W1, from 1935 to 1938.

2    Anne Wood[§] (b. 1907), English contralto and a friend and colleague of Pears's in the BBC Singers during the 1930s.

3    Eric Greene (1904–1966), English tenor, noted for his interpretation of the role of the Evangelist in the Bach Passions.

4    The Lyons Hotels were an extension of the company's famous Corner Houses and teashops, popular centres for eating and meeting in the 1930s.

5    Charles Lamb (1775–1834), English essayist and humourist. The *Dictionary of National Biography* reports that Lamb 'was afflicted . . . all his life with a bad stutter, and the eagerness to forget the impediment, which put him at a disadvantage in all conversations, probably further encouraged the habit.'

2. Calverley,[6] progged at Cambridge, said to the proctors who detained him, "Gentlemen, may I just say one word?" "Certainly, sir, what you like." – "Damn!"

3. Casals[7] before a concert (with George Reeves)[8] quietly smokes his pipe until the boy calls him, then gently takes his pipe out of his mouth, puts it on the table, walks over to Reeves, picking up his cello and bow, and saying "Calm! now keep calm! quite calm!", he walks on to the platform and plays like an angel.

According to Eric, Dorothy[9] is the complete prima donna who must be petted and looked after continually, or else she gets depressed and doesn't sing well.

Lovely greys of receding Southhampton docks. A ship with a purple hull and vermilion funnels looks lovely from about 300 yards. The tracery of the cranes is like Bruges lace – very fine and spiky. Very sleepy at about 5 p.m. Read Proust[10] lazily till excellent supper 7.30, lovely melon. Little rehearsal after. Wrote to Ma,[11] Anne, & B[asil] & T[revor].

*von Zu Mühlen*[12] (?) famous lieder singer and teacher, when asked if he sang French songs: "Yes: I sing French songs! I wriggle my bottom a leetle and I sing French songs!"

Sylvia Townsend Warner[13] is just like Lolly Willowes; witch-like, with broad hat and high heels, she grows herbs in a cottage in Dorset.

*Saturday November 7th* (1st Letters to Ma; P.C. to T&B, & Anne.)
A poor night. Ship rolling a good deal. Very hot in the cabin, and Eric and I slept two hours between us. Took Mothersill – soothing result, but no need really. Happy lying down, not so good sitting and standing. Reached Queenstown [Cóbh, Eire] at about 10. 3hrs late. Most beautiful

---

[6] Charles Stuart Calverly (1831–1884), English poet, parodist and Latin scholar.
[7] Pablo (Pau) Casals (1876–1973), Catalan cellist, who was well known for his extreme nervous tension before playing in public.
[8] English pianist (1895–1960).
[9] Dorothy Silk§ (1883–1942), English soprano.
[10] Pears was reading *A la recherche du temps perdu* during the voyage, in C.K. Scott-Moncrieff's English translation (published between 1922 and 1931).
[11] Pears's mother, Jessie Elizabeth de Visne Pears (1869–1947).
[12] Raimund von Zur Mühlen (1854–1931), German tenor who settled in Britain and became a prominent teacher.
[13] English writer§ (1893–1978), whose second novel, *Lolly Willowes*, is described in the *Dictionary of National Biography* as a 'deft and fanciful elaboration on the themes of witchcraft', and was an immense success on both sides of the Atlantic after its publication in 1926.

with lovely downs round it – all very brown and green. Wind getting stronger every moment, rough crossing in prospect. Sweet old man with lovely daughter played cornet on the tender, which came to fetch and bring passengers. Queenstown rather lovely, old slate and stone town with a big church in a good position; a few houses with coloured washes. A lovely green island in the bay.

Eric: Steuart[14] is essentially an intelligent artist, but in his younger days his voice was better than any of the Heddles and Parrys.[15] Gervase Elwes[16] used to stand as still as a post, with an occasional sway or shutting of the eyes. Always sang Gerontius without a score. E. thought there was a good part for me in John in [Elgar's] The Apostles.

Cinema started at 11.45 in the lounge. Looked in but packed for a bad Powell–Harlow–Loy–Tracy film,[17] and rolling uncomfortable. All the travellers on this boat have sallow complexions: why? Cuthbert adores ice cream, perhaps the Americans do too. Two g-l bell boys: q?[18]

Proust going along nicely; very disturbing but far more fascinating, occasionally overdone. All his love complex for his mother rings absolutely true. Will he turn homosexual? Perhaps H.'s always love their mothers so much that they renounce everyone else of her sex, for her, and in frustration go H. Not very likely.

Cuthbert: "These seems seem wondrous, yet more wondrous I".[19] True of every artist; the person counts, not the thing painted.

Why is A so difficult to sing, while A♭ & B♭ are much easier (out of proportion)? Should like time to practise, but my voice can still do with no singing.

---

[14]  Steuart Wilson§ (1889–1966), English tenor and administrator, and a distant relative of Pears (he was the son of Pears's father's first cousin).

[15]  Heddle Nash§ (1896–1961), English tenor, and Parry Jones§ (1891–1963), Welsh tenor.

[16]  Gervase Elwes (1866–1921), English tenor, who was closely associated with the name role in Elgar's The Dream of Gerontius, which he sang for the first time in 1904.

[17]  American actors William Powell (1892–1984), Jean Harlow (1911–1937), Myrna Loy (1905–1993) and Spencer Tracy (1900–1967), who starred together in the 1936 comedy Libelled Lady.

[18]  I.e. 'good-looking' and 'queer' (gay).

[19]  Recte: 'These things seem wondrous, yet more wondrous, I', a line from the refrain of Thomas Weelkes's six-voice madrigal, 'Thule: the period of cosmography'. The piece was in the repertory of the New English Singers.

Memorata: Gerhardt:[20] Harty[21] is a little mad, but a fine musician, and the best English accompanist since the war.

I must remember even in talking to push out my lower jaw to the full. Six more days on this boat is like being condemned to stay in one hotel for a week, without going outside it; or doing nothing but singing one song all day for a week. Quite comfortable but limited. Thinking of setting "She's like the Swallow" for 6 voices.[22] Lunch. Then lie down and good sleep. Tea and crossword in Dorothy's cabin. She is holding out well. Mary [Morris] has not appeared since lunch.

Ship moving more and more. A small breather on deck then supper and bed. A note from Frau Mayer[23] asking me to meet her if well enough, but won't risk it yet. Slept like a log.

---

[20] Elena Gerhardt (1883–1961), German mezzo-soprano (originally soprano), who settled in England in 1934. Pears studied with Gerhardt for a short time in 1937; her name first appears in his pocket engagement diary on 16 January.

[21] Sir Hamilton Harty (1879–1941), Irish composer, conductor and pianist. Although chiefly remembered today as a conductor of remarkably diverse repertory, he was also a gifted accompanist from his earliest days as a professional musician.

[22] It would seem that Pears was contemplating an arrangement of the Newfoundland folksong for the New English Singers; however, no such arrangement survives. We are reminded here of Pears's early ambitions as a composer. Earlier in 1936, Anne Wood had already included a song by 'Luard Pears' in a recital at the Grotrian Hall, London, on 27 March, a setting of Robert Nicholls' 'When within my arms I hold you', and Pears composed several other songs during this period. Some of these are now lost, but at least one, 'Take, O take those lips away' (1931), survives in manuscript at BPL and was revived in 1984 by Graham Johnson and the Songmakers Almanac at a Wigmore Hall concert celebrating Pears's career. The programme also contained an arrangement by Pears of the Appalachian song 'Soldier, soldier won't you marry me', dating from July 1936. Among Pears's other compositions at this time was an unfinished orchestral setting of T.S. Eliot's *The Journey of the Magi*, a text that Britten was to set in 1971 as his *Canticle IV*, Op. 86.

Pears himself recalled his efforts as a composer to Donald Mitchell in 1985: 'At Lancing I was interested in the idea of being a composer, and I did write a few songs, and in fact I went on a very, very little; I mean, it was only a handful of songs; I knew I was never really going to be a composer.' (*The Tenor Man's Story*, by Donald Mitchell and Barrie Gavin, Central Television, 1985.)

It is of interest to note that in 1976, during the last year of his life, Britten set 'She's like the swallow' for Pears and the Welsh harpist Osian Ellis, very possibly at Pears's behest. It was subsequently published as the second of *Eight Folk Song Arrangements* (Faber Music, 1980).

[23] Elizabeth Mayer$ (1884–1970), who with her husband, the doctor and psychiatrist William Mayer, and their family – two sons (Michael and Christopher) and two daughters (Beata and Ulrica) – were to become the most important figures in Pears's and Britten's lives during their period in the United States between 1939 and 1942.

*Sunday November 8th*
An excellent bath at 8.45 (9.45, clock back one hour each day). Up for breakfast. Went on deck afterwards. Huge rollers: rough perhaps very rough sea. Ship moving a lot. Fresh air lovely, but bed more comfortable. Atmosphere below quite odious after fresh sea air, but I find myself altogether too self-centred to worry about what is good for me. Give me comfort every time. So back to my cabin and my bed. Passenger list shows a collection of the oddest names possible, and a news sheet gives one an idea of American journalist. A good heading: "Landon admits [*illegible word*] paddling was helpful", and a very funny article about Abyssinian Missionaries. Noticeable mixture of scientific earnest information of the more remote type and undigested sensationalism. Notice: on German circular about baggage wichtig spelt wichtich, c.f. socks and sox.

I can see myself lying down for the rest of the week. How long is it before one loses the use of one's legs?! Why do they try to behave on board ship as though they were on land. This is pure hotel life: tea with music at 4, ping pong and bridge tournaments, like a hotel on a rainy day, when one unfortunately can't go out. One ought to have fishing from the deck, surf riding and other nautical sports! though perhaps not in seas like these (they grow heavier every moment). Why don't they build the whole of the body of the ship i.e. all except the chassis as it were the frame, on grooves which work on the theory of a gyroscope and kept the whole body level, no matter how the rest of the boat heaved?! One does little but eat and sleep. Lunch then sleep then tea and talk then supper, a little fresh air, sleep.

Interesting talk after tea.

Cuthbert: If I read through the Matthew Passion with anyone, I could shew that there was one way and only one right way of reading it.

I: No; each person has his right way of reading it. But there is only one right way of approaching it.

Cuthbert (in effect): There is only one right technique of reading it.

I: No, each performance has its own technique.

We are not expected to reach New York till Sunday.[24] Introduced myself to Frau Mayer at supper. Nice.


*Monday November 9th*
An excellent night. Slept like a log. Ship rolling less, but started again this morning, after some sun early.

---

[24] The *Washington* docked in New York on Saturday, 14 November: see p. 13.

Mary appeared later in the day. A little rehearsal. Bridge and other card games after supper, when we sang [Morley's] "Now is [the month of maying]" to the Steward.

Interesting talk to Frau Mayer. Two stories about Knappertsbusch[25] leaving Munich. 1. He refused to allow swastikas on the stage in the last act of Meistersinger. 2. The portrait of Hermann Levi,[26] a great Munich conductor, was being removed from the opera for obvious reasons, and Knappertsbusch insisted on it being taken to his own private room.

Lent Cuthbert Peacock's Crotchet Castle.[27] I read a little aloud – the scene of Dr Folliot's being waylaid on the way home – but I am not very good at reading aloud and it fell rather flat.[28]

*Tuesday November 10th*
Ship going better from noon yesterday till noon today 513 miles, almost double what it was before. Cuthbert much enjoyed Crotchet Castle, especially "Sir, I do not care a rush or any other aquatic and inesculent vegetable". Also T.L.P.'s proposal to Jane Griffith which really is a model of what a proposal by letter should be. Rehearsed "Corpus Christi"[29] this morning. I must make it more free.

Just remembered 2 good stories of Nelly[30] about negress.

1. Employer persuaded old negress to put her money out of her mattress (already sold) into bank. Bank crashes. Sorrow. "Ah, you see, sir, de day after you opened an account for me, I took it all out, & put in my mattress."

---

[25] Hans Knappertsbusch (1888–1965), German conductor, who was musical director at the Munich opera house from 1922 until 1936, when the Nazis revoked his life contract.

[26] Hermann Levi (1839–1900), Jewish-German conductor and a leading figure in Munich's musical life for over a quarter of a century.

[27] Thomas Love Peacock (1785–1866), English novelist and poet, whose satirical novel, *Crotchet Castle*, was first published in 1831.

[28] In later years, after illness forced his retirement from singing in 1980, Pears was especially fond of reading in public. He devised and participated in programmes at Aldeburgh and elsewhere that incorporated prose and poetry, and commissioned Robin Holloway and Peter Paul Nash to write works for speaker and chamber ensemble.

[29] Peter Warlock's *Corpus Christi Carol* (1919). A programme for their 1937 tour of the United States shows that the New English Singers included Warlock's carol in both of their 'joyous yuletide programs' at Carnegie Hall, New York. See also Personalia: Anne Wood, p. 226.

[30] Nellie Carson,§ second soprano of the New English Singers, and second wife of Cuthbert Kelly.

2. Negress asked about her 6 children: 2 by my 1st husband, 2 by my 2nd husband and de rest all by my self ⎫
on my own ⎭ ?

Played cards with Mary afternoon. More rehearsal. Sea much rougher. Uncomfortable. Bed early. Sleepy and bored. What a very dull diary this is! For C's sake, feel & think a little more!

*Wednesday November 11th* (Armistice Day!?!)
Very little notice taken of the above. I deliberately (quel snobbisme) ignored it.[31] Apparently a wreath was thrown into the water: surely very primitive symbolism: it must merely have gone the way of the waste paper and food, the drains and the dust. Rehearsal.
Cuthbert's stories of Tovey:[32]

1. Speyer[33] asking for Brahms quartet of which viola part had .been deliberately left behind, T. supplied it at piano.

2. T. at piano, talking of preludes played a chord, turned about, digressed for 1¾ hours on preludes, then turned back & played the 48 straight through (?)!

C. (to me): You are so like my David![34] That is why I like you so much. You have the same fastidiousness over words. (Oh! dear, have I? I have great interest in words, but a purely aesthetic one, like Mervyn[35] with his medicine.)
Long discussion quite profitless with Eric and Nellie about chorus girl's legs!
*Cuthbert*: Did the shape of folksong perhaps come from the shape of a dialect! Certain turns of speech corresponding with turns of tune? What about the drone of Scottish folk music? not from speech but from instrument? C. underlines the folksingers interest in the words, but e.g. The Brisk Young Widow is too B.Y.W. to be used for any other words, except perhaps (my suggestion) a B.Y. Sailor (not Soldier! but perhaps

---

[31] Pears's firmly held pacifist beliefs, partly from conviction and his Quaker background, are in evidence here.
[32] Sir Donald Tovey (1875–1940), English musicologist, composer and pianist.
[33] Eduard Speyer (1839–1934), German musician and businessman, and son of the violinist Wilhelm Speyer, who lived in the UK from 1859 where he organized concerts in London and founded the Classical Concerts Society. He was a friend of Brahms, Clara Schumann and Elgar; Strauss dedicated *Salome* to him.
[34] Presumably Kelly's son.
[35] Mervyn Horder (b. 1910), English 'gentleman composer'.

Air Force Man!?). Apparently a lot of tunes had interchangeable words. E.g. what?

Cuthbert hinting possibility of American future prospects of New English Singers might keep me from going back to the BBC. I fear not.[36]

Why am I not more interested in fundamentals?

Interesting point about vulgar swimming pool here. *Objection* Too much ornament and good timiness à la Lido of girl spectators. Eric counters doesn't notice. He takes it as it is: doesn't bother him, suggesting doesn't matter. Surely the sharper one's taste, the more pure one's artistic performance? (or not necessary). Personality is a different thing from Artistry. Gigli[37] is Personality. Schumann[38] Artistry?

*Story*: Chaplain to the King (at service): Let us pray! Duke of Cumberland (gruffly): By all means.

*Incident*: Beastly American Jew, annoying girl with Hungarian man; more & more insulting, Hungarian angry, words, blow, Jew saying ad lib. "if I liked, I'd kill you". Mary interposing a hand, Eric fetching purser. Jew led off. Later as we played cards in the Saloon, the Jew passes. Nellie: He's got his eye on you, Mary. Mary: Ay knoo! (Bursts into tears.)


*Thursday November 12th*
Sea very much calmer. A little shuffle board. Good talks with Cuthbert about Dick Shepherd.[39] Pacifism. C: This [Peace Pledge] Union starts on the wrong lines. I would try to stop the next war but 2, by teaching in schools a proper sense of value; music better than motorcars.

*Cuthbert*: Is there anything to be said against the world being the creation of our senses? So that when I die, it dies. In other words, only one person died in the war, but God knows that was enough.

---

[36] Although Pears resumed his work with the BBC Singers on his return home, he did indeed terminate his contract with the BBC in October 1937 before departing on a second North American tour with the New English Singers (October 1937 – January 1938) (CHPP, pp. 76–9). Before leaving the BBC he had already begun to build up a small amount of freelance solo work, mainly oratorio, and from the beginning of 1938 he was reliant on solo engagements and the New English Singers for his livelihood, although his time in the Glyndebourne Chorus during the summer of that year widened his experience further. In September 1938 he was to ask the BBC for an audition as a soloist, 'as I am confident that my voice has improved ... particularly since I left the Singers last year'; although an audition date was set, Pears would seem to have had it postponed owing to a heavy cold. A new audition time does not appear to have been arranged.

[37] Beniamino Gigli (1890–1957), Italian tenor.

[38] Elisabeth Schumann (1888–1952), German (later naturalized American) soprano.

[39] The Very Revd Hugh Richard ('Dick') Sheppard$ (1880–1937), English clergyman and peace-campaigner.

Life, to be sure, is nothing much to lose,
But young men think it is, & we were young. A.E. Housman.[40]

*Cuthbert*: The Appreciation of Poetry is the Realisation of the Perfect arrangement of the Stresses.
*I*: Yes, that is the intellectual appreciation of the means; but the Mystery of why it is right is inexplicable, as of Music.
*Cuthbert*: Quite so: it is some Rhythm in both us and it: a vibration.
Later. C.: Keith Falkner[41] dull as ditchwater. Campbell McInnes[42] loveliest sound ever heard. Really great craftsman. Dorothy Silk a first-class singer of lieder, if it hadn't been for a knock out blow at her first recital. (What?)[43] Dorothy's voice like a chameleon. It changes colour to an oboe when accompanied by one: same with a flute.
Exquisite description of the river in Proust. Really most moving masterpiece, but one wants more time to read it slowly. Just starting Swann in Love. Extraordinary description of Mlle Vinteuil and the Lesbian.

*Friday November 13th*
Changed £5 of dollars at $4.80 to the £.
Very interesting conversation with Frau Mayer. Thomas Mann[44] greatest German writer: really German; lives in Zurich merely because in '32 he forecast the rise of the Anti-spiritual Forces (as represented by the Nazis). Frau Mayer knew D.H. Lawrence well, and admired him.[45] Says Germany is fundamentally not 1 nation. Many Bavarians would like an independent Catholic state. "Hitler is the only Pacifist left in Germany."
C.K.: In the Erl-König[46] the boy is the only excited person.

---

[40] The quotation is from Housman's *More Poems* (1936):
　　Here dead lie we because we did not choose
　　To live and shame the land from which we sprung.
　　Life, to be sure, is nothing much to lose,
　　But young men think it is, and we were young.

[41] English bass-baritone (1900–1994), particularly well known as a soloist in oratorio.

[42] (James) Campbell McInnes[§] (1873/4–1945), English-born baritone who settled in Canada in 1919.

[43] The unusual circumstances of Silk's first recital have not been identified.

[44] German novelist[§] (1875–1955).

[45] Lawrence first visited Germany in 1912 and left England permanently seven years later. In 1914 he married Frieda von Richthofen and it may have been through this connection that Mrs Mayer knew him.

[46] 'Erlkönig', Schubert's famous setting of Goethe's poem.

C.K.: In the spacing, rhythm, emphasis of word delivery there is a right way, which is organic in the poem, not imposed from outside. The only difference in great performance is the difference in quality of tone. Steuart is wrong Evangelist because he takes hold of Bach, instead of letting Bach take hold of him.

Myself: A song is different each time we look at it.

C.K.: (in effect) Yes. But there is always a right way (??)

C.K.: The Keats sort of poetry is onomatopoeic, but not musical in the bigger sense. By musical, I mean the arrangement of vowel stresses etc for the content. (Subject: The proper appreciation of Poetry.)

I: The Keats poetry is like Representation in Pictures, where Representation (Naturalness) is held up as good; merely the Clothes. The good Representational Picture is the one that is R subordinated to Design etc. The Thought content is little. I suggest that the Secret of Great Art is the Relating of Truth to Sound.

If I want to change other people's opinions, I must have standards, by which to measure them, i.e. I must go after perfect performances.

V. Interesting talk with Cuthbert.

(CK). I (PP.) am sensitive and not a fool singer: but I must learn to be a natural singer. Exercise giving out emotion. I am introspective, which is alright; but it must come out. Exercise suggested of reciting poetry. Also muscular exercises with tongue and lips. A large part of emotion must become purely muscular so that I can go further after finer points. How wrong it is for fool singers to win! How marvellous it is when an intelligent brain is behind the emotion is shown when Steuart lets the music run away with him.[47]

---

[47]   Kelly's assessment here of Pears as a singer reminds us that he was not yet the fully mature artist – either vocally, intellectually, or emotionally – that he would become by the time of the première of Britten's *Peter Grimes* in 1945. Trevor Harvey recalled Pears in the mid-1930s in an interview with Donald Mitchell (1980): ' ... in those days I could never conceivably have imagined Peter as an opera singer, or even a lieder singer or anything, because he had quite a small voice. He was frankly pretty lazy and I very seldom ever heard him practising or anything like that at home, and he didn't seem to have any great ambition'. Basil Douglas remembered (again to Mitchell, 1987) Pears 'getting increasingly dissatisfied with his singing, because he had a very small voice – charming, marvellous, and very musical – but he obviously couldn't express what he wanted with it'.

Britten however, when he first knew Pears, evidently thought the voice had potential. In his diary entry for 15 October 1937 he notes that Lennox Berkeley and Christopher Isherwood visited him and Pears, 'to hear Peter sing my new songs [*On this Island*, Op. 11] & are considerably pleased – as I admit I am. Peter sings them well – if he studies he will be a very good singer. He's certainly one of the nicest people I know, but frightfully reticent.' It was his association with the composer from 1937 onwards that encouraged Pears to develop his voice more fully than before and to widen his artistic horizons. During his stay in the

12

*Saturday November 14th*

Arrived N.Y. 9.30 AM. Marvellous sky line covered in mist, with just 3 scrapers peering through. Like a Monet. Selective & lovely. Better than when we saw it all, when it was shapeless. Noises in planes admirably like the planes of the Skyline. Memorable. Serene, lofty, peering. Dashed through N.Y. to G.[rand] Central Terminal. Incredible like a cathedral. Oyster stew – too much. Trouble with luggage (put in a separate taxi). Met Brockways;[48] charmers. Caught 3 o'c to Boston. Incredible number of cars in America. Wooden houses. Vile fast driving in New York. Good musical criticism, reasoned, of Barbirolli[49] in NY Times, N Yorker, Time. Mess of towns. Met Schary[50] at lunch: very attractive.

Arrived Boston 8 p.m. went straight to Hotel Statler. Marvellous hotel, room $4 (16/6). First class service. (On train one had tea, always iced water, attentive polite coloured servants, a peppermint after.) Slept like a log. Very comfortable.

---

United States with Britten between 1939 and 1942, he passed through the hands of a number of teachers – Campbell McInnes, Therese Behr (Frau Schnabel), and Clytie Mundy – all of whom helped him on the path to full vocal maturity. It is telling that Britten's *Seven Sonnets of Michelangelo*, Op. 22, written in New York in 1940 for Pears (and dedicated to him), were not publicly performed until Pears's and Britten's return to the UK in 1942, although they did occasionally perform them for friends while still in the States and made a private recording in 1941 (*GB-ALb* 3-9000026). A comparison between their 1942 HMV commercial recording of the *Michelangelo Sonnets*, made shortly after the première, and the private New York recording unequivocally demonstrates just how far Pears had developed as an artist in two years. In the HMV recording we can revel in what Basil Douglas, to his surprise when hearing Pears again for the first time after three years, refers to as a voice with a 'wonderful round, golden quality' to it.

Pears's words 'how marvellous it is when an intelligent brain is behind the emotion' provides an apt description of his own particular brand of artistry when at the height of his powers, more especially in his searching interpretations of the lieder repertoire, with Britten as his equally intelligent partner at the piano. Although he was never the possessor of a supremely beautiful voice *per se*, Pears was undoubtedly a remarkable singer in respect of what he could make of a particular song – words and music – his expressive, thoughtful, musical delivery going straight to the meaning.

[48]  Unidentified.

[49]  John Barbirolli⁵ (1899–1970), English conductor, who was principal conductor of the New York Philharmonic Orchestra, 1936–42.

[50]  Unidentified, but Pears was to dine with Schary again on 15 December when the Singers returned to New York.

*Sunday November 15th* (1st Letter to Iris)[51]
Slept late. Went down for breakfast 10.30. Wrote long letter to Iris. Lunch. Then off to the Fine Arts Museum. Two El Greco (one surpassing marvellous) & Vincent (one v.g. Postman) several Monets, one or two Sisleys, Pisarro's, Renoir landscapes, Millet Pastorals, Manets, Gaugins, Van Dycks, Velazquez, Chardins, etc etc. Marvellous collection. Then Elizabeth Gardner Museum. Extraordinary collection of 1st class things, crowded together in 1 house. Must at any cost return to these 2 collections & the Fosq Museum at Harvard.

   Boston itself v. ugly. Mess. Vile architecture. No significance. Like stones beside the road.

   Caught 9.30 sleeper to St. John N.B. [New Brunswick]


*Monday November 16th* (1st Letter to Anne with PS. after Concert. 2nd
   Letter to Ma.)
Arrived here (St. John) at 11. after going through some very beautiful wooded lake and sea country. The houses uniformly impossible. St. John is uglier even than Boston. Comfortable hotel (Admiral Beatty). Concert tonight in School at 8.30. Well looked after. Wrong programme printed, but we sang it all the same. Concert a success, spoilt by having to share it with a violinist, who playing nothing but trash queered our pitch.


*Tuesday November 17th* (Postcard to PB.)[52]
Crossed the Bay of Fundy at 8.0 AM from St John, to Digby & thence Sackville.[53] Admirably plain decorations on boat (pleasant contrast to the Washington).

---

51   Iris Holland Rogers$ (d. 1982), a friend of Pears who shared a flat with Anne Wood.
52   Peter Burra$ (1909–1937), English writer on art, music and literature.
53   Digby, on the west coast of Nova Scotia. Although Pears clearly writes Sackville in this diary, his pocket engagement diary, in which the itinerary for the New English Singers is given, suggests that it was at Wolfville, further up the west coast of Nova Scotia, where they gave their next concert; the Sackville concert was next on their itinerary.

# THE NEW
# ENGLISH SINGERS

Director : CUTHBERT KELLY

| DOROTHY SILK | ERIC GREENE |
| NELLIE CARSON | PETER PEARS |
| MARY MORRIS | CUTHBERT KELLY |

on their return from
their recent tour in Canada and
The United States

●

WIGMORE HALL
19TH FEBRUARY 1937

IBBS & TILLETT
124 WIGMORE STREET, W.1

PROGRAMME 1/-

Programme for the New English Singers' concert, Wigmore Hall,
19 February 1937.

15

# 2  Far East Diary (1955–56)

On 31 October 1955 Peter Pears and Benjamin Britten left England for a five-month world trip, sailing on the night boat from Harwich to the Hook of Holland where they were met the following morning by Peter Diamand, their agent in the Netherlands. After giving concerts in Europe, including their first recitals in Yugoslavia (see pp. 22–5), Pears and Britten travelled eastwards to Turkey, India, Singapore, Indonesia, Hong Kong, Japan, Ceylon (Sri Lanka) and India again, before returning to England on 17 March 1956. For part of the trip they were joined by their friends the Prince and Princess of Hesse and the Rhine. For Britten, there were three events that would prove to be of lasting influence on his output: the colourful sounds of the Balinese gamelan, the imperial court music of Japan, and the overwhelming impact of the restrained, formal idiom of the Japanese Noh-play tradition.

While making this journey Prince Ludwig kept a diary which was privately published as *Ausflug Ost* (Darmstadt, 1956); a few extracts appeared in translation in Britten's fiftieth birthday *Festschrift*, published in 1963. Pears also made his own idiosyncratic account of their adventures; his diary, unlike Prince Ludwig's, is incomplete and remained unpublished in his lifetime. It is published here for the first time. Two sections of Pears's text exist in a conventional narrative form, namely those covering their first visit to India and the first part of their stay on Bali; only sketchy notes or a précised form of text survive for the other parts of the tour. There is one exception to this: the first section of Pears's account, written in Istanbul but describing their time in Holland, West Germany and Switzerland, takes the shape of a letter (now incomplete) to Janet Stone. It seems possible that Pears intended the whole diary as a gift to Mrs Stone: for example, when he writes about meeting her brother, Robin Woods, in Singapore (see p. 38), she is openly addressed in the text. At some point after his return from the Far East, Pears acquired a crudely typed copy of all that apparently survives of this letter which he then kept with all his other papers relating to the diary of the world trip. The single extant folio of his handwritten original letter can be found among Janet Stone's papers at the Bodleian Library, Oxford (*GB-Ob*, Stone, Box 20). Mrs Stone, however, never received the complete text, and after his return Pears showed no interest in reviving his account of his and Britten's extraordinary journey.

Pears's diary was discovered in The Red House, Aldeburgh, after his death in 1986. Most of the different sections had been kept by him in an envelope labelled 'Far East Diary / *unfinished*' (*GB-ALb* 1-9500030), while the material for the Japanese leg of the trip had been inscribed in a single notebook (*GB-ALb* 1-9500031). Pages from the notebook were first exhibited at Aldeburgh in June 1991, as part of an exhibition of the source materials and other related documents for Britten's *Curlew River* prepared by Paul Banks and Philip Reed. In the present edition, the sections of text are indicated by separating rows of asterisks; the changing types of notepaper used by Pears, often taken from one of the hotels in which they stayed, have been indicated on their first appearance. Pears's orthography has been followed as accurately as possible, although occasional editorial interventions have been made for clarity. Those sections which remain in note form have occasionally proved difficult to transcribe and in a few instances Pears's intentions have eluded the editor and his sharp-eyed colleagues. Illegible words or passages have therefore been indicated within square brackets [ ].

Extracts from Prince Ludwig's *Ausflug Ost* appear in translations made variously by Mervyn Cooke, Kara Lyttle, Syd Swann and the editor, unless otherwise stated.

Istanbul Hilton
ISTANBUL, TURKEY

This was begun in Istanbul about December 1st!

Dear Janet,[1]

There have been so many jolly excuses in the last month for not writing to you that it has become quite natural to say to myself "Oh no of course there is no time for *that*!" But in fact now that we have settled down in this hyper-super-everything great pub for a day or two, the pricks of conscience are too painful (besides, everything goes septic in this climate!). So here goes! But where do I start? right at the beginning with Farewell to Clytie?[2] or even earlier with Have you the Passports or What have you done with my Sleeping Pills? or still earlier with How many Aertex Dress Shirts does one need for 4½ months Tour to the Far East? Let's skip all that. Good crossing: weak efforts at Last Cine-views of England: the setting sun on the mud at Rotterdam turning it into chocolate junket: the excellent smoothness of Dutch trains: familiar Amsterdam faces: why is it that though we have given oh twenty recitals in Amsterdam in the last 8 or 9 years we are always shaking with nerves there? The audience is always very warm and we have lots of friends but somehow each time one feels more responsibility, & less confidence in shouldering same. Well, the concert was adequate, I suppose, & then there were two blessed days without work, in which we could see our friends.[3] Ben practised the Mozart 2 Piano Concerto and the Schumann Andante & Variations for 2 Pianos for the Aldeburgh Festival next year[4]

---

[1]     Janet Stone[5] (b. 1912), Pears's distant cousin (they are both descendants of the prison-reformer Elizabeth Fry), wife of the artist and engraver Reynolds Stone.

[2]     Pears's and Britten's dachshund named after Clytie Mundy, Pears's singing teacher in New York in the early 1940s. A photograph of Britten with Clytie appears in PFL, Plate 324; the same volume includes a reproduction of Mary Potter's 1959 portrait of the composer with Clytie on his lap (Plate 229).

[3]     Pears and Britten gave a recital on 1 November in the small hall of the Concertgebouw, Amsterdam. On one of their two free days in Amsterdam they visited the British Ambassador Sir Paul Mason and his wife at The Hague, 'most musical, kind, and amusing people. They gave us names of ambassadors and people we may meet in the Near and Far East' (Britten to Roger Duncan, 12 November 1955).

[4]     Britten and Maria Curcio (Peter Diamand's wife) were to perform these works at concerts during the 1956 Aldeburgh Festival. While in Amsterdam Britten clearly took the opportunity to rehearse with Curcio.

(one can't escape Suffolk so quickly) & we visited Simon Goldberg[5] & his wife, and had a very happy "Yes" as answer to our invitation to him to come to the Festival. On the journey to Düsseldorf, a passport man shook us by telling us that we needed visas to perform in Germany. We had none. However he was kind and let us in. The whole of the Ruhr is immensely prosperous; the big Mercedes-Benz is known as the Volkswagen of the Ruhr. But whatever you find to say against the Germans, they love Music, & our audience at the Robert Schumann-saal was wonderful.[6] Nice German couple took us home in their car; talked about contemporary German painting: next morning they had sent us a woodcut by Gerhard Marcks,[7] and a medallion by Ewald Matare;[8] both very distinguished contemporary German artists. Most kind and generous. Our life in Düsseldorf was very much helped by the extremely pleasant & helpful British Consul General, and his wife, who gave us a lift to our next concert in Wuppertal, which was again extremely pleasant, in a small hall.[9] Asked back in April: Ben can't do it, so offered Julian Bream[10] and me instead: accepted. On by train to Stuttgart:[11] met by local agent, fat & white; staying at new hotel (how many new hotels have been built in Germany? Thousands). Visited local music shop to buy Bach Cantatas as word has come that I was asked to sing 6 evenings of them at Ansbach in July![12] Lunch with British consul general & wife, Sino-phile, very nice. We plot to go to Peking instead of Tokyo. N.B. All British Councils & Consuls (Generals & otherwise) have been

---

5    Szymon Goldberg (1909–1993), American violinist and conductor of Polish birth. On 23 June 1956 in Aldeburgh Parish Church, as part of the Aldeburgh Festival, he participated in a concert of music by Bach, Britten and Telemann, with Pears, Britten, and the cellist Terence Weil.

6    Pears and Britten travelled by train to Düsseldorf on 4 November on the evening of which day they gave a recital. The programme comprised six canzonets by Haydn, lieder by Schubert and Schumann, and Britten's *Seven Sonnets of Michelangelo*, Op. 22, and *Winter Words*, Op. 52.

7    German sculptor (1889–1981). Pears's and Britten's art collection includes five woodcuts by Marcks and a pencil drawing of a standing male nude.

8    German sculptor (1887–1965). The circular medallion, depicting a horse and rider, survives at the Britten–Pears Library.

9    The concert in Wuppertal took place in the Stadthalle on 6 November.

10   English guitarist and lutenist[§] (b. 1933).

11   Pears and Britten travelled to Stuttgart on 7 November where they remained until the 9th.

12   Pears was to make his second appearance at the Ansbach Bach Festival in July 1956 when he participated in four concerts of Bach cantatas under the direction of Karl Richter. See also Chapter 3, Pears's account of the 1959 Festival.
         Pears may have had little success in purchasing scores of Bach cantatas in Stuttgart. His pocket account book (*GB-ALb* 1-9400531), which he assiduously kept throughout the trip, indicates that he bought some cantatas in Zürich during their brief stay in the city (11–12 November).

enormously helpful on this tour. Stuttgart concert[13] took place in rather too large newish hall; the audience was kind if not enormous; "but next year –"!; mad young man who spent whole concert photographing us off stage. On from Stuttgart to Geneva.[14] I fell & deeply scraped my shin on a Swiss railway carriage step: not painful but won't I get tetanus later on? Welcomed by dear Pat Fuller and Sidney Shaw, and spent 36 hours as her guests.[15] Ben started one of his tummies, apparently very bad, visions of operations, cancelling concerts etc. However he got through with the help of old friends Brandy & Glucose. Concert in rather dreary little theatre, run by hard-faced impresariette, who gave us out of stinginess an appalling piano, 1890 Steinway continually used for Boogy-woogy;[16] Ben almost overcome but managed somehow. On to Zurich which seemed particularly Swiss-li after Geneva.[17] Nice comfortable hotel, nice good piano, nice kind audience, nice supper after at the Hürlimanns.[18] Next day flight to Vienna, arriving after dark in the rain. P: "There is a movie-camera man; who are they after?" B: "Ambassador or so, I expect." Horrors no! after *us*: pursued by flashes, collecting and losing baggage, trying to change money, getting into & waiting in bus; television, it seems; we behave very self-consciously and unphotogenically; dull for viewers, I fancy. The real old Wien-erish atmosphere is captured immediately upon entering historical Sacher hotel. Birthplace of the world-famous Tart, its amenities are as cosily grand as ever and the food is divine. My blue suit, built for me in 1944, is the measure of my girth. When I am exercising forbearance and doing my Namaskans, it fits me easily and to spare, but I can't go on with mayonnaisy hors d'oeuvres and world famous Tarts without feeling the pinch.

*******

[13] On 8 November.

[14] Pears and Britten travelled by train to Geneva on 9 November.

[15] Patricia Fuller was the wife of Frederick Fuller, the singer and translator. Her correspondence with Britten and Pears suggests she ran a theatre in Geneva. Sidney Shaw remains unidentified (but see also p. 22).

[16] Their recital took place on 10 November at the Théâtre de la Cour St-Pierre. The programme included English canzonets by Haydn, lieder by Schubert and Schumann, and Britten's *Winter Words* and French folksong arrangements.

[17] Pears and Britten travelled by train to Zürich on 11 November, giving their recital that same evening.

[18] Martin and Bettina Hürlimann§, directors of Atlantis Verlag, Zürich, who had commissioned, translated and published the first book on Britten's life and music, Eric Walter White's *Benjamin Britten: eine Skizze von Leben und Werk* (1948) which was subsequently published in English by Boosey & Hawkes.

CATHAY HOTEL
CATHAY BUILDING
SINGAPORE


*Vienna*:
Meistersinger – [Karl] Böhm[19]
Concerts
Emmie von Sax:[20] Chand'eau
Egon Seefehlner[21]
Fritz Reiner, [Bruno] Walter[22]
Bruce Flegg
Party at B.[ritish] C.[ouncil]
Josef Marx[23]


[Pears and Britten flew to Vienna from Zürich on 12 November, remaining there until the 17th when they travelled to Salzburg. On the 14th they lunched at the British Embassy and in the evening attended a performance of Wagner's *Die Meistersinger von Nürnberg*, conducted by Fritz Reiner, at the newly opened, reconstructed Vienna Staatsoper, on which occasion they met Bruno Walter who was present in the audience. Britten wrote about the occasion to Anthony Gishford (of Boosey & Hawkes) on the 19th: 'We went to the Opera – wonderful house, but dreary performance (Meistersinger)'. (It was the role of David in *Meistersinger* that Pears was to tackle just over a year later, in January 1957 at Covent Garden, the only occasion he sang Wagner.) Pears and Britten also met Karl Böhm and Egon Seefehlner of the Vienna Staatsoper. On the 15th Pears and Britten were guests of honour at a reception given by the British Council. While in Vienna they gave two concerts: a recital on

---

19  Austrian conductor (1894–1981), director of the Vienna Staatsoper, 1943–5 and 1954–6.
20  The sister of Erwin Stein, Britten's publisher and adviser.
21  Austrian musical administrator (b. 1912), deputy director of the Vienna Staatsoper under Böhm and Karajan, 1954–61. Britten wrote to Anthony Gishford (19 November 1955):

> . . . saw a lot of Seefehlner . . . a remarkable chap, with remarkable ideas for a Viennese, but struggling rather helplessly against usual Viennese intrigue & incompetence. We've known him for ages as head of the Konzerthaus (which he still is). I think he deserves encouragement. He wants very much to do the Screw next year (at the Redoutensaal) & possibly Lucretia too . . . I was non-committal about the former; & definitely the Ballet (!) [*The Prince of the Pagodas*, Op. 57] too . . . I think he & Böhm *really* mean to do it, but whether they will succeed is about as doubtful as – well, the Scala, for instance!

22  Fritz Reiner (1888–1963), American conductor of Hungarian birth; Bruno Walter (1876–1962), German conductor and an honorary member of the Vienna Opera.
23  Joseph Marx (1882–1964), Austrian composer, particularly of lieder.

13 November which included Britten's most recent cycle for Pears, the settings of Thomas Hardy, *Winter Words* (1953), and an orchestral concert on the 16th, the programme of which included music by Purcell – the Chacony in G minor (edited by Britten) and the Suite of six songs from *Orpheus Britannicus* (edited and arranged with accompaniment for small orchestra by Britten) – as well as Britten's *Serenade*, Op. 31, for tenor, horn and strings, and the *Sinfonietta*, Op. 1. Britten reported to Anthony Gishford on the 19th: 'The Concerts have been really very successful – Winter Words much liked everywhere, especially Vienna! . . . with a really good performance of the Serenade – & the old Sinfonietta too!']

*Salzburg:*
Arrival in rain, nice M^r Gmachl,[24] sweet hotel, Americans, shape of Austrians head, clothes, Sidney Shaw, drive up to Bad Aussee, cold, awful supper party with Fells, concert Mozarteum, "Zigeuner Baron"

[Pears and Britten journeyed by train to Salzburg on 17 November, remaining there until the 19th. They gave a recital in the Grosser Saal of the Mozarteum on the 17th (Haydn's English canzonets, Schubert lieder, Britten's *Winter Words* and folksong arrangements), and on their final evening attended a performance of J. Strauss's *The Gypsy Baron.*]

*Ljubljana:*
Train journey, American without passport, woman & customs,[25] arrival in Ljub, confusion over hotels, nice Andrzejič, radio, concert in nice hall, visit to radio, sweet old town, extra concert. Brit. Coun Dr. Thompson[26] lent car.

*Maribor:*
sweet sunny town, mayor etc to meet us, solemn slivovitz, then rest, concert, small chandeliery room packed with students, visit in morning to art gallery, v. interesting, nice director; sliv. sliv. sliv. drive onto Zagreb, lovely country (opera house)

---

[24] Julius Gmachl, who was responsible for organizing Pears's and Britten's recital.
[25] Britten described the journey to Roger Duncan in a letter written from Istanbul on 3 December:
> Train was packed with people – many going home, and bringing with them lots of things you can't buy in Jugoslavia. One woman seemed to be carrying everything *including* the kitchen stove, and the customs man made her unpack everything . . . One poor man, an American, had clean forgotten to get himself a visa, and was turned off the train. God knows where he spent the night; it was already late, and a pretty terrible place.
[26] Drummond Thompson, the British Council representative in Zagreb.

22

| | | Jugoslavia | 840 Din total $\sqrt{}$ |
|---|---|---|---|
| | 2218 | | |
| Hotel (Bill) | 747. 00 | Ljubljana Nov. 20-22 | Dinars. |
| Lunch. | 140 .00 | Breakfast | 380.00 |
| Tips (Hotel) | 45 .00 | Lunch + tip | 800.00 |
| Taxi. | 25 .00 | Party (6) | 2000.00 |
| Porter. | 10. 00 | Hotel Bill (nights 4?) | 5,434.00 |
| Postage | 12. 00. | Manila 22-23 | |
| | 3197 00 | Lunch | 1,148.00 |
| 480 A.S left in cash | | Tea | 100. 00 |
| | | Party 6 | 1,500 .00 |
| | | Hotel Bill | 10·0.00 |
| | | | 500. 00 |
| | | Zagreb | 500. 00 |
| | | | 500. 00 |
| | Din | | 650. 00 |
| Received in Ljubljana £ 40.000 | | Suitcase. | 10,900. 00 |
| " Radio Interior £4.850 | | Lunch (7) | 4.000. 00. |
| " " Broadcast. 30.000. | | Hotel (3 nights) | 6. 000 00 |
| " " Beograd (Radio) 12.250 | | Tips | 500. 00 |
| Received in cash in Jugoslavia 962.130 | | Porter | 400. 00 |
| Ticket: Zagreb to Reynold 6/704 (Jugo Konzert) | | Extra ticket | 600. 00 |
| | | | 36,422. 00 |

Two pages from Pears's pocket account book which he kept throughout the trip.

*Zagreb*:
old fash French pros. hotel, mad keenness hospitality, Peter Grimes,
1 act of [?*Ero the Joker*], *Wed.* PG.[27] *Thurs.* Concert.[28] *Fri.* Jeunesse
Musicale. Habunek's[29] party. Off to Belgrade. Dr. Thompsons

*Belgrade*
6AM arrival posse of greeting. Sleep all day in Hotel Moscow & concert
that evening apparent success but agony of tiredness: composers supper
after: no English.
Rumanian concert.
National day at opera house Tito[30] present. young artists
Reception at Tito's palace.[31]
Broadcast. Embassy lunch.
Univ. choir
Air travel. *Jugoslavia*

[Pears and Britten arrived in Ljubljana, Yugoslavia, on 20 November, where
they gave a concert on the 21st. While in the country they also visited Maribor
(22nd–23rd; concert on 22nd), Zagreb (23rd–25th; concert on 24th) and
Belgrade (26th–30th; concert on 26th and radio broadcast on 29th). Pears
described some of their experiences in Yugoslavia to the artist Mary Potter in
a letter written from Istanbul on 1 December:

The first part of Jugolsavia was absolutely heaven – ravishing weather
– beautiful country – sweet welcoming people – lovely audiences – no
advertisements so that you could really *see* the landscape – nice looking
peasants, dear oxen, an occasional lorry with a puncture, stately geese,
silly turkeys, bony horses, all fair game for our driver who enjoyed
near misses, except for one chicken who had it. Nice old place called
Ljubljana with an open market by a fine river, & a nice piano; darling
old place called Maribor (we were suddenly told when we arrived that
we had an extra concert – oh dear!) with a terribly nice crowd of

---

[27] Pears and Britten attended a performance of *Peter Grimes* on 23 November. The
composer wrote to Imogen Holst on 1 December that the production was 'not
alas very good, but, thank God, enough good that one needn't be only critical
afterwards.' Pears thought the performance 'wasn't half bad, though I don't
believe Croat is a very easy language to translate into!' (letter to Oliver Holt,
24 November).
[28] Their recital in Zagreb would appear to have been the same programme as in
Salzburg.
[29] Vlado Habunek⁵ (1906–1994), Croatian theatre and opera director.
[30] Josip Broz Tito (1892–1980), President of Yugoslavia from 1953 until his death.
[31] Britten described their encounter with President Tito on 29 November, in a letter
to Imogen Holst: 'We went to a reception given by Tito, curiously attractive
personality, & met quite a few members of his government, all cultured &
sympathetic.'

provincial professors etc. who welcomed us, & a chandeliered room in the opera house, holding at a pinch 300 seats into which were *squeezed* two hundred standing students as well (my! the heat & the smell) & a piano which Ben played throughout with the soft pedal down & it still jangled like an old barrel organ; then Zagreb, which was heavenly – terribly nice pair at the Brit. Council, & a wonderful producer called Vlado Habunek whom we both fell for & "Peter Grimes" in Serbo-Croat! *Very* slow *indeed*, & an Ellen with a cold, a dull production, but a good-singing rather dim Grimes & an enormous loud good chorus: then Belgrade, a ghastly grey hotel, with endless official luncheons etc., questions to Ben (what is the future of modern music?), one or two terribly sweet occasions, a students' choir singing English songs (wonderful sound) & terribly keen & grateful! Oh! it's all been most moving & exhausting, & now for a day or two off before we tackle the Turks!]

*Istanbul*
arriving 1 hour early
[*illegible word*] Rich in Istanbul
Trip up Bosphorus
Mosques. Santa Sophia, Kaigh Djamal

Ankara – New city. Snow.
Huge endless party of 200 people
Opera – Ballo[32] – good Turkish soprano. Hittite museum – old Roman antique temple
Ambassador (jaundice) – Concert in opera house

*Hilton Hotel*
Back to Istanbul – [*illegible word*]
Turkish music – in cinema
Turk Philharm Concert Private
Cinema 11AM Sunday morning

Ghastly night journey to Karachi – Beirut.

[Pears and Britten arrived in Istanbul on 30 November where they stayed at the Hilton Hotel. They visited Ankara, 5–7 December, returning to Istanbul on the 8th where they remained until the 11th. Pears described his first impressions of Istanbul in a letter written to Mary Potter the day after their arrival:

---

[32] A performance at the local opera house of Verdi's *Un ballo in maschera* on 8 December.

Well, we have reached this glossy glamorous pub. & from our windows we can see Asia! It looks pretty good, as we see it from the 7th floor on top of a hill, and the Bosphorus which flows between is very beautiful with twinkly ships at night, & extraordinary layers of dusty pink and grey at twilight. We arrived yesterday from Belgrade . . . by plane *two* hours early in the rain with no one to meet us, and a little Turk was very helpful (he was clearly either a pimp or a secret police agent or both) in finding us a taxi & we ploughed through the mud of half made roads to this great slab of House & Garden. It was opened in June & is surrounded by swimming pools – bedroom furniture by Hille of London, close fitting carpets in lemonpeel, Siamese pink or gunmetal, coffee & rolls in bed costs £1 and a hair-cut and-wash 30/-, but it's worth it (we hope!) for a few days anyway, after our very gloomy hotel (the Moscow!) in Belgrade.

Apart from making the usual sight-seeing trips, Pears and Britten attended a concert of contemporary Turkish music at an Istanbul cinema on 4 December which included music by at least one composer – Cemal Resid – in whom Britten took an interest. They gave a recital in Ankara at the local opera house on 6 December, where they returned two days later for a performance of Verdi's *Un ballo in maschera*. Back in Istanbul, Pears and Britten gave two concerts: a short, private recital to the members of the Istanbul Philharmonic Society on the 10th, following which there was a reception and dinner, and another on the morning of their departure (11th) in a cinema.

The flight to Karachi via Beirut departed at 10.15pm on 11 December, arriving in Pakistan at lunchtime the following day. After spending one night in Karachi's Palace Hotel, they travelled on to Bombay on the morning of the 13th (see Plate 3) where they stayed at the Taj Mahal Hotel.]

*******

[Unmarked paper]

Karachi – heat – leg – first whiff of Indian colour. Servants

*Bombay*
Arrival. Colour of India – green trees, white clothes, light saris – white or light houses – brown skins.
I had heard so much – childhood.[33]

---

[33] Pears's paternal grandfather had spent much of his life in India serving in the Army, and Pears's father had also worked abroad for much of his life as a civil engineer in India and Burma. Pears's parents were married in 1893 in Bombay.

They say Bombay not India, do. Delhi, do. Calcutta. How is one to find India?

1st Act to have tropical clothes made. Lovely cloth made in England. Fairly well copied.

Energetic Parsee ladies – strange names of Parsees – capable – public spirited – Parsees look after their own people, hospitals, etc.[34] Tala foundation.

Time & Talents Club.[35]

Drive to Poona (dusty) via Kalah caves.[36]

No alcohol.[37]

Elephanta – Hindu sculpture.[38]

\*\*\*\*\*\*\*

---

[34] Britten commented to Roger Duncan in a letter written from Agra, 26 December: 'In Bombay we were literally *run* by Parsees (an old sect of Indians, originally Persians, who live mostly in the West, and are the business back-bone of the country) and once a Parsee lady gets her teeth into you, there's no hope. They are charming, intelligent, brisk, and business-like.'

[35] Pears and Britten gave a recital for the combined charities of the Time & Talents Club at the Regal Theatre, Bombay, on 15 December. The programme comprised five of Haydn's English canzonets, lieder by Schubert, and Britten's *Winter Words* and folksong arrangements (see p. 28). Britten wrote about the concert to Roger Duncan on the 26th: '. . . we didn't enjoy our concert there much – an enormous cinema, and we both felt that people had come [more] for snobbish reasons than for musical'.

[36] An excursion to Poona and the Khale caves took place on 18 December.

[37] While in Bombay Pears and Britten were obliged to have an official permit to consume alcohol.

[38] Pears and Britten made an excursion to Elephanta Island on 16 December.

**The Time & Talents Club**

**Combined Charities**

*Sub-Committee*

*Presents*

# BENJAMIN BRITTEN

# &

# PETER PEARS

**At the REGAL THEATRE**

on *Thursday December 15th 1955,*

at *9 - 30 p.m.*

Programme for the recital in Bombay, 15 December 1955.

*Delhi*: rather dull flight from Bombay over brown landscape dotted with trees:[39] airport a long way from town: drive in with Parsee lady secretary of Music Club & Sikh founder, late of Cambridge: have chosen to stay at Hotel in old Delhi, miles from New Delhi, which is modern centre: pity in certain ways, involves long drives in every direction: nice old Cheltenham type hotel, large rooms; much cooler here than Bombay, downright cold in evenings, no question of thin suits: nice British Council Robinsons, helpful: afraid we are bad sight seers, always arrive at a mosque five minutes before closing time; easily daunted by distances, e.g. Red Fort v. impressive (& red) from outside but vast. Can one face tramping all through its interior? Sikh gentleman kindly lends car, reception for us at Gymkhana Club,[40] dry (no drink in Delhi on Tuesdays), various Ambassadors etc, nice, supper after with B. Council – very agreeable. Concert on Wednesday went well in pleasant small Y.W.C.A. hall.[41] Nice Indian situation – Wonderful new Bösendorfer concert grand bought a year ago, always tuned by one particular tuner, but piano was moved by a certain firm who insisted on *their* tuner doing the piano. So when we arrived to rehearse, No.1 was in middle of tuning; we stopped him & worked & balanced for radio; enter No. 2 tuner: everyone busy hiding one from t'other: delicate situation, unsolved. Also memorable moment in evening – P & B arrive for concert, glance at piano & mike to make

---

[39]  Pears and Britten arrived in Delhi at lunchtime on 19 December, staying at the Maiden's Hotel until the 23rd. Oddly enough, Pears makes no mention in his diary of their meeting on 22 December, in Delhi, with Jawaharlal Nehru (1889–1964), India's first Prime Minister following independence in 1947, and his daughter, Indira Gandhi (see n. 6, p. 87), to follow in her father's footsteps as leader of her country. In a joint letter to Mary Potter, Pears and Britten wrote on the 23rd:

> We had lunch with Nehru & his daughter – what a man, & so gay too! – considering what responsibilities & problems, & that he'd just made an hour's speech in Parliament. Imagine Churchill relaxing, petting his Panders, talking gay nonsense, followed by discussing what he's said – & insisting we should eat some Melon brought by Bulganin! – to absolute strangers!

[40]  The reception was held on 20 December.

[41]  Pears's and Britten's recital in Delhi took place on 21 December at the YWCA Constantia Hall under the auspices of the Delhi Music Society. The programme, like so many of the others on this tour, comprised five of Haydn's English canzonets, Schubert lieder, and Britten's *Winter Words* and folksong arrangements. The concert, which as Pears's diary makes evident was recorded by All-India Radio, was widely and most favourably reviewed in the English language press.

sure in same place, Indian radio-lady at first sure not moved but P. thinks it has been, Indian r-lady worried suggests re-balance; as audience in hall already, r-l draws curtain *behind* mike, P & B utter a few chords & squeaks ppp with thick curtain between music & mike; radio-lady eagerly listening with headphones 2½ yards off-stage, expresses complete satisfaction. Stifled laughter from P. & B. Next day two minutes of tape recording showed Indian radio-lady's balance-judgement not reliable. Invitation to tea next day by I.r-l. (name Mrs. Dutt): accepted: went & were treated to many sandwiches & rich cake, in company with Indian general & others, also 2 Americans. Hostess played on piano excerpts from Ballet written for Pavlova! also sang long song about the Ascent of the Soul: music mixture of Alec Rowley and Ketèlbey: composer said sadly, coyly "I try to fuse Indian ragas with Harmony. I am a Rebel!" This tea-party mercifully was preceded by an hour or more of the real thing. Ravi Shankar, a wonderful virtuoso, played his own Indian music to us at the Radio station & we attended a Broadcast.[42] Brilliant, fascinating, stimulating, wonderfully played – first on a full orchestra of about 20 musicians, then solo on a sort of zither. Starting solo (with a plucked drone background from 2 instruments always) & then joined halfway through by a man playing two drums; unbelievable skill & invention. Then another nice cosy evening with Brit. Coun. We spend restful mornings, writing & reading round swimming pool in nice warm sun, observing Indian bird life, a vulture hovers greedily overhead, our ribs can feel its beak, darling parrots green & yellow squawk, kites float, monkeys caper, butterflies soar, Pernod soothes.

---

[42]   Indian sitar player and composer (b. 1920). The broadcast took place on 22 December. The next day Britten and Pears wrote to Mary Potter:

Yesterday we had our first *real* taste of Indian music, & it was tremendously fascinating. We had the luck to hear one of the best living performers (composer too), & he played in a small room to us alone – which is as it should be, not in concerts. Like everything they do it seemed much more relaxed & spontaneous than what we do, & the reactions of the other musicians sitting around was really orgiastic. Wonderful sounds, intellectually complicated & controlled. By jove, the clever Indian *is* a brilliant creature – one feels like a bit of Yorkshire Pudd. in comparison.

As Mervyn Cooke has noted, Britten's interest in Indian music (which began in the 1930s) had to wait until 1968 to surface in his compositions when, in the third church parable, *The Prodigal Son*, Op. 81, Britten made explicit borrowings from a gramophone recording of two *ragas* performed by the flute player Pannalal Gosh. (See MC, pp. 371–8.)

*Agra.*[43]

Awoken at 6.45, we take a small aeroplane (a Heron) from one of the Delhi aerodromes. Confusion intense at getting off from hotel, paying bill etc. Tips are a burning problem in India; there is a row of entirely unknown faces, eager, perhaps worthy, people who have cleaned one's shoes, washed one's clothes, mended them, dusted one's room, brought breakfast, laid the fire, made the bed, liftboys, porters, waiters, all different, how many does one tip & how much? Embarrassment on all sides. B and P mutter furiously "Have you any small change?" "I've told you once, No!" Finally one tips two people far far too much & the others not at all. Impossibly difficult.

Journey to Agra allright over progressively more fertile plain: signs of floods but not excessive. Arrival at nice colonial-style hotel. Snake charmer immediately noticeable, with python & mongoose. Whenever B or P are visible on way to or from room, he blows a squirl at us from his absurd shawm. Irresistible. When will we succumb? Arrange to visit Taj [Mahal] with dear old guide, in taxi, also Red Fort. Both turn out v. impressive. Red Fort vast walled palace built by Akbar in 1569(?) in red sandstone: ravishing marble mosque-let & wonderful carved lattice screens. Taj quite perfect, noble elegy: gentle & not oversize: exquisite inlay work throughout: dome superb & yet not oppressive. Late lunch, lazed in garden all afternoon. Early to bed. Hotel has several (10?) English guests. We don't speak.

Dogs bark loudly most of night; uncomfortable beds, pillows filled with cotton-wool rocks. B. sleeps little: P. enough. Tea brought by ex-Sepoy at 7.30 A.M. After breakfast, off with guide in taxi to Fatehpur Sikri, Akbar's capital for 16 years, built in 20(?) years employing 20,000 workmen: vast city, depressing, only beautiful thing, tomb of Holy Saint who foretold Akbar's son, in marble again. Gosh! how good marble is, compared to red sand-stone? Man dived from roof 70 ft. into dirty water for us: curious what tourists pay for! Back for Christmas Day lunch; mincepies etc. Forced into conversation with British pair, man & wife, doctors, caravanning from London to Singapore; Druids, prefer Stonehenge to Taj Mahal; hair-raising stories of punctures in Afghanistan, etc: very odd: on to Calcutta in their Land-Rover. Lazy in sun all afternoon, tea, drinks, then dinner (plum pudding, oh dear, my waistline.) Then to the Taj by moonlight. Too much mist, too many silly noisy people, too little moon, but grand, beautiful, haunting, touching all the same. Another deafening night with dogs howling near & far and a terrible cough just outside the window; Indian music on the wireless

---

[43] Pears and Britten left Delhi on Christmas Eve when they travelled to Agra where they stayed at Laurie's Hotel until the 26th. They returned to Delhi for one more night (26th) before journeying on to Calcutta the following day.

starts at 7 A.M. and goes on to 9 P.M. with few breaks. Ultra-lazy morning in the sun. Ben: "I want to do just this for three weeks". Great decision: asked snake-charmer to perform at a charge of Rs 5. (7$^s$/6$^d$). Appeared with a sleepy python, 3 cobras, a krite(?) (you're dead in 20 minutes!) a two headed snake (rather a dear) and a depressed mongoose. Charmer rather like a one-eyed Malcolm Sargent,[44] limited repertoire; dull tune, snakes didn't dance, merely sat up & spat. Malcolm Sargent offer to drape python round one's neck, no danger, refused; cowardly?

During the wait for the Air-Bus, succumbed to another Tourist lure. Man with three little so-called Indian canaries, attached by the leg to a cross-stick. He frees them & throws coins, rings etc into the air which they catch, they put betelnut into his mouth, cottonwool into his ear, one threads half-a-dozen beads with needle and cotton, another picks up the card with the number you chose on it; very talented, dear little creatures; owner learnt it from his father, produces fat book of references and appreciations, signatures & photographs. Charges 7$^s$/6$^d$ for demonstration. Reasonable? Early at the Airfield, we lie for half an hour in the sun in a ruin – not of a 4th century temple – but of an open air film theatre. Oh India! Land of contrasts!

Good flight to Delhi, met by nice Eric da Costa, Economist, who motors us to see two more of the 9 (at least) cities which have been built on or near Delhi in 1000 years. Very curious tower called Q'tub [Qutab] Minar – part of vast mosque built in 12$^{th}$ century by Turkish invaders – very tall and – as it were – waisted with pleats at every storey – most curious and beautiful effect. Thence to Tuglakabad [Tughlaqabad] – immense fort built in 13$^{th}$ century (in 18 months) – with vast impressive panorama – left empty after 3 years. India full of such deserted horrific ruins, always reminding one of the length of this continent's history and its vast scale and senselessness.

Stayed the night with Philip Wade, of Burmah-Shell in house which used to be inhabited by my brother-in-law John.[45] Extremely comfortable, & kind host. Roaring open fire most acceptable. Nevertheless I started a cold which was not helped by 1¾ hrs. shivering wait from 7. A.M. to 8.45 at Delhi airport, nor by the ventilation of the Skymaster which bore us towards Calcutta[46] & which swung wildly from icy breeziness which made one cower under a rug, to blasts of heat

---

[44] British conductor (1895–1967) with whom both Pears and Britten had an uneasy relationship, Pears most recently during the rehearsals and first performances of Walton's *Troilus and Cressida* at Covent Garden in December 1954, for which Pears created the role of Pandarus.

[45] The husband of Pears's sister, Jessie.

[46] Pears and Britten arrived in Calcutta at midday on 27 December, staying at the Grand Hotel until 2 January 1956.

which set one gasping. Arrived shattered. Ben Watt of Bank, Casanovas & Jacob, conductors, to meet us. Very amiable; taken to hotel. Party in evening at Watts for mostly British music lovers, followed by most pleasant dinner at Lady Mookerjee's (friend of Leonard Elmhirst).[47] Family of son daughter & d-in-law, all arguing furiously and presto about everything. Sir Brien M.[48] holds forth lengthily about finance & socialism. House built 1880? full of wild Victorian pictures & furniture, surprising since Lady M. is a great patron of contemporary painting. Next day our concert, in surprisingly acceptable theatre-cinema.[49] Went allright, though I was so hot during first part that I imagined that the great drops of sweat splashing off me were clearly audible and visible from gallery. Not so, I'm told. After concert, dinner with Ben Watt. Next day, went to tea with Lady Mookerjee & then on to Fine Arts Exhibition with her. On the whole very poor standard of painting and drawing; either trad. Oriental or efforts at European. One good old man, & one very young man. Then change and on to dim official party,[50] & thence to Martha Graham's Co[mpan]y.[51] Surely here are two ingredients: 1. gifted inventive woman with well trained coy, 2. basically pretentious and sentimental American folksiness. Music awful. In the afternoon just as we were going to Lady M. got a message (re invitation to the Hills) that only plane left at 4.A.M. Decided to take plunge, therefore after M. Graham, went to bed for 2 hours & were roused at 2.15 to drive in Black Maria-like van to Dumdum aerodrome. Waited 1½ [hours] in hangar, got off at 4.0. Reached Grassmore at 6.30AM. Met by Martin Hawes, our host, with whom we spent a delightful 24 hours.[52] The Doars are the beginnings of the Himalayan foothills, Kanchenjunga was partially *just* visible. Here tea is the thing, miles of flat topped 3 ft. high bushes. Climate delightful, never too hot, 250 inches of rain, all in 3 months, lovely sun, fresh breeze. M.H. lives in delightful bungalow with a brilliant garden created by himself, bright reds, purples, yellows, really inventive, with a tiny water pool. Distances are great, the railway

---

[47]  Leonard Elmhirst (1893–1974), patron of the arts and founder of the Dartington Hall Arts Centre, near Totnes, Devon, where Pears and Britten gave numerous recitals from the early 1940s onwards, had many connections with India. The reception and dinner took place on the 27th. The Mookerjees were described as a 'charming family' by Britten in a letter to Imogen Holst (4 January 1956).

[48]  Sir Birendra Nath Mookerjee (1899–1982), Indian businessman and politician.

[49]  The programme details of this concert have not been traced.

[50]  A reception hosted by the UK High Commissioner on the 29th.

[51]  The American dancer and choreographer (1900–1991) whose company set new standards for contemporary American dance.

[52]  Pears and Britten left for this excursion on the 30th, returning to Calcutta on New Year's Eve. Martin Hawes was later described by Britten as 'a fan of ours' who had contacted them 'out of the blue suggesting we should go' (letter to Roger Duncan, 18 January 1956).

or airport is 30 miles off, there are only 200 Europeans in a section 10 x 200 miles. Life must hang on the congeniality of one's fellows, whether Indian or British; not always forthcoming. One can manage it, like our host, by being genuinely fond of & interested in the Indians, and exerting himself to find the best in his colleagues from Aberdeen and Dundee. We were shown a Tea Factory: much dust; and figures which I can never remember (Produce? 1¾ million lbs. of tea a year??). Also taken to jungle lookout, high up over clearing in jungle, waited for 2 hours at dusk, saw nothing but heard a wonderful pattern of jungly noises, all sorts of birds, jungle cocks, toucans etc, an elephant moving through the forest, a tiger coughing, very tense and electric. Off back to Calcutta by plane next morning after breakfast in warm but balmy sun in Martin's garden. Altogether most memorable visit. After 2 hours wait for plane, flew back over most interesting Bengal landscape. Very visible that Nature has not yet stopped tinkering with her work: riverbeds' courses changed by floods, rice fields in previous course; they are waiting for two more earthquakes in the mountains before they settle down, earthquakes which may easily change whole rivers and hills; unlike our tight little island which is now more or less settled for a bit – or isn't it? Plane much later in Calcutta than expected; therefore almost immediately whizzed off to visit Jamini Roy, G.O.M. of Bengal painting.[53] House a series of quite white box-rooms, with white low book-cases to sit on. J. Roy (until 1942) was financially struggling as most Indians are, but the Yanks arriving during the war descended on him & bought everything. His answer was to employ son & ?nephew to copy his pictures without cease, so now it works as a sort of factory (cf. Rubens, Vandyck etc.) with the old boy doing one & the others copying & perhaps altering slightly. It was as clear as day which were copies & which were originals, or so it seemed to us, and we bought a line drawing which I'm sure is original,[54] partly because it has had so many drawing pins stuck into the corner (? to hold the tracing paper down for the son to copy!), also because it has real vitality in the drawing & the others had *not*.

After visit, home to rest & change, then dinner with Emmerson (Lit. Editor of The Statesman) & wife (sister-in-law of W.H. Auden)[55] very Pernod-y and voluble, with nice J. Roy paintings and others. Then on at midnight to New Year Party at Desmond Doig's (friend of Martin Hawes) who had Tibetan & Nepalese dancers. Tibetans: sweet square family 3 women with drums 4 males large & small, dancers, whizzing

---

[53]  Indian artist (1887–1972), one of the founders of the modern school of Indian painting, particularly known for his studies of Christ. 'G.O.M.' = grand old man.

[54]  The drawing does not apparently survive at the Britten–Pears Library.

[55]  The *Statesman* was a Calcutta (later Calcutta and Delhi) English language newspaper. Emmerson's wife was the sister of W.H. Auden's brother John's wife.

round-over, round-over: simple & touching, very intent on doing their best. Nepalese: ill sorted group of 5 or 6, two double-ended drums, touching, but spoilt by paralytic shyness of them all, particularly man dressed & dancing as woman who had to have his moustache shaved off before they started; also singing very bad indeed – they had never *performed* before, I think. We left early but not before Ben had been cornered by Martha Graham & asked for a Ballett about Heloise & Abelard, to be made as a Coloured Film![56] Next day out to lunch with Ben Watt to Tollygunga Club, ravishing spot, old lofty house, Nabob-type, classical & white; one can see what colonial life could have been in the good old days. One is embarrassed by the excess of servants in even quite simple households; one would like to think that one is being bourgeois in thinking that they want tips. One is not: they do.

[Unmarked notepaper]

Leaving Calcutta Jan. 1st–2nd 1956 took place at one of those forgotten times-of-day so much beloved by International Air Lines – 2.40 A.M. We had to be at Dum-dum Airport at 1.45, so we had a very late dinner indeed (of course all drink ceased at midnight) & finally were driven off stupid & sleepy by our friend Ben Watt and M^r. Jacob. Earlier in the evening we had done a half hour broadcast for the Calcutta studio of the All India Radio, with a small audience of friends, & had overheard a few minutes of Indian female singing – very peculiar – a sort of hard-pressed low squeal, full of controlled flourishes but not nearly so immediately sympathetic as the instrumental music. The lady squatted eastern fashion on the floor. (*Memo*: I must learn to squat; I am sure the Indians owe their wonderful figures to it!) One of the features of Calcutta life which we were most sorry to leave was the very persistent pimp outside the Grand Hotel, who might whisper ardently to us at any time of day or night we appeared. At first his words were quite unintelligible, (possibly Hindi or German?) then after a day or two "You like girl?" was audible, which grew into "school girls?" (con espressione) and then "English school girl?" (ah! that's got him); finally, in despair, to a quite unresponsive Ben, "FRENCH SCHOOL GIRLS?!!" We got rather fond of him.

The air journey to Singapore was the usual procession of meal-lets, drink-lets, and sleep-lets. When we emerged from the plane, we were aware that we had reached the Tropics! In one minute all one's stuffing

---

[56] Although Britten did not collaborate with Martha Graham on a ballet based on Abelard and Heloise, it was a story that had attracted him, oddly enough, on more than one occasion during the 1940s. See DMPR, p. 1205.

was gone; in half an hour one was sweaty and cross, and not because of the heat but (our old friend from New York), the Humidity. We were in Singapore for 5 days (Jan 2$^{nd}$–7$^{th}$), and all the time that one was out of doors one was bothered by this beastly damp heat. Quite hopeless for the poor old vocal chords [sic], of course, and I sang like a pig at both concerts (one including Dichterliebe and the other Schöne Müllerin)[57] in one of those ghastly good-for-nothing great halls built in the middle of the nineteenth century to glorify municipalities, useless for meetings (speaking voice inaudible) vile for concerts (music goes up to the ceiling and stays there, churned around by fans). The artist's room icy with air-conditioning, the hall stifling with airlessness, sweat pours down one's shirt, and one shouts oneself hoarse to be heard by the poor people at the back of the great hot barn of a place. Ugh!

But we met some very nice Singaporeans and were well looked after, particularly by Roy Benger & his wife, & the Van Heens.[58] Singapore is a ¾ Chinese city, (Footnote: In Chinese, the 1st name is the Surname, e.g. Ah Chum (a Tailor in S.$^{pre}$) wld. be called Mr. Ah, until you got to know him better when you could call him Chum. Also there was a nice firm called Wee Wee Dry Cleaners.) & we were shewn some appalling modern Chinese temples, with a hideous great Buddha and sickening smells. We also met Chinese food for the first time in the Chinese Restaurant of the Cathay Hotel where we were staying. As we went in, there was a band making a hellish noise, while a Chinese balanced another Chinese on his head the top one upside down, scalp to scalp, while the top one consumed a glass of beer and kept it down (or should one say up?) until the turn concluded. The band went on making a frightful American-type noise, the lights went dark blue, & we tried to eat our first Chinese food in the noisy darkness. I had been bold and had ordered fascinating things like fried prawns, & some sort of odd meat in rice, but Ben thinking of his tummy had ordered safe sounding things which turned out to be identical dishes i.e. Chicken Soup with beans, beans with noodles, & chicken chop suey or something, all quite uneatable with chopsticks. After an hour we went to bed, Ben exhausted with frustration and still hungry, to our ice-cold air-conditioned bedroom, where one sleeps better as it is cooler but where one is regularly de-conditioned for the outside oven-temperature. A breeding-ground for split personalities?

We were very kindly entertained on various occasions in Singapore; we consumed a great deal of very weak whiskey and soda, some fascinating little Chinese cocktail-goodies, minute ravioli filled with

---

57   The first concert took place on 4 January (Schumann's Dichterliebe), the second on the 6th (Schubert's Die schöne Müllerin).
58   Unidentified, although Benger may have been with the British Council in Singapore. See also p. 52.

shrimps and chutney, & little balls of chopped sweet nuts, and we started on the Great Rice Consumption which will continue now I suppose till we get back to England. But there were three events at Singapore which stood out from the rest of our visit to this fundamentally rather characterless city. First, our visit to the Rubber Plantation, about 35 miles North of Singapore, in the State of Johore. We were picked up by Jane & Roy Benger and drove straight North to the end of Sing.[pre] Island, across the causeway, through Johore city out into the country. Immediately one leaves Johore, one is in Bandit country and *could* be attacked even on the main road.[59] However – – after 30 miles of unadventurous journey, we were met by the Planter, Bill Vincent, in an armoured car, and we were escorted two miles down a very rough side road (past the English school run by 2 indefatigable English spinsters) to the Factory Area, a village entirely enclosed in barbed wire, with the Planter's house on a hill above, again enclosed with a barbed wire fence, and flood lamps which are on all night. Bill Vincent, aged about 34, ex-RAF, from Surrey, fairhaired, nice looking, had been planting 8 years. All that time the Bandits had made periodical incursions, mostly for food, occasionally to kill a foreman. If a worker had refused them food, he might have his head sawn off. There had been just such a visit in the month before we were there. We were shown the factory where half a dozen simple processes "convert the cream-like latex into pure rubber squares ready for dispatch in a day". (Compare any documentary film, put out by Dunlops.) Quite crude machinery involving such little expense must bring in vast profits for the Investors (if the price of rubber is high). We were shown the Rubber Trees, always shadowed by two Gurkha types with machine-guns. Our host then gave us some gin & tonic (excellent tonic water from Singapore) much appreciated! followed by an admirable lunch – rice, of course, etc. & a fascinating sago sweet with molasses. To live alone in a bungalow, with jittery Malays as your servants and employees, behind barbed wire, waiting for anything, needs tremendous spirit, and Bill Vincent, admirable fellow, has that allright. We left again under armed guard as far as the main road, and thence proceeded alone. After ten minutes towards Singapore, a downpour occurred. In a minute there were rivers in the ditches, the road was a-flood, and one could see nothing through the wind-screen. We went through a vast puddle and in 30 yards came to a stop – water in the plugs – quite dead. It teemed

---

[59]  The bandits mentioned here by Pears were Chinese Communist guerillas led by Chin Peng. After the disbanding of the Malayan Peoples' Anti-Japanese Army in 1945, these guerillas had infiltrated trades unions and attacked European rubber planters. A state of emergency was in force in the country from 1948 and was not to be lifted until 1960. Leaving the safety of Singapore was – at the time of Pears's and Britten's visit – a potentially hazardous excursion.

and teemed. Roy pressed the starter for twenty minutes – nothing. Hot inside & wet out. Off to the right of the road was a large house with its shutters up from which bandits would clearly emerge at any moment; on the left was rather thick jungle – ideal cover for them. We sat and sweated, and the rain teemed. At last a Singapore car with 2 Chinese in it stopped. They weren't bandits and they offered us a lift, and Ben & Jane & I gladly took it and left Roy with the car. After various further delays, we reached the Bengers' house an hour late for a date but that didn't matter! We had come unscathed through our terrible ordeal! More weak whisky & water ...

The second major event in Singapore was a visit (after a nice dinner out by the sea) to the "Happy World" one of 3 (The others being called "The New World" and "Out-of-this World"(?)) sort-of-Fun Fairs which the Chinese have built for themselves in S. It is roughly on the lines of the Tivoli at Copenhagen, being a large enclosed space to which you pay for admission, filled with shops, cafés, restaurants, stalls of all sorts, and revues and opera theatres. To one of these Chinese operas we went – or for half-an-hour of it. The stage was at one end of a large garage which was fairly well filled with an audience largely of young women & children who showed a fair attention but not enthusiasm for the very odd entertainment. The story appeared to be some sort of family quarrel – a young man was crouched on the floor in disgrace, a young woman was howling, a father-character was holding forth grandiosely. We went up off-stage. O.P was a small percussion band which crashed & banged between speeches. We crossed over Prompt side in time to meet the young actress crossly demanding a prop, whereupon a fair-haired, blue-eyed, large doll was thrust into her arms, & she went back onto the stage. No-one seemed surprised. The orchestra on the Prompt side consisted of a flute, a cigar-box-violin, a xylophone, and a soft drum and guitar. This made a very gentle background for a nasal singer. No one was audible from the front of the house, I'm sure. After a bit, the whole entertainment seemed too curious and we left, bought some junk & went home.

The third event in Singapore was meeting and seeing something of my cousin the Archdeacon of Singapore.[60] (Dear Janet, your brother couldn't have been less bossy and boring! It would be wonderful to have someone like him in every city we visit. Alas! not enough Robins to go round! P) He is a man of considerable charm and enormous energy who has built up a large and enthusiastic congregation (may one call a congregation enthusiastic?) in his vast parish. He has the major

---

[60] Rt Revd Robert (Robin) Woods (b. 1914), Janet Stone's brother (see note 1, p. 18) and a friend of Britten's from his public school-days at Gresham's, Holt, in Norfolk. Woods was Archdeacon of Singapore and Vicar of St Andrew's Cathedral, 1951–8.

advantage of a large and really splendid Victorian Gothic cathedral (c. 1850) built by some civil engineer (from a book of plans by Pugin,[61] I should think). Standing in a green grassy close and shining brightly all over with white paint, it makes a typically-English but v. successful contribution to the Singapore sky-line. The next best building in Singapore is the Cricket Club, just along from the Cathedral, which looks like a bit of St. John's Wood. Altogether a very "homey" corner of the Empire!

Conclusions after Singapore: How easy and what fun, in a way, to be pioneers, but oh how difficult and drab to be 4th generation consolidators, batting on an exceedingly sticky wicket with no one paying much attention to the Rules of the Game. Hats off!!

On January 6th, the Hessens (Lu and Peg) joined us in Singapore for the rest of the tour,[62] and on the 7th we flew on to Djakarta.[63] A certain confusion was caused in the last days at Singapore because Peg's brother, John Geddes, had, from well-intentioned enthusiasm, inveigled out of a rather unwilling-sounding Governor, an invitation for us all to Dine at Government House on Saturday, January 7th, the day on the *morning* of which we were to leave Singapore. General retreat in disorder. Much face-saving, letter-writing, book-signing, amid gubernatorial umbrage!

Djakarta (formerly, under the Dutch, Batavia) is the capital of the Republic of Indonesia. No one knows how many inhabitants it has; some say three million, some four. It spreads a huge distance, and at 5.30 p.m, the time we arrived, the traffic is impossible. There are very many large American cars, but they say that in Djakarta alone there are 50,000 Tricycle-Rickshaws. These are Tricycles, ridden by a boy, with a seat hitched onto a frame in front, holding 2–3 people. We saw these things for the first time in Karachi where we were told that the machines were hired out to the boys at 10 Rupees a day. The boys charge ½ a Rupee a Mile (or maybe less) so that they have to go 20 miles at least a day before they have covered the Hiring Fee. Think of it, in tropical heat. No wonder that the incidence of T.B. is very high among these boys. Yet you see them in their thousands throughout the Tropics and the East, toiling away pushing families of fat Chinese. In India there is a move for banning them, but they are too popular.

---

[61] Augustus Pugin (1812–1852), English architect whose *Contrasts*, advocating Gothic as the only truly Christian style, was published in 1836.

[62] Prince Ludwig of Hesse and the Rhine[s] (1908–1968) and his Scottish-born wife Princess Margaret[s] (b. 1913). The Hesses had left Frankfurt on 27 December 1955 and after eight days in India had joined Pears and Britten in Singapore.

[63] The party flew to Djakarta (Java) via Palembang (on Sumatra) where they changed planes.

In Djakarta we stayed with Eric Corrin and his wife Hazel[64] whom we knew well when she was in the British Council in Amsterdam. New house, sensibly designed with open verandahs and plenty of through-draughts, and a garden full of fabulous tropical plants, paw-paws, banana trees, palms, hibiscus, vast cannas, elephant ears, and an extraordinary fern which shrivels right up and droops directly you touch it, another plant with yellow berries and blue flowers on it at the same time, called "Pretty Girl and Naughty Boy!"

Our patrons in Indonesia are "the Union of Art-circles" (Kunstkring Bond), a Dutch organisation consisting of 30 centres in Indonesia, a membership which pays a little subscription, the whole thing heavily subsidised by Holland. I propose to write more of this (seemingly) enviable set-up at the end of our visit to Indonesia.[65] Enough for now that they are arranging all travel, accommodation, etc for BB., PP., & the Hessens, and have provided us with a mentor, guide, & musical-lexicon in Bernhard van Ijzerdraat,[66] of whom also more later. The Kunstkring asked us in the first place to do *30* concerts in In^d; that meant at least 2 months here. We said NO but we might do 5 or 6. They said "Yes".

---

[64] Working for the British Council in Indonesia. The Hesses did not stay with them but at the Indonesian Hotel.

[65] As the diary remained unfinished, Pears wrote no further of the work of the Kunstkring Bond. However, in a joint letter to *The Times* (6 June 1956) supporting state aid for the arts, particularly in connection with the exposure of British music and musicians abroad, Pears and Britten wrote: 'We now know that we would have never got to Japan or Ceylon or Turkey without the British Council. As for Indonesia (with its Dutch-supported organization – Kunstkring) . . . concert life would simply cease without State support.'

[66] Bernard 'Penny' Ijzerdraat (d. 1986), Dutch ethnomusicologist, who for a time played in the famous gamelan at Peliatan (near Ubud, Bali), a rare distinction for a westerner. It was under Ijzerdraat's guidance that Britten heard much Balinese music first-hand, an experience that immediately fed into the composition of his three-act ballet *The Prince of the Pagodas* (1955–6), and which was to have further long-range consequences to his musical vocabulary. See MC, pp. 10–195, Mervyn Cooke, 'Britten and Bali', *Journal of Musicological Research*, 7 (1987), pp. 307–39, and Cooke's sleeve notes to the Virgin Classics recording of *The Prince of the Pagodas* (VCD 7 91103-2), and Donald Mitchell, 'What do we know about Britten now?' and 'Catching on to the technique in Pagoda-land', in Christopher Palmer (ed.), *The Britten Companion* (London: Faber and Faber, 1984), pp. 39–45 and 192–210. Britten commented in a letter to Imogen Holst (17 January 1956):
The music is *fantastically* rich – melodically, rhythmically, texture (such *orchestration!!*) & above all *formally*. We are lucky being taken around everywhere by an intelligent Dutch musicologist, married to a Balinese, who knows all musicians – so we go to rehearsals, find out about & visit cremations, trance dances, shadow plays – a bewildering richness. At last I'm beginning to catch on to the technique, but it's about as complicated as Schönberg.

We have met our Secretary, Treasurer, etc and all seem agreeable.

(Jan 7th) On our first evening in Djakarta, we were taken out by the Corrins to a restaurant in Chinatown. As everywhere in S.E. Asia, the Chinese are the most industrious, successful, reliable part of the community (and therefore richest) but not, I fancy, the most imaginative or sympathetic. Certainly their cooking is better than the Indonesian, & this meal was a very nice one, close by a market where everything from bamboo flutes to bicycles was being sold up to 9 at night.

First concert in Djakarta in long narrow hall:[67] awkward for singing: Dutch officials being very Dutch and stiff in interval and after concert: my voice *hates* the tropics: very wet and hot: more weak whisky and water after concert: "Kidneys must be flushed frequently in tropics."

On Monday, January 9th, we flew on up to Bandung in an old Dakota, facing crossways. No one sick. Very pleasantly situated place in mountains but very near to bandits. (During the Asia–Africa conference there, the entire Indonesian army was called on to keep the bandits well away.) Driven around in afternoon by local Dutch to see scenery; Dutch driving, as in Amsterdam, furious and noisy, bad example for Indonesians; Ijzerdraat put on some very sweet music for us, a bamboo flute and a sort of zither played by two teachers, gentle, charming, skilful, civilised; also witnessed class of tots (5–9) being coached in dance – much finger–wrist–arm-movement, slow, control-needing.[68]

---

[67] Given on 8 January.

[68] This occasion in Bandung was Britten's and Pears's first live contact with Indonesian music, an event also recorded by Prince Ludwig in *Ausflug Ost*, pp. 30–31:

> Siesta. Then Mr Ijzerdraat . . . takes us to a schoolhouse situated behind our hotel. From outside one can already hear music and drumming. All the rooms inside are full of little girls learning to dance to the sound of a small orchestra consisting chiefly of percussion. They şwing their bodies and move hands which are bent backwards, gliding then standing still. The youngest group is about five years of age. They all wear, over European children's clothes, batik sarongs and waistbands from which sashes hang at both ends . . . A zither- and flute-player come into the adjoining room. The zither is very large, shaped like a ship, with many metal strings stretched over it. The bamboo flute has six fingerholes . . . The zither begins, a sound like groping around. The flute follows suit. I am unable to comprehend the overall effect, hearing only the waterlike tone of the flute and the sound of the zither changing direction, seemingly independent of each other. Then a song, where they both come together in a strident melody. The pieces die away slowly and without a final emphasis. Ben and Peter distinguish between the tune (which stays firm) and the decoration which the performer adds himself. My aural ability and musical knowledge do not allow me

Concert in school hall holding 1000;[69] pleasant; a number of Indonesians in audience; torrential downpour before and just after concert. Usual stiff Dutch party afterwards.

New (to us) features of hotel-life, indigenous to Indonesia: (1.) The climate being constantly very warm (75°–95°) one is provided at night with a single sheet only: with this there is also (besides usual pillows) a longish fat bolster, laid down the middle of the bed. I understand that one is expected to hug this thing all night: why? something to do with perspiration. It is called a Dutch Wife!

2. The Indonesian bath room consists of a tiled square room with a drain in one corner and a tall open tiled tank in another. This tank is filled with cold water (in which one often discovers spiders, sand, mosquitoes etc) and a tin scoop is provided which is dipped into the tank, filled with water and then emptied over one's back in the middle of the room. This of course leads to much splashing, and not only the walls but one's hairbrushes, razor blades and towels are always wet. The floor is more often than not 3 inches deep in water which is awkward for the lav. (usually in a 3rd corner of the room)! The hours I spent with my shoes awash!

We left Bandung on Tuesday 10th. Or rather, we went to the airport at *8 A.M.* to catch a plane to Surabaja, and finally took off at *5.30 p.m.* & got as far as Semarang. (Is there any day less well spent than one at an airport – waiting?) We were of course not expected at Semarang. However the Bandung Dutch had telephoned to warn the local Kunstkring of our plight, and we were met and entertained by 2 local Dutch who arranged for the Hessens to be put up by the Dutch Commissioner, & us by a v. nice British BAT chap called Beckett. The whole thing was a very good example of organised and yet spontaneous hospitality, which one continually meets in the East. They put us all to shame with their kindness.[70]

Communications of all sorts are very inefficient in Indonesia, post, telephone, telegraph, hotel and air reservations, arrangements of any sort can go far astray. So the next day (11th) from Semarang, there were only 2 air tickets (for Ben & me), and Lu & Peg had to go by train to Surabaya (very decent and air conditioned.) In Surabaya we were staying

---

such an appreciation. The players are happy when Ben sings out to
them the scale on which it is based. They laugh.

[69]   The recital in Bandung was given in the 'Aula Christelijk Lyceum'. The programme comprised Haydn's English canzonets, lieder by Schubert and Schumann, and Britten's *Winter Words* and French folksong arrangements.

[70]   One excursion while in Semarang not recorded by Pears was a visit to a famous gong factory (Semarang is traditionally regarded as the centre of gong manufacture in South East Asia), an event which gave the travellers their first encounter with gamelan instruments.

with an exceedingly nice couple (De Waal) particularly the wife, very comfortable cabin: jolly good food: after concert (in a circular hall with one side open to allow overflow outside to hear, and continual traffic-bangs-squeaks-tinkles-screeches)[71] we drank chez Dan & Peggy Hubrecht, a wholly delightful (Dutch) English couple who gave us lots of introductions to Bali.

The next morning we ran around Soerabaya buying beach-shoes, thin shirts, socks, drink, soap, razor blades and torches (!) and finally took off by a Heron plane (pleasant little 14-seater 4-engined creatures) for Bali.[72]

The G.I.A. (Garuda Indonesian Airways) provided us with lunch consisting of: 1 piece of cold breaded fish, 1 potato croquette, 2 creamy cakes, 4 biscuits and 1 cup of chocolate milk. In spite of this, we arrived at Bali none the worse!!

## BALI! BALI! BALI!

BALI
January 13<sup>th</sup>–25<sup>th</sup>

When is an island not an island? When it's as big as Java or Sumatra. But when it's Bali, my goodness it's an island. Bali is quite big: same sort of shape as Isle of Wight, but 100 miles across and 70 up & down, (and you don't have tigers at Shanklin or little girl dancers at Osborne.)

From the moment we arrived at the airfield which is about 200 yds wide & situated bang on an Isthmus, we didn't get out of the sight & sound of water. It was hot & a bit humid; although their summer, it was the rainy season, and no day passed without at least one torrential downpour lasting from 20 minutes to several hours. The best time to go is *not* now: one *should* visit Bali in the dry mild-ish time of July & August. However – it isn't bad even now – not half! The landscape always has a mountain in the background (there are 3 or 4 volcanoes, 10,000 ft) and then are always coconut palms, (neat, well drawn, Henri-Rousseau-like trees) and always rice-fields. The rice fields are small

---

[71] A programme survives at the Britten–Pears Library for a recital in Surabaja promoted by the Kunstkring Bond. However, it bears no date and may therefore represent the programme for this occasion or the other recital given by Pears and Britten in the town on 25 January. The programme shows that songs by Purcell, Schubert and Frank Bridge were performed, as well as the Second Lute Song from Britten's *Gloriana* and folksong arrangements. See also Plate 4.

[72] The party flew to Bali on 12 January. During their first evening Ijzerdraat introduced them to the music of Bali, Borneo and Java by playing several tape recordings.

squares, very varied in size but much smaller than our fields; generally in terraces up a hillside, they can also be on the flat. In the hills, they drain from one field to another all the time as the water *must* change always. The colours vary from wonderful pale yellow to bright vivid green and ripe gold. As the climate is much the same the whole year, you have these colours always with you. The houses are mostly made of woven rush screen-like walls, sometimes with brick too, & thatched roofs over bamboo beams. The people are far the most beautiful we have met and although the March of Mind has created a fashion for shirts and vests and brassières, still most Balinese, male & female, are bare from the waist up, and most beautiful and simple and convincing it is. There are 4 million people on Bali, but village life is very highly worked out. Temples are very much in evidence; rather disappointing we thought; very elaborate carving in a very soft stone, over all walls, pillars, flat surfaces. The Balinese are Hindus, whereas the other Indonesians are Mohammedans. The stone is so soft that temples are always falling down, and new ones have to be built, which keeps the style alive. The immediate superficial impression is that in spite of its beauty and charm (and in spite of the endless glossy photographs) Bali is *not* glamorous, and those who expect and demand Hollywood-type technicolour glamour will be disappointed. It is adorable, but essentially simple.

There's one quasi-first class hotel – boring, bad food, though very nice helpful manager.[73] But they have an annexe at the sea-side (Sanur) about 7 miles from Den Passar (where the capital is, & the big hotel). And to Sanur we went when we arrived and stayed there for 3 nights. The annexe was close to the beach, separated from it by coconut palms: the beach itself is pale honey coloured, and composed entirely of minutely crushed shells, rather prickly for the feet, and you find all sorts & sizes of lovely shells. Bathing is possible here because of the reef 200 yds out on which the surf breaks gloriously white. This keeps all but the smallest sharks out but means that the water inside is very shallow, and swimming difficult. Mostly one splashes and flops – very agreeably. Often the water, the air, and the earth seemed to be of exactly the same temperature & one only changes elements and textures. It is a mistake to think of Bali (anyway in January) as being perpetually sunny. There were nearly all the time clouds, beautiful swelling shapes, but seldom was the sky quite free of them. But even so one could quickly get burnt, lying in the haze.

---

[73] The Bali Hotel, Denpasar, served as their base on the island, although they were to spend periods outside the capital, notably at the beach resort of Sanur and in Ubud, Bali's artistic centre.

One could hardly have spent those three days more blissfully: lazing, bathing, sleeping and going to listen to music. As Ben was announced as being engaged in making a study of Balinese music, and as we had as our cicerone Bernard Eizerdraat [sic], the best young Dutch authority on Indonesian music, we were all set for a course of intensive music listening. The evening of Friday (our 2nd day) we heard no less than 4 different sorts of Balinese music and 4 different orchestras!

We started off in the house next door, belonging to M<sup>r</sup>. James Pandy, art-dealer, sophisticated Indonesian, who had travelled all over the world. He gave us drinks (araq (spirit) and tuak(?) (rice wine) pleasant & sweet) and entertained us with music on the GENG-GONGS.[74] These are miniature Jew's harp-type instruments, played most ingeniously with mouth and throat resonance. The noise is rather like frogs, very small, & the pieces played are short and descriptive such as "The dragonfly dipping over the waves" or "The deer trying to climb the banana-tree" or just "The Frogs". It is real chamber music; there were eight players, sitting on the ground, earnest and intense; the dark was lit up by little wicks in oil. An adorable experience.

After supper (Balinese food is *not* very good) we drove some miles to witness a PURIFICATION DANCE, done to purify a village after an epidemic or so. In this, two lines of young girls (5 years old up to 17) moved *very* slowly forward with slow intricate arm movements. All the Balinese can dance, it seems, but some were better than others. The orchestra playing for it was a good big one of gongs, metallophones (like xylophones, only with metal strips and bamboo resonators) and drums, also one or two flutes. The music was splendid, but in fact the dance was one of the less interesting ones we saw, although strikingly intense because of its extreme slowness. We were, of course, surrounded by very inquisitive villagers who looked at us as if they wondered why on earth we were there & giggled & wandered on. There were also a large number of very quarrelsome and extremely thin, grey dogs. The theory is that when uncles and aunts die, their souls transmigrate into the bodies of dogs. I'm not sure that this is fair; but we seemed to meet all our dreariest aunts and uncles, in the earthly envelope of the greyest skinniest brutes you can imagine. They *always* wandered across the most remarkable dancing; they *always* howled or barked when the most

---

[74] 'Gangong (Jew's Harp)' forms one of the sketches Britten took down from some of the musical performances he and Pears attended during their stay in Bali. The names of two of the remaining three musical events of their second evening – 'Redjang (Purification)' and 'Sang Hang Dedari (Trance dance)' – were noted on the same sketch page as *gangong* but no musical sketches were made (*GB-ALb* 2-9300894). For a discussion of these important sketches, see Mervyn Cooke, *Britten and the Far East* (Woodbridge: The Boydell Press/Britten–Pears Library, forthcoming).

exciting music was on. And at night it was a perpetual plaint from an aunt on one side of our hotel to an uncle on the other. And they were all (poor dears!) so very very thin. Please feed me better when I become a dog!

On the way back from the *Purification Dance*, we struck a *Sanjang detan* or Trance dance, where two little nine years old girls were dancing themselves silly. The heat was considerable, and after a lot of dancing, they would eventually get dopey and utter some important phrases which the priests would interpret in their way. We stayed for 20 minutes while huge hot rain drops fell & then drove on to stop for a little while at a *Shadow-play*, where we didn't stay long. It was raining hard by now and it was almost impossible to see what was going on. By the time we got back to our hotel the rain was blowing through the windows and doors and dripping through the roof onto the beds, but no one cares. It all dries up very quickly, as far as anything is ever *quite* dry in such a humid climate.

The next day we had news that there was going to be a Cremation at a place called Klentang, a rather grand cremation of an important priest, and we hurried across in a car to catch it. Unfortunately rain was about all the time and it came down in buckets before the cremation began and finally we left after two hours soaking. We therefore missed the actual ceremony but witnessed many preparatory rites, & heard much music & saw the splendid many coloured bier which was to take the corpse on its journey.[75] There were constant streams of splendid Balinese women carrying offerings on their heads, bananas on leaves, rice on leaves, & fruit etc. These offerings were put down in front of an

---

[75] It was on this occasion that the travellers witnessed for the first time a full gamelan taking part in a temple ceremony, described by Prince Ludwig in *Ausflug Ost*, pp. 43–4:

> Beneath the roof of the meeting place in front of the entrance to a complicated and highly ornate temple sits a gamelan (that is to say, an orchestra that has at least one gong and one drum). There are about twenty instruments: metallophones, gongs, drums. They play beautiful, complex music without looking at each other; they have the confidence of sleepwalkers and smoke cigarettes. The gamelan gradually gets to its feet and moves off in a small procession round the area. An old priest mumbles nasally from a high bamboo stall in front of the temple. He plays skilfully with his fingers, spraying water from stalks of flowers and ringing a small handbell here and there.

As Mervyn Cooke has pointed out, the processing of the gamelan on this occasion may well have stayed in Britten's mind to resurface ten years later in his second church parable, *The Burning Fiery Furnace*, Op. 77, when he instructs the small group of instrumentalists to process around the church. See MC, p. 73 and Cooke, 'From Nō to Nebuchadnezzar', in Philip Reed (ed.), *On Mahler and Britten: Essays in Honour of Donald Mitchell on His Seventieth Birthday* (Woodbridge: The Boydell Press/Britten–Pears Library, 1995), pp. 142–3.

image & at once were devoured by the dogs or the pigs who disputed possession with the dogs and generally won. We saw again here a number of American tourists most curiously dressed, & one felt ashamed to be doing what they were doing so obviously, simply intruding, with curiosity undisguised, on a friendly people's solemn ceremony. But the Balinese do not seem to mind. There was some chanting too but not very impressive: there is very little singing in Indonesia, it seems.

*******

*SANUR* [12 January] (Thursday afternoon) tape recordings

*Friday* [13 January]
Evening
1. Ganggong at Pandy's (Jew's harp)
2. By car to Purification Ceremony (Redjang) at Batuan. Virgins
3. on way back. Sanjhjang dedari
   Trance dance – two girls
4. Shadow play. Wajang

*Saturday* [14 January] Cremation (Rain) Klentang.
1. Dinner at Pandy's: gandér wajang (4 metallophones)
2. Djogéd (girl attracting men)

[The evening was spent with James Pandy, an occasion recorded by Prince Ludwig in *Ausflug Ost*, p. 45:

> We take our seats behind a gamelan made up of many bamboo xylophones [*rindik*]. Music strikes up and entices a girl, isolated from the others, out from behind a curtain. She then creates her own individual dance, the same thing happening with the other girls in turn. The Djoged 'bung-bung' is free . . . Single girls ask men up to dance with them. Ijserdraat [*sic*] . . . can dance gracefully: he has elegant hands and is eminently musical. Some idiot has a try and is naturally clumsy and comical. I make my excuses, Ben declines.

The 'djoged' is the only social as opposed to religious dance in Balinese culture. Mervyn Cooke has suggested the style of the music played by the xylophones in the 'djoged' subsequently influenced the gamelan textures in *Death in Venice*, Op. 88 (1973).[76]]

---

[76] See MC, p. 74, and Mervyn Cooke, 'Britten and the gamelan: Balinese influences in *Death in Venice*', chapter 9 in Donald Mitchell (ed.), *Benjamin Britten: Death in Venice* (Cambridge: Cambridge University Press, 1987).

*Sunday* [15 January] Selat. *Ubud.* Evening rehearsal 5 little girls (Legong)[77] new tunes by Djokorde Mas

[The main part of the 15th was devoted to a visit to the foothills of Gunung Agung, Bali's famous volcano. Visits were also made to Klungkung, the island's eighteenth-century capital, and to Selat. The party spent the night at Ubud as paying guests of a Balinese prince. Princess Margaret described their location in a letter home dated 16 January:

> A temple gate and courtyard separates us from Ben and Peter's house. We are "paying guests" with a Bali prince who though no longer ruling but has many feudal rights. Each "house" has its bathroom, a W.C. and bath. The W.C. is only a C and made out of stone, as if done by Henry Moore! The "bath" is a sort of horse trough in the corner and one sloshes the water out of it, over oneself and everything else. No light (coconut oil light in one open courtyard only), no furniture except two small hard beds covered with mosquito nets with holes in it, hard pillows and a "dutch wife".

According to Prince Ludwig, it was Britten who made the joke about the Indonesian *mandi* looking like a Henry Moore sculpture (*Ausflug Ost*, pp. 48–9).]

*Monday* [16 January]
Girls in the courtyard for films.
(Den Pasar – bathe –)
Rehearsal.

[After breakfast on the 16th a small gamelan and three girl dancers came to be photographed by their dancing instructor. The party lunched in Denpasar

---

[77]  A reference to the *legong* dance, described by Prince Ludwig in *Ausflug Ost*, pp. 49–50:

> Already during the evening meal there is a gurgling and growling from the distance – the gamelan is rehearsing. We go then with pocket torches through the pitch-black, slippery night to a small hall with bamboo fencing as walls where, under the petrol lamp, the whole orchestra of about thirty to forty men squats on the ground and hammers away . . . Then comes the skilled 'Legong'. There appear five child dancers, each exercising in minute detail for about three-quarters of an hour a pre-composed dance made up of graceful, decorative, insect-like movements.

Britten was especially excited by the quality and type of dancing he encountered while in Bali, describing it in a letter to Imogen Holst (17 January 1956): 'The dancing would thrill you – usually done by minute & beautiful little girls, & of a length & elaborateness which is alarming, but also by wonderful elderly men with breath-taking grace & beauty; & little boys with unbelievable stillness & poise.'

*en route* to an afternoon's relaxation on Kuta beach. In the evening they returned to Ubud where they attended the rehearsal of a children's gamelan; after eating they returned to see the *legong* rehearsal. As Mervyn Cooke has noted, the children's gamelan seen and heard on this occasion may have influenced the choice of a percussion orchestra as the accompanying medium for the children – and in particular, Tadzio – in *Death in Venice*.[78]]

*Tuesday* [17 January]
(Sacred forest)
Djogéd

[After a second night in Ubud, Britten, Pears and the Hesses spent most of the 17th walking through the rice fields to nearby villages examining temples and shrines on the way. In the afternoon they visited a museum exhibiting Balinese art. Prince Ludwig writes in *Ausflug Ost*, p. 52:

> At the museum, we meet Rudolf Bonnet, the painter (he is Dutch) who has been living in this quarter for many years. A good-looking older gentleman who, as a patriarch, knows all about the islands. He leads us to his bamboo house across the street, with the wonderfully lushly flowering garden. He has cleverly collected Balinese art. Shows a few things, powerfully painted nudes and portraits, belonging entirely to the art trend around 1910 and quite good.

Although not specifically mentioned by Prince Ludwig in his diary, it may well have been on this day that the party passed through the village of Peliatan, whose gamelan had toured the West with great success a few years earlier. During their tour two long-playing gramophone recordings were made from live performances (Argo RG 1–2; *GB-ALb* 3-9401051–4/3-9401055–60), both of which were in Britten's possession during the composition of *The Prince of the Pagodas*.[79]

In the evening they attended another dance performance, described by Prince Ludwig in *Ausflug Ost*, p. 53:

> Then, in the evening, in the village barn, a single beauty dances to the bamboo gamelan. The group comes from the neighbouring village. The dancer grabs individual partners, which give rise to gales of joy among the numerous spectators.
>
> The bamboo sounds somewhat muted; it does not have the impact of bronze. The dance is called the *Djoged* and is the forerunner of the modern *Djoged bun-bung* that we saw at Mr Pandy's.]

---

[78] See Mervyn Cooke, 'Britten and the gamelan: Balinese influences in *Death in Venice*', in Donald Mitchell (ed.), *Benjamin Britten: Death in Venice*, p. 115.
[79] See Donald Mitchell, 'An after word on Britten's *Pagodas*: the Balinese sources', *Tempo*, 152 (March 1985), and MC, pp. 103–4.

*Wednesday* [18 January]
Ben's sharks
(Visit to Den Passar: bathe.)
back to lunch.

*Thursday* [19 January]
Long drive to Hills, Temple, Bats etc
Dinner [Rudolf] Bonnet. Ganggong.

[18–19 January were spent at the coastal town of Kuta as guests of Djokorde
Gde Agung. On the way to Kuta they called in at Denpasar where, according
to *Ausflug Ost* (p. 53), they bought Javanese sarongs. On the 19th the party
dined with Rudolf Bonnet, an occasion Prince Ludwig describes in *Ausflug Ost*,
pp. 59–60:

> In the evening, invitation to Rudolf Bonnet's. We drink good rice wine
> beneath the arbour with the large yellow Alamanda flowers. The frog
> and cicada concert begins and is augmented by 14 men with jew's-
> harps (guimbards). The painter asked them to come, as before, i.e.
> before the war. Shirtless, in sarongs and coloured waist scarves, white
> head cloths, coquettishly knotted, a large flower behind the ear. The
> slim young people with their brown lithe bodies, looked quite glorious
> by the light of a few lamps. It is understandable that people can fall
> uninhibitedly in love with these savage beauties with their somewhat
> sad faces. They all look like 16 to 19 years old, although there is many
> a well-established paterfamilias of over 30 among them. Their chirping
> and frog music merges with the surroundings and the night with the
> moon and the bright stars.]

*Friday* [20 January]
Lazy morning. Barong dance in afternoon. Back to Ubud.
Children's gamelan. Ghastly American.

[On the morning of the 20th the party posed for photographs in traditional
Balinese costume: see Plate 5. They witnessed a *barong* dance in the afternoon.
(The *barong* is a legendary figure of good fortune.) Prince Ludwig recorded
the event in *Ausflug Ost*, p. 61:

> On the ground to the left is the gamelan. Music: the Barong appears
> at the gate. Two men are inside a wild caricature of a lion . . . At the
> end there is a great combat between the Barong and an evil demon.
> The Barong disappears through the gate . . . It is over. Magnificent –
> a performance lasting about an hour and a half. The gamelan
> accompanies and augments what is happening . . . Ben, who is indeed
> the most sensitive amongst us, is strongly moved by the realistic mad
> rage of a beautiful warrior.

On their final day on Bali, Prince Ludwig noted: 'Peter let Penny [Ijzerdraat] present him with a whole miniature barong at the last moment at the airport. The rest of us can foresee endless difficulties in dragging along this voluminous souvenir. In the end, Peter carries it under his arm, like a Balinese Skye-terrier' (*Ausflug Ost*, p. 67). The miniature *barong* is now at the Britten–Pears Library.

In the evening of the 20th they attended a performance by a children's gamelan.]

*Saturday* [21 January]
Drive to Den Passar. Lunch; on to Sanoer [Sanur].
Back to Ubud for Supper. Legong.[80] Back to Sanoer.

*Monday* [23 January] recording

[In his entry for the 23rd, Prince Ludwig writes in *Ausflug Ost*, p. 65:

> In the morning to Denpasar where Penny [Ijzerdraat] sets up tape-recordings with the best gamelan from Ubud of pieces which particularly interest Ben. In the little studio hall it is like a turkish bath. After about two hours the instruments are at last disposed to everyone's satisfaction. Two pieces are played, each of about 26 minutes' duration. Our skulls boom at the fortissimo sections, but there is a great impression of fantastic discipline and of astonishing empathy in tone and rhythm. We are soaked in sweat and the performers, who are at work from nine to one, are in the same state. In the afternoon a further three pieces were given without me.

Mervyn Cooke was the first to explicate the significance of this tape-recording (*GB-ALb* 3-9401043–64) to the composition of *The Prince of the Pagodas*, for some of the Balinese music on the tape provided the basic material for Act II of the ballet on the composer's return to Aldeburgh. Indeed, one track, *Tabuh-telu*, was incorporated virtually intact into the score of *Pagodas* (as the theme associated with the Prince disguised as the Salamander).[81]]

*Tuesday* [24 January] Special village performance

[On their last full day in Bali, the party returned to the same studio where the recording session had taken place to attend a Balinese shadow play (*wayang kulit*). They left the island for Java (Surabaja) the following day (25th) where

---

[80] Djokorde Gde Agung organized specially for the party what Prince Ludwig calls a 'Monstre-legong'. The following day they witnessed further dancing (the *baris* and *kris*) in the vicinity of Sanur.

[81] See MC, pp. 78–81 and 103–19, and Mervyn Cooke, 'Britten and Bali', *Journal of Musicological Research*, 7 (1987), pp. 307–39.

they remained until the 31st. (Pears and Britten gave a recital on the 28th in Djakarta at the residence of the Dutch High Commissioner.) Britten wrote to Imogen Holst (8 February 1956): 'Bali was heaven, scenicly, musically, dancicly. It was a glorious holiday of 12 days too. Unfortunately the holiday was rudely dispelled by our return to Java, where *everything* went wrong, & I got ill & had to cancel a concert . . .']

[Notebook]

*2nd visit to Singapore*[82]

[31 January]
Chinese dinner Lieu Chou's house hideous. (wife).

[1 February]
Dinner German ambassador, daughter. British CG [Consul-general] Pritchets?
Tiger balm garden. Lunch Tanglin Club.
Roy Benger's film

[In the evening of 1 February the party dined with the German Consul-general, Dr Granow. That afternoon, after lunch, they had visited the Tiger Balm Gardens, described in one guidebook as 'a gaudy grotesquerie of statues illustrating the pleasures and punishments of this life and the next, plus scenes from Chinese legend'. The gardens were financed by the fortune Aw Boon Haw made from the miracle panacea Tiger Balm. Prince Ludwig describes the gardens in *Ausflug Ost*, p. 76:

> Siesta and tour of the Tiger Balm gardens. The latter are truly amazing in their naive Chinese surrealism, their sensuality, comic effect and coloured demonic element. One large hill-garden is inhabited by thousands of large and small concrete figures which are painted most colourfully with oil paint; with innumerable grottos, flights of steps, little temples, pagodas, which seem to have sprouted from the imaginations of insane first-formers. In the steamy heat, one really imagines oneself to be in a feverish dream.]

*Flight on to Hong Kong*[83]

---

[82] The party flew to Singapore from Djakarta on 31 January to spend two days of sight-seeing. On their way home, Britten and Pears called in at Singapore for a third time when they gave a concert at the request of Robin Woods on 23 February to celebrate the centenary of the Anglican Cathedral.
[83] The party flew to Hong Kong (via Bangkok) on 2 February where they remained for five days.

Met by launch David[84] & O'dell. Lunch Gomersall.
First concert Empire Theatre. Lunch. HE [His Excellency the Governor]
(crowded)
Radio. Shopping (Cat St).[85] Gomersall Concert.

[Pears and Britten gave a recital to an audience of 1300 at the Empire Theatre
(Cinema), Hong Kong, on 3 February in the presence of Sir Alexander
Grantham (1899–1978), Governor of the colony, 1947–57. The programme
included songs by Dowland and Purcell, Schubert lieder, and Britten's *Seven
Sonnets of Michelangelo* and folksong arrangements. Three days later, on the
6th, Pears, Britten and the Hesses had lunch with the Governor and his wife;
on the same day Pears and Britten gave a broadcast recital and a joint
interview with Peter Sharp for Hong Kong Radio's weekly *Music Magazine*
programme.
    'Gomersall Concert' is probably a reference to the performance of
Schumann's *Dichterliebe* which Pears and Britten gave on 7 February
(according to the composer's pocket diary), 'in a private house of a curious
man' (Britten to Roger Duncan, 8 February 1956). Prince Ludwig notes in
*Ausflug Ost*, p. 84:

> In the evening, a concert at the unpleasant finance manager's home.
> The clever and really very nice governor with his petite wife were also
> there. One cannot get rid of the feeling that the sinister nabob had
> harnessed famous English artists and foreign royalty, in order to lure
> the important governor into his den.]

Maçao – ship [*illegible word*] Hotel. Mr. Coonez. Shadowy Dr Lobo.
Club Theatre. Fantan. Governor. Supper after. Drive.
Lunch in Ch. [Chinese] ¼. Crab & Pigeon. [*illegible words*]
"Foreign Maid" [*illegible word*]

[The party travelled to the Portuguese colony of Macau on 4 February, where
Pears and Britten gave a recital that evening for the Music Circle in the
eighteenth-century Pedro V Theatre. The programme was identical to their

---

[84]   David Geddes (b. 1917), Princess Margaret's brother and a director of Jardine
    Matheson Hong Kong (1953–7). In a letter home (5 February 1956) Princess
    Margaret recounted their arrival:
       We were very V.I.P.-ish, Ben and Peter surrounded by press and an
       interview for the radio. Dave whipped us away into smart Jardine
       motor boat across the bay into cars and up and up on winding steep
       roads to their house on the Peak.
    To Imogen Holst, Britten wrote (8 February 1956); 'Hong Kong is a sweet place,
    very interesting, & we've been beautifully looked after by Peg's charming brother
    David & sister-in-law (Norwegian dancer, whom you'd love).'
[85]   A well-known market for traditional arts and crafts.

Hong Kong recital. (See Plate 6.) After the concert they all visited a gambling den (a feature of Macau), an experience which Britten found horrifying.]

*Japan* arrival. Photo crazy. Drive miles through heavy flat Tokyo. Hotel Imperial (Lloyd Wright 1922).[86]
Chat about finance. Formal. Bowing.

[The party flew from Hong Kong to Tokyo during the afternoon of 8 February where they were met by a representative of the British Council and Dr Löhr of the West German Embassy staff (see Plate 7). According to Mervyn Cooke, Kei-ichi Kurosawa, a Japanese Anglophile, and his son Hiroshi (known to his English friends as 'Peter') were also there to greet the visitors and took them to the Hotel Imperial. Kurosawa (d. 1978) had connections with the British Council and NHK (Nippon Hoso Kyokai, the Japanese Broadcasting Authority), the two organizations which were sponsoring Britten's and Pears's visit to Japan. On their arrival at the airport they were greeted by a batallion of press photographers, as Britten told Roger Duncan (20 February 1956): 'We . . . were met by hundreds of cameras and reporters. Japan is photography *mad* – Peter and I had every moment photographed on our first few days there . . .']

*Next day* to NHK. Finnikaki. Poet-painter. Press interview.
Teleconcert: makeup girl, nice hall. Party after.
Clive's daughter. HE.[87] Then Jap meal w. Redman & MacAlpine.
Feet in warm pit. Charcoal pots. sit down
Little dishes, exquisitely served. Lacquer. Sake warm (Hasty 3) no more after Rice. Colour schemes, waitresses sitting by you. Fish, cold hot raw. Strawberries!!

[At 11.00 am on 9 February, Pears and Britten gave a press conference (see Plate 8). Later that day they gave the first of two concerts for NHK, a recital broadcast simultaneously on radio and television (see Plate 9). (A film of the occasion survives in the NHK archives; a video-tape copy can be consulted at the Britten–Pears Library.) The programme comprised two songs by Purcell, Britten's *Michelangelo Sonnets* and folksong arrangements.
    Princess Margaret wrote the day after the broadcast:

    Yesterday Ben and Peter were televised – we went along to watch them being made up and then in front of 3000 *invited* guests we enormously enjoyed their concert. Programmes hand printed on sort of velvet flock

---

[86]    The hotel where they stayed was designed by the American architect, Frank Lloyd Wright (1867–1959), between 1916 and 1920 and proved to be one of his most distinguished early large buildings.
[87]    HE = His Excellency the British Ambassador, Sir Esler Denning (Ambassador in Tokyo, 1947–57), who had attended the NHK recital.

paper! All this sounds very dry, but we 4 laugh and fool so much and so many funny things happen we are a sort of travelling circus!

Following a reception after the recital, Vere Redman and Bill MacAlpine (Deputy Director of the British Council in Japan) took Pears, Britten and the Hesses to a restaurant for their first authentic Japanese meal. Prince Ludwig describes the occasion in *Ausflug Ost*, pp. 86–8:

The antechamber is a kind of stable, marked by buffalo heads, and a store room from where a sharply raised threshold leads into the dining room. We leave our shoes at the threshold, walk on bast matting through the sliding door on which paper is glued. A quite low, lengthy table around which we seat ourselves on the floor. Feet and legs go under the table into a hollow which is heated from below with charcoal and where a kind of fine grille separates the embers from your socks. Wonderfully warm. Cloth hangs from the sides of the lacquered table, so that the heat cannot escape. The three nice girls climb about behind us and pour hote sake from earthenware jugs into the little earthenware beakers. One drinks it down in one gulp and immediately gets a refill. If one wants to show goodwill toward someone, especially servants, then one takes the beaker, rinses it out in the water in the red lacquered dish in the centre of the table and hands it to the other person. Then one takes up the little jug and fills the beaker. The other drinks up and rinses out the beaker in turn. This may also be omitted, as a sign of special familiarity. The beaker, handed back, is now filled by the other person and one empties it, smiling in a friendly way.

As an hors-d'oeuvre, there is delicious raw fish and pieces of shellfish that look like carrots, with a hot vinegar-sauce to dip into. The Japanese chopsticks are easier to handle than the Chinese, because they are flatter at the end, made from lightweight wood, whereas the Chinese chopsticks are made from heavy bone and ground round at the end. Then a chicken dish with rice is prepared at table, in a beautiful brass vessels with black enamel lids. The brown lacquer table looks like an exhibition of exquisite brown, black and yellow earthenware vessels with some tile-red or black enamel things among them; an enchanting sight. Beside us stand large rough earthenware heating pots with glowing charcoal. No more sake is served from the moment when rice is put on to the table. Rice in two forms is not allowed. Finally, there is tea from beakers, on which a kind of millet floats. Quite excellent.

Leave-taking from the nice hostesses with laughing and bowing. They fit quite wonderfully into the whole Asiatic Rembrandt-picture, with their dark red, brown and black kimonos, with yellow and white sashes. We, unfortunately, fit into it less well.]

(Cold!) Museum: Wooden figures (Gods Nara) Masks –

Dinner H.E. 2 Pianos. Sitwell ugh![88]

[On the 10th the party visited the National Museum. In the evening the visitors were the guests of the British Ambassador at a dinner held in their honour. The occasion is recalled by Reg Close (Director of the British Council in Japan) in an unpublished memoir (copy held by the Britten–Pears Library):

> It was as a duty that Sir Esler Denning . . . gave a formal dinner for Ben and Peter; but it was also a personal pleasure, for His Excellency was quite a good pianist. The Embassy residence had two grand pianos, on one of which Sir Esler practised regularly, hoping that somebody could be appointed to his staff who could accompany him on the other. Ben saw the situation as soon as he entered the ambassadorial drawing-room, and felt the same nervousness that overcame him when he entered the Headmaster's study to see the cane lying on the table. Sure enough, when the gentlemen joined the ladies after dinner, one of the guests asked if His Excellency and Mr Britten would favour the company with a duet. The performance was more metronomic than musical. Both players, no doubt for different reasons, decided that there should be no encore.

Prince Ludwig noted in *Ausflug Ost* (p. 89) that it was music by Bach and Mozart that was played.]

Shopping kimonos. Lunch G. Amb. Nôh. Chanting solo: then 5 dancers. Sumida river. Foot movement: Intoning. 3 Instruments (Flute, two perc.) & 2 Singers. Chorus. Mask of widow.

---

[88]  An inexplicable reference to one of the Sitwells, perhaps Edith with whom both Pears and Britten were on particularly close terms during the 1950s.

Geisha entertainment: Furukaki:–[89] moderate, sweet – (not enough saké!). "Samisen"

[On 11 February the party lunched at the West German Embassy with Dr Kroll (the Ambassador), his wife and Klaus Pringsheim (Thomas Mann's brother-in-law; conductor and teacher at the Imperial Conservatory, Japan, from 1931). Pringsheim contributed an extensive appreciation of Pears's and Britten's concerts in Tokyo to the English language edition of one of Japan's leading newspapers, the *Mainichi Daily News* (3 March 1956). Pears also notes here the party's attendance at a performance of the Noh theatre which, according to Peter Kurosawa, was given at the Suidōbashi Noh Theatre and that the play *Sumidagawa* (Sumida River), from which the entire conception of Britten's church parables came, but *Curlew River* in particular, was performed by the Umetani Group of the Kanze School (see MC, p. 212). Pears notes many of the salient features of Noh convention, including the instrumental ensemble of a bamboo flute (*nōkan*) and drums.

Prince Ludwig recorded the occasion – without doubt one of the most significant of the entire trip in terms of Britten's subsequent musico-dramatic development and, by implication, for Pears's operatic career – in *Ausflug Ost*, pp. 89–91:

. . . we come to an art school. Inside is a roofed stage to the right of a rectangular auditorium with tiered seating.

---

[89]   Tetsuro Furukaki, President of NHK. Reginald Close recalled in his unpublished memoir:

As a representative of the British Council in Japan, I received a cable from Head Office asking if I could find someone to sponsor a concert by Britten and Pears in Tokyo. The British Council, struggling to survive on a shoe-string in those days of stringent economy after the war, had no money for unexpected opportunities. On the other hand, post-war Japan, despite its own problems, was so keen to see and hear whatever up-to-date western culture had to offer that its leading newspapers and media could usually be relied upon to stage concerts and exhibitions by well-known western artists. Furukaki . . . immediately agreed to be the sponsor of this occasion and I cabled London accordingly. Head Office, ever conscious of the Treasury's eagle eye, cautiously replied telling me to ask for a guarantee that all the necessary expenses would be covered.

In his palatial office, Furukaki sat like a feudal samuri. Much embarrassed, I put the request to him as I had been told to; but before the volcano could erupt, I hastily added, 'I will of course give the guarantee myself.' That was not too rash. Having been in Japan since 1952, I knew that Japanese students would starve themselves, even sell their blood, to pay to hear live western music. Furukaki showed no sign of the indignation he must have felt. He walked with me to the door, bowed slightly and once only, saying, 'Thank you for your visit. You are beginning to learn.'

The audience sits to the front and left of the stage, which is of the same height throughout, with a bridge furnished with a rail and small trees leading to a door in the rear left-hand corner of the auditorium. There hangs a curtained entrance through which the players come onto the bridge with an exciting jerking of the curtain. The stage area has in its rear right-hand corner a little door through which the chorus enters and exits. There are no decorations. In front, to the right, the stage is enlarged by an extension-like balcony on which the chorus of about twelve men dressed in black squat on the ground. Two drummers sit, somewhat higher, in the middle of the stage. Now and again they play drums bound with a network of lateral and diagonal strings with short, pounding strokes. In addition, they chant with a curiously strained and strangled tone . . . The chorus recites in this fashion, but often sings properly on an urgent monotone . . .

The players move with slow steps, lifting up their white-socked feet and putting them down carefully in front of them. They wear clothes which are obviously very old but generally opulent in shape and colour. Overall, the whole effect is strangely comic to us. But it turns out that, although the recitation of the text is entirely nonsensical up to the last syllable, it is nevertheless a humanly moving art form. This is especially true of the piece called 'Sumida River'. There is a ferryman on the river; a traveller arrives, drawing attention to a woman. This mad mother is looking for her lost child and turns up on the river bank by the ferryman, who makes a point of refusing to take her with him. Finally, he conducts the traveller and mother across, and relates on the river a long tale about a child whom a thief kidnapped and who died of exhaustion on the other side of the river. The mother weeps, and then finds the grave of her child on the other river bank. She mourns. The mother is played by a large man in woman's clothes with a little wooden female mask. Props are used in the presentation of events: a bamboo frond represents madness, a staff for the ferryman, a little gong to represent sorrow. The mother's grief, a high, swelling Sprechstimme, the gesturing of the hand to the weeping eyes, the little stroke on the small gong . . . the mourning at the grave, the curiously strained and expressive voices, the sudden stamping with a white foot . . . At the end, the impression of the piece is moving and profound. It has greatly affected Ben.

In the evening they were entertained by geisha singing to the accompaniment of the *shamisen,* a traditional three-stringed lute. Prince Ludwig recorded the occasion in *Ausflug Ost,* p. 91:

In the evening, a banquet at the best Japanese restaurant. Host: Furukaki. About 10 guests, at least 20 women for serving and amusement. Waitresses and geishas. The latter present boring dances, to bawling singing accompanied by metallic noises. Much sake. Delightful banquet.]

Evening: Geisha party: Baseball dance:[92] Presents of Prints – more amusing than Tokyo one.

[On the morning of 13 February the party visited the Imperial Palace, a collection of separate buildings linked by corridors or galleries that includes the Nijo Castle, housing the Ninomaru and Katsura Palaces. Before lunch they also visited – with less enthusiasm – the Nishijin Textile Museum. In the afternoon a visit was made to the detached villa of Katsura-rikyu on the outskirts of Kyoto, with its exquisitely designed gardens. The Shokin-tei contains a number of rooms including a tea-room in which natural light can reach every corner. A second evening of geisha entertainment for the party was hosted by the Kyoto office of NHK, an occasion recalled by D.J. Enright in his *Memoirs of a Mendicant Professor* (London: Chatto and Windus, 1969), p. 45:

[We had] some visitors who gave as good as they took, like Benjamin Britten and Peter Pears, at a magnificent dinner which the Broadcasting Corporation of Japan gave for them at the Tsuraya, a notable Kyoto teahouse. The most highly regarded samisen [sic] players and singers were brought in to entertain the guests. As they performed, Britten scribbled down the musical notation while Pears (an even greater feat, I should think) swiftly made his own transliteration of the words. Then Britten borrowed a samisen and plucked at it while Pears sang – the result being an uncanny playback. The effect on the geisha, a race who tend to be excessively conscious of their inimitability, their cultural uniqueness, and aggravatingly assured of the pitiable inability to understand their art inherent in all foreigners, was almost alarming. They paled beneath their whitewash. A more violent people would have seen to it that their guests' throats were cut the moment they left those sacred halls. This was one of the few indubitable triumphs for British art or artists which I noticed in Japan – and probably the most striking.]

*Tuesday* Drive to Nara at 8.30 (Sun) (NHK men press photo)
(Tired legs & knees)
Park: deer: shrine orange & green: priest.
Ho? Buddha temple. Splendid guardian figures.
Huge Buddha temple: *v.* impressive: size: eyes: hands:
Lovely Fountain (?) Lantern in front:
Dirty pond. ?Wrong season

[In the morning of the 14th they visited the Nara Park within which lie numerous historic buildings, including many shrines, and large numbers of tame roe deer considered sacred by the Japanese. Among the sites visited by the party was the Todaiji Temple containing the Great Buddha, the largest

---

[92]    Pears's reference to a 'Baseball dance' remains elusive.

bronze statue in Japan. They entered the temple precinct through the *Nandai-mon* (Great South Gate) in whose external walls are a pair of *Nio* statues (guardian figures) eight metres high. Pears notes that in front of the *Daibutsudan* (Great Buddha Hall) is an octagonal bronze lantern with fine relief decoration.]

Back to Kyoto for lunch Chekes, then talk with K. Musicians. Questions: "advanced age", compliment (Jap dilemma w. music – copyists argument: lost soul: eternal rectangle! insect: insincere:)
Tea ceremony – !! Formal aesthetic
Shopping. Hot Bath. Sake. Home Kumagei.
Family: wife, daughter, 3 boys. Flowergirl (Press). Tea ceremony
Noodles & Sake. Flavour of fish
Music Son flute: daughter Tosca with me.
Rounds. Brahms with Ben. Press!! Tape recorder after, supper at Kyoto Hotel: seafood & argument.
Bed. Inn gave presents as farewell.

[The party lunched at the Kyoto Hotel as the guests of the British Consul-general, Mr Cheke, after which Pears and Britten met members of the Kyoto Music Club. Later that afternoon they attended a traditional Tea ceremony, described by Princess Margaret in a letter home (23 February 1956): 'We ... took part in the most impressive, complicated and full of deep meaning ceremony – the Tea ceremony – it takes (or took us) about two hours and at the end one has drunk three mouthfuls of very bitter and strong and excellent green tea.' They spent their last evening in Kyoto with a Japanese family (the Kumageis) with whom they partook of a second Tea ceremony, following which the occasion was enlivened by an impromptu performance by Pears of an aria from *Tosca* (accompanied by the daughter of the household), the singing of rounds, and a Brahms song from Pears and Britten.]

Wednesday: shopping. Train 1.0
in Tokyo bed –

*Thursday* Rehearsal: shopping prints
Kai Tokyo Mad. Soc. Brit. Council party: Dinner H.E. (Singing)

[Pears and Britten joined the members of the Tokyo Madrigal Singers at an informal performance conducted by Kei-ichi Kurosawa, an entertainment organized at a cocktail party hosted by the British Council in the Council's library on the evening of 16 February (see Plates 10, 12–13). Prince Ludwig noted in *Ausflug Ost* (p. 105): '. . . the charming Mr Kurosawa conducts his fine madrigal group. He is overjoyed that Ben and Peter sing with them.' Mervyn Cooke reports that Peter Kurosawa, who also sang in the choir on this occasion, remembers Pears specifically requesting a rendering of Wilbye's 'Sweet Honey-sucking Bee'. Kei-ichi Kurosawa founded the Tokyo Madrigal Singers in 1929, shortly after his return to Japan after studies at Trinity

College, Cambridge; his son now directs the group (MC, p. 215). After the drinks party, they once again dined at the British Embassy. After the meal Pears and Britten performed some lieder and Britten's *Mazurka Elegiaca*, Op. 23 no. 2, for two pianos, the latter for the Ambassador's benefit.]

*Friday* Rehearsals: Kabuki 4.30 onwards

[On the 17th the party made a visit to the Kabuki theatre, a genre incorporating elements from various dramatic forms in which acting, dance and music are combined to achieve maximum variety and dynamic force. In almost every respect Kabuki represents the antithesis of the Noh tradition. Mervyn Cooke has suggested that the experience of Kabuki theatre may have influenced Britten's second church parable, *The Burning Fiery Furnace*, and in particular Pears's interpretation of the role of Nebuchadnezzar.[93]]

*Saturday* Imperial Court Music. Palace:
Lunch. Sleep – Rehearse – Concert.
Furakaki – Japanese meal. He late. Cross

[On 18 February a second visit (according to Mervyn Cooke) was made to the Music Department of the Imperial Household Agency (*Kunaicho-Gakubu*), where Britten, Pears and Prince Ludwig experienced the sonorities of the Gagaku orchestra. Hiroshige Sono, an authority on Gagaku, acted as their guide. Prince Ludwig recalled the occasion in *Ausflug Ost*, p. 109 (an entry subsequently translated by the author as part of his contribution to *Tribute to Benjamin Britten on His Fiftieth Birthday*, edited by Anthony Gishford (London: Faber and Faber, 1963), pp. 61–2):

> In the morning we go to a performance of the Imperial Court orchestra which has been specially organized for Ben to hear. Dignified old gentlemen in blue suits, like generals in mufti, play two long pieces for us on unknown and strange instruments. Bronze age serenades probably sounded like that. One realises that this music follows some pattern, though I for one cannot discern it. European 'music lovers' like myself are always on the look out for something they have heard before. Hence that hankering for 'expression' and romantic gusto. We cannot penetrate this kind of music, though there is some attraction in its hidden pattern or form.
>
> It is disconcerting to see the dignified musicians take up penny whistles to let off sudden shrieks, or others beating boat-shaped harps without much sound. I feel not educated or musical enough to judge this ancient art.
>
> The concert takes place at the theatre building in the gardens of the Imperial Palace.

---

93   See MC, pp. 338–9, and Cooke, 'From Nō to Nebuchadnezzar', in Philip Reed (ed.), *On Mahler and Britten*, pp. 140–41.

Britten's interest in the Gagaku led to the purchase of two gramophone recordings of the repertoire and a volume of transcriptions, both of which are at the Britten–Pears Library (Columbia BL 28–9; *GB-ALb* 3-9401031–2/3-9401041–2). Mervyn Cooke has drawn attention to the importance of the *shō*, one of the principal instruments of the Gagaku ensemble, to the organ-writing in the church parables. It is a free-reed mouth organ comprising seventeen bamboo pipes mounted symmetrically according to height on a wooden cup-shaped wind-chest. Unmentioned by Pears (or, for that matter, by Prince Ludwig) is Britten's purchase of a *shō* from Tōzaburō Satake's 'Japanese Old Musical Instrument Company' while in Kyoto. He learnt how to play the instrument with the aid of a manual by Leo Traynor entitled – for the composer's amusement – 'A Young Britten's Guide to the Shō'.[94]

Pears's and Britten's second concert in Tokyo took place at 8pm on 18 February, with Britten conducting the NHK Orchestra and Pears as soloist in *Les Illuminations*, Op. 18; Pears was also the narrator in *The Young Person's Guide to the Orchestra*, Op. 34. The programme began with Britten's *Sinfonia da Requiem*, Op. 20, composed in New York, in 1940, to celebrate the 2600th anniversary of the founding of the Japanese dynasty. It was rejected by the Japanese authorities at the time on the grounds of the inappropriateness of the work's overtly Christian sentiments. This performance in 1956 was the work's Japanese première. For a full account of the turbulent history of *Sinfonia da Requiem*, see DMPR, pp. 703–5, 805–6, and 881–4. The concert was recorded for broadcast the following day on NHK Radio 2.]

*Sunday*: Pearls: Radio interview:
Nôh play 12.30–4.30
Back to Hotel. Party. Drinks. Ewing[95]
Imperial Ducks eaten at Closes. Farewell.

[The party attended a second performance of *Sumidagawa* on 19 February, when they were accompanied by Reginald Close. Prince Ludwig noted in *Ausflug Ost* (p. 110): 'We see another performance of the piece called Sunigawa [*sic*] River at Ben's particular wish. It is magical once again, although in my opinion the time from noon to 2pm is not ideal for dramatic profundity.' Close recalled:

As we were leaving the theatre, Peter put a wad of notes into my hand, begging me to get them a record of the *Sumidagawa* music [*sic*]. I got the Noh company to make a recording, and Lady Gascoigne, who was then on a brief visit to Tokyo, took it back to London and delivered it personally to Ben and Peter, who were then living in Chester Gate, Regent's Park.

---

[94] See Mervyn Cooke, 'Britten and the *Shō*', *Musical Times*, 129 (1988), pp. 231–3.
[95] The party had lunched with the Ewings on 16 February; however, they otherwise remain unidentified.

The tape recording of the *whole* play – not just the music – survives at the Britten–Pears Library.

After dinner with the Closes, the party was taken to Haneda airport; they were seen off by Kei-ichi and Peter Kurosawa, Bill MacAlpine and Reginald Close. The next day Pears wrote to Close from Hong Kong:

> Ben and I cannot thank you enough for all your help and kindness to us, not only officially as the British Council but personally as yourself, and not only *during* our stay in Japan but also those frantic days before we arrived. As you must have realised, we had no idea of the trickiness of the situation, and although the Japanese sensitiveness has been fairly well publicised, the individual in this case was someone quite unusually awkward. We do realise what a strain it must have been for you. Anyway, we want to send our warmest thanks to you and tell you how very keenly we appreciate all you did for us . . . I am quite determined to come back to Japan for a longer visit . . .

Neither Pears nor Britten ever returned to Japan.]

*Hong Kong* 24 hours: hotel. David & Pitt dinner.

[The party spent twenty-four hours in Hong Kong (staying at the Gloucester Hotel) before flying on to Bangkok on the 21st. Apart from the usual sight-seeing in Bangkok, they lunched with the Ambassador, Sir Barclay Gage, on the 22nd. They continued their journey on the evening of the 22nd, returning to Singapore (see note 82, p. 52).]

*******

Japan is in many ways the most curious & fascinating country we have visited: it is also the most baffling & enigmatic. In 1856 (?) it suddenly westernized itself. Now trains are excellent & electric; 99.5% of pop. is literate; electricity is laid on in smallest, remotest village; techniques are very advanced. But underneath the surface is much mediaevalism.

Cultural plusses are 1. the *NOH* plays; 14th century dramas (religious in flavour, stories mythical, actors Buddhist (near)-priests) of the *utmost* refinement, intensity, skill, power. 2. *Kabuke dramas*: developments from Noh, popularised, colourful, dramatic, brilliant, dazzling, amusing, skilful. 3. Beautiful temples and shrines (Nona, 5–9th centuries. Kyoto 9th–19th cent). 4. Exquisite garden landscaping of a most superior order. 5. Charming houses. 6. Minor arts (flower arrangements, tea-ceremony). 7. Strong survival of craftsmanship.

*Enigmas to Europeans*
Endless formalism of social intercourse.

1. Bowing, bowing, bowing.
2. Answer to *every* question is "Yes", e.g.

> *Ben*: (to 1st Trumpeter in Orchestra) Would it not be better to play this passage with a mute?
> *Trumpeter*: Yes!! (plays with mute: awful)
> *Ben*: Perhaps it might be easier with mute *half* in?
> *Trumpeter*: Oh! Yes!! (plays with ½ mute: ghastly)
> *Ben*: Or would it sound stronger *without* mute?
> *Trumpeter*: Yes! yes!! (plays without mute: frightful)

### STALEMATE!

Or,

> P.P. (at Television Studio): Shall I come on before Mr. Britten takes his applause?
> *Announcer*: Yes, please.
> P.P.: Or would you rather I came on afterwards?
> *Announcer*: Oh yes! yes please.

\*\*\*\*\*\*\*

[Unmarked notepaper]

*Ceylon* B. Council party Kelly
Staying Mt Lavinia Hotel. Wild storms of rain.
Sea. Little beggars. English [*illegible word*] guests.
Excursion to Negombo, bathing, servants, waiter insisting
(cheese pineapple)[96] – Churches.
Lunch gynecol. ?Thiaganaja. Antonypilai.
Rucks.[97]

[The party flew from Singapore to Colombo, Ceylon (now Sri Lanka) on 24 February. Their arrival was announced by a report and photograph in the Colombo edition of the *Ceylon Times*. They stayed at the Mount Lavinia Hotel, formerly the British Governor's residence, described by Britten in a letter to Roger Duncan (11 March 1956) as, 'not a wonderful

---

[96] Pears notes in his characteristically abbreviated form an exchange with a waiter recorded by Prince Ludwig in *Ausflug Ost*, p. 122: 'Peter asked him: "Have you got some cheese?" The candid answer: "Yes, master, pineapple". He then brought some pineapple.'
[97] According to Britten's pocket diary, Pears and Britten lunched with the Rucks on 7 March in Colombo; however, they otherwise remain unidentified.

hotel, but a superb position with lovely bathing, and big waves, and *hot* sea!'
On the 25th they were the guests of John Kelly, British Council Liaison Officer
at the UK High Commission in Colombo. They made a visit to Negombo
(about twenty-five miles north of Colombo) on the 26th.]

Up to Kandy – John Gibson's bungalow; butterflies, birds (?banbette,
drogon), elephants. Botanical gardens. Drumming (amateur) George
Keyt. Taperecorder.
On to Polonanura via Siginja (rock early [*illegible word*]); bees.
Resthouses. Tank & birds at P.
Sculpture: Buddha & ?Branda. King.
Leopard civet cat mongeese monkeys.
Rum omelette.

[A trip was made to Kandy, the ancient capital, between 29 February and
2 March when they were the guests of John Gibson, a tea-planter, with whom
they stayed for two nights (the 29th and 2nd). On their first day there they
visited the Peradeniya Botanical Gardens. On their first evening in Kandy
Gibson introduced them to local musicians, dancers and drummers, as well as
to the well known Singalese painter George Keyt. (It was in fact through Keyt
that contacts were established with the musicians.) Princess Margaret noted in
a letter home written on the same day: 'We have even borrowed a tape
recorder for Ben and Peter to record the new music'. A tape labelled
'SINGALESE DRUMMING (KANDY)' with a typed list of its contents survives at the
Britten–Pears Library (*GB-Alb* 3-9500154).

Britten described their adventures on 1 March to Roger Duncan (11 March
1956):

The next day we motored to another even earlier capital of Ceylon
called Polonnaruwa which was abandoned in the 8th Century, and
completely over-run by the jungle . . . It was re-discovered about
50 years ago, and the jungle cleared away, and the ruins of temples and
shrines, with most wonderful stone Buddhas (one enormous one lying
on its side) are now visible in a glorious park. We stayed the afternoon
there and then drove back through the jungle to Siginja [*recte:
Sigiriya*]. On this journey (of about 50 miles) we saw some exciting
things: lots of monkeys of course, sitting on the road and leaping
through the trees, some wild cats (with long striped tails), the car was
charged by a large water buffalo (luckily it missed!) and, finally just
after it got dark, a *LEOPARD* streaked across the road in front of the car!
We couldn't believe our eyes, so we stopped the car and sat waiting,
and it came back onto the grass verge and watched us, for nearly two
minutes, and we could see it baring its teeth at us in the light of the
car! People consider us very lucky since they are now very rare –
although, personally, I was glad to be in the car, safely!

We spent the night in a rest house (very simple, hotelly hut place)
in this village Siginja, and then climbed to the top of the famous lion

67

rock, which is shaped like a gigantic lion. 1,000 years ago it was plastered and white-washed, but now all that remains of the details is the lion's paws, about two thirds of the way up. In the cool of the morning we climbed nearly 1,000 steps to the top, with a wonderful view over a great deal of the island.]

Back to JG. Ceremony of Octagon at Kandy elephants (little one trumpfart) during speeches. PM., colour, dancing v. poor.
On to Haputale. Garden vast view, drink.
T. Lipton's summerhouse (boy tea, late, throw over)

[The party attended a Buddhist ceremony, described by Britten in a letter to Roger Duncan (11 March 1956): 'That evening we went to a big ceremony in Kandy, when the Prime Minister made a long speech in Singalese, but with a little bit at the end in English, sort of summing it up – a kind of rather dreary political speech.' Prince Ludwig described the occasion in detail in *Ausflug Ost*, pp. 135–6:

Again to Kandy in the afternoon, where we take part in the folk festival in celebration of the return of the high octagon, by the government, at the Buddhist temple. Everything is variously hung with pennants, flagged and decorated with coloured paper garlands. Many drummers, like those we know from the dance evening, greet the prime minister. Six or eight elephants lift their trunks, but trumpet only moderately. Only one, a particularly small youngster manages a few powerful hoots, then, however, immediately sniffs embarrassingly at his much larger neighbours again . . . Endless, completely unintelligible speeches that are heard with a fine indifference by the public . . .
    Later, in the dark, we went to the same square again, where dances to drum-beat were presented on a small stage, between closely pressed masses of spectators. These dances were, again, not very well performed, the whole thing, despite the glorious old costumes, approximating the level of a schuhplattler group at an October funfair.

On the 3rd they made an excursion to Haputale to visit one of Lipton's tea plantations.]

Down to Colombo, oh so hot. Galle Face fuss over rooms. Hot concert. Ben's tummy. Party after, oh! Rehearsal for St. Mat. perf., heat, amateur, fans. Tea with Suya Senje (Bach [*illegible word*]) songs folky v.
Cake; young men. Seneja's own songs (work).
Party at Donovan Andrée: v. curious mixture. Memory man.[98]

---

[98]  Britten wrote to Roger Duncan (11 March 1956) that at one reception, 'there was a bewildering trick – rather boring too, when a man memorised a whole pack of cards spread out in any order'.

[Pears and Britten returned to Colombo on the 4th, leaving the Hesses behind, where they gave a recital at the Ladies College Hall on the 5th. On the day of their recital they lunched with the UK High Commissioner, Sir Cecil Syers. On the 7th Pears and Britten participated in an amateur performance of Bach's *St Matthew Passion* given by the Colombo Philharmonic Choir (conductor: Gerald Cooray) in the Church of St Michael's and All Angels (see p. 70). Prince Ludwig described the occasion in *Ausflug Ost*, p. 142:

> In the evening the Matthew Passion, without orchestra, with choir, piano (that was Ben) and organ in a medium-sized church. Peter sings the Evangelist quite indescribably beautifully, with Ben accompanying very well on the continuo. Otherwise the performance is a very mediocre Passion, greatly mutilated by cuts. The quite nice choir stretch out the holy chorales in unbearable sentimentality. The soloists are scarcely adequate.

Britten remarked to Roger Duncan (11 March 1956): 'We did it really to encourage the Singalese musicians, who were putting it on, because they have so little Western Music (as opposed to their own). But they didn't show much skill or understanding, and it was a pretty dreadful evening, as well as being gruellingly hot.' A photograph of the occasion appeared in one of the local Colombo newspapers the day after the performance.]

Whole day coping with income tax in heat.
Kindness of Kelly.
Off at 5am.

*Madras* Crescent House v. beautiful colonial Italianate white-red carpet red white & gold; connecting rooms pale green, p. terracotta, p. blue white swing doors half height, fretwork coloured photos of Indian leaders. Comfy; new ADC.
   Mikado!! costumes! M. Music Assoc. founded by Uncle Steuart.[99]
Colours of skin of chorus.
Billows[100] wife & ma.

---

[99] Steuart Durand Pears (1859–*c.*1950), sometime Superintendent–Engineer of Public Works, Madras. See also CHPP, pp. 144–5.
[100] Lionel Billows, who first got to know Britten and Pears while posted with the British Council in Switzerland during the late 1940s. Lady Billows in *Albert Herring* takes her surname from him. In the 1950s he was working for the British Council as the Regional Representative in Madras.

## COLOMBO PHILHARMONIC CHOIR
*(Patron:* Dr. R. Vaughan Williams, o. m.)

J. S. BACH

# ST. MATTHEW PASSION
WEDNESDAY, 7th MARCH, 1956

at 6.00 p. m.

SOLOISTS

PETER PEARS *Tenor*
RICHARD WILDING *Baritone*

JOAN COORAY
*Soprano*

MAURICE LEA
*Tenor*

PHYLLIS SHEPPARD
*Contralto*

LYLIE GODRIDGE
*Baritone*

★

*Organ*
LUCIEN FERNANDO

*Pianoforte*
IRENE VAN DER WALL
BENJAMIN BRITTEN (*Continuo*)

*Violin*
CHRISTOPHER CANAGARETNA

*Ripieno Chorus of Boys*
From ST. THOMAS' COLLEGE, MT. LAVINIA

*Conductor*
GERALD COORAY

★

CHURCH OF ST. MICHAEL AND ALL ANGELS
POLWATTE — COLOMBO.

BOOK OF WORDS: ONE RUPEE

Colombo, 7 March 1956. Programme for the *St Matthew Passion,* a performance
in which Pears sang the role of the Evangelist and Britten played continuo
(on piano).

[The party flew to Madras on the morning of 8 March where they stayed at the Governor's residence, Crescent House, until the 12th. On their first evening, they attended an amateur performance of Gilbert and Sullivan's *The Mikado* given by the Madras Music Association.]

Excursion to shops & homes. Music at Radio. Sing driving & potting (!) N. Menon[101] v. nice.
Excursion to Mahabalipuram ½ success v. hot, too many people. Billows, Khanna, N.M. [Narayana Menon], ADC, Mouse. Hot. Sculpture; descent of Goayes. Bathing.

[On the 9th a visit was made to All-India Radio at the invitation of the directors to hear local musicians. The following day an excursion to Mahabalipuram took place. It was described by Prince Ludwig in *Ausflug Ost* (an entry subsequently translated in Anthony Gishford (ed.), *Tribute to Benjamin Britten on His Fiftieth Birthday*, p. 64):

> . . . we leave for Mahabalipuram where we have lunch and then ·inspect the fascinating surroundings. The place is close to the sea, and was a seaport in its great days about twelve hundred years ago. Temples and statues were cut out of the great monoliths at that time. Most impressive is a cliff carved with innumerable human beings and animals. The animal figures are amazing. They show simplification and at the same time great naturalism in movement and characterization. They remind me strongly of this morning's first dance. There, as here, an animal was first represented by a few external characteristics, and then by its movements which represent its deeper character. Here these movements have been caught in stone.]

*Sunday* Dining chez Menon. Pictures of Khano/Khame. Lunch Danielou,[102] odd man. Jack Hughes.
Concert: hot, fans. Party after, long wait Gin. Chinese food. ?Melonjuice.

[The last concert of the tour was a broadcast recital from the British Council, Madras, on 11 March, following which Lionel Billows hosted a reception. The next day the party flew to Bombay for a few more days sight-seeing before beginning the long return journey home. They arrived at Frankfurt on the 16th, and after spending the night with the Hesses at Wolfsgarten, Pears and Britten returned by boat-train to Aldeburgh (via Harwich) on the 17th.]

---

[101] Narayana Menon$ (b. 1911), Indian music administrator, writer and composer. Britten, Pears and the Hesses were to encounter him again during their second trip to India, in 1965 (see p. 86).
[102] Alain Daniélou (1907–1994), French musicologist and oriental scholar, who was director of a research centre into Sanskrit literature at the Adyar Library, Madras, 1953–6.

# The Regional Representative

invites

*Dr, Mrs Narayana Menon*

to a Broadcast Recital

## PETER PEARS (tenor)

accompanied by

## BENJAMIN BRITTEN (piano)

at 150-B, Mount Road,

on Sunday, March 11th, at 7-30 p.m.

R. S. V. P.

### Programme

| | |
|---|---|
| Anon. c. 1600 : | Have you seen but a white lily grow ? |
| Philip Rosseter (1597) : | What then is love but mourning ? |
| Joseph Haydn : | The Sailor's Song |
| | She never told her love. |
| Franz Schubert : | Liebesbotschaft. |
| | Gesang des Harfners. |
| Robert Schumann : | Des Sennen Abschied. |
| | Mondnacht. |
| Benjamin Britten : | 1.  At day close in November. |
| | 2.  Midnight on the Great Western. |
| | 3.  The little old table. |
| | 4.  The Choir Master's Burial. |
| | 5.  Proud Songsters. |
| (from " Winterwords " Lyrics and Ballads by Thomas Hardy). | |
| Folk Songs, arr. Britten : | Down by the Sally Gardens. |
| | The Ploughboy. |

*Guests are requested to be seated by 7-15 p.m.*

The invitation/programme card for Pears's and Britten's recital in Madras,
11 March 1956.

# 3 Ansbach Bach Festival (1959)

Pears first sang at the Ansbach Bach Festival in 1955, and returned in 1956, 1957 (when Britten accompanied him), and 1959; he made his final appearance at the July 'Bachwoche' in 1963. At Ansbach he was one of very few non-German singers invited to participate (and the only English singer), a sure indication of his high reputation on the Continent. In his mid-forties Pears emerged as one of the most distinguished and distinctive interpreters of Bach's vocal music, but in particular of the role of the Evangelist in both the Passions, where his shaping and pacing of the complex recitiatives constituted something quite remarkable in the history of Bach interpretation in the post-war years. His recordings of both the *St Matthew* and *St John* Passions (he recorded each twice) testify to his stature as a Bach singer. Alongside Britten and Schubert, Bach must be counted as one of the three composers who meant the most to Pears; how curiously fitting therefore that on the day preceding his death in April 1986, he gave an inspired masterclass on the interpretation of the recitatives in the Passions.

His understanding of Bach's music – characterized by 'the necessity for rhythmic accuracy', as Janet Baker recalled Pears once telling her (PPT, p. 4) – was occasionally at variance with some of what he encountered at Ansbach. A letter to Britten from the 1955 Festival gives an account of his first impressions, particularly of the shortcomings of the performance tradition there:

> This Festival is very instructive. Gosh! what lots of money there is for art here! The tickets are very expensive & the audience smart, snob to a certain extent, but Bach is safe that way! Performances frightfully efficient, jolly accurate in every way & with about as much charm as a type-writer. The great rage is a young man called Karl Richter, played a complete organ recital by memory on a hideous organ. The line seems to be straight & narrow Bach with no room to expand – an occasional, very, ornament played pokerfaced to show we know about them. Plenty of lively down-beats but precious little living rhythm. My players were as usual better wind than strings – oboe good, flute young & a bit silly, violin a shy adequate Brucknerian from Munich, rather sweet girl harpsichordist. But all the musicians are young and passionately keen, and play for their lives. It is in many ways curiously touching. It makes me sure that we ought to have our musicians at Aldeburgh for the whole of the week before the Festival – !

It was under Richter's direction that Pears was to sing virtually all his Ansbach concerts, including performances of church cantatas, both

Passions and the B minor Mass. If the experience of singing for Richter was not always inspirational (it was, however, a relationship that improved a little over the years), Ansbach certainly afforded Pears the opportunity to work with many fine instrumentalists and singers, some of whom he enticed to Aldeburgh for its annual June festival. For example, it was at Ansbach in 1956 that Pears first sang alongside the German baritone Dietrich Fischer-Dieskau, a singer whose own extraordinary artistry was later to draw him into Britten's and Pears's circle.

The experience of Ansbach and its festival devoted to Bach were to play a major role in Pears's and Britten's decision to establish their own highly successful Bach weekends at Long Melford, Suffolk, between 1962 and 1967. This annual short series of concerts gave both musicians the opportunity to explore a rich repertory and develop their own ideas on Bach interpretation.

Pears gave his diary of the 1959 Ansbach Bach Festival, originally written in German and here translated by Marion Thorpe, to Princess Margaret of Hesse and the Rhine in 1963, possibly as a fiftieth birthday present. He mentions the diary in a letter to Britten (28 July 1959): 'I'm trying to do a diary auf Deutsch in the Lu style! [a reference to Prince Ludwig's *Ausflug Ost*] I thought it might amuse them.' With the diary he sent a short (undated) note to the Hesses: 'Here is the absurd Ansbach doodle! Quite not-worth-while! so pay no attention to it.'

The diary was unpublished in Pears's lifetime (he kept no copy), and it remains in Princess Margaret's possession; a photocopy supplied by her is held at *GB-ALb* (1-9500032). A transcription of Pears's German text can be found in the Appendix (pp. 207–13).

# ANSBACH BACH FESTIVAL (1959)

*July 23rd*

*Thursday*: In Munich at 8 in the morning punctually to Sixt's Auto Hire-Service; after a wait of ¾ of an hour (why? don't ask me) I am on my way in an Opel "Olympia" (a little non-U, I think). It goes quite well, on the right side of the Autobahn, and I arrived at Neuendettelsau without further incident. Beautiful weather, beautiful scenery, beautiful people, and now here, naturally, specially good people. First rehearsal with Richter;[1] O.K; I find that I overlooked one aria, so I must sight-read it. But it is not difficult, and terribly beautiful; so far so good! In the evening I took a little "walk" in the car, to Schwabach[2] (very beautiful late gothic Parish Church, with seven girls and two young men singing a service – & a placard "If you do not believe, do not come". I hesitated.)

We eat together, all the musicians, in a warm hall, filled with plants & trees & our menu is a little like school:

Thick semolina soup
Pork cutlets with dumplings
Pears with chocolate sauce

Good for growing tenors!

*Friday*. Two more rehearsals for these terribly difficult arias. I hope it will go well. My colleagues are:

1. *Ursula Buckel*[3] (German, but from Ghent) Soprano – with her husband. Bourgeois charm. I imagine her sitting room to be beige & spinach-greens. I have not heard her yet – singing.

2. *Hertha Töpper*,[4] beautiful alto, nice person, with her husband, a cross face, without charm (perhaps an Icelander?)

---

[1] Karl Richter[5] (1926–1981), German organist, harpsichordist and conductor. Pears wrote to Britten on 24 July 1959: 'Rehearsal here for the first time with Richter, wonderful music, performed very much as usual, with virtues & defects . . . [Ernst] Häfliger was here yesterday recording the Arias I am doing on Sunday . . .'

[2] Approximately thirteen miles east of Ansbach, half-way on the main route to Nürnberg.

[3] German soprano (b. 1926), a noted Bach singer from the 1950s onwards.

[4] Austrian mezzo-soprano (b. 1924), who studied singing with Franz Mixa whom she later married. As well as being a noted Bach singer, Töpper had a distinguished career as an opera-singer.

3. *Keith Engen,*[5] bass, American, with his wife (is she German or American?) Nice but boring.

With these excellent people I shall have to partake of thirty more meals. Dear Lord!

This evening's menu:

Stuffed pancakes with salad
Cheese & meat with bread
Period.

In the evening it becomes cooler. One hears young Protestant girls practising Mozart and Dussek. Faint, distant laughter. Two fifteen-year olds are running around the building with a colleague on a bicycle – six times – seven times – now ten times. It is not as in Jokmotik, it is getting dark. The Sisters[6] are already in bed – only one stays the whole night in the toilet, probably – she is always there, when I want to be.

*Saturday.* Each morning at six o'clock a lorry drives round the corner by my room and wakes me from my dreams. At 6.30 the farmers follow with their oxen; at 7 the Sisters water the flowers and a calm activity surrounds us. Also at 7 o'clock today M. Nicolet[7] started to practise. He sleeps in No. 8. I am in No. 10. But he did not play in his room. He was far away, in the Augustana Hall, 100 metres away, but I could hear every note. Up I get! I take my breakfast at 8 and go to the Aug. Hall after M. Nicolet & practise from 8.30–9.30. Then the rehearsal. God, how difficult Bach is, but always beautiful. Tonight, the main rehearsal in the Gumbertuskirche. Quite good. I have a beautiful aria with cello obbligato, and he plays it very beautifully.[8] "Very elegant", said a Mr. so-and-so Friend of the Bachwoche [Bach week], small and slim, a somewhat English type, his face familiar from the previous year. After

---

5  Kieth Engen (he adopted the German spelling of his first name) (b. 1925), American bass, who was a member of the Bayerische Staatsoper, Munich, from 1955.

6  The sisters of the religious order who were accommodating some of the Festival artists. See also Pears's poem to his hosts on pp. 83–4.

7  Aurèle Nicolet (b. 1926), Swiss flautist, who was principal flute of the Berlin Philharmonic Orchestra (1950–59). He appeared at two Aldeburgh Festivals (1958–9), where he participated in concerts with, among others, Yehudi Menuhin and Britten.

8  'Wo ferne du den edlen Frieden für unsern Leib', from Cantata No. 41, *Jesu, nun sei gepreiset.*

BACHWOCHE ANSBACH 1959

(11. Jahr) 26. Juli bis 2. August

SONNTAG, 26. JULI

17 Uhr – St. Johanniskirche
Eröffnungsgottesdienst
Landesbischof D. Dr. Hanns Lilje

20 Uhr – St. Gumbertuskirche

Kirchenkantaten
Weihnachten – Neujahr

Nr. 63 Christen, ätzet diesen Tag
Nr. 124 Meinen Jesum laß ich nicht
Nr. 41 Jesu, nun sei gepreiset

Leitung: Karl Richter

\*

MONTAG, 27. JULI

11 Uhr – Orangerie im Schloßpark

Kammermusik
Sonate g-moll für Flöte und Cembalo
Toccata c-moll
Sonate a-moll für Flöte allein
Toccata fis-moll
Sonate h-moll für Flöte und Cembalo

Ralph Kirkpatrick – Aurèle Nicolet

20 Uhr – Münster zu Heilsbronn

Toccata d-moll – Pastorale F-Dur
Präludium und Fuge c-moll
Orgelchoräle „Ich ruf' zu dir"
„Das alte Jahr vergangen ist"
Fantasie und Fuge g-moll

Orgel: Karl Richter

\*

DIENSTAG, 28. JULI

11 Uhr – Prunksaal des Markgrafenschlosses

Bachs Kantaten – Auslegung des Wortes Gottes
Vortrag Professor Dr. Hans-Rudolf Müller-Schwefe

Bachwoche, Ansbach, 1959. A page from
the brochure.

the evening meal (spaghetti with meat, bread & cheese, a ¼ of much needed wine) to bed.

A blessed parcel from the saintly Peg arives today with two Horrors, Mozart letters and Knut Hamsun:[9] a well balanced menu!

*Sunday*

All quiet! No oxen carts! Only bells at 7 o'clock – & Sisters going to church. Also no Nicolet. A very lazy day. Enormous lunch:

Thick soup
Pork, with a hundred dumplings
Wine crème.

Sleep. At 5, half an hour practice – then change for the first Cantata Evening.[10] Terribly hot – have sweated profusely – heavenly music – have sung partly well – familiar faces – Frau Klarwein – Klaus Hoesch – old horsefaces – tall ladies.

---

[9]    Probably E. Müller von Asow's German edition of Mozart's letters (Berlin, 1942). Knut Hamsun (1859–1952), Norwegian writer.

[10]  Given at the St Gumbertuskirche. The programme comprised three cantatas for the Christmas and New Year season: No. 63 *Christen, ätzet diesen Tag*, No. 124 *Meinen Jesum lass' ich nicht*, and No. 41 *Jesu, nun sei gepreiset*. Pears wrote about the concert in a letter to Britten (28 July):

Bach goes on. He is quite wonderful & monumental. Richter has improved – not so overpushing – more modest – makes mistakes, sometimes big ones – it is of course German but this solidity is very useful to build up & away from! The first Cantata Evening [on] Sunday went well enough. Marvellous music – including the Cantata "Meinen Jesum lass' ich nicht" 124 we did at Bideford [a] year ago, v. beautiful with oboe d'amore. (I want to direct some of these Cantatas!)

After the concert I dined with Hans Ludwig[11] and lady friend at the "Schwarzen Bock". What memories of Lupeg, Mrs. Clewes, Yehudi etc![12] I didn't see Mrs. C. A nice evening.

Richter somewhat better than before, perhaps he does not know the Cantatas as well as the Passions. Also, one can hardly overdo these. He is a little cross with me because I am engaged in Hamburg on Good Friday, instead of Munich.[13]


*Monday.* ½ past 5: oxencarts.

Free day – Bachless – for me. After an hour's practice (8.30am–9.30) I went to Nuremberg; for the first time I drove the car slowly. Very hot. The city is still terribly destroyed. But I visited three very beautiful churches.

1. Frauenkirche; beautiful shape, nothing special inside, but a lively west front[14]

2. Sebalduskirche: stark Romanesque and high Gothic combined. Beautiful sculptures, and a very rare "Sebaldus Tomb" from the 16th century. Figures of classic heroes & gods with saints, putti & Barbarossa, animals and angels, Joshua and "Simson". I find it all goes a bit too far.[15]

---

[11] Professor Johannes Ludwig§ (b. 1904), German architect and friend of Princess Margaret. According to a letter from Pears to Britten (28 July 1959), Ludwig had been responsible for designing the re-modelled Johanneskirche in Ansbach.

[12] Lupeg = Pears's and Britten's affectionate compound name for Prince Ludwig and his wife, Princess Margaret. In return, the Hesses too had a similar name for Britten and Pears: 'Benpet'.
Yehudi = Yehudi Menuhin (b. 1916), the American-born violinist and conductor. For a time, Menuhin appeared regularly at the Aldeburgh Festival (1957–9, 1963), often with Britten in the role of accompanist or conductor.
Mrs Clewes remains unidentified.

[13] Richter presumably wished to engage Pears to sing the role of the Evangelist in one of the Bach Passions. Pears's entry for Thursday, 30 July (see p. 81), indicates that he was already booked to sing the *St Matthew Passion* in Hamburg for Richter's rival conductor at Ansbach, Joseph Keilberth.

[14] Pears may be referring to the porch of the Frauenkirche which is noted for its richly carved decorations and sculptures.

[15] The Shrine of St Sebaldus, masterpiece of Peter Vischer (1455–1529), stands in the centre of the choir. It is in the the richest style of Gothic architecture, entirely of bronze, consisting of a fretwork canopy supported on slender pillars beneath which lie the relics of the saint.

3. Lorenzkirche: splendid wide Stoss Annunciation and also an expressive Crucifix.[16]

All three churches beautifully restored. (Good fish and wine for lunch.)

*Germanisches Museum*: very beautiful things; early Gothic sculpture and this fabulous Golden Evangelic Book of Echternach. That's really something. Celtic influence: the colours still wonderfully bright.

At 4 o'clock, dead tired, back to Neuendettelsau.

8 o'clock *Richter Organ Concert* in Heilsbronn Minster.[17] Brand new organ, which is half broken in the first piece. I dined with Bishop Lilje. Charming man, excellent English, very nice & complimentary to me. He had heard the Cantatas. I only exchanged ten words with him, but he made a big impression on me.

After a short little scented country-air stroll with the contralto (and husband) to bed.

The wife of Keith Engen comes from Vienna! & how!

*Tuesday* A long rehearsal in the morning. It should have been the main rehearsal in the Gumbertuskirche, but it was occupied by a Bach lecture. A rest in the afternoon. Another half hour rehearsal. In the evening second Cantata Concert.[18] A thunderstorm as I drive to Ansbach: rather nervous, did not sing very well; pity! beautiful arias; my nice spinach and beige soprano sang a wonderful aria very beautifully.

Terribly hot.

---

[16] The largest and finest Gothic church in Nürnberg. As Pears notes, the Lorenzkirche includes a carving by Veit Stoss (d. 1533) depicting the Annunciation, which is suspended from the ceiling, and a wood gilt crucifix on the high altar also by Stoss.

[17] Richter's recital of organ music by Bach took place in the nearby town of Heilsbronn. Pears wrote to Britten on the 28th: 'Last night Richter had an organ concert at Heilsbronn – the organ misbehaved – an ugly brute anyway – but he played quite well.'

[18] Like the first concert, the second programme of cantatas – this time for Passiontide – was given in the St Gumbertuskirche. The programme comprised four works: No. 127 *Herr Jesu Christ, wahr' Mensch und Gott* (with the soprano aria, 'Die Seele ruht in Jesu Händen', which Pears mentions); No. 73 *Herr, wie du willt*; No. 22 *Jesus nahm zu sich die Zwölfe*; and No. 182 *Himmelskönig, sei willkommen*. Pears described the occasion to Britten (30 July 1959): 'The Second Cantata evening went quite well. Lovely arias for me – fair, not fizzy. Wonderful Soprano one.'

*Wednesday.* A free day!

The weather has broken. Everywhere grey. It will rain. Bonjour, M. Nicolet. But I follow. ¾ hour practice. After breakfast off to Bamberg over small roads and Pommersfelden. But there were so many diversions and the roads were so often closed that I never reached Pommersfelden. I always had to drive towards Bamberg; and just as I stopped in Bamberg, I saw that my front left tyre was flat! Thanks be to God that it did not happen half an hour earlier, in the middle of the Oberfränkischen Forest, on terrible roads, in the desert! So, while I had my lunch, my car was being looked after – everything in order. But I was a little nervous about it, and abandoned Pommersfelden. Back via Heilsbronn where there was a good cold lager-beer!

Did not go to the concert.[19] Early to bed after a very silly and disappointing practice.


*Thursday.* Also free. Nothing to do, except BACH! And that …

.Practise the whole morning. (Did not go to the Prunksaal for Richter's Goldberg Variations.) A little further with these difficult arias.

In the evening to the concert in the Orangery. (The Viennese girl sewed on a button for me, very attractive – very charming.) Keilberth[20] conducts Bach like a real Bavarian beer-drinking peasant. If Richter is not our "cup of tea", what can one say about Keilberth? I am trembling for my "Matthew Passion" with him in Hamburg.

A very gifted violinist – Szeryng[21] – also Nicolet played as always.

In the interval, I listened endlessly to Frau Rosenkrantz from Wuppertal. She babbled and chattered and chirped and squeaked and murmured and squawked. I believe I promised to visit the Rosenkräntze in November after our Wuppertal concert. What will Ben say?

After the concert, a reception in the Prunksaal. Very beautiful. Much to eat, much to drink. Spoke with the enormous Frau Klarwein (customs(?) lady). Difficult to understand. My German gets worse every day, and Frau K. has little English. Many people dressed in black. All of us singers were perhaps a little tipsy. I drove home very quickly. Ssst!

---

[19]  A concert of Bach's solo violin music given by Henryk Szeryng in the castle orangery.

[20]  Joseph Keilberth (1908–1968), German conductor, during the 1950s conductor of the Bayerische Staatsoper, Munich, and at the annual Bayreuth Festival. At Ansbach, Keilberth conducted Bach's Second, Third and Fourth Orchestral Suites (with Nicolet as soloist in No. 2) and the E major Violin Concerto (with Szeryng).

[21]  Henryk Szeryng (1918–1988), Mexican violinist of Polish birth.

*Friday.* The weather remains cold – rain – thunderstorm. A long morning rehearsal and practice. The wine last night was not actually very good. Another short rehearsal after a post-lunch sleep. Evening – Third Cantata Concert.[22] Again wonderful music. I thought I sang badly. The soprano sang "Mein Gläubiges Herz" [from Cantata No. 68] very beautifully; there is an enchanting postlude, so gay, and light and clear. Wonderful J.S.B.

After the concert, something to eat with Hans Ludwig. Very cosy and friendly.

*Saturday.* Cold, grey, ugly. Half past nine rehearsal, difficult arias. Then to Ansbach to the newly renovated Johannes Kirche. Well done, though not brilliant. A horrible modern tapestry on the wall. Good acoustic. Concert by the Thomaner Choir from Leipzig.[23] Beautiful voices, charming sound, but Kurt Thomas[24] too boring a conductor. Richter always drives, is too subjective, and has a mediocre ear. Thomas is cool & clear, objective, without musical feeling. Who is the best? or the worst?

Much rain the whole morning. I got very wet. Then with Hans and niece to Rotenburg for lunch, and Creglingen and D.?–gen to see the Riemenschneider Altars.[25] Very beautiful, but a thousand horrible tourists everywhere, in buses etc. and rain, rain, rain. A bit coldy, early to bed.

*Sunday.* The last day. Pity.

I long to fly back to Aldeburgh (the influence of Bach texts!) but the Bachwoche is always an experience, truly. This old Protestant, so deeply rooted, so faithful, and so dear is a unique companion – although damn difficult to sing.

---

[22]  Given in the Gumbertuskirche. The programme comprised four cantatas for Easter and Whitsun: No. 4 *Christ lag in Todesbanden*; No. 67 *Halt im Gedächtnis Jesum Christ*; No. 104 *Du Hirte Israel, höre*; and No. 68 *Also hat Gott die Welt geliebt.*

[23]  A morning concert of Bach motets, including *Jesu, meine Freude.*

[24]  German choral conductor (1904–1973), director of the Thomaskantorei and the Thomaskirche, Leipzig, 1955–61.

[25]  Tilmann Riemenschneider (*c.*1460–1531), German sculptor, whose famous decorative altar, the *Ascension of the Virgin*, is at the Herrgotteskirche, Creglingen.

After the concert,[26] back to Neuendettelsau. Goodbye sisters,
deaconesses, novices, the old, the young, bells, flowers.

two glasses of Nackt-Arsch
    a last piece of bread and cheese.
        Adieu
           Ursula
                Hertha
                      Keith
                            Adieu!
        Both Karls[27] –
        and both wives
        Bye-bye Bach.

\*\*\*\*\*\*\*

FAREWELL WORLD! I AM WEARY OF YOU,
   I WISH TO GO HEAVENWARDS
WHERE THERE WILL BE REAL PEACE
   AND ETERNAL, PROUD REST!
WORLD, WITH YOU THERE IS WAR AND STRIFE
NOTHING BUT SHEER VANITY;
   IN HEAVEN, FOREVER
   PEACE, JOY AND BLISS.

Final Chorale: Cantata 27
"Who knows, how near is my end?"
J. S. Bach

\*\*\*\*\*\*\*

POEM.[28]

Nuns? why are you not
Eva and Elsa and Elisabeth[29]

---

[26] The final evening of cantatas – for Trinity – was, again, held in the Gumbertuskirche. The programme comprised: No. 45 *Es ist dir gesagt, Mensch, was gut ist*; No. 27 *Wer weiss, wie nahe mir mein Ende* (from which Pears includes the text of the finale chorale as part of his diary: see above); No. 8 *Liebster Gott, wann werd' ich sterben*; and No. 79 *Gott, der Herr, ist Sonn' und Schild*.

[27] I.e. Karl Richter and Dr Carl Weymar, administrative director of the Bachwoche.

[28] An amusing poem by Pears written in honour of his hosts, the Sisters of the 'Diakonissenanstalt'.

[29] The female characters from Wagner's *Die Meistersinger von Nürnberg, Lohengrin* and *Tannhäuser*, respectively.

Under this Bavarian sun?
It was – perhaps – the heavenly clamour
Resounding in these Sunday bells
Which one day turned your so-blond souls
Into black and white.
Virtuous, pious, but not cold
You thus dip us into your shadow
'Ere our evening sun suddenly fades.


Herewith, I lay my English greetings
Sisters, at your industrious feet;
Agnes and Anna and Marta-Maria*
Unknowing witnesses of the Christian German power.

   *Also Diakonisse[30] Thusnelde Schmid,
   Leader of the Kindergarten Teachers Seminar

---

[30]   *Translator's note*: the dictionary translates Diakonisse as 'Lutheran Nurse';
       Diakon, however, is a deacon.

# 4  *India (1965)*

As has already been noted in Chapter 2, India – the land, its people and culture – played a significant role in Pears's formative years. After his first visit to the sub-continent in 1955–56 and the evident pleasure that it gave both him and Britten, it is not therefore surprising to find that when planning their sabbatical year of 1965 a return trip, far more extended than was previously possible, was placed high on the agenda. Britten and Pears spent over six weeks on holiday in India during the winter of 1965. They left London on 16 January, flying to Frankfurt where they joined the Prince and Princess of Hesse and the Rhine who had accompanied them on their first visit. The next day the four companions flew to Delhi, from where the party travelled to Udaipur, Madras, Bombay, Ootacamund, Cochin, Kerala, Thekkady, Mysore, and the former Portuguese colony of Goa, before returning to Bombay for the homeward flight on 2 March.

1965 was broadly intended as a sabbatical year for both Britten and Pears, with the principal exception of the Aldeburgh Festival in June. However, while in India they gave one concert (see p. 88) and Britten continued to work on new pieces: his *Gemini Variations*, Op. 73, were completed there, as was the German translation of *Curlew River*, Op. 71, prepared by Prince Ludwig with Britten's assistance; time was also found for a complete reading of Tolstoy's *Anna Karenina*, a novel that Britten intended at that time to forge into a major new opera for Galina Vishnevskaya and Pears.

As in 1955–56, Britten wrote a sequence of diary-letters to a young friend (the recipient on this occasion was John Newton, who had sung in *Curlew River* the previous year) and Pears attempted to keep a diary. In fact, the diary proper survives in an incomplete state – it covers only the first week or so – but he effectively continued it in a short series of letters to Helene Rohlfs (1892–1990), widow of the German artist Christian Rohlfs (1849–1938) whose paintings Pears much admired and collected. These letters are used in conjunction with the unfinished diary to provide a fuller account of the visit.

Pears's original diary text can be found in *GB-ALb* 1-9500033; photo-copies of Pears's letters were supplied to their author by Frau Rohlfs (*GB-ALb* 4-9500336).

Wolfsgarten[1] the 1st upbeat, the preparing for the plunge – then we're off.

Excellent Maxim's lunch – as we look down on Yugoslavia & Vlado [Habunek], and to the Greek coast (Mt Attus below) and Olympus and its inhabitants over far to the right.

The steward who recognised us (not the purserette) is the owner of a gramophone company[2] – who has so far put out 2 records, one of Eric — ,[3] bass of the Met, the other of our old friend Ted Uppmann[4] 1st Billy Budd. Without any backing or ads. he hopes to make money after 1000 copies have been sold of any record – plans for unrecorded music, & young singers very typically American! no evidence of taste or genius but good intentions. He left us at Beirut, and another crew took over. A half hour's wait in Beirut and then on to Karachi, which was thick in fog, rank and hot; stayed on plane & then in 1 hour on to Delhi, where we arrived (?) a.m. local time, & were met (angellically!) by Narayana Menon, our old friend, secretary and mainstay of National Music Academy here. He saw us to our hotel large and somewhat shoddy and we sank into a bed (too hard to sink into) and tried to sleep: woken many times by new noises, dogs howling, monkeys & parrots chattering: emerged for lunch in hotel restaurant for excellent lunch with Narayana, kindness itself. Drove to see Red Fort, were shown round by charming old guide, and haunted everywhere by beauty, the grace of the Indians, the colour of their dresses, the touching appeal of their expression. One boy followed us from first to last, observing & listening though he spoke no English; with thick short sighted glasses and nicely dressed he seemed to regard us as some vehicles to a wider world, full of respect; Ben's heart was touched, so was the boy's. After a rest, Narayana and Rekha came and we ate again in the restaurant, delightful man, intelligent sensitive graceful, the best of India influenced for the best by the best of England (Cambridge etc.). We hear of his new schools for music & drama (4 for music 2 for ballet & 1 for drama now beginning).

*Tuesday* [19 January] After deep if broken sleep, off to see the Gandhi memorial, on the place where he was cremated, quite simply done. Inside a park, where a bullock was pulling a grass mower, and along a ramp, through an earth wall, a plain grass square, with, in the centre, an

---

[1]   Schloss Wolfsgarten near Frankfurt, the Hesses' principal home.
[2]   The steward was Kurt Stenzel whose company, Internos Records Inc., was keen on issuing recordings of American artists in repertoire that had not previously been recorded.
[3]   *Recte*: Ezio Flagello (b. 1933), American bass.
[4]   Theodor ('Ted') Uppman[5] (b. 1920), American baritone, whose record (INT. 0001), with Allen Rogers (piano), included music by Schumann, Mozart and Verdi. See also Plate 23.

enclosure surrounded by large low stone slabs, a paved rectangle with a black marble square tombstone, many red & yellow garlands and his last words in script 'God'. Very simple & touching; far removed from the splendour of the Red Fort. The mosque is a splendid quadrangle with the bulbous domes on pinnacles at the corners so characteristic of Moghul art, so refined and so disastrously copied or adapted by Lutyens[5] in New Delhi where they can only remind one of solar topees. Little chipmunk animals playing & fighting in a corner. Very beautiful stone carving of flowers: how does the ogee curved arch persist & what is at the back of it? Flowers in pots in stone. All India has been spoiled so many times.

In the evening to Mrs Gandhi's[6] home for dinner: some film producers, a Festival is on; otherwise family. The beauty & charm of Indian women. Simple home. Jamini Roy of Tagore & Ghandi. Couldn't get talking: stiff, dull: but afterwards taken to rehearsal of Dancing for Independence Day. Just as little girls with candles had perched on pots, rain came; we had to adjourn to a tent: v. awkward for the dancers, from all corners, pale, dark, tall, tiny mongol, aryan: stunning boys as girls; Himalayan dance on shoulders; the spring in an oldish man's foot; chocolate skins; behinds with horse tails; sort of sanusaphone with 2 notes.

[Pears described the dancing in his first letter to Helene Rohlfs (23 January 1965):

[We] were taken to see the folk dancers who were gathered from all over India from the Himalayas & Assam to the far South & the Laccadive Islands; they were to perform on Independence day (Jan 26th). They were going to perform for us on a special stage – but just as they began (4 little girls dancing with candles alight, they came from near Burma) the rain poured down; poor little things they were soaked & so were we a bit, & we went into a tent, where they all did their best in a small awkward space; all amateur folk dancers, some marvellous, some v. simple, dark brown, quite fair, bass oboes, flutes, drums,

---

[5]   Sir Edwin Lutyens (1869–1944), English architect whose early reputation was founded upon his large-scale domestic architecture but whose greatest work was undoubtedly the building of New Delhi (1913–30), a final flowering of aristocratic imperial architecture. His daughter was the composer, Elisabeth Lutyens (1906–1983).

[6]   Indira Gandhi (1916–1984), Indian political leader and only child of the nationalist leader Jawaharlal Nehru, independent India's first prime minister (1947–64), whom Britten and Pears met when visiting India in 1955–56. Among the other dinner guests were 'an excellent Indian painter & his wife Krishen Khanna' (Pears to Helene Rohlfs, 23 January 1965), and Britten remarked in his first letter to John Newton (24 January 1965) that Mrs Gandhi was 'charming and intelligent, with a house full of pictures'.

a strange brass horn, huge from the far North, some slow wriggling, springing, stamping, terrific fast circling, everything you can imagine, tinkles, bangs, cries, silence, clashes, infinitely touching.]

*Wednesday* [20 January] Concert day! rehearsed at excellent new Akademi building:[7] 1st class little theatre: charming director; lunch at High Commissioner,[8] nice company, Mr Norman Butler (Bach Choir), Mrs Cazalet Kei. Macao (Sekers' friend), Austrian Ambassador – NO. Then evening concert.[9] OK nervous – on to drinks at Narayana's & K. Kannen.[10] S. Ray.[11] (films). Moti Mahals for superb food chicken Tabouri? Butter'd chicken***

*Thursday* [21 January] Drive to Agra through greenish fertile country most of the way. Akbars milestones. Road medium with awful patches. Owing to fuss over money & bills, late starting & arrive at hotel at 2.30, new efficient internat. hotel. Taj after lunch, v. beautiful as before.

---

[7]   Britten wrote to John Newton (24 January 1965):
      *Jan. 20th.* Today . . . is the only work-day of our trip. A great friend of Peter's and mine is a famous Indian musician – head of the Academy of Music, Art and Dancing here, Narayana Menon. And to please him we have agreed to do a concert in the Library of his Academy. We rehearsed a little in the morning – not as much as we should have done, perhaps, because it was hot and we were lazy and rather cross!

[8]   Sir Paul (later Lord) Gore-Booth (1909–1984), British High Commissioner to India, 1960–65, described by Britten as 'charming and musical' (letter to John Newton, 24 January 1965).

[9]   The concert at the Sangeet Natak Akademi comprised songs by Purcell and Handel, five of Haydn's English canzonets, and Britten's 'Fish in the unruffled lakes', the Second Lute Song from *Gloriana*, *Sechs Hölderlin-Fragmente*, Op. 61 (dedicated to Prince Ludwig on the occasion of his fiftieth birthday in 1958), and folksong arrangements. Pears wrote to Helene Rohlfs (23 January 1965): 'We gave a concert in the Academy, in a long low hall to a nice audience and had a wonderful Indian meal afterwards'; while Britten told John Newton (24 January 1965): 'We gave the concert at 6.30 and it wasn't too alarming – 200 invited guests, and very friendly – but we were rather out of practice . . . and got nervous a bit!' See also p. 89.

[10]  Khrishen Khanna (b. 1925), Pakistanian painter, whose *Town landscape* Pears already owned.

[11]  Satyajit Ray (1921–1992), Indian film director, whose work is celebrated for its depiction of Indian life.

sangeet natak akademi

# peter pears tenor
# benjamin britten pianoforte

rabindra bhawan, new delhi

wednesday, january 20, 1965

New Delhi, 20 January 1965. Programme for Britten's and
Pears's recital.

*Friday* [22 January] British parks & houses etc. slept at Agra & on by early plane to Udaipur via Japan-Dakota. Picked up T. Cazalet Kei & Mrs Norman Butler. They left at Jaipur. Reached U. by taxi from airport 13 miles. Wonderful reds & yellows of saris. The hotel a white meringue in a lake.[12] Wonderful courtyard with trellis work in marble, charming rooms, mirror glass inlay; excursion into town; huge palace built round vast rock, mirror glass inlay, elephant painted, open air rooms on top with columns, for water and colour throwing, teeming bazaar, Hindu temple with well preserved statuary, scenes of lakes, fine embankment: two excursions on lakes, birds, crocodiles: heavenly quiet day with no excursions; on to Ahmedabad, day with Geeba Sarabhai excursions in A., charm, kindness, v. pretty daughter, *teeming* bazaar, v. little cripple or illness *apparent*, textile institute. Bombay, dinner at Juhn beach with Sarabhai's, endless journey in little taxi to Ritz H, 2nd class, tarts, inefficiency, etc.

Next day [26 January] to Madras. Hideous poverty & squalor en route to Bombay airport. Madras green contrast. Met by Mrs Clubwala with Ben's child: beautiful:[13] hotel Oceanic medium pleasant: garden party at Raj Bhavam where we stayed 9 years ago: met by H. Comm. Patterson:[14] party stopped by sudden shower; dinner with Pattersons at Madras Club: huge steak etc.; charming colonial houses.

*******

---

[12]  The Lake Palace, Udaipur, where the party remained until the 25th when they travelled to Bombay. See p. 91 for Pears's description of the hotel in the first of his letters to Helene Rohlfs.

[13]  Britten wrote to John Newton (1 February 1965):

A remarkable Indian woman, called Clubwala, has started many homes for orphans, or unwanted children, and gets people to pay for their keep. Peg Hesse (Princess Margaret) and I "adopted" one when we were here last, and today we see them for the first time (they were only babies before). I have been writing to mine occasionally, and we have a very touching re-union. He is a sweet boy of about 13, very dark, good-looking, but shy ... We go to the home where he lives, and they all perform for us, doing some dances and gymnastics – they are very lithe creatures, and perform brilliantly and neatly.

[14]  William Paterson (1911–1976), British Deputy High Commissioner, Madras, 1961–5.

Sunday (?) 23rd Jan [*recte*: 24th]    Lake Palace Hotel
*Udaipur*

Dearest Helene,
   It wasn't until our fifth day in India that we reached Paradise! "It is here, it is here, it is here, if it is anywhere on earth," as an inscription says in the most beautiful room in the Red Fort at Delhi! Well, this white palace is in the middle of a large lake; not far from one side is the mainland with a towering white castle: we have been here two days and go on tomorrow – too soon – too soon – too soon! It was originally the Maharana's palace in summer[15] – he is the greatest, bravest, most honoured of all the Hindu princes because on three occasions at Chitorgarh his many wives burnt themselves while their husbands dashed out of the city against the enemy and together with his nobles and followers threw themselves onto the lances of the invaders! However they also made beautiful things besides! And there are fascinating rooms and courtyards both in this modernised hotel and in the old palace on shore. But best of all is the lake on which we have now twice boated, and seen all sorts of strange birds of every shape, size and colour, from brilliant greeen paraqueets with long tails which fan out quickly as they land (they *all* collect on the second island at sundown 6 p.m. & spend the night there – fascinating to watch their noisy meeting – thousands of them) and storks and cranes, bright blue big kingfishers, curlews, ibis, paddy-birds, little waders, pelicans (huge yawns!), vultures, many kinds of long legged grey birds, standing up on their nests on the tops of trees. And also crocodiles – two very big and one baby ¼ grown! The far side of the lake slowly climbs ridge after ridge to high hills, which go all shades of gray and chocolate when the sun sets behind it. But now the sun is high and hot and we are sunbathing.


*Monday* morning [25 January]
I have just woken up to another glorious sunny day of golden silence – not a movement on the lake – pigeons cooing – slowly the town and palace wake up – shuffling steps of the servants, who are dressed in khaki shirts and berets left-over from the war, I should think. Everything here is white marble, with much Moghul influence, courtyards with fountains which go at different speeds to imitate light or heavy showers of rain; pinnacles like umbrellas at the corner of every wall; marble

---

[15]   Britten told John Newton (24 January 1965): 'It was originally the Summer Palace of the Maharana of Udaipur (the Prince of the district) until quite recently when (as is so often the story today) it was too much for him to keep up as well as his other Palace – a little affair of about a mile in circumference! – on the mainland. So he turned it into the most exquisite hotel you could imagine.'

trellis-ed screens, with coloured mirror-glass inlaid; huge mango trees shading geometrically formal grass squares, all within a tiny island like a L 40 yards by 50 yards! Blue blue sky, shivering lake, white arches and parapets – magic! only the radio played by the Japanese in the next room (or is he American?) is a pity . . .

The British have always been in love with India, they say, and I can very well understand why. Poverty – yes – of course, but some of what seems like poverty is endurable in this climate. *Not* many signs of disease etc. That, I think, is really better than it used to be. But problems! My God, what problems & how vast it all is & so different, yet 500 million people *do* live under one rule . . .

I shall post this from Bombay this evening & write again from Madras next week.

Much love to you my dear from us all
Peter


Jan 29th                                                    Oceanic Hotel, Madras

Dearest Helene,
I think I said in my last letter posted in Bombay that poverty was not *so* bad here. One car ride to Bombay airport was enough to contradict that *for ever*. Most of the miles out from the city consist of shacks put up on sewers – the filth and conditions of huts cannot be described – and yet the human beings themselves are *clean*, their white clothes are *much* whiter than London or Manchester's grey & black suits. This is part of what touches one so deeply in the whole human situation. Here has been for many thousand years a beautiful people (they *are* that) with quick warm human instincts but with very little real education for the vast majority, and as yet no real basis for improved education. Much is being done for the exceptional and gifted – technical schools are being built, and in Madras there is great building activity in schools and institutions. It is only scratching the surface. The difficulties are vast. A huge population increasing alarmingly prevents any apparent improvement. The Government is doing its best, I think; they make mistakes of course (just now a stupid decision to insist on Hindi as the national language at once has brought tragic days here – already they have realised their mistake & will try to slow down, I think) but *what* difficulties they have! India is a place where *all* countries meet, the main technological institutes are directly equipped by Russia, U.S., W. Germany & Britain. Here in Madras, in the homes for destitute children, Canadians, New Zealanders, etc. etc. adopt or sponsor the children. Last time we were here (1956) Ben sponsored a little boy and now saw him for the first time – a dear chap, 13 years old now, and doing so well in this marvellous

home run by excellent Indian people. And now I too have sponsored a "son" – a little 12 year old called Vadjravel (Diamond spear). His father is dead; his mother deserted him some years ago; he is a nice good chap, and so happy to have someone who is interested in him. I shall try to write to him regularly (a hard task for a wicked old sinner in correspondence such as me!). He was deeply moving.

Madras is the most beautiful of the big Indian cities; a wonderful sandy beach and splendid colonial buildings from the early British days, and many fine gardens. Madras is always green. We have driven out quite a bit – to temples along the coast – and have been entertained – mostly rather boring parties (today lunch at the Governor's house, a marvellous colonial 1800 mansion outside Madras, where we stayed when we were here before – a pleasant dinner last night at the Br. Council rep.'s house, another at the old Br. Club). I visited the Cathedral to find the grave of my nephew Martin (Cecily Smithwick's[16] only son, who died of polio here in 1952); it was nicely cared for: and I found Baptismal Entries of 4 or 5 cousins of mine! My family was much in India and mostly in Madras: empire-builders!

This morning we spent some hours at Kalakshetra (the Theosophical Centre) and heard a lot of Indian music and dancing – absolutely fascinating it was: a very good singer and an old old instrumentalist, charming, witty, moving, complicated, very Indian.[17] Tomorrow we go at dawn to Ooty [Ootacamund], where my father was born and where my mother used to take my brothers & sisters in the hot weather. It is high up in the hills & will be cool. Here in Madras it is Maximum 28°C. strong sun ...

We are really enjoying the trip very much. Ben had one or two days of terrible tummy upset & pain, but Peg always has a remedy for every ill in her "muttitasche".

I must post this, otherwise it will be much longer getting to you from Ooty.

Much love to you, my dear, from us all. Look after yourself!
Peter

---

[16] Pears's older sister, to whom Britten dedicated his carol for women's voices, *The Oxen* (1967).

[17] Britten wrote to John Newton (1 February 1965):
Spend fascinating morning at the Kalahshetra [*sic*] School of music and dancing, which was started a dozen years or so ago by a remarkable woman Ruhurein Devi, a famous dancer in her time. We attend classes of folk dancing and classical dances, all done by young girls. And then, most interesting of all, go to a class of music which was being taken by a wonderful old player and a singer. There were about 3 boys and 4 girls in the class, and we were allowed to join in and ask questions! We leave this place feeling somehow "refreshed" by what we saw and heard . . .

7/2/65 *Cochin*
posted 9/2/65
[Envelope addressed from:
Taj Mahal Hotel, Bombay]

Dearest Helene,

I posted my last letter to you in Madras airport on our way to Ooty, I think.

Well, we flew off just as the sun came up, after a long slow drive in the dark out to the airport, with shadowy figures always in white, on the way to work or more essential natural functions, with smells of burning or jasmine or drains in one's nostrils, an odd mixture of magic and horror. An hour's flight took us to Coimbatore at the foot of the Nilgiri mountains, & then 2½ hours in an ancient taxi (all taxis are ancient, all Indian drivers hate to change gear, they drive in the middle until the last possible moment and use their (ancient) horns ceaselessly!). In India human beings don't listen to horns until the car is on top of them and the cows, dogs & waterbuffalos pay no attention at all! You just have to wait & drive round them. The road to Ooty is up the sheer side of a mountain covered with forest. It is really marvellously built with 13 hairpin bends, used by huge lorries. Our car knocked and bubbled all the way, but we made it – & found up there (8000ft up, nearly 3000 metres) a glorious climate, cold at nights but hot sun in the day, huge eucalyptus trees and conifers, and of course oleanders & bourgamvillas, & mimosas, and English houses and cottages built eighty or a hundred years ago, which made up corners of Sussex, with names of villas on the gate which you find retired Englishmen fancying everywhere. I could well imagine my father's father working there or going up from Madras in the hot weather. In fact my father was born there, perhaps in "San Remo" or "Lynmouth House" or even the Savoy Hotel, where we stayed and were given real British food of Scotch Broth, Fried Fish, Roast Lamb (as well as curry) & Steamed ginger pudding! Our breakfasts too are enormous, twice as much as the Wentworth Hotel [in Aldeburgh]!

In India everyone passes one on to their friends in other towns, so in Ooty we were kindly looked after by a highly intelligent wife of a man in charge of a huge new film factory being built. She took us up to the highest peak in the neighbourhood, Dodabetta, with the most glorious view I have seen anywhere. The clear air with the sun produces cloud formations and intensities of endless variety, and there the land is greener than below, with these gigantic trees, which at dawn are tinged with silvery grey against a pinkish blue sky. We went to visit a settlement of ancient aboriginal people, the Todas, in appearance similar to the Indians but taller and with more aquiline features. They worship no images, only the spirits of nature, and build circular covered cones of bamboo & grass in which a priest lives (chosen by the month, I think) with a buffalo, the chief supplier of their food. They are pastoral & eat only milk, fruit, nuts and millet, a charming simple peaceful people. (Their buffaloes are especially splendid.) Of course they will disappear. Their land, the grazing downs, are being planted with quinine trees by the government & they wont be able to wander as they used to. There are only 1600 of them left. Sad.[18]

We spent 4 lovely days in Ooty. One is reminded of several things: the absurd drink laws by which foreigners have to get permits & may not drink in public. Everyone agrees that prohibition is a good thing on the whole. In the old days they used to distill spirits at home, which was lethal: now the poor are fitter without it. Most Indians don't drink or eat meat, but European sinners need it!! (at least drink!) Ooty was the chief meeting place in the hot months for South Indian society, & there is still an air of nostalgia for the good old British days, parties, picnics, riding, the race course, shooting, hard drinking etc.

Round the lake are the palaces of the Maharajahs who can't afford to pay high taxes for living in their palaces, so they will slowly fall down. We went to tea with our hostess who brought several Parsee friends to meet us. The Parsees are the richest and most efficient group in India, it seems; certainly intelligent, educated and benevolent. From Ooty we drove off at 5.15 a.m. to catch the plane at Coimbatore for Cochin. The drive down the mountains was less alarming although dark, and our flight was comfortable in one of the small planes which they use much in India. Here in Cochin it is by the sea, & much hotter, rather too hot at first, though now we are getting used to it. A pleasant hotel on the water of the inland harbour, with constant activity of ships great & small. The coast line is flat with low houses with red tiled roofs, tall coconut palms; Kerala is a small province but very ancient. The Jews came here in A.D. 72, & the Christians had long been settled when Vasco da Gama reached Cochin round the Cape. 40% Christian & the most literate of all the states, it is Communist: very beautiful & lush: 8 months rain a year, but thank God, now it is sunny, with glorious twilights! It is a particular pleasure to drive in a motorboat through the enormous harbour & islands, all fringed with green palms and rice

---

[18]  Britten described the encounter with the Toda people to John Newton (9 February 1965): 'The women, who wear their black hair done in ringlets, sang a song of welcome to us: the tune (repeated over and over again) ... I couldn't catch the words, I'm afraid, which were in one of the 225 quite independent languages they have in India!'

A sketch of the 'Toda Welcome Song' survives among the fragmentary material for Britten's second church parable, The Burning Fiery Furnace, Op. 77 (1966). The theme was not incorporated into the parable nor elsewhere in Britten's oeuvre, but its inclusion among the preliminary sketches for The Burning Fiery Furnace surely points to Britten's latent interest in Indian music (see n. 42, p. 30).

fields, sweet naked children, beautiful, finely built beautiful men punting or rowing boats with a grace which makes all of us seem gross and clumsy. The Indian women are very charming, we find, with their lovely clothes and sure friendly un-shy manners and quick intelligence. We went out to dinner with a civilised (Indian) tea-taster and his beautiful Indian wife, and they drove us along the coast, coconut trees all the way, the richest of all crops, when every bit is good for something, the husk for fibre (mats, rugs etc), the liquid for various drinks & butter & oil, the meat for cocoanut, the shells for firewood. Again the Indians always drive 40mph through children, animals, puddles, holes, ditches, villages – very alarming to us old Europeans. Again poverty, poverty, poverty – *far* too many people in this rich country. What problems. Also elephantiasis of the legs very frequent here caused by some fly. But they have almost entirely eliminated malaria which is a great triumph. Next must come family planning.

We have reached half-time in our holiday – 3 weeks gone and three weeks to come! I am enjoying it enormously, but I know I shall be happy to be home . . .

Much love my dear and from Ben
dein Peter

P.S. ... We probably stay here until 20th then Mysore & Goa & Bombay.


18/ii/65 DOLCE FARNIENE Aranigia Nivas
*Thekaddi*

My dear Helene,

We have only two days – or less – still to live in this Paradise! We came 10 days ago and each day has been like a new adventure, and yet a wonderful and soothing holiday. The annex in which we live now is across the water from the main hotel, through a long water-passage through which submerged trees stick up, dead but still solid. Water is on three sides of us. Every sort of flower blooms in our little garden from European rose-bush to glorious creepers which climb up the tall tamarisk trees and hang down 30ft to the ground. I have no idea of the names of most of these trees & flowers, poinsettias yes and bourgainvilleas, but there is a large tree with grey black trunk and darkish green leaf which produces brilliant orange clusters of blossom and then when they drop, huge long sharp pods appear sticking out stiff from the tree, which the blue and green parrots greatly enjoy opening, and the seeds float out over the roses. (I enclose some seeds!)

Each day we go out in the motorboat for some hours either at dawn or dusk to look at bison or wild pig or deer or the elephants – but them we feel we know already as old friends. We can watch them from our breakfast table, pulling the tufts of grass and dusting them over their knees before they stuff them into their mouths, washing and spouting in the water, splashing & drinking, and rolling the babies over in the mud and washing them. Yesterday a noble old tusker prepared to defend his herd against some people in a boat who teased him with noises & got too near. He trumpted splendidly and banged his foot & curled his tail at them, looking very righteous and splendid. The monkeys we hear but do not see much – black chaps who go hooping-hoop hoop hoop (crescendo ed accelerando) up the scale like a contralto practising in the bath! The birds are glorious – we have seen nearly 70 different varieties in India, quite new names like the Drongo, the Minivet & the Concal, and also rare European birds like the osprey. Three beautiful kingfishers – and the blue Roller – but also some whose song is deadly monotonous and disturbs Ben, who is working on a piece for the Hungarian twin boys who are coming to the Festival with Kodály.[19] Lu has been busy translating "Curlew River" into German. Peg writes letters and reads, I read and write letters – and programme-notes for the Aldeburgh Programme-book! All very industrious, as you see – in a perfect place for a holiday! . . .

Much love to you
Peter

---

[19] Zoltán and Gábor Jeney, the thirteen-year-old Hungarian twins whom Britten and Pears had met in Budapest in 1964, for whom Britten composed his *Gemini Variations*, Op. 73, a 'quartet for two players: flute, violin, and piano 4 hands'. The talented, extremely musical Jeney boys gave the first performance of the *Gemini Variations* at the 1965 Aldeburgh Festival. Britten's set of variations was based on a theme by the Hungarian composer Zoltán Kodály who also attended that year's Aldeburgh Festival, and who was present at the première of the new Britten work. See Humphrey Carpenter, *Benjamin Britten: a Biography* (London: Faber and Faber, 1992), pp. 448–9.

# 5   Armenian Holiday: A Diary (August 1965)

In September 1960 Britten attended the first British performance of Shostakovich's Cello Concerto No. 1, with the thirty-three-year-old Mstislav Rostropovich as soloist. This was not quite the first occasion on which Britten had heard the Russian cellist: a few days earlier he had caught part of a broadcast on the radio, 'and thought this was the most extraordinary cello playing I'd ever heard'. Introduced to Britten after the concert by Shostakovich, Rostropovich 'attacked Britten there and then and pleaded most sincerely and passionately with him to write something for the cello'. Britten called at Rostropovich's hotel the next morning and said that he was very keen to write a sonata for cello and piano for himself and Rostropovich on the condition that Rostropovich would give the first performance at the 1961 Aldeburgh Festival.

The Sonata in C, Op. 65, proved to be only the first of several major Britten works for Rostropovich – the Cello Symphony, Op. 68 (1963), and three solo Suites (1964; 1967; 1971) followed – and a warm friendship between Rostropovich, his wife Galina Vishnevskaya, Britten and Pears developed over the years. Other works planned in the late 1960s, but never composed, included a Shakespeare sonnet sequence for tenor (Pears), cello and piano, and at his death Britten left unfinished a final work for Rostropovich to conduct, *Praise We Great Men* (1976), a setting of a poem by Edith Sitwell, for soloists, chorus and orchestra, which was intended for Rostropovich's debut with the National Symphony Orchestra of Washington D.C.

Britten and Pears first visited the Soviet Union in March 1963 for a Festival of British Music, and the English Opera Group made an important tour there the following year. In 1965 Rostropovich invited his English friends to spend a summer holiday in the Soviet Union, an invitation which, while not troubling the warm-hearted Rostropovich for one moment, appears to have given his more practical wife some cause for concern. As Vishnevskaya recalls in her autobiography (GV, p. 370), a solution was found:

> While I was racking my brains trying to figure out what I was going to feed Ben and Peter, Shostakovich gave me a wonderful piece of advice. He had recently been in Armenia, where he had vacationed at the Composers' House in Dilizhan, located high up in the mountains, and he was greatly impressed by the Armenians' hospitality. So he suggested we take our foreign guests there, assuring us that the Armenians wouldn't disappoint us, whereas in Moscow we'd hardly manage on Russian grub. And indeed, when Slava called the Composers' House and said they might have the honour of playing host to Benjamin Britten

himself, along with us, they were so overjoyed they were ready to declare a national holiday.

Thus Britten and Pears spent August 1965 in Armenia as the guests of the Armenian Composers' Union, the visit concluding with their reluctant participation in a Britten Festival at Yerevan (see pp. 125–30).

The original handwritten manuscript of Pears's account of the trip survives at the Britten–Pears Library (1-9400532), as does an incomplete typescript draft (1-9400533). Extracts from *Armenian Holiday* appeared in the 1966 Aldeburgh Festival Programme Book (pp. 71–3), and in December of that year Pears privately published the complete diary in a soft-back edition of 1000 copies, typeset and printed by Benham and Company Ltd of Colchester. Copies were distributed by him and Britten as Christmas gifts. The text of the present edition corresponds to this private publication, which Pears prefaced with the following cautionary note:

This casual record of a very happy month is left as it was written, inconsistent in spelling and punctuation. Such interest as it has would not be increased by editing!

*Saturday, 7th August 1965*

Yesterday we arrived at our furthest point, the south-eastern most limit of our journey. Here is where our holiday begins, and today, with the sound of always running water in our ears and wispy grey clouds in our eyes, clouds which have not yet ceased contributing their tears to the ever-running streams, today is a perfect moment to begin a Diary.

But first, the Prelude. Arrival at London Airport, driven by Jeremy[1] from Aldeburgh on the Sunday in time for Slava's[2] concert at R.F.H. with Ben's Cello Symphony, party after, at the Festival Hall, given by the Russian Embassy; Monday spent in usual last-day operations, a party for Faber Music at the flat[3] and dinner with Marion,[4] Basil,[5] Slava and Galya[6] at Prunier's. At the Airport in good time on Tuesday, to find Galya and Slava surrounded by seers-off and loaded down with purchases from Harrods (which must do very well out of Slava) – food-mixers, hair-dryers, in all eight parcels which travelled on our First-class tickets. For some odd reason, Slava and Galya always fly Tourist class (at any rate in Russian planes). We took some time getting through – tickets, etc. – and there was not too much hanging around before getting to the plane, apart from a moment when Victor Hochhauser[7] had to persuade the customs man that he was not either stowing away to Moscow or recently smuggled into England.

Once on board, our holiday had started: we were in Russia. The immensely solid plane with few, if any, frills; the nice serious stewardess, not in uniform, a sort of auntie-type; the plentiful vodka; the plentiful medium-good food; the small incompetences (why hang a curtain over a door on the side to which the door opens? why have a tray all slotted

---

[1]  Jeremy Cullum (b. 1931), Britten's secretary for eighteen years from 1951 to 1968.

[2]  Mstislav ('Slava') Rostropovich[§] (b. 1927), Russian cellist, pianist and conductor. The concert at the Royal Festival Hall, London, on 1 August 1965, was given by the London Symphony Orchestra conducted by Gennady Rozhdestvensky. As an encore, Rostropovich played the last movement of the Cello Symphony (the passacaglia) but with Britten, rather than Rozhdestvensky, conducting.

[3]  Held at Pears's and Britten's London home, 59c Marlborough Place, NW8 (see PFL, Plate 166). Faber Music, Britten's publishers from 1964, began trading in 1965 as a department of Faber and Faber before being incorporated as Faber Music Ltd in December 1965.

[4]  Marion Thorpe[§] (b. 1926), the Countess of Harewood at the time of Pears's writing.

[5]  Basil Coleman[§] (b. 1916), English opera producer who worked extensively with the English Opera Group in the 1940s and 1950s.

[6]  Galina ('Galya') Vishnevskaya[§] (b. 1926), Russian soprano, married to Rostropovich.

[7]  English music agent and impresario (b. 1923) who, with his wife Lilian, acted for many Russian musicians – Rostropovich and Vishnevskaya included – when making concert tours in the West.

and pitted for cups, etc., and a thick napkin over it which doesn't fit and upsets the balance?) – but a very smooth 3½ hours flight non-stop to Moscow (except for a half-minute maelstrom over the Baltic). Slava had organised everything for us the other end; it had involved for him, we gather, a special trip to Armenia to make sure that everything was possible, putting the fear of God into the whole Union of Soviet Composers, and when we came down in Moscow the only reason why the Armenian Prime Minister was not there in person to greet us was that he had to attend a highly important conference in Yugoslavia! Even P.M.s find it very, very difficult to say No to Slava. Instead of the Prime Minister there was the Sub-President of Goskoncert,[8] and two of Armenia's leading musicians, with flowers galore. Taxis took us at once; no customs, very little waiting, all Harrods got through, no questions asked. Through Moscow we sped, past the Kremlin, to Slava's flat, where we spent some waiting and resting (Galya had gone off to the Datchya with most of the luggage in a taxi from the airport) and proceeded after some hours to the Georgian Restaurant, to a private room, and had the best dinner imaginable – caviar (vodka, of course) and a delicious mess of liver and nuts, and ham, beetroot and cabbage salad, superb cucumbers and tomatoes and onion, an excellent bortsch soup, and a small crushed grilled whole chicken (a little too lifelike!), grilled rather peppery, to be torn apart and eaten with fingers, very good ice-cream (Russian possibly world's best) and Turkish coffee. Slava then drove us out to the Datchya where Galya, Slava's mother, another family relation, Galya's aunt(?), a furry dog, a very unworried cat, and Slava and Galya's adorable daughters, Olga and Helena (9 and 7) welcomed us. The Datchya 'country (house) cottage' about which we had heard so much, really requires a chapter on its own. Wherever we had met Slava for years, he had been acquiring things for the Datchya. There had been a copper roof he had flown from Amsterdam, crates of furniture from Spain, aquariums from Harrods complete with cases of English sand and stones (on which Ben had paid £100 overweight when we agreed to fly it with the English Opera Group last September to Russia),[9] everything from everywhere. The House itself has 2 large sitting rooms (dining and drawing) plus kitchen, etc., on the ground floor; 3 large bedrooms and bath, etc., on the first floor, and a large panelled playroom–bar–music–children's room on top, full of Spanish furniture. It is a far bigger home than I imagined and really very pleasant, with a wild bit of garden leading immediately into the forest of birch and oak. In the same estate are houses for artists and intellectuals all built

---

[8]  The state-run concert agency of the Soviet Union.
[9]  The EOG had toured *Albert Herring*, *The Rape of Lucretia* and *The Turn of the Screw* to Leningrad, Moscow and Riga in September–October 1964.

20 years ago according to Slava; they looked a bit older to me. The famous aquariums were on the window-sills in the drawing-room – very active – though one looked dreary and discoloured, the fish were swimming happily. On the landing by the staircase was a small granite-encased chip-covered and well-laid-out cactus desert, nine feet square, in a place of honour. Mexican plunder, I presume.

The air was marvellously fresh and clean, and after late tea (11 p.m.) we all went to comfortable beds with striped Irish linen. The next day, after a late breakfast, Slava took us into Moscow where with great pride we visited OUR bank and cashed a cheque from OUR accounts and came away with several hundred roubles.[10] How we shall spend them, I don't know, as Slava insists on buying everything for us. After lunch we drove out for about 2½ hours, to see the Tschaikovsky Museum at Klin,[11] an excursion which Slava had arranged for us (including, I think, a lunch for which they were expecting us and he had forgotten to call off). The house where Tschaikovsky lived the last years of his life is a charming and nicely arranged wooden home, and we were shown round by a sweet English speaking great-niece. Lots of photos and documents, his copy of the Mozart Gesamtausgabe, his piano, his narrow high bed, the desk where he wrote the 6th Symphony, programmes, clothes, his pupils, his family, diplomas, wreathes, Modeste (his brother who looked after the home after Tschaikovsky's death), Modeste's room with Greek statues and a signed photo of Nijinsky. A touching and well-worth-while excursion, from which we drove back in Slava's smart new Mercedes bought in West Berlin, along roads partly good, partly appalling, and on to the Datchya and an excellent dinner of stuffed cabbage and liver. Afterwards (or was it before?) the children had given us their repertoire on the piano up in the playroom, Olga, the elder, very brilliant and virtuoso, looking round for applause before the last chord had died; Helene, more sensitive, if not so advanced, giving a charming performance of 'The Sick Doll' by Tschaikovsky.[12] Afterwards, a projected ballet danced by Helene to Olga's original music came to grief in a typical family way owing to forgetfulness and fury – only temporary, however. Slava proudly served us vodka from his bar

---

[10] In the 1960s – as now in the 1990s – it was forbidden to take Russian currency out of the country. Pears and Britten had already given concerts in Russia in 1963 and 1964, when they had evidently placed their unspent fees in bank accounts. Occasionally such fees were used to make expensive purchases: for example, on one occasion, they bought a set of the complete Tchaikovsky edition (now in the Britten–Pears Library) in an attempt to use up their accumulated roubles (see p. 150).

[11] Approximately 50 miles north-west of Moscow.

[12] No. 7 from *Album pour enfants: 24 pièces faciles (à la Schumann)*, Op. 39.

(installed from Sweden?) and in due course we tumbled to bed, full of vodka, Bisodol and sleeping-pills.

The morning dawned stormy; when we went down to breakfast, there was no Galya, but Slava, on tip toe, tending to disappear upstairs. We ate our eggs alone nervously, with an occasional banged door from upstairs keeping us alert, forte soprano, piano calmando legato baritone. The theme was roughly: 'How can a mother leave her house and children to a pack of silly women who spoil them and don't look after them and quarrel and let them run wild and don't do what I tell them to do? And why has this been done and hasn't that? And I can't possibly go away to Armenia. I must stay here and clear it all up.' It was basically a struggle between Slava's mother and Galya's aunt.

However, by 11.45 we were all in the car, with mountains of luggage, and a transistor TV set from America, and the cello, and a vast picnic-basket from Harrods, and a cinecamera from Japan, and a triple pocket-flask with cognac for S. and B. and P., and Cinzano for Galya. I rather think we missed the plane we were booked on and went an hour later on the next; it was never clarified.[13] However, we were whizzed out in due course to the plane before everyone else, and took off for Yerevan, the capital of Armenian S.S.R. accompanied by the conductor of the Yerevan Philharmonic. A charming hostess with a very little English made us as comfy as she could. (Our presence on board was announced and applauded by our fellow-travellers, and all announcements were thenceforth made first in English.) We had 3½ hours in a 4-engined plane, before coming down over the Caucasus mountains into a sandy desert with green valleys here and there. New Yerevan is being rebuilt as fast as possible, of a local soft red tufa, and the effect is, and will be, quite good in some years; we were put in bungalows for V.I.P. visitors, all very decent, with the usual rough plumbing, but a warm-hearted lot of composers.

At the dinner there were about 14 of us, all musicians. Cognac (Armenian and very good) flowed, likewise Armenian wine; toasts galore; everyone kissed everyone, local composer Mirzoyan[14] and handsome wife, Leningrad pupil of Shostakovitch, Ouspensky[15] and pretty blonde wife, anonymous local musicians; endless toasts during all courses. I can't remember what we ate – caviar, of course, Armenian roquefort and milk cheese (excellent), good rather heavy pastry with honey, some meat or fish I can't remember. Toasts to us, to them, to the occasion, to friendship, gulp gulp down goes another whole glass –

---

[13]  In his pocket engagement diary (entry for 5 August), Britten noted: 'Fly 1.30 to Erevan. arr 6.20. Dinner Composers Union in evening'.

[14]  Eduard Mik'aeli Mirzoyan (b. 1921), Armenian composer and teacher; head of the Armenian Composers' Union from 1957.

[15]  Vladislav Alexandrovich Uspensky (b. 1937), Russian composer and teacher.

help! mineral water – tea. Immense good-will, translated into Aldeburgh-Deutsch[16] by Slava. The wine here is very light and fresh and good and wouldn't hurt a fly, and somehow vodka and cognac don't seem to hurt one either! So far, we thrive on it.

In the morning on we drive to Dilidjan, a small town 3 to 4 hours away, where two years ago the Armenian Composers built a summer colony of about a dozen houses in a lovely lonely valley of thick woods under high grassy hills. The journey was not very comfortable. Some roads in the U.S.S.R. are perfectly good. Others are in the process of being made, and in this vast process vast holes are simply left for cars to break their axles in, until the time comes to fill them up. There was a lot of traffic, about 95 per cent of it trucks and lorries, carrying stones, gravels, cement, machinery up and down from the hills, which most of the way were brown and parched. Gradually the crops got thicker and better, and we came to the big lake Sevan, which is spoiled by a large electrical works, but has an amusing little island near to the shore with two churches on it. There was a new hotel, full of holiday-makers, some bathing. On we went, up into the mountains, meeting trucks and buses on hairpin bends. The wild flowers grew more and more extraordinary every mile. Then when we were all green, down we fell into a valley across a rough bridge up a gritty road, through a sort of lodge gate where welcoming children threw flowers at our taxi, up to the communal building to be greeted, semi-officially, and on to our little house (bedroom, bathroom, dining-room, music–drawing-room and balcony).[17] The clouds closed around us for 48 hours.

*Wednesday, 11th*
The sun cleared on Sunday and showed us glorious green woods of all sorts of trees, oak, sycamore, beech, birch, crowned above the trees by sunny downs, with sheep and cows visible on the sky-line. Before the weather improved, our walks were short and uncomfortable on thick, red clay layered with grit. Since then we have gone further afield, up the

---

[16]   Britten's and Pears's lack of fluency in Russian, matched by Rostropovich's and Vishnevskaya's in English, led to the development of a highly personal *lingua franca* known as 'Aldeburgh Deutsch'.

[17]   In an article for the *Sunday Telegraph* (24 October 1965), 'A Composer in Russia', Britten described their accommodation and surroundings:

>   There was a bungalow for us, with Slava and Galya in another, 20 yards along the lane; here we ate a succession of superb meals produced from rather primitive conditions in the cellar by the top Intourist chef, a charming character called Hachik who had cooked for Khruschev and Nehru. And here we settled in for three weeks, 5000 feet up in a circle of wooded mountains, reading, sunbathing, swimming and picking mushrooms.

hills, through barley and oats (I think), up paths hedged with wild flowers of every description. After our first long fine walk I brought back a bouquet which I put in a jar. It ranged from enormous viper's bugloss, great yellow headed thistles on top of round brown heads (no prickles), scotch thistles red and white, large minty herbs with strong smelling leaves, scabious white and mauve (huge), great canterbury bells blue and white, great wild hollyhocks pink and yellow, large-scale thyme (I think), wild pinks, some leguminacae, little, white pink and yellow, and large red, near orchid-like flowers on non-orchid stems with non-orchid leaves, vast marigolds, wild sunflowers, daisies, dandelions of every sort, yellow daisyish floribundas (?), heavily armoured thistles with silver leaves, down to coltsfoot and our old friend, bindweed, some rock roses and large crane's-bill. The fields were multicoloured. There were orchid leaves (but no orchids). What it must be like in spring I can't think. They were cutting a (second?) hay crop. How the cows must love their food! I have never seen anything like it. We have a house-martin nesting on our balcony and flocks of goldfinches flash past us as we sunbathe. Yesterday outside our front door lay, neatly on its face, a 2½-foot-long little fox, white and yellow, killed by the dogs (audibly) in the night.

Yesterday we made a long, memorable excursion.

I had expressed the desire to get up on to the grassy downs high above our local woods. No sooner said than put in motion. We started off walking down the hill at about 11.30 a.m. and were picked up, late, by a bus (small-capacity about 16) with windows all round, none of which were designed to open. The sun shone hot and we stifled down the hill, across the river, up the hairpin bends the other side, in and out of potholes. After half an hour we alighted at the tree line and changed into a heavier bus with a very powerful engine, in which we groaned and bumped on an impossible track over the downs, driven with great *brio* by Marcel, the lynch-pin of the Composers' Village. His dog insisted on coming too, but the bumps were altogether too much for its digestion! After 20 minutes we reached a point where another bus had unloaded a vast picnic, already displayed on the grass, the seats of the bus round a large american-cloth. Further off, over a crackling fire, a cauldron bubbled superb smells and our cheerful cook and waiter soon plied us with vodka. We ran down the hill to taste a local spring (the water is glorious here) and clambered back in time for more vodka and (as always) caviar, cucumbers, dried thin sliced veal with marvellous flat unleavened (?) bread (Armenian speciality) called lavash, also a delicious herb called rehan. After about an hour of this, we went on to the cauldron – lamb stew with peppers, etc. etc. Fearfully good, but my cup was nearly full, and I thanked God for coffee. The view was staggering: all round green-topped hills with wooded valleys rich in trees and not a conifer among them. The mountains are not higher than 5–6,000 feet, I think, but are very open and broad, and one sees far-off walls of rock everywhere. The air was superb; one breathed flowers and sun, and Ben and I climbed up higher still after our coffee, and somehow the whole world was explainable, so dizzy and beautiful it was. In due course down we had to come. In fact we had ended up not so very far above our own valley, and our Armenian host decided the direct road was easiest, though I knew he was wrong. So we bumped, rolled, slid and scraped our way down through steep wet woods, swamps, over sharp stones, sticky clay – with much laughter and all in good spirits. Ben had on sandals with leather soles, hopeless;[18] Galya bedroom slippers; I, plimsoles; Slava, tremendously smart white leather pumps bought in Rome, and only when we got home after 3 hours, did we realise just how much vodka we had got through. Today we ache: Slava is feverish and his legs and arms are on fire; Madame's nose is scarlet; one of Ben's toes is raw and in Elastoplast, and my knee, which was not good when I left London, is now *very* not good. However, it was a heavenly day.

*Thursday, 12th*
The kindness of Slava cannot be exaggerated. It is dangerous to express an interest in anything: I am fairly sure the nice coffee-cups which I have admired here, simple brown, nicely shaped, will be in my baggage to Aldeburgh; Ben regretted not having his camera; one will probably arrive tomorrow. But everyone is kind. We visited Dilidjan, the little

---

[18] Vishnevskaya relates in GV, p. 371, the lengths to which her husband went to have Britten's inadequate footwear, which was ruined by the expedition, repaired:
> One couldn't buy shoes for any amount of money: there simply weren't any in the stores. Slava called a 'council of elders' – the Armenian composers who were taking care of us – and, holding up the gentleman's pair of shoes, said, 'What are we going to do? Britten doesn't have another pair. Right now he's sitting at home in his slippers writing – in Dilizhan – music that will bring you fame. I can hold him off for a few more hours, but what then? Will I have to call the Georgians? They always have everything.'
> Then the oldest got to his feet, clutched Britten's worn-out shoes to his chest, and, rolling his eyes ferociously, said that only over his dead body would a damned Georgian touch them. 'Faust and Othello will repair them so they're better than new. It is a matter of honour for the Armenian people.' (Apparently, almost all the shoemakers in Armenia are called either Faust, Othello, or Caesar.)
> And indeed, after Ben finished working for the day and asked Slava where they could go to buy shoes, Slava placed before him a beautifully repaired pair, polished and gleaming like new. 'Why buy a new pair? You're used to your favourite shoes. Just look how Othello knocked himself out for you. You must admit that you have never had your shoes repaired by Othello before!'
> Ben was delighted.

run-down ex-Turkish spa, 2 miles away, and while we were inspecting its curious and sad shops, we couldn't find postcards. A nice musician overheard and offered to send us some from Yerevan which he was on the way to. Today a pile of them has come for us. There is always a new bottle of cognac in the cupboard and wine in the fridge. We make tea (from Ceylon) in an electric kettle, and I put into my cup instead of sugar a delicious syrup made with rose-petals, called varenya, always available – as are two other syrups made with walnuts and baby aubergines – too rich for me. The food is really superb in its way. Sturgeon every third meal, grilled on charcoal (glorious), boiled with potatoes for Ben, cold. Today, marvellous aubergines, peppers (very sweet) and tomatoes stuffed with rice and meat and sour cream. The fruit is very plentiful but not very good, not really ripe, except for grapes. One breakfast we had dvorok (curds) and smetana (sour cream) with honey: num num!

*Later:* the man with the camera from Yerevan arrived, bringing 2 possible models: we have chosen the smaller, fool-proof, very good, and Slava, of course, has paid for it. One can do nothing against his over-affectionate lavish kindness.

I have given my knee as an excuse for not going up-hill and rather tiring walks. I expect tomorrow a doctor will arrive, hot from Moscow. It must be stopped somehow.

The three Armenian composers of whom we have seen most are Mirzoyan (President of Armenian Composers' Union), Babajanian[19] and Akazunjan.[20] All good friends, they seem to run Armenia's musical life, even though 2 live largely in Moscow. They are all here with their families on holiday, and Mirzoyan comes and eats with us, handsome, charming, a fair composer. Can one imagine Arthur Bliss, William Walton and Ben and lots more taking their holidays together on Windermere and entertaining Fischer-Dieskau[21] and [Hans Werner] Henze for a month? Not quite.

Above the houses, a very good swimming-pool has been built for the musicians with (much too-) heated water, and the base of a tennis-court has been laid. Most of the day, except at meal-times, bodies of many shapes and sizes lie or splash at the pool. Our favourite time (very English) is either at 7a.m. or 7p.m., when we have it to ourselves. In the morning the air is crystal clear and you can count the individual haystacks on the top of the hills, wonderfully still. There are two largish birds of prey that float all day up and down the valley. They have yellow

---

[19] Arno Harutyvni Babadjanyan (1921–1983), Armenian composer and pianist.

[20] *Recte:* Alexander (Kotic) Arutunjan (b. 1920), Armenian composer. Pears would appear to have experienced some difficulty in transliterating Arutunyan's name: later he is referred to as 'Adzunian' (p. 109).

[21] Dietrich Fischer-Dieskau⁵ (b. 1925), German baritone.

beaks, handsome brown plumage, splendidly marked under the wings, and they cry a lot in a high short squeal. Their wing-ends have feather-fingers, like a hand. Buzzards? Slava calls them oryols (eagles) but I am sure they are not big enough. We have a nut-hatch living near, and a dark bobbing chap with a red rump (red-start?).

Slava has explained to us (as best he can, in Aldeburgh-Deutsch) something of the status and standing of Soviet musicians. His main claim is that in Russia the artists say what they want to do (in the way of concert tours, etc.) and the State concert Agency (Goskonzert) *must* arrange it for them If Slava wants to do a week's concert in Siberia, it shall be done. Artists are paid a salary (graded according to age, fame and experience) and are expected to do so many concerts a year. If they do more, they are paid to scale for them, and if only 15 people come to each of those Siberian concerts, niechevo, he is paid his full fee, and Slava's is very handsome indeed by our standards. When he goes abroad, his usual (Russian) fee is paid to him in Russia out of the foreign currency, but he is free to spend the rest of the local fee locally as he wants to. (Many Russian artists don't.) But this explains the copper roof, the Spanish interior, and Harrods.

After a composer or artist has passed his exams, etc., he is elected to the Union, and from then on gets a salary, which is increased according to the amount of work he does, teaching or performing or composing. If a composer wants to write a big-scale work, he asks permission to do so from the Committee of his Union, I think, and expects to get paid for it when it is finished. The Committee considers it and if it decides to publish the piece, the composer gets payment for it, and again for any possible performances later he receives a fee. So that composers can be extremely wealthy persons and the most popular of them unquestionably are. On the other hand, there are mountains, cupboards-full, of scores at the Union of Composers which they have paid the composers for and will never get printed or performed. There are about 1,500 members of the U.S.S.R. Union of Composers, paid on salary, but not a great many who are any good, like in any other country or any other art. But I do not think a sure future should make one compose any the worse.

### Sunday, 15th

When we first aired the idea of this Armenian holiday, or rather when Slava first told us our plans, 18 months ago, one of his great highlights – the finale – was to be a Britten Festival in Yerevan.[22] We squashed this with horrified laughter, but Slava's ideas are not so easily thrown away;

---

[22] Held between 28 August and 1 September: see below, pp. 125–30.

and so when we squarely faced him with return dates and arrangements for the end of the month – always vague if attractive – he had to confess that there *was* to be a Britten Festival of 5 concerts, in Erevan,* with Slava, Galya, the Philharmonic Orchestra of Armenia plus a String Quartet. Four of B.B.'s music, one a Recital (Moussorgsky–Tschaikovsky) by Galya and Slava, 'dedicated to us'. There will be talks, receptions, etc., all in a town without charm at a probable temperature of 95 in the shade. The prospect is simply not to be dwelt on.

* Yerevan, Erevan, Yrevan are all the same place!

*Monday, 16th*

Last evening Slava attended a ceremony connected with the composer Adzunian[23] and his god-child, the chief feature of which was the roasting and eating of a complete lamb, accompanied with much brandy and wine and speeches. He returned after an hour and a half and as a result of excess food had a bad night with his heart. All the village was audibly enjoying itself late.

Adik Kudoyan,[24] small lively composer, gave Ben a copy of his newly published Solo Cello Sonata (dedicated to an Armenian pupil of Slava). Ben made a great hit by discovering some misprints, since when Adik not only kisses him each time he meets him (everyone does that) but goes down on his knees to him.

Everyone is delighted that Ben is setting some Pushkin! The last thing he bought at London Airport was a Penguin Pushkin with literal translations.[25] Beautiful poems, a lot of them make marvellous lyrics for songs, and Ben is plunging ahead setting them for Galya.[26] Already she

---

[23]  Possibly the composer Arutunjan, here mistranscribed by Pears; or Alexander Adzhemyan (1925–1983), Armenian composer, also wrongly transliterated by Pears.

[24]  Adik Gegamovich Khudojan (b. 1921), Armenian composer.

[25]  The volume of Pushkin's verse, one in the Penguin Poets series, introduced and edited by John Fennel (Harmondsworth: Penguin Books, 1964), survives at the Britten–Pears Library (1-9104809). There are a number of significant pencil annotations by Britten and Pears relating to the musical setting, and the volume is signed on the flyleaf: 'Бен Ажам' [Benjamin]. Britten recalled in 'A Composer in Russia':

> On the way to the airport we found we were short of things to read, and a hurried search at a bookshop produced the Penguin edition of Pushkin's poems. With the verse in Russian and an English prose translation, this was the ideal supplement to our pre-breakfast struggles with irritatingly forgettable vocabulary and irregular verbs.

[26]  In 'A Composer in Russia', Britten wrote:

> I decided that setting some Pushkin might help my obstinately bad Russian. I got Slava and Galya to read the poems I chose from the

and Slava have decided to do them in Moscow in October – if they are finished, says Ben![27] I, meanwhile, as soon as he has started one, begin trying to translate it into singable English – a fascinating job. How often an exact translation will fit, but the rhyme is what throws one.[28] Ben is now on his 4th!

*Later*: Between us and the river which we look down, there are about 100 hilly yards, the woods have been cleared and the hill planted with fruit-trees; the grass, or to be more exact, the flowers were scythed yesterday. I watched this difficult operation with much pleasure; the man's movements, the time he took, his lunch under the tree; his strawberry-coloured shirt; most of the inhabitants are very swarthy; he must have come from the north, quite fair. A woman has just come out of the house below us and shaken an apple-tree, with strong arms: solid, like most Russian women, she pocketed a few, put one in her mouth, and went on her way up the hill. The brilliantly blonde and pretty wife of Ouspensky, the Shostakovitch pupil from Leningrad, has just walked by; she has a charming smile and has nice bright clothes. Our servant-woman has just emptied our dustbin into the bigger communal one down on the road. She is very well set up, fair in a gypsy way, strong, good smile and teeth. She cleaned our muddy shoes this morning by washing them; they will never be dry by lunch. This afternoon we are to go on an excursion.

The fifth member of our party whom I have not yet mentioned (though she is delightfully and positively memorable!) is Aza.[29] She is

---

English crib in my Penguin, and painstakingly they set about teaching me to pronounce them properly. I worked out a transliteration of six of them, and began setting them to music.

I would write a song, then play it over and get Slava to correct the prosody. It is not perhaps the method I would recommend to composers setting foreign words: it is best to learn the language first. But it was nice to find that I seemed to have caught something of the mood of these vivid, haunting poems: if I haven't, Pushkin still remains intact!

[27] *The Poet's Echo*, Op. 76, completed in Dilizhan, 23 August 1965 (see below p. 120). In fact, the songs received their first complete performance at the Moscow Conservatory on 2 December 1965, by the work's dedicatees, Galina Vishnevskaya and Mstislav Rostropovich.

[28] On their publication (Faber Music, 1967), the songs appeared with an English singing translation by Pears.

[29] Aza Amintayeva, described in GV, p. 355:
Aza was a fine pianist. Slava called her Osya. She was from Daghestan, had jet-black hair and a faint moustache. Slava glanced into her room one day in Dilizhan, saw her sleeping, and shouted: 'Iosif Vissarionovich!' She bounded up in bed, too sleepy to understand, and he chuckled. 'Ioska! Osya! You resemble Stalin

Slava's accompanist and Galya's coach, and will play Ben's Sonata with Slava at Erevan, and is teaching Galya *Lady Macbeth* (Shostakovich's opera), which she will make a film of, starting in October.[30] One can just hear them practising in their house 50 yards away. Aza is stocky, dark, 35-ish and comes from the Caucasus and a particular 'tribe' of people. Though she learnt English at school for 5 years, she doesn't talk it, and we communicate with eyes, hands, lips and half a dozen Russian words. She gets easily melancholy, having had some tragic events with a drunken ex-husband, but her laugh comes easily and is splendid, an ancient black laugh. We all go for walks up the hills together and much to Ben's horror search at slow length for mushrooms.[31] Mushrooms, of course, *are* Russian. The woods, thick in leaf-mould, silent, damp and mild are prolific in a hundred sorts, the yellow crinkly pfifferlinge, the brilliant pink and red ones, nondescript browns, and a particularly unattractive dirty grey sponge-like growth, which is greeted with triumphant cries and is considered No. 1. We come back each day with nylon-net bags full of *greebwee*.

To eat, they are, whatever Ben may say, absolutely scrumptious. Recipe: First, scrape and clean the mushrooms (preferably removing the actually deadly ones) and boil them for 20 minutes at least (boiling also counteracts poison). Then fry, in butter, only a little very finely sliced onion, and add the mushrooms, frying (in more butter) for a further 10 minutes. Finally, as you serve, pour sour cream (smetana) over them. Smetana (sour cream) is simply the top of sour milk, I think. The rest of the sour milk may be strained in a bag, then held in the bag for a few minutes in boiling water. Then it turns crumbly when dry, and is delicious with some cream poured over, and honey! The sight of Galya and Aza, with their heads done up in squares, sitting at a table on the balcony cleaning *greebwee* is very dear and very Russian.

Two more women have just shaken the apple-tree: none fell this time, the earlier one had been so tough with it. The handsome secretary of the Armenian Composers Union has just passed leading his baby son. Midday quiet descends for lunch.

---

frightfully!' After that, we all called her Osya.

[30] Shostakovich's *Lady Macbeth of Mtsensk*, revised in 1956 as *Katerina Izmailova*, was filmed by Lenfilm (Leningrad Film Studio) later in 1965. See GV, pp. 349–61; GV also includes three stills from the film. The opera was familiar to both Pears and Britten: in 1936, while still a member of the BBC Singers, Pears had taken the role of Second Foreman in the UK première (a concert performance); Britten had attended this performance and written about it with tremendous enthusiasm in his diary (DMPR, pp. 409–11).

[31] Britten's fondness for 'nursery food' is well known, as are Pears's more adventurous epicurean tastes. However, mushrooms, along with pears and tomatoes, were one of the more everyday foods that Britten thoroughly detested.

*Later, Monday*: Our (my) camera (I am not sure which) which was delivered on Saturday is a great success. In order to test the results, I had to take 36 shots in a few hours so that they could be quickly developed and returned. I have just seen the film and it looks rather impressive. The camera is (to my mind) hideously complicated and I had to work hard, but some Art-Photography of the woods I had done has turned out triumphantly, and now I suppose I shall have to take it seriously! The nice man who sold it to us is soon off to England and Edinburgh to photograph and confer. He was very gracious to me on my first steps.

We are very near here to Mt. Ararat and Noye's Fludde;[32] it is actually in Turkey, much to the Armenians' chagrin, and they would very much like to have it back. They put pressure on Moscow from time to time about it, but Moscow isn't having any, it seems. The Armenians are Christians, and we have seen marvellous shots of ancient churches, also Roman and Hebrew ruins. The Azebaidjanians to the north-east, the Turks south and west, and the Persians south-east are all Muslim; uncomfortable, but here it seems O.K. Religion may not be encouraged in the U.S.S.R., but religious differences are also not encouraged.

We are looked after by two special Intourist staff, a cook and a waiter, Hadyi and Michael, both first class and charming. No trouble is too much for them. Michael thinks he speaks English, French, German, Italian as well as Russian and Armenian. I am not so sure. We eat much parsley (petroushka) and a delicious herb, rather minty, for which the English name, according to Michael, is anise. (I just wouldn't know: the Russian is *rehan*), also Tarxhon (tarragon) very good with poached salmon-trout.

*Later*: We went for our excursion. It had been my suggestion. On a map which we had been given were depicted some of the Touristic Interests of the District, ancient monasteries, etc. Among them on the top of a pass was a Pushkin monument; this seemed appropriate and not too far off. So at 3 p.m. (no, 3.30 p.m. – it should have been 3) we drove off. Our driver, who had driven us car-sick in 20 minutes last week, was warned. But I imagine that an Armenian chauffeur is insulted if he is seen driving less than 40 m.p.h. by his fellow countrymen, and so, say what we might, we were driven round hairpin bends and curving rivers at 40 all the time. The country was extremely fine; large-scale valleys under large parallel ranges of mountains. The villages (such as Lermontov) were full of blond Russians. These we were told were

---

[32]  Mt Ararat is allegedly the place where the ark came to rest when the floods subsided. Britten had commemorated the story of Noah in his opera, *Noye's Fludde*, Op. 59 (1957), a setting of the Chester Miracle Play, first performed at the 1958 Aldeburgh Festival.

Makhanites (?) Protestants protected in Christian Armenia by the Tsar. I should like to learn more of them, for while in Dilidjan, our local town, 90 per cent are dark and middle Eastern, these Makhanites could come from Sweden. The villages were touching, vivid with good houses, most of them on the same oblong pattern with a covered first-floor balcony, often glazed with small panes. In most cases washing hung from lines across these balconies. There were some small gardens with huge hollyhocks and sunflowers; the whole feeling was fresh, free and lively, if simple. The countryside was carefully cultivated with a variety of crops; sheep on the precipitous rocky hill-side; we drove hooting through cattle on the way back.

The Pushkin monument turned out to be a fountain of beautiful water with a bronze relief of a scene in Pushkin's life, which in spite of many explanations in Armenian, Russian and Aldeburgh-Deutsch I could not fathom. Perhaps it will emerge later. Attached was a restaurant (!) built in the Classical style, filled with travelling types, bus-drivers, local shepherds, soldiers, some drunk, and we were served (inevitably) with very good light cognac, gherkins, peppers, tomatoes, bread, milk, cheese – none of which, after those hairpin bends, seemed quite the thing, apart from cognac. The scenery was superb; an Armenian composer with an extraordinarily loud voice told us the whole Pushkin story in Russian. Very confused, we did our best to understand. Another Armenian composer took many photographs. I took Ben, who doesn't like hairpin bends, to the gents, where he was quite understandably immediately sick. I wonder if the Russians have much sense of smell. Our return home in some rain was very much quieter, as our chauffeur had been considerably chastened by our hosts. Galya had been very alarmed and uncomfortable on the drive up and displayed her displeasure perfectly clearly. On the way home we stopped at an open mineral water spring (very delicious) along with half a dozen army boys of all complexions and a local family of three, father and 2 sons; armed with scythes, who had been cutting hay. These great scythes carried by the youngest, aged 12, were age-old in effect and touching. All three males were fairest blond, on their way back to Lermontov, we thought. What a country of extremes! All these villages and villagers might have been here since Noah bumped into Ararat. But we had driven through the new industrial town of Kriovakhan, of a deadly boring squareness which will take a very long time to mature. Factories belching fumes, town parks, cultural centres, blocks of flats, unfinished roads – maybe one day – no, they never will compare with the villages and farmlands and streams, with children bathing naked in them, against these majestic steeps and wide green valleys.

*Tuesday*

The weather has let us down, one has to admit. The last four days have been cloudy most of the time, too cloudy for sun-bathing, and no going to the pool; cold baths at home instead. That other barometer, Ben's tummy, has of course reflected this. Today again we have had to postpone an excursion with a barbecue reception by the Armenian Composers on that account. Edik Mirzoyan has been angelic about it and we hope that tomorrow all will be well again. We think it may have been caused by the very cold mineral water spring at Lermontov yesterday.

I have hardly mentioned two familiars here, Gilbars and Jacko. They are dogs of a sort you see often in Russia, of medium large size and varying colour, with longish hair, and very Siberian in looks. Gilbars is the name of a famed patriotic general of I don't know which century, and the animal was called after him before he was discovered to be a bitch – and a very engaging bitch the General is. She is greenish yellow in colour and has a Clytie-ish[33] way of insinuating herself through the door into the house – forbidden – while we are having lunch, and with her protruding yellow eyes and vast grin, she crawls, thumping her tail, a foot or two forward at a time, resting her chin on her paws as she ogles us. She gets all she wants, including handfuls of chicken bones, which do her no harm.

The other dog is a very nice fellow too, but he is not so bold or so charming as the General. They both come for walks with us, but Jacko won't come in the car. He really should be pulling a sledge.

*Wednesday*

After our expedition to Pushkin's memorial, Ben spent 24 hours in bed with tummy *in extremis*. Every imaginable remedy was proferred and taken, Alka-Seltzer, Enterobioform, manganese in solution and stewed pomegranate leaves. All of which, in ensemble, proved effective and Ben was O.K. in 48 hours. Well enough, yesterday, to go for a gentle drive down the river past Dilidjan to Idjevan, through high mountains of bare rock on the west side and craggy, bristling rocky precipices all covered over with forest on the east side. Superb trees of all sorts, and willows in the rushing, clear pebbly water. Our driver has been chastened and we went seldom more than 30 m.p.h. It was, of course, much more pleasant and we could really look at this superb and 'horrid' country.

Ben's two days' *hors de combat*, one in bed and one on sofa, produced, as it so often does, intense creative energy. He has now just written his 5th Pushkin song, and Galya, who is to sing them, heard

---

[33]  See n. 2, p. 18.

1    The New English Singers, 1936. Left to right: Mary Morris, Eric Greene, Peter Pears, Dorothy Silk, Cuthbert Kelly and Nellie Carson.

2    A new English singer: Pears in the 1930s.
(Photo: Polyfoto)

3    Arrival at Bombay, 13 December 1955: Pears and Britten with their hosts.

4    Britten and Pears after one of their recitals in Surabaja.
     (Photo: Nikola Drakulic, Surabaja)

5    Ubud, Bali, 20 January 1956. Pears, Prince Ludwig, Princess Margaret and Britten pose in traditional Balinese costume.

6    Macau, 4 February 1956. Britten and Pears are congratulated by the Portuguese Governor after their recital in the eighteenth-century theatre.

7    Arrival at Tokyo, 8 February 1956.
     (Photo: NHK, Tokyo)

8    Press conference, Tokyo, 9 February 1956. (Photo: NHK, Tokyo)

9    Tokyo, 9 February 1956. Pears's and Britten's first recital on television.
     (Photo: NHK, Tokyo)

10   Pears and Kei-ichi Kurosawa.

11 After *Sumidagawa*: Prince Ludwig and Pears mimic the playing of the Japanese drum, the *o'otsuzumi*, using wastepaper baskets!

12 Pears and Britten (partly visible) with the ladies of the Tokyo Madrigal Singers.

13  Tokyo, 16 February 1956. Pears and Britten (back row, seventh
    and fourth from the right respectively) join the members of the
    Tokyo Madrigal Singers, conducted by Kei-ichi Kurosawa.
    Prince Ludwig noted: '. . . the charming Mr Kurosawa conducts
    his fine madrigal group. He is overjoyed that Ben and Peter sing
    with them.'

14  Pears at Ansbach in the 1950s.
    (Photo: Eva Jaenisch, Munich)

15 Mstislav Rostropovich and Britten. (Photo: Peter Pears?)

16 Britten's caption: 'The Amphora picnic, Dilidjan'. Left to right: Arno Babadjanyan, Rostropovich, Pears, Britten and Eduard Mirzoyan.

17  Eduard Mirzoyan (centre) and Pears; the figure on the left –
    another Armenian composer perhaps – is unidentified.

18  Armenia, 1965. Britten and Galina Vishnevskaya.
    (Photo: Peter Pears?)

19 Rostropovich, Pears and Britten. Britten's caption:
'On the balcony of our Bungalow, Composers'
Colony, Dilidjan'.

20 Days of British Music Festival, Moscow, April 1971. Left to right: Rostropovich,
Dmitri Shostakovich, Britten and Vishnevskaya.

21 Pears as Gustav von Aschenbach. (Photo: Anthony Crickmay)

22 Pears outside the Met, New York, 1974.
(Photo: Victor Parker)

23 New York, 1978. Pears with Ted Uppman (left) and Richard Stilwell (right).
(Photo: Jean Uppman)

them for the first time this afternoon. She was deeply affected, as I knew she would be, and wants to get at them at once. Slava, too, was highly excited. I am pegging on at the translations.

Last night after dinner we had heard a record of Edik Mirzoyan's Symphony for Strings and Timps on a very bad gramophone which didn't give the work much chance, to his distress.[34] It has some nice sounds and is felt and tense, though the last movement was played too slow and sounded ineffective. Tonight another leading residing composer is going to play a piece of his to us.

### Thursday

He came and played – Bobajanian – large solid 35-year-old with a great nose – and played his own Six Pieces for Piano with tremendous gusto and agility. Lively, strong music, rhythmic and edgy, in the style of post-Bartók folk-based Armenian. How much he has beyond these I don't know, but certainly good as far as he goes.

### Tuesday

The next morning, Friday, we were due for another longer excursion to the part of Armenia which lies S.E. between Azerbaijan and Persia. This is to take the place (alas!) of a projected trip to Georgia (Tbilisi and Vladicafcas) which would have shown us some of the world's most majestic mountain scenery which is so marvellously described in Lermontov's *A Hero of Our Time*. This will not take place, largely because of inter-Republican tetchiness and pride, at least as we understand it, listening to elaborate Armeno-Russian telephone conversations. Had we gone unofficially to Georgia, the Georgian composers would have been mortally offended and probably sabotaged us in some lethal manner; on the other hand, had we flown in on a red carpet, we would never have survived it, as the Georgians, as well as being passionately proud are prodigiously hospitable, and more spirits are consumed in Georgian toasts than even in Armenian ones. So, from a medical point of view, it is perhaps as well that we shan't go.

However we *did* go to the south-east. We started off at 9.15 in the car to Erevan (all cloudy here, 90°F. there) and the country looked its best, particularly Lake Sevan glittering in the sun. Through the city where we paused for a few minutes for photographs outside the Theatre with its vast advertisement for the Britten Festival in 3 scripts and languages. On to the little airport where the commander plied us with

---

[34] An inscribed study score of this Symphony, presented to Britten by the composer, is at the Britten–Pears Library (2-9401242).

lemonade, and off in an Aeroflot 12-seater plane to Goris, a little town charmingly situated in a high green plain, in rocky country. Indeed all the country in our hour and five minutes' flight was rocky, some of it wholly barren, some sparsely cultivated with crops, spread out underneath one in irregular smears of yellow, brown or green, on foothills of streaky sulphurous grey-green mountains, looking from the air as if they were lichen-covered stones with pink stains in their folds, sometimes precipitous, always arid. Up in the hills some dams had been made for the precious water and the green dribbles lit up the dusty landscape. There is no flight pleasanter than in a small plane and we all enjoyed it, even when we started to come down over a ravine, with nothing like an airstrip in sight. However, the field of clover we landed in was pretty smooth, and all of Goris was there to meet us, the Mayor of the District, the First and Second Secretaries of the Party and other local dignitaries, with several cars. The town itself was laid out and built by a French architect in the eighteenth century, and is a charmingly designed place with nice houses and good gardens and lots of trees. The roads are not nearly as wide as they are in the new towns (too wide) and there are avenues of trees down the streets which are clean (as most Russian cities are, as opposed to the countryside where litter – and worse – is rampant). We had half an hour in our hotel for washing and a nip, before we drove off into the country for a picnic, up into the woods above the town, out of the cars into fields where clear water was running from a mountain spring and charcoal was already burning for the shashlik. A little copse of 50 fir trees had been carefully planted near the water, spaced for picnics, and here was a huge trestle-table spread out with sliced cucumbers and tomatoes, white cheeses, great wheels of brown bread, sheets of lavash, olives, butter, sour-cream, honey, yoghourt, peaches, grapes and fruit of all sorts, on which we were to start before the shashlik appeared (pieces of lamb pierced on to swords and grilled over the charcoal). In the stream, great green water melons were cooling along with bottles of wine, mineral water and vodka, a special sort, of high alcoholic content, made, I was delighted to hear, from mulberries. It was now about 3.30 p.m. and we were all hungry and thirsty, and we fell to with gusto. Toasts followed one another in the usual fashion with rambling speeches, toasts to Armenia, England, the guests, the hosts, international friendship, music, the ladies, etc. I found the vodka a little disappointing but good, and surely not fearfully strong. We tucked into the warm brown bread, the butter which was sweet to the palate and tasted of the flowers that were the cows' daily food, the best I ever had anywhere; the sour cream was lighter and sweeter than I can describe, the honey was nectar, the yoghourt cold and fresh, the cucumbers crisp, the woman serving us had a straw hat on straight out of Watteau; Slava is making a speech and drinking too large a glass of vodka, so I lean over and knock it out of

116

his hand; the lamb is not too tough, the bread is superb, the butter – hullo! there seems to be feeling of challenge in the air – all these toasts and emptying of glasses – I must make a speech – the air is wonderful up here – we have a mulberry tree at home too – a final toast to vodka – a high alcoholic content, did they say? – well here we are, to friendship – how many is it – nine or ten? Not a scrap – time to go – some photographs – yes, all in a group – wait, let me get further away – now – hullo whoops and over I go backwards into the best bed of nettles I ever fell into – never mind – click-click and up we get and down the hill we go into the cars and off to see the views of great broken rocks, in a shower of rain and hermits' caves in a rainbow, and back to the hotel where we spend a quiet, gentle, unruffled (quite well, thank you) hour on the balcony of our room, witnessing Goris' sparse night-life, before I dare lie down for an hour; for at 9.30 p.m. we are – once more – to eat.

I cannot pretend that when I awoke (with some persuasion from Ben) I had any interest in food – or drink – at all. It was perfectly clear to me now that the mulberry vodka was none other than that most dangerous of drinks – slivovitz – in disguise, and I had to pay the penalty of a thick head. Vodka and aquavit are both perfectly harmless in my experience, but I never mean to touch slivovitz again; not even in Yugoslavia. So help me!

The next morning, however, everything was right as rain, except that our efficient and impressive hosts insisted on conducting us to the boundary of their territory, some miles into the mountain, and offering us cold chicken and vodka at 10.30 on a rock covered with a tablecloth hard by a delicious mineral water spring, which I sampled freely with much relief. After still another pause to collect a frame of the honey which we had so much enjoyed earlier (we were already supplied with some of their divine butter and celestial cream) we set off towards our next stop, Djermuk, a famed Kur-ort and mineral springs. This was 100-odd km. away.

In spite of my brief headache, we all had the happiest memory of Goris and our hosts, the only regret being that we had no time to see the town which, judging by our own spotless hotel room, might have had real charm of a rather dotty order.

The journey to Djermuk had something of a nightmare quality. There were 7 of us in a large saloon Intourist car, and while Slava, Ben and I in the back-est seat could stuff down together fairly all right, Galya felt the heat greatly in front with the driver, and for Aza and Edik Mirzoyan in the folding seats it must have been hell. Edik had very sweetly taken charge of the frame of honey and had to hold it upright with both hands on the back ledge of the front seat, yet so that it didn't touch Galya's head. Edik himself refused to put the back of his seat up in case it cramped us. He therefore had no back to lean against, and for

4 hours or so bump after bump he had to keep the honey upright. No wonder he looked worn out yesterday.

The roads, for nine-tenths of the way, were appalling, varying from the slow comparative ease of Golf Lane, Aldeburgh,[35] to pure virgin ploughed or unploughed hill-side. Our chauffeur drove quite magnificently; he found the road where it was being remade, and when he lost it at one place, he found someone to advise him, and casting aside a rock or two took us gently forward. It was the hottest time of the day, and the time when the landscape had lost its shadows and colours. Lit by an overhead sun, the hills failed to charm, and the dust in one's eyes and hair was hateful.

After an age of 3 hours, we dipped down into a green valley to find 2 dignitaries who had been waiting for 2 hours to lead us up a beautiful river to Djermuk. The stone gorge was cut out into wild shapes, organ pipes, abstract sculptures, mothers and childs; we stopped to sip at a sulphurous spring. Up high in Djermuk a hospital welcomed us for a wash – typical international matron type – (Djermuk – 9 years of building; holidays, hospitals, etc.) – before a 4 p.m. picnic lunch with the mayor and secretaries and families amid pine trees in a garden. The fare was exactly similar to the previous day's without (thank goodness) the slivovitz. The toasts were similar, the speeches similar, the company similar – all admirable – charming – but the day was getting long and we were happy to drive to the field where the plane was waiting to take us 35 minutes' flight to Erevan, where chauffeur Stefan was waiting to take us the 3-hour car ride to Dilidjan, up out of the heat of the plains into the cool mountain, where after a bath and a simple pot of tea with bread and butter (what butter!) and honey (what honey!) we could fall gratefully onto our beds.

The following morning (Sunday) at breakfast, Edik rang Slava to say with regret that we *must* all go and be the guests of the Mayor of Dilidjan for lunch; he had always been determined to invite us and that day was a special annual Flowerday, and he wanted to show us the town. So down we went at 1 o'clock and inspected the Flower show and several tables of dahlias, asters, roses, yesterday arranged by the children of the surrounding villages, and at the end a special flower piece with in the middle a plaque with Ben's name picked out in mauve phlox petals. It was absurd and very sweet; we were given flowers and took photographs [see Plate 16], and then went off up the hill to the town's botanical gardens, very bright and varied, and there we were taken to a circular bower of an iron frame entirely covered with virginia creeper or some such, large enough to hold a vast circular table and the twenty

---

[35] The rough track adjacent to the Aldeburgh Golf Course on which The Red House, Britten's and Pears's home from 1957, is situated.

people who had collected to eat the familiar Armenian food. The company consisted of our party, 5, plus Edik Mirzoyan, Arno Babajanian, the Mayor, the First Secretary (?) and his wife and four children of identical features, the Curator of the Museum, another official and his doctor wife, a female musicologist who spoke some German and knew her *Peter Grimes*, and a student of photography with a camera. Inevitably, the routine was as familiar as the food, except for red caviar as opposed to black. Though the flavour of shashlik lamb is generally delicious, we have not yet had any outside Moscow which our teeth could master. There was in fact one change in routine in the lunch, and a big one. After various more or less formal toasts, the Mayor announced that he wished to give us a souvenir of this our visit which was of such momentous importance to them, etc. etc., and forthwith from under the table, the Museum Curator produced what must have been their Museum's chief treasure – a superb large almost perfect amphora – which had been dug up in excavations at Dilidjan and was reckoned to be 5,000 years old. This, of course, left us quite speechless; it was the most touching moment. They were giving us one of their most priceless possessions as a gesture of friendship to two English musicians. It was an act of spontaneous natural hospitality which one had really never met before. We could only stumblingly say our thanks and that we would make sure that as many people saw it and knew where it came from.[36] It is a marvellous thing and we long to know more about it. If we can get it back unbroken, we shall ask the British Museum for expert advice and try to treasure it as I am sure it should be treasured.

## Monday
Monday was a day of calm routine with a very long walk in the afternoon up and down the woods and hills looking for mushrooms. Babadjanian came in after supper and talked music. These composers are all perfectly well aware of the latest movements in music, but just as Schoenberg never meant anything (Slava and Mme Furtseva,[37] the Soviet Minister of Culture, were deeply shocked by [Schoenberg's] *Moses and Aaron* by the Bad Taste of what happened on the stage and the poor production) so Webern and his followers have passed them by.

---

[36] The amphora can be seen at the Britten–Pears Library.
[37] Ekaterina Alekseyevna Furtseva (1910–1974), Soviet Minister of Culture from 1960, and between 1957 and 1961 the only female member of the Soviet Politburo. Britten and Pears met Furtseva many times over the years during their official visits to the Soviet Union for concerts. Britten first encountered her when she was embroiled in the political manoeuvrings to prevent Vishnevskaya singing in the première of *War Requiem*, Op. 66, in 1962. See GV, pp. 263–5 and 365–8.

Mussorgsky, Shostakovitch, Bartók and perhaps Mahler, as well as folk-music, make the seed-bed for them.

*Tuesday*
Today took place the twice-postponed picnic given to us by the Composers and Musicians resident here. So at 1 p.m. we drove off in our 2 cars through Dilidjan down the river some kilometres, and turned off the good asphalt Tiflis road into tracks up into the mountains towards a small lake surrounded by fine green trees. A bus was waiting to take us the last 5 km. The road was deeply lined with ruts and small ravines, thank goodness it was not very wet or our wheels could not have circulated. Even so, it needed a skilful driver to get us along and we lurched at frightening angles. The lake is very pretty and supposed to be phenomenally deep and quite transparent. As to the first, we did not test it; transparent it certainly was not, though the reflections of the overhanging trees perhaps made it seem so. Nearby was a grassy meadow and here in thickening clouds we had our picnic, some 40 of us squatting round a long piece of American cloth. The main feature of the lunch was Slava's determined and wholly successful campaign to quieten an over-talkative if sweetly-silly lady musicologist by insisting on drinking 'Bruderschaft', with arms entwined, in large mugs of vodka. In due course, poor dear, she became a good deal more piano! Our return along the same violently rutted roads was memorably hilarious and gay. Slava on all these occasions is the life and soul of the party, and brings out the best and gayest in everybody. Alexan [Arutunjan] of the unbelievably loud and grating voice kept us all in stitches. There was an air of excitement about the whole day, for Ben had promised to play the Pushkin songs which he has now finished, six of them, to a handful, Slava-picked, of composers, etc. This took place at 7 p.m. when we had had time to rest and bathe. It was most touching how these musicians all respect and revere Ben. We went through the songs, with me vocalising the voice-part with an occasional Russian word, after Slava had read the texts and explained the plan of the cycle.[38] One and all were immensely impressed and moved, and after a drink of brandy, we went straight through them again. Apart from astonishment at the feeling Ben shows for the language and Pushkin, not a foot wrong anywhere, their chief emotion seemed to be simply admiration for these moving, lovable songs, and pride and thanks that Ben should have written them in their Dilidjan and for them. The whole place bubbled

---

[38]  Vishnevskaya offers her own account of this remarkable occasion in GV, pp. 374–5. Britten presented the manuscript of *The Poet's Echo* to the Armenian Composers' Union in return for their generous hospitality.

with excitement and still does, and though we have seen very little of the residents apart from the 3 composers, we sense a strong friendliness. Smiles greet us, and invitations would abound if Slava, our jealous Cerberus, allowed them to.

*Wednesday*

Wednesday was a quieter day, with not much beside a drive in the evening to re-find the charms of Lermontovo and the other villages of Makhanite Russians, with their pretty painted houses, neat enclosed gardens full of sunflowers and hollyhocks, and their dazzling blond inhabitants and bearded old men. The rain drizzled disappointingly but we walked down the village street and visited the shop where we were thanked for the honour of our visit and wished well. One noticed high prices for anything of any quality; an excellent pair of good strong shoes cost 28 Rs (£9). Slava explained on the way home, that while rents are negligible, transport very cheap, and food generally cheap, other consumer goods are really very expensive. The summer frocks one sees on the girls are often very pretty, though the peasant-farmer types obviously stick to working clothes. Slava's own flat in Moscow is in a block of several apartment houses, which was built co-operatively. The money was borrowed from the State and is paid back in rent over 15 years, in Slava's case (5 rooms) £500 a year inclusive (light, telephone, etc.) until the 15 years are up, when the rent will be simply upkeep, a few pounds a month. We asked about pensions: there are two – an old-age pension at 60–65, and a work pension, which functions after 20 years of work, when no one need work any more, though they mostly do, I fancy. Galya, for instance, has been 'working' now for 20 years; she started very early. And this relieves her of having to renew her contract at the Bolshoi, where she finds conditions very boring and trying. She has to sing boring operas, and has to spend ludicrous long hours in production and musical rehearsals. This seems to be a tradition there. *Falstaff* took over a year; Ben's *M. Night's Dream*, due for production in October, started musical rehearsals in February and daily production rehearsals in May.[39] Galya plans only to sing at the Bolshoi after next year as a guest, being then free to go abroad more, which is at present restricted for her.

In the evening, the third of the composers, Alexan, came up to play his Symphony and some Piano Pieces to Ben and us all. He is not, to my mind, so interesting. This Symphony was a highly national affair, heavily under late Tschaikovsky symphonic influence and using some

---

[39] *A Midsummer Night's Dream*, Op. 64 (1960), was performed at the Bol'shoy Theatre, Moscow, on 28 October 1965, the first occasion a work by a living composer had been given there. The production was conducted by Gennady Rozhdestvensky.

very beautiful Armenian tunes. Very noisy and seldom subtle, it is almost hysterically passionate and rhetorical, though not without some moving moments. (The piano pieces were nothing.) This is the sort of music which has never been written in our country, I think, though Elgar's symphonies occasionally vibrate to the same feeling.

*Thursday*

Glorious sun. Coddled eggs and caviar for breakfast. Baked on the verandah all morning.

In the evening, off in the cars down our familiar road to Dilidjan, past the new handsome pink school with the stiff cement mother and children in front, down the slowly macadamising road, the sheep and goats, to the town lake-bathing-pool with the plaster flamingo statuary (not bad), past the village-for-soldiers to the Tiflis road along the adorable tumbling willow-lined river. Soon we turned off to a lesser road through a superb wide gorge, and then again up in a steeply mounting narrow valley, thick with apple, plum and damson trees, with wooded sides, and wherever there was room, tobacco or sweet-corn. The road was over simply a ledge at the bottom of the rocks overhanging the little gorge of the river: there was no surface to it other than its natural rough rockiness. Extremely tough and resilient, our little Moscovitch car climbed most gamely at all angles, round every corkscrew. As the valley widened up, it looked less like a bit of Devonshire, and on more open spaces houses had been put up, stone walls with wooden verandahs, tobacco was drying under the eaves, sweet corn standing up in the garden, a cow, geese, children, old men populating the yard. Small pigs and a donkey with her foal allowed us to lurch by, and after much scraping, reversing and sudden stops and starts we dragged ourselves up a rock, and beheld a good-sized semi-ruined stone church of the tenth to twelfth century. Here a holy man had retired in the sixth century; I don't blame him, for the view was even now superb, a semi-circle of kind, smiling green wooded hills, with an open vista spreading over the valley, which we had just climbed, and over it retreating folds of stony heights. The holy man's name was Gosh, so was the village's. His church had been very ruinous but is now being (rather roughly) repaired as a national monument. The west door opened into a cruciform centrally domed space, through whose western wall an arch led to a smaller square choir with apse and sanctuary, with east wall red with Armenian texts. There were signs here and there of coloured decoration: two monks' cells and a cloister and a free-standing chapel gave one an idea of the main buildings. The main dome and tower were good solid plain structures of a hardy unadorned simplicity, touching in this high remote place. We took pictures and Galya and I sang in the choir which had a superb acoustic. Our Armenian colleagues were very touched at hearing this

122

little shrine brought to life in sound for a moment; with the Pérotin *Hymn*[40] I was at the same date as the church. The Armenians are supposed to be Christians but their religion has shrunk much. Church bells can be heard but rarely. The drive back was even more frightening, but the valley was so charming with its fruit-trees and wild hollyhocks that I would not have resisted overmuch being pitched into it for good.

Back at Dilidjan, we had invited the Mayor to be our guest for dinner; and up he came with his mute, cottage-loaf of a wife. Mayors serve and are elected for two years at a time, and are of course paid. If they are honest and modest and efficient mayors they may be expected to serve a life-time. Toast followed toast as usual and in due course we broke up, having promised to send the Mayor a sack of Benjamin Britten and Peter Pears gladioli to remember us by.[41] A poor return for the beautiful old amphora.

*Friday*

Tremendous news – Gilbars, who had been seen to be swelling daily, disappeared last night and produced five enormous black, white and brown puppies. Dear creature, she was delighted when we all visited her with burnt (meat) offerings. We couldn't photograph them; they were hidden away behind piles of wood and old doors, but we extracted two of them and solemnly christened them Clytie (a brown) and Jove[42] (a black). Everyone was delighted; and we wrote the names down in Russian characters.

At one o'clock we set off for Lake Sevan, past which we had several times driven, for a picnic. The Armenians call it their country's heart and love it dearly. Forty miles long and 5–10 miles wide, its waters are sweet to taste and dazzlingly kingfisher-blue and wine-dark violet. Our picnic on a glorious day in the shade of a cliff was idyllic. Surrounded by wild rock-pinks and yellow hollyhocks as well as a good deal of litter, our salmon trout tasted delicious poached (1st course). And following

---

[40] One of Pérotin's monodic settings, 'Beata viscera Mariae virginis', composed in about 1190, to which Pears had been introduced by Imogen Holst. Pears often included it as part of his solo contribution to Purcell Singers' concerts. Rosamund Strode has suggested in PPT, p. 90, that it was a piece that 'always seemed to suit him best and which he sang with extraordinary flexibility, passion and concentration'.

[41] Varieties of gladioli named after Britten and Pears were developed in the late 1940s and 1950s: Britten's was a deep-toned lavender in colour; Pears's, pale salmon. Although the Britten strain has now ceased to be available, the Pears variety still flourishes, appearing annually in the horticultural catalogues. Examples of both types were, naturally enough, to be found in Britten's and Pears's own garden at the Red House.

[42] Britten's and Pears's second pet dachshund (black), an off-spring of Clytie.

on, came salmon trout grilled over charcoal on a sword; this will not be forgotten. With light Armenian wine and fresh crisp gherkins, nothing could have been tastier. After our lunch, a hydroplane was waiting at the bathing beach to swish us for an hour over the lake. There were 150 or so seats (very comfortable) downstairs, but we stood alone on the bridge. Clouds shadowed the pink brown mountains, the sun shone gloriously, and very proud of their Russian-invented boat, our hosts showed us how it works on some sort of jet principle, and we admired the narrowing wake as our speed mounted, and we almost took off.

As always in Russia, time limps and totters, and the clock races. We were supposed to be home by 4.30 to hear the Quartet and singers for tomorrow's opening concert in Yerevan. At 6.15 we fell rather tired into a quick bath, and for the next 2 hours advised, corrected, despaired, explained, were encouraged and finally exhausted by six singers and their accompanists and a solo pianist, who had come out specially from Yrevan. A very mixed bag, with a very musical and intelligent high baritone (ought he not to be a tenor?) and a sweet older-fashioned dear soprano. Quantities of Ben's and Purcell's songs and folk-songs and the 'Holiday Diary' by a quick-fingered insensitive pianist. The String Quartet was ill, didn't come. At about 9, they all left to take the bus back to Erevan, where they would arrive about 1 a.m., foodless, I suppose (perhaps not).

*Saturday*
Saturday, the day of departure. Our three weeks in this lovely and – now – sunny valley, where we have been spoiled by everyone, had to exact one boring duty before we left, and instead of spending our last morning with Gilbars and her puppies, or baking on the balcony, or searching in the silver green silent woods for mushrooms, or finding a new wild-flower (I found an orchid, but not a very beautiful one, I thought), we had to listen to an endless tape of an Armenian composer, Edgar Oganessian,[43] the director of the theatre in Erevan. Pretentious, bombastic, rhetorical, with minimal ideas and a maximal display of pseudo-energy, listening to it in a fairly comfortable chair paralysed one's hind-quarters and made every muscle contract with bored fury. We got quickly away and solaced ourselves at an early lunch with what we call Moscow-mineral-water, i.e., vodka (water in Russian is voda, without the k). Farewell kisses to all, the chauffeur, the manager (Marcel), our superb cook, Hadjik, who had cried with indignation at the idea of a tip, our little nut brown cleaner who had not been kissed

---

[43]   Edgar Sergeevich Oganesjan (b. 1930), Armenian composer and director of the Armenian Theatre of Opera and Ballet, 1962–8.

by a man for 25 years, I think, and off we had to go to Yrevan and the Britten Festival.

*Yrevan.* We arrived in time for some tea, drink and a bath, and for Ben an hour's rehearsal with the String Quartet, before we had to prepare ourselves for the opening Britten Concert at the Philharmonic Concert Hall. This, built in the 30s, is under the same roof as the Theatre-Opera. Unfortunately the hall is not beautiful nor is the acoustic. We were installed as guests of honour in the box along with other composers and the No. 2 (woman) from Moscow Ministry of Culture, and the concert was duly announced by an M.C. First came Ben's First String Quartet played by the Prokofiev Quartet from Moscow (all women): the cellist is good, the others moderate. However, the performance had greatly improved since Ben's rehearsals. After this came our charming older singer with some French folk-songs, and the promising baritone with some *Michelangelo Sonnets*, 'Fish in the unruffled lakes' and 'Heigh-ho, heigh-hi'.[44] After an entr'acte we had our other singers and the pianist from the evening before, also a grand and condescending old People's Artist singing 'The Miller of Dee' and 'Hee baloo',[45] with Slava and Asa finishing with 3 movements of the Cello Sonata. The pleasantest surprise was the young soprano, who yesterday had sung 'Music for a while' and the difficult 'If Music be the food of love' so stiffly that I despaired.[46] I had, however, worked hard with her, and talked a lot afterwards – and as a result, I like to think, she sang them really beautifully, paying great attention to every point I made, with great expression and style. The voice is stiffly produced, particularly at the top, but it has a fascinating timbre. I said to Galya, was it characteristically Russian? She said, No, No. The little girl was the success of the evening and after terrific long claps and stamps, she had to repeat 'Music for a while'. I was, of course, delighted.

Lots of people in the artists' room afterwards, including the charming Leningrad conductor and admirer of Ben, whom we met with the E.O.G. in October, Dalghat,[47] conductor of *Peter Grimes* in

---

[44] Presumably the unidentified baritone sang a transposed version of Britten's *Seven Sonnets of Michelangelo*, Op. 22 (1940), as they were originally written for tenor and piano. 'Fish in the unruffled lakes' (1938), a setting of a poem by W.H. Auden, also for high voice and piano, was also almost certainly transposed downwards. 'Heigh-ho! Heigh-hi!' is one of Britten's French folksong arrangements ('Eho! Eho!', in French).

[45] 'The Miller of Dee' is from Britten's third volume of folksong arrangements. 'Hee baloo' = 'The Highland Balou', a setting of Burns, the second of Britten's song-cycle *A Charm of Lullabies*, Op. 41 (1947).

[46] Two of Britten's Purcell realizations.

[47] Djemal Dalgat$^{§}$ (1920–1992), Russian conductor, who did much to promote Britten's music in the Soviet Union. In a private communication (29 September 1989; written in English) Dalgat recalled:

Leningrad and Moscow. We hope to see more of him here. The concert was an enormous success and huge applause for Ben ended the first evening of Britten week in Erevan.

The next day, Sunday, was almost as hot, 90°, and sleeping is not easy for us. At one o'clock, after a quiet morning, we went along to the Composers' House for some Armenian music. This is a house built about 8 years ago for the lucky musicians. There are flats for about a dozen composers, as well as offices of various sorts, practice rooms and a small concert-hall with a new organ from Prague, and a vivid, good long rectangular decorative painting by Seryan,[48] their G.O.M. of painting. We heard the following works on tape in this very pleasant if unbeautiful hall:

1. Ter-Tatevoian's 2nd Symphony[49]
2. Ballet Suite by Gregor?
3. Song Cycle for Soprano and Baritone with Orchestra
My Country – Terterian[50]
4. Sonata for Cello Solo – Kudoyan.

No. 1 has a few interesting sounds. 2 was terrible. 3 was more sympathetic, though diffuse. 4 was shorter and clearer and less pretentious. They are all still too wrapped up in history and emotional patriotism to be able to present continuous and clean shapes. Rhapsodical nationalist symphonies are hard to make and hard to take.

Lunch at 3 p.m. and a little rest before Djemal Dalghat brought his intelligent art-historian wife and pretty pale daughter to tea and to show us the Leningrad *Peter Grimes* story in press-cuttings and photos. He did two performances at the Kirov theatre and then one in Moscow, at the end of last season. It will now be in the repertoire for many more performances.

---

The days we spent together in Armenia during Britten's festival, organized by Rostropovich in Yerevan, were really unforgettable. At that time I was on a holiday there with my family, and my wife, professor of the Academy of Fine Arts, introduced Britten and Pears to Sar'yan, whose paintings delighted them, and at the closing concert of the festival the artist presented them with one of his paintings. (See n. 60, p. 130.)

[48] Martiros Sergeevich Sar'yan (1880–1972), Armenian painter, particularly noted for his landscapes.
[49] Hovhannes Gurgeni Ter-T'at'evosyan (b. 1926), Armenian composer, whose Second Symphony ('The fate of man') was composed in 1960.
[50] Avet Terteryan (b. 1929), Armenian composer, whose orchestral song-cycle *The Motherland* was composed in 1957, the year he began his studies with Mirzoyan.

The evening brought Galya's and Slava's song-recital of Tschaikovsky, Moussorgsky and two of Ben's new Pushkin songs as encores.[51] The Tschaikovsky songs in particular were quite wonderfully done; each time one hears her sing them one realises his greatness as a song-writer, and how bad translations have managed to wipe them out of the English repertoire. They are big, original, varied songs and we must try to do some. Tremendous reception for them (Galya looking very beautiful in green and gold Sekers silk and her hair piled up) and Slava as always an eloquent introducer of Ben's songs which were repeated and hugely applauded. The heat was stifling; everyone in white shirts except us in thick best grey flannel suits. I mopped and wiped. With us a highly intelligent and charming No. 2 to Furtseva, Minister of Culture.

*Monday*

Slava and Galya had a bad night, poor dears, because of a wretched young man playing a transistor to his sweetheart in the large and resonant square outside the hotel. Indeed, nights are very hot and restless, and today is 95°F.

This morning our composer friends arranged an excursion to Echmiadzin, the ancient holy city of Armenia, half an hour away, where the supreme head Catholikos of the Armenian world-church has his palace. The cathedral was the oldest in the world, built (the foundations remain) by Gregory the Illuminator in A.D. 301, when Christianity became the State religion of Armenia. The German-speaking Catholikos received us all most kindly, giving us a delicious peach from his well-kept garden. The palace (not big) was being redecorated, and the throne room had just been fitted with walls of beige marble, with reliefs of the finest Armenian churches and names of Catholikoses – finely and restrainedly done, with good lettering. All this as well as a great deal more had been achieved in the last nine years when large sums have been forthcoming from the State. Relations with the State were good, we were told, and certainly the complete marble reflooring of cathedral and palace must have cost a great deal, and could not have been done without the State's active help.

This year is the 50th anniversary of the ghastly 1915 Armenian massacres, when the Turks coming in with Germany against Russia, took the opportunity of murderously expelling two million Armenians from the southern half of their country; and this, of course, remains a monumental date in their history, and much music, painting, poetry has

---

[51] According to Edgar Oganesjan's notice of the Festival concerts, 'Britten Days in Armenia', *Sovietskaya Musika*, 12 (1965), pp. 109–11, Vishnevskaya and Rostropovich performed 'My heart . . .' and 'Epigram', the second and fifth songs from the cycle.

had this theme in this year. Whatever the politics, it is clear that Armenia is greatly encouraged in its own culture and pride in its past. The Institute, where the superb collection of MSS. from the fourth century on (including some splendid illuminations and miniatures) is housed in a grand building built 9 years ago, with air-conditioned rooms, reading rooms, private cells, etc. We have seen this and admired it and liked the enthusiastic Director and charming assistants. The Theatre and Concert Hall was built in the 30s, not very alluring, but at least the Opera is lively enough to put on one of Ben's operas next season and is now starting its season with a more standard repertoire. September 1st is the day when all schools and conservatoires start their year; on that day every child comes to class with a bunch of flowers for the teacher. We shall be in Moscow that day so that Slava can clock in and receive his bouquets!

From Echmiadzin we came back in time for my hour at the Composers' House, I spoke to my audience a little of English musical life and my career; Slava eloquently flattered me, flowers galore, the State Capella Choir appears (60–70 strong), and under a tiresome virtuoso conductor, sing terrible elaborate folk-song arrangements for half an hour with skill and good-ish voices. I reply with 'I wonder as I wander'[52] and Pérotin. Very sweet reception, kisses, flowers, for Slava and me, and I quickly break it up for 3 p.m. lunch. At 6 we wake up to visit two painters' studios: (1) a younger man whose name I haven't got, had done some awfully good landscapes and pictures of peasant life, with that bright palette which suits this dramatic country so well, also some less good formalised 'modernish' constructions; (2) the old Seryan, 85, 20 years in Paris, with a charming old wife, difficult past, but now nationally recognised and acclaimed, obviously an uneven painter, but at his best (in landscape) very exciting and touching. The light here is wonderful for painters, and though I have seen in the hotel boring old landscapes, the newer lot of this century have real vitality and colour.

The concert was Slava and Aza: Schumann, Tschaikovsky and Ben (Sonata: and 1st Russian performance of Solo Suite);[53] marvellous playing, overwhelming reception. Interval employed by Ben sitting for a sculptress, sweet but rather hopeless. Back for supper; all feeling the heat and the strain!

---

[52]  In the early 1940s Britten made an arrangement of 'I wonder as I wander' by John Jacob Niles, in the mistaken belief it was a folksong and therefore in the public domain. Because Niles's song was still in copyright, Britten was unable to publish his version. In recitals, Pears sang Niles's tune unaccompanied (as he evidently did on this occasion in Armenia) with Britten interpolating interludes of his own invention.

[53]  The Suite for Cello, Op. 72, which Rostropovich had premièred at the Aldeburgh Festival in June 1965.

*Tuesday*

The amphora is proving difficult; somehow or other we have got to make sure we get it home safe. One case made for us proved far too big, my overnight air-bag is a bit small, and Erevan is not overfull of such amenities. We are expecting someone to arrive and save us. They came bringing a large cardboard box with much stuffing, and cut it down to a reasonable size. Then they started tying it up. Two composers, two workmen and our floor-lady vied in knots and glue and flaps and handles for two hours. It now looks absurd but safe, I trust. After this exercise of skill and energy, we went to the Philharmonic to pick up Ben after his final rehearsal for tonight's orchestral concert. Only to find Ben, alas! in despair and, fortified by our arrival, he had to make a scene and *forbid* the performance of the Cello Symphony tonight. The silly young conductor[54] from Moscow had spent his four rehearsals on the *Peter Grimes* Interludes and the *Young Person's Guide*, regarding the Cello Symphony as accompaniment, easy and unimportant, which it is not. He did not know the piece and the orchestra could not play it, so Ben had to be firm. Slava had suffered and was very relieved at Ben's action, though ashamed of the situation. The conductor was only allowed to conduct *Grimes*; the local man[55] took over Y.P.G. and conducted it from memory perfectly all right. Ben and I volunteered to fill up the 2nd half of the programme with songs, old English, Purcell and Folk Songs, which suggestion was accepted most gratefully.[56] After this rehearsal with all its fuss and fury, we were beflowered and speechified and toasted in the aid of the Young Pioneers (the Russian boy scout–girl guide movement – white shirts or blouses, and scarlet ties or scarves) and the Armenian New Twins played us some Handel duets. The New Twins (my title! – successors to the Hungarians!)[57] are violinists and 13 years old and authoritative and lively and engaging – in fact, jolly good. This (plus vodka) helped to raise Ben's spirits and we felt better at lunch. The evening concert duly took place. It was a horrid hall to sing in and I was miserable; however, we got through, and Slava joined us in the Bach Aria as an encore,[58] and there were terrific scenes of enthusiasm. The TV lights were switched on; Arno and Alexan played

---

[54]  Yuri Aranovich, who conducted the Armenian State Symphony Orchestra.

[55]  V. Aivazyan.

[56]  According to the notice of the Festival in *Muzikal'naya zhizn*, 20 (1965), p. 17, six Schubert lieder were given in place of the Purcell songs mentioned by Pears in his diary.

[57]  Zoltán and Gábor Jeney: see n. 19, p. 97.

[58]  'Wo ferne du den edlen Frieden', from Cantata No. 41 *Jesu, nun sei gepreiset*. Pears, Rostropovich and Britten had together performed this aria as an encore to Rostropovich's first Aldeburgh Festival recital, in 1961, a concert that included the première of Britten's Cello Sonata.

a smashing new 2-piano dance[59] specially written for Ben's honour – played it superbly; Seryan's picture (given to us by him) was presented to us in front of the cameras;[60] speeches, flowers, kisses, very hot. Slowly we got away to the artists' room, the stage-door, and thence to the hotel where a reception by the Armenian Minister of Culture awaited us. This followed the usual festive pattern, was not unduly protracted, and in the morning we woke up none the worse. Our plane left at 9 a.m. and we were collected, accompanied to the airport, and seen off by all our delightful Armenian friends, by Edik Mirzoyan, Arno Bobajanian, Alexan Arakinian, Adik Kirdoyan, the Minister of Culture and his sister and many more musicians, the lady sculptress who was very sad that Ben wouldn't actually carry her large bust of him back to England, the Art Keeper who gave us a picture of his, and so on – all warm, friendly, hospitable people who had given us such a wonderful welcome and treated us so friendly. Their goodwill is boundless.

The flight (2½ hours) to Moscow was spent in relaxing after these 5 hectic days, in accustoming ourselves to a change in temperature from 95° to 60°F., and in Slava revealing to us that he was going to buy a large motor-cruiser and wanted us to go down the Volga with him and Galya in 1967 or 1968!

Uneventful arrival in Moscow: Mercedes waiting; delayed drive into town because of traffic regulations owing to Nasser's visit;[61] lunch at the flat, and we got off on to the road again at 3.30 p.m. This time we were to drive across Russia – 'the real heart of Russia' – to Pushkin's birthplace – 'not far from Pskov'. The curator was Asa's brother-in-law and was expecting us that night late. It was a long way, Slava knew, but never mind. Off we set: Slava was determined to drive with special care on account of his precious cargo, not too fast, no risks, and the boot was stuffed with bottles and the great Harrod's picnic basket, which we opened and shared at about 7.30 by the side of the mosquito-infested road. Every few miles along the road you find little pavilions for picnics, some classical with painted columns, and tiny, formal beds of petunias or salvias, others mushroom shaped and Disney-like, or as, in Armenia, almost Chinese Chippendale, out of 'Seraglio'. They each have a table

---

[59]  Part of their *Armenian Rhapsody*.

[60]  It was Sar'yan's *Sunny Day* that was given to Britten and Pears (information from Professor Ludmila Kovnatskaya, St Petersburg). A photograph of Sar'yan presenting his painting to a grateful composer can be found in Edgar Oganesjan, 'Britten Days in Armenia', *Sovietskaya Musika*, 12 (1965), p. 110. The painting no longer forms part of the Britten–Pears collection.

[61]  Gamel Abel Nasser (1918–1970), Premier and later President of Egypt, 1954–70. Although initially a champion of non-alignment, Nasser became increasingly dependent on the Soviet Union for arms, aid and wheat supplies during the 1960s.

with benches round, but never a litter basket. Litter abounds but the Russian countryside has room for it. The road quite straight shines ahead of you as far as you can see up and down and over gentle great undulations: on either side there are thin woods of silver birch or thick mixed conifer forests, widely spaced villages with bright painted wooden log-houses, with small fenced gardens, fields of thin crops, marshes, occasionally lakes. This landscape, which stretched with few variations for 700 km. to Leningrad and thence south for another 700 km. to Pskov and the same again home via Smolensk, was after Slava and Galya's own heart. They sighed and exclaimed with pleasure; their souls seemed ready to expand to the ends of the horizon. By 11.15 p.m. after 8 hours' driving we had reached Novgorod; and it was raining and had been for some hours; there were 200 km. still to go. Galya suggested we stop; all, even Slava, agreed, and so we asked about a hotel. We found one, and Slava, by cajolery, charm, insistence, personal authority and by swearing to find the receptionist another job in case she was sacked, persuaded her to give us two large rooms reserved for Mexican diplomats who had not yet arrived. Here *we* slept and *they* did not arrive, thank goodness. We had a double bedroom, a sitting-room and a large bathroom filled with pipes going in all directions and ending in taps, all of which gave us scalding water, especially through the shower-spray which would turn itself on suddenly and soak the walls: the lavatory seat was deeply and dangerously cracked. In the morning the rain teemed down, and when our nice receptionist told us that the road was unusable to Pskov and advised us to go via Leningrad, we were glad we hadn't gone on the previous night.

We were glad too to have a chance of seeing Novgorod, one of the very oldest great Russian trading cities on the fur route from the far north to the Black Sea and the West. We were shown round by a charming admirer of Slava and Ben who got her pretty shoes and feet terribly wet. The Kremlin has a wonderful Verona-like brick wall all round it, also a big, fine cathedral full of wall paintings being restored, some good, some not, and superb Romanesque bronze doors; also a theatre and a large sculptural group of Peter the Great in glory, which was taken to pieces during the war and hidden, and which the Germans never found. The city is full of churches and we were taken to a charming one where the fine but damaged frescoes by the mediaeval Feophan Grek were being repaired by painters who had seen *Peter Grimes* in Leningrad. There is only one (church) which is in use, it seems. Novgorod was very badly destroyed in the war but the new city is one of the better-designed ones, we thought, with good streets and flats in a pleasant stone.

At about 11.15 a.m. we set off for Leningrad, leaving a party of British students passionately discussing Communism in the foyer of the hotel. The rain slowly slackened and by lunch-time we were able to suggest trying a possible short-cut round Leningrad. On the map the road looked good. In fact, after two or three miles of asphalt, it turned to wood-blocks in desperate need of repair and potted with holes. So we made use of the glorious quiet and mushroomy woods to have our picnic and then turned back on to the main road. The Leningrad route was said to be only an hour longer than the direct way; of course this was quite untrue. Four hours was nearer it. We did drive round Pskov, a charming old city full of little bulbous domed churches and a grand walled Kremlin, for an hour; but it was not until 8 p.m. that we reached our destination, Pushkin's home, just 24 hours later than we were expected. Our hosts had waited for us all night. Slava had not thought to telephone; but we were welcomed and greeted as if they had been in no way inconvenienced or put out. He was a poet and man of letters, of some achievement, I think, with an arm lost in the war, a fine, witty, lined face; she had a beautifully shaped face, oval, with brown hair, sensitive, lovely eyes, in all a little like dear Olive Zorian.[62] Their wooden clap-board house was built by Pushkin's son; four or five rooms leading into one another, and a large verandah where we eat. No mod. con., one tap in the middle hall, and lavs. in the garden. The quiet was extraordinary; there were lilac-bushes brushing the gutters, the beds of white phlox along the garden paths filled the Library with scent where we slept deep in books. Before we retired, our host took a torch and showed us Pushkin's house and museum, and outside the front door was the clock tower and its cracked clock which was there in Pushkin's time and still struck its old hours. Simple six-roomed one-floored house, while the two caretakers, a man and his round wife, held up candles to the dark pictures and framed MSS. on the walls, and the brass bedstead and the fastenings on the stove glittered. We saw the little house where Pushkin's beloved Nana lived, her ikons on the shelf by the stove, her spinning-wheel and the clasp which held the thin strips of wood which lit the little rooms in those days. There was too the house of the bailiff, simple and austere, all wood, neatly clean.

After a meal of soup and excellent cold leg of lamb, and a sort of barley with meat balls (so good), marvellous coffee and plum syrup, our host begged to hear the Pushkin songs. We moved into the lamp-lit sitting-room with an upright piano in the corner, and started on the songs (after an introduction by Slava). Galya sang her two,[63] and I hummed the others. The last song of the set is the marvellous poem of insomnia, the ticking clock, persistent night-noises and the poet's cry

---

[62] English violinist (1916–1959), leader of the EOG Orchestra (1952–7), and founder of the Zorian String Quartet, which gave notable performances of works by young British composers (including the première of Britten's Second String Quartet).

[63] I.e. the two settings that Vishnevskaya had performed in Yerevan (see n. 51, p. 127).

for a meaning in them. Ben has started this with repeated staccato notes high–low high–low on the piano. Hardly had the little old piano begun its dry tick tock tick tock, than clear and silvery outside the window, a yard from our heads, came ding, ding, ding, not loud but clear, Pushkin's clock joining in his song. It seemed to strike far more than midnight, to go on all through the song, and afterwards we sat spell-bound. It was the most natural thing to have happened, and yet unique, astonishing, wonderful. In the morning, from our windows we could see the still silver pond beyond the field, with clumps of silver birches far away, and the great forest of enormously tall, enormously thin fir-trees. Not far off was the village church, to which Pushkin in his exile was commanded to report for worship every day at 1 p.m. (so we were told). It is a simple, pleasant and spacious little country-church with a bulbous dome, and is approached up a flight of steps. In front is Pushkin's tomb, a curious un-beautiful, masonic affair, which the Germans ineffectively tried to mine as they left. They also destroyed most of the church walls and roof, and blew up the great bronze bell which summoned Pushkin to worship. The church has been rebuilt and turned into a museum – pleasantly enough. We paid our respects, and set off in uncertain weather back towards Moscow. Our hosts to whom we said farewell with much regret (such kind sympathetic civilised souls) recommended the Vitebsk–Smolensk route, and thence the great Minsk–Moscow highway. Unfortunately for us, a lot of the earlier part was being remade, and so we were left simply to get through as best we could. In one place soldiers were working on the road and helped us, shifting the surface for us; in others, we had to plunge out into ankle-deep mud and let Slava drive while we walked. We had a good morning's exercise this way, in pleasant wooded country. The sun shone through the leaves and made pine-trees smell. Later, when we reached the Highway, a drizzle began and Slava drove as fast as he dared along this very broad good road, covering the last 400 km. in 4 hours. We were due for dinner at Shostakovitch's datchya at 6 p.m.: we arrived at 9.20. After a quick wash, a large meal awaited us; various caviars, cold meats, pâtés, yoghourts, cheese, chicken casserole, hot and cold fish, pastry, tarts, éclairs, vodka, brandy, wine, all at once! As soon as Shostakovitch heard that Ben had set Pushkin, he was all tense to hear them; and his nice young wife[64] had to restrain him until we had eaten. He himself had just set some satirical jokes from 'Krododil',[65] which didn't stop him from admiring Ben's songs: he was, as always, physically strung-up, but personally most welcoming and amiable; he is clearly fond of Ben and

---

[64]  Shostakovich's third wife, Irina.
[65]  The *Five Romances on texts from 'Krokodil' magazine*, Op. 121, for bass and piano.

was glad to see him. We did not stay terribly late as we were all tired after our 10 hours of driving, but we were imperatively invited back to breakfast, and it seemed a very short night before we were sitting at 9 a.m. at the same table covered with much of the same food. Ben and I both found chicken casserole perfectly possible, preceded by cognac or vodka, an important prelude, I fancy. Shostakovitch told us with pleasure that his 13th Symphony (the one with the Yevtushenko 'Babyar' test, which had had a poor performance and reception last year)[66] was to be revived in October; and we discussed, in various broken languages, Armenia, composers, music, performers. Shostakovitch is mad about football, and wants to come to England in 1966 for the World Cup. He also wants to come to Aldeburgh in 1967: we hope he will.[67] Our hosts gave us a very warm send-off, and on we sped in the Mercedes to Moscow. Galya took us shopping for presents in one of the big shops in Gorky Street, before we fulfilled our last social engagement in Russia, which was lunch with our dear Aza Amintieva at her flat. She had prepared a splendid lunch in her charming one room (glorious chicken done in the Georgian style, looking as if it had been rather carefully run over) and loaded us with bottles of home-made sauces to take home. From her flat, just round the corner from Slava's, we drove out to the airport, and there we took leave of our very dear Slava and Galya who had given us such a wonderful, exciting, new holiday-month. Never could any two guests have been more royally treated; never can any country be more generous and hospitable to us than the Soviet Union was; every person we met was friendly and welcoming; no trouble was too much, and we came back with much increased friendly feelings for these marvellous people, and especially of course for Slava and Galya with whom, in spite of all language difficulties, we were sympathetically happy and at ease every minute of our stay.[68]

---

[66] Shostakovich's Thirteenth Symphony, 'Babi Yar', Op. 113, a setting of Yevgeny Yevtushenko's poem about the Nazi massacre of seventy thousand Jews outside Kiev in September 1941, was a bold and highly controversial indictment of contemporary Soviet anti-Semitism. After the first two performances in 1962, the Soviet authorities banned the work. The occasion proved to be Shostakovich's last major clash with the Soviet authorities.

[67] In fact, Shostakovich was invited to the 1968 Aldeburgh Festival when a number of his works were featured in the programme, including the first UK performance of his *Seven Romances on Poems of Alexander Blok*, Op. 127 (1967). He was, however, prevented from attending owing to ill-health. Shostakovich paid a single visit to Aldeburgh, in July 1972, when Britten showed him what he had written of his final opera, *Death in Venice*, Op. 88, to be completed later that year.

[68] On their return, Britten and Pears sent a telegram to their Russian hosts:
WE CAN NEVER THANK YOU ENOUGH FOR OUR GLORIOUS HOLIDAY SO HAPPY SO FULL SO KIND. ALL ALDEBURGH IS PREPARING FOR YOUR CHRISTMAS.

# 6 *Moscow Christmas: A Diary (December 1966)*

Britten and Pears spent their Christmas and New Year holidays of 1966/7 in Moscow and Leningrad, once again as the guests of Mstislav Rostropovich and Galina Vishnevskaya. Apart from making some of the usual sight-seeing trips and spending time with their Russian friends, including visits to Shostakovich, they gave two important recitals at prestigious venues in each of the cities. As Pears reveals (see pp. 146), it was also during this visit that, after seeing Rembrandt's magnificent *The Return of the Prodigal Son* at the Hermitage, Britten conceived the idea of making the New Testament story the subject of his next church parable with William Plomer.

As Pears notes in a postscript to his main text, the notebook in which he inscribed *Moscow Christmas* was given to him by Rosamund Strode, Britten's music assistant. To enliven his text, Pears pasted into the volume some postcard illustrations of the Kremlin, their concert programmes, and his Aeroflot airline ticket, and presented the diary to Miss Strode on his return. Extracts appeared in the 1967 Aldeburgh Festival Programme Book under the title 'Russian New Year' (pp. 99–102), and in time for Christmas that year, Pears had *Moscow Christmas* privately published in an edition prepared by Benhams (Colchester), the company who had printed *Armenian Holiday* two years previously.

The original notebook is at the Britten–Pears Library (1-9300457), a gift to the Library from Rosamund Strode in 1993. The text used in the present edition adheres in the main to that of the published version; in one or two instances, however, material omitted from Pears's published diary – principally concerning the identity of Khrennikov (see note 28, p. 150), which was very thinly concealed in the original publication – has been restored. Pears clearly sanctioned such changes to protect not only himself but, more importantly, his many Russian friends and colleagues mentioned in the text, all of whom were living under a difficult and often oppressive political regime.

It is Christmas Day, 1966. The Pekin Hotel is one of those buildings exclusive to Moscow which soar straight skyward for eight storeys or so and then fine off into fairy-tale towers and pinnacles, which proliferate in every direction open to all the winds of heaven. There are 13 floors, and we are on the eleventh, snow-blown and only rarely visited by lifts, and we leave our keys on the 8th with the blond concierge-lady, not ill-tempered. As I lie on my bed, I look up twenty feet or more to the ceiling, with its *Empire* moulding. The walls coming down from the ceiling are orange. Our bedroom is 14 ft. square. To reach it we traverse a hall with a bathroom etc. off, and a writing-room, and a reception-room, all very lofty and orange. All the rooms above the 8th floor are lofty. The furniture tries to match it, but only half succeeds, the ceiling is out of reach. Why are we here? Because Slava and Galya spent last Christmas at Aldeburgh and they insisted on returning the hospitality. We arrived yesterday, Christmas Eve, two days later than we had planned. Ben had had some bad days and I had a very tired, relaxed throat – we had agreed to do two concerts, one in Moscow, one in Leningrad, and the Moscow one had to be put off until today. We arrived alright yesterday via Helsinki, but no Slava to meet us. Instead, Toya, familiar as friendly helper and interpreter on many occasions, AND a real Father Christmas who dispensed small packages of postcards and dolls. Slava is in disgrace. Back on Friday, late, from Israel, he promised to drive Toya out to meet us. No go: he had disappeared, Galya had no idea where, and she had to sing 'Cio-cio-San'. Grumbles from Toya all the way to the Hotel. Slava is impossible but you can't be angry with him when you see him. We reached our hotel and our orange suite and sat grumbling, cursing Slava, telephoning uselessly, and drinking our whisky. At last, a call from Slava, apologies, explanations, he had trouble with his Opel on the way to the Airport. Finally Slava himself. By now we were prepared to sulk, and teased him for a bit. But, Toya is right, you can't be cross with Slava. So in no time at all, he was charging us in his No. 3 car (a puce Opel) down opposite one-way streets, his windscreen dense with ice, passed on both sides by buses and trucks. We were to see 'ten minutes' of Galya's Butterfly at the Bolshoi and then home to eat. In fact, we got there at the last Intermission and had to face the whole last Act. Galya glorious, in splendid voice and looks, in a typical Bolshoi set, vast, expensive and incredibly un-Japanese. A young, very immature Pinkerton with a pleasant timbre, and a routine Sharpless in a real Savile Row morning coat. Terrific ovation for Galya, curtains galore. On the stage we met the v. promising Mezzo who sings Oberon there.[1] Unfortunately there is no performance of M.S.N.D. for

---

[1]  Yelena Vasil'yevna Obraztsova (b. 1937), Russian mezzo-soprano, who sang Oberon in the Russian première of Britten's *A Midsummer Night's Dream* at the

another 3 weeks, long after we shall have gone. After the performance and hand-shakings with Chulaki[2] (Bolshoi Intendant) and others, back to Slava and Galya's flat. Olga and Helene have grown quite a bit and are beautiful and sweet-mannered children. By now we were hungry and thirsty and enjoyed our dinner (N.B. beetroots sliced and chopped small in a garlic mayonnaise!) Toya drank too much and never stopped talking. Glad to get to bed, Moscow time 1 a.m. Ours 10 p.m. This morning I lie and look at the ceiling.

*26th.*

We had determined that we would go to church on Christmas Day. But it wasn't possible. The only time we could use the hall at the Conservatoire for rehearsal was half an hour before our 4 p.m. concert. So we arranged to rehearse at Slava's at noon, he to fetch us at 11.45. At least that is how I thought it was, Ben was not so sure. In fact, breakfast ordered for 9, came at 10. In other Moscow hotels 3-minute eggs arrive barely warmed through. So 5 minutes would be safe, I thought. In the Pekin, 5 is 5 or more, and they were strong, unbreakable. After breakfast we waited. No Slava. I practised in despair for an hour. At last Slava, at 1 o'clock. I had particularly asked if we could eat early, not later than 1. We sat down at 1.45. The concert got nearer and nearer. We finished with strong coffee at 2.50. Drive to Hotel, through thick snow of course, quick change, drive to Conservatoire, five minutes on stage for practice, and lights. Fuss with nice intelligent woman who will announce *Dichterliebe* as first half, instead of Dowland–Purcell–Schubert. Last minute crowd in artists' room until I sing them all out fortissimo. Apologies for non-full house (it was over-sold before change of date, and Sunday – Christmas Day) and we go on to perform. It is a big lofty hall but beautiful, with a fine acoustic and a marvellous warm feeling. Heavenly audience, quiet as mice, and immensely warm and enthusiastic. 'Wonder-wander' and 'Plough-boy' as encores.[3] Could have done six more, but tired after a strong programme. Went well on the whole, and my memory wasn't too bad at all. Crowds in artists' room, Shostakovich, Koslovsky,[4] Nina

---

Bol'shoy. The role was originally designed for the counter-tenor voice (Alfred Deller sang it in the first production at Aldeburgh in 1960), at the time a peculiarly English phenomenon; in the published score, Britten wisely offered the alternative of using a mezzo-soprano instead.

[2] Mikhail Ivanovich Chulaki (b. 1908), Russian composer and teacher; director of the Bol'shoy Theatre from 1955.

[3] 'Wonder–wander': see n. 52, p. 128; 'The Plough Boy' comes from Britten's third volume of folksong arrangements. The second half of the recital began with Britten's *Seven Sonnets of Michelangelo*, Op. 22.

[4] Probably Ivan Semjonovich Kozlovskyi (1900–1993), Russian lyric tenor and member of the Bol'shoy company.

Richter,[5] many familiar faces. Ben gives interview, and is presented with a Russian printed copy of his Violin Suite, very rarely played in England, but pirated and popular in Russia.[6] Three keen singing students ask me questions such as 'What is the difference between opera singing and concert singing?' 'Do you breathe in the day-time as you do when you sing?' i.e. I think that was the question, though they looked a little discouraged by the answer. They wanted records and I suggested a meeting at the Hotel. Another charming chap gave me a souvenir pin, with, I found later, a picture of the Cathedral of the Assumption on it in crimson enamel. We extricate ourselves, give our bouquets to Toya (her mother is coming to visit her), say *Das Vidanya* to the photographer (image of Rimsky-Korsakov) and drive back to our orange suite for an hour's break and change before Christmas dinner at Slava's.

From our eleventh floor we look down on a white townscape. Opposite is a theatre and the vast Tchaikovsky Hall to the left, and a broad boulevard stretches for miles off to the right towards more faery-palace hotels and party-offices. A kino stands back, and in front of it, small remote figures move to and fro buying Christmas trees which are dragged off down the pavement. The Russian Orthodox Christmas remains in the middle of January (hence no Church Bells at all audible in these days) but the Orthodox Soviet Atheists are only interested in the New Year. All Russians love Christmas trees however, and Father Christmas (if not Santa Claus) is in evidence everywhere. At Slava's, there was no tree, but the dinner table was brilliant with candles, and the chandelier over the table (a very beautiful old one bought 'from a very old woman in Leningrad') sparkled. Dmitri and Irena Shostakovich were there, punctual as always, and we exchanged presents which we had brought from Aldeburgh (a Victorian coral pin for Galya, Swedish glass and a china white-and-gilt putto playing the cello (found in Woodbridge) for Slava, amber pendants for the girls). I received a typical Russian lacquer box, and Ben a great buffalo horn from Georgia. We sat down to a splendid spread, with an excellent goose, and talked of many things. S. in good form, talkative, nervous, Irena gentle, quiet, a marvellous foil for him. After dinner, we produced a specially brought

---

[5]    Nina Dorliak (b. 1908), Russian soprano and wife of Sviatoslav Richter (see note 10 below).

[6]    At this time the Soviet Union was not a signatory to the Berne Convention, and as such was able to publish copyright music by Britten and other Western composers free from prosecution. With the non-existence of copyright protection, a number of Britten's works appeared during the 1960s under the imprint of the Soviet Union's music publishing house, including *War Requiem* and the Suite, Op. 6 (1934), for violin and piano.

pack of 'Happy Families' (not the old original illustrations alas!).[7] Slava had been champion at Aldeburgh Christmas '65, but this time in Moscow it was Dmitri who triumphed. We all enjoyed it, a great success, much laughter, every breach of 'Thank you ver' much' pounced on and punished. Talk about Stravinsky and the drivelling muck written about Dmitri by Nabokov, etc.[8] Ben tells his recent dream of Stravinsky as a monumental hunchback pointing with a quivering finger at a passage in the Cello Symphony 'How dare you write that bar?' Dmitri quickly excited and depressed. We drink healths and break up not too late, and back to our orange suite and the too short bed and the pillows stuffed with woollen pebbles, and a deep deep sleep.

*Later.* I suppose we woke up, but not entirely. All day we yawned. Breakfast never came at all: yesterday's still remains on the table, egg shells, half saucers of jam and glasses rimmed with dried tea-leaves. Later Toya drove us to the Kremlin and we walked up through the Troiska Gate on glassy cobbles, against a searching windy snow, across the splendid square (16th–18th–20th centuries all blending impressively) to spend ½ hour in the Cathedral of the Assumption. How small to be called a Cathedral, a series of ambulatory-chapels round a central chamber, with a superb great Iconostasis, figures by Feofan Grek and his master Rubliov.[9] Now a Museum, well-kept. A constant flow, most hats are removed, some stomp through with vacant gaze. Every inch of wall covered with events and figures: many very beautiful and curious, the central dome going up and up to the great benevolent, just, face of Christ watching us. A tall lame oldish man with intelligent eyes sends his

---

[7]   A reference to the unique set of 'Happy Families' cards, devised by Mary Potter and given to Britten as a Christmas present in the mid-1950s. In place of the usual illustrations, Mrs Potter's cards depict Aldeburgh families well known to Britten and Pears.

[8]   Nicholas Nabokov (1903–1978), American composer of Russian origin, whose dislike of Shostakovich's music was well known: see Nabokov's malicious description of Shostakovich at the 1949 New York Peace Congress, reprinted in Elizabeth Wilson, *Shostakovich: A Life Remembered* (London: Faber and Faber, 1994), pp. 238–41. Nabokov had recently published a book on Stravinsky (Berlin, 1964) and was to contribute some important reminiscences in *Cosmopolite* (Paris, 1975).

    Both Britten and Shostakovich had a curious, often uneasy relationship with Stravinsky, and it is of some interest to find here that Pears reports the two composers discussing their senior colleague. See also Bayan Northcott, 'The Fine Art of Borrowing: Britten and Stravinsky', Aldeburgh Festival Programme Book, 1994, pp. 14–19.

[9]   Feofan Grek [Theophanes the Greek] (c.1340–1405), whose finest work can be seen in the Kremlin Cathedral of the Annunciation. Andrey Rublyov (c.1360–c.1430), Russian painter, who joined Theophanes in his work on the Cathedral.

139

grand-daughter to ask the time, perhaps in English, hoping for an English answer. Watchdog Toya intervenes and helpfully gives the right Russian answer: Confused frustration all round: T. is very useful and well-meaning, but sometimes too much of a Cerberus.

Back through icy wind (we are definitely sub-under-clothed!) to car and 2.30 lunch with Slava, Galya and Toya at the Georgian Restaurant in Pushkin Square. Superb food (that crushed chicken again). Back to hotel at 4.45, over-fed, to relax before being collected at 7 o'clock by Nina to spend evening with her and Slava Richter[10] at their Datchya. This is a simple cottage-bungalow, 4 rooms in all, belonging to an actress, and while Slava was away in Italy, Nina rented it for some time. How long I don't know, but she has had a piano brought down from the Conservatoire. Richter has a flat in Moscow in the same group of blocks as Slava Ros. All musicians live there, but Richter found the practising of the occupants of the flat above him (3 pianists together, including our old friend Aza Amintieva) so distracting, so over-whelming, the foot stamping and pedal banging so shattering, that he can't work there. Who can blame him? I should go mad.

Slava Ros. knew we were going to Nina and Slava Rich. for the evening, and I think deliberately filled us up to the brim in the afternoon. Anyway we (and Ben in particular) never recovered from the Georgian meal.

We drove over frozen snow past the Ukraine Hotel and the Borodino Panorama out into the country, slowly, carefully for 40 minutes, with the adorable, gentle, sensitive Nina, until we came down lesser lanes to a quiet snow-bound little home, dimly-lit and very simply furnished. Slava lit the Christmas-tree and he and I talked about Rimsky-Korsakov's operas, while Ben sat glass-eyed, and sipping whisky, struggling against sleep. We had agreed to order a taxi for 10.15, but we kept him waiting until 11.0, until we had finished our slow, simple, excellent dinner, and I had worked out with Slava his programmes for Aldeburgh, Ben agreeing monosyllabically. (We had learnt earlier that Slava Rostropovich cannot after all come to Aldeburgh next Festival '67 – Too many English visits – and if we want him in '68, then '67 is off). We arrange four concerts – one solo (Chopin and Debussy), one Mozart Concerto, one Ben's concerto, one with BB (2 pianos) plus me (Debussy Songs) – sweet chap! he is being very generous.[11] Back to Moscow in a taxi, driven with great panache by one of those who loves to show off

---

[10]   Sviatoslav Richter[§] (b. 1915), Russian pianist.
[11]   At the 1967 Aldeburgh Festival Richter gave a recital (Haydn, Chopin and Debussy: 16 June); performances of Mozart's E flat major Piano Concerto, K. 482 (13 June) and Britten's Piano Concerto (18 June), both conducted by Britten; and a joint recital with Britten and Pears (Mozart, Britten and Debussy: 20 June), including Debussy's *Ariettes et chansons* with Pears.

their skid-control round corners. Quite good fun when there is no traffic, and there is not too much at midnight. (In the middle of the day, though, Gorky Boulevard is nearly as bad as Regent St. with taxis, buses and trucks).

The night air strikes very cold, although it is only 10° below zero. But it is dry and sparkling.


*Tuesday*
The telephone woke us at 7.45: a persistent *Pravda* lady. Ben, who had had a nasty previous experience with *Pravda*'s false interviews, staved her off when she telephoned again later. Another journalist, friend of Slava's, came later and had an interview with Toya's help. Also a pair of musicians, one the leader of the Bolshoi orchestra who has formed a group of 17 solo violins (sic!) who play standing in a long row, in unison, 2 or 3 or even 4 parts! This sensational but musically unattractive notion has a Circus flavour, and the Programmes shown us were *very* ordinary. Ben found the inevitable request for a composition not too difficult to side-step. We heard later from Slava that Ben shouldn't dream of it (but then Slava really doesn't think that Ben should write music for anybody but him!).

Dear Nina Richter made a special visit to our Hotel to bring a warm over-coat-lining for Ben and a pair of woollen socks. Such kindness!

In due course the time came for our departure for Leningrad at 13.30. Slava was to drive us to the Leningradski Station and arrived ON TIME. He is in the middle of a series of All Soviet Cello Congresses (I think) as well as fitting in his usual Conservatoire Pupils (20 in all) before the New Year Hols. After a Congress Session today finishing at 5 pm, he will teach until 1 am, ditto Wednesday and Thursday. Galya has already gone to the Datchya; she has not to sing until Jan. 2nd (Pique Dame). (Slava Richter said she was marvellous in this part [Liza] and it was the only Bolshoi production he liked at all. He did not think too much of the M.S.N.D. at the Bolshoi. Grandiose Kitsch.)

We had decided to go on the day train to Leningrad, as one doesn't expect to sleep on a night-train starting at midnight and stopping at 6 am. People were sympathetic but surprised: no-one goes by day. But we wanted to see the country and Ben likes long train journeys, and six hours is not too long. Toya told us there was only one stop. So we boarded the train; all seats bookable and booked. Twelve great coaches, holding about 100 (more?) passengers each, 2 each side of a gangway, spotlessly clean, a linen drugget right down the gangway was removed from a smart blue carpet (dirty from entering passengers' boots) as we started off. A no-smoking coach, rigidly observed; many exitings for a puff in the cold-ish entrance hall-let. All one class, of course – No, one sleeper carriage which was probably dearer. Very smooth and quiet journey, with not a great deal to look at out of the window. Solid carriages, reasonably comfortable seats, warm but not stuffy. Fellow travellers very agreeable to look at – an amorous sweet pair behind, across, an old couple, rather prosperous country types, she spreading everywhere, he shrewd with a long flat nose, snoring gloriously together for two hours; two glamour girls behind him, one dark and handsome (Armenian?) dressed in good colours, with thick pencillings from the eye-corners, the other henna-ed, in orange and green, not so much my cup-of-tea: two quiet serious friends in front of us, and ahead a good looking soldier who arrived hot and panting just in time.

This train costs (?) three roubles to Leningrad, while the night train is (?) eight roubles (sleeper included). Each carriage has a guard – a girl-guard – dressed in smart sky-blue tights? trousers? stockings? Black coat and skirt and fur cap. Our blonde guide looked smashing, and gave us each a book in German about Russian Festivals, i.e. Music, Theatre, Ballet, etc. filled with glossy photos, including the 17 piece Violin-Group all lined up in front of the Bolshoi Drop-cloth.

After the second stop, it was clear that the train was not *all that* express. Toya enquired, and yes! in summer it takes six hours, but in winter 8, and stops several places. We easily resigned ourselves, and enquiring for tea, we were taken down the train, past a little over-crowded buffet to a guard's sleeper-carriage where we drank a welcome hot sweet tea, for which our kind girl refused payment.

At each stop, people dashed out and bought sandwiches or pop or cakes at the little station buffet-cabin on the platform. The two friends in front of us got great chocolate éclair-shaped cookies, splendid with pink and green, which they devoured with amused appreciation. On we went, all good-humoured, and, ages before Leningrad, everyone began to get dressed and get down parcels and bags and stand waiting. We sat and got out later, greeted by nice cheerful Mr. Mendelson,[12] of the Philharmonic Hall (& Orch) and the Horn Player (Ben thinks) who made that fabulous record I played at the Aldeburgh Club last year.[13] At first we thought Leningrad was warmer than Moscow but I am not quite so sure. Damper, they say. Not such deep snow as Moscow, but a

---

[12] Yuryi Michailovich Mendelson (d. 1981), deputy director of the Leningrad Philharmonic Orchestra.

[13] Vitalii Mikhailovich Buyanovsky (1928–1993), Russian horn-player and principal horn of the Leningrad Philharmonic Orchestra. While at the Philharmonic Orchestra, Buyanovsky formed a wind quintet which he subsequently linked to the idea of chamber ballet (see pp. 144–5). Several of Buyanovsky's recordings survive at the Britten–Pears Library, including a recording of Britten's *Serenade*, Op. 31, for tenor, horn and strings, in which he is the horn soloist, with Karel Zarins (tenor), and the Leningrad Chamber Orchestra conducted by Lasar Gozman (Melodiya SM 03829–30; *GB-ALb* 3-9400585).

glorious city, and the yellow buildings shone out in the snow. We drove to our hotel, our old friend the Europe(-an?), and after our hosts left us, settled down into the lofty suite, a hall, a passage, a sitting-room, a bedroom, a great bath-room cum-lav. and basin, the whole suite hollow with hanging-cupboards. The beds (alas! the same length, though slightly softer pillows) have gold coverlets (as at the Pekin) and the bedroom has gold rayon shiny curtains (drapes?!) but the walls are a delightful *lilac* – much more agreeable, and we have a beautiful Edwardian marble lady in the corner, shamelessly and entirely nude. (Memo: I must ask K. Clark[14] for instruction on 'the Russian Nude'.) First, we have our charming room-mate (if we may so call her). Then downstairs in the Buffet, there is a Soviet Arcadian gilt relief (over the door into the cloak-room) of 'Music and Dance' with tauntingly nude ladies accompanied by the double-flute of a stuffily tunicked shepherd. On the other hand, in the first-floor reading-room, rather good antique marble copies of Ganymedes and Discusthrowers display themselves fearlessly. Of course, the dreadful athletic statues dotted over the whole Soviet countryside and ringing every Stadium, are all too decently covered, male and female, to the obvious embarrassment of the sculptor. I presume that, while it is fairly easy to 'drape' the female figure and not so easy to 'drape' the male, either sex dressed in vests and drawers is sculpturally insoluble. The men seem to come off worse every time, and always the result is – to say the least – peculiar.

Not a word however against the pictures in Russian hotels! Large, gold-framed, landscapes of Russia, they suggest a high level of academic painting with no discernible influence later than that of Sisley.

*Wednesday*
Toya tells us that our solid corn-haired waitress is worried that we don't eat our breakfast. Cold underboiled eggs are not the thing for Ben any time, and soft toast is easily resistable. In Russia, you must order exactly everything you want, including salt, pepper, and sugar: milk, too. It is advisable to order it for at least 20 minutes before you want it.

It gets light terribly late here. The street lamps are on until 9.30. Our room looks exactly across onto the door of the Philharmonic Hall, so we only have to cross the road for our concert. Posters of concerts include Rozhdestvensky conducting Igor Oistrakh[15] in Mozart, Hindemith and the IIIrd Act of Prokofiev's Flaming Angel on Thursday. We may go to

[14] Sir Kenneth (later, Lord) Clarke⁵ (1903–1983), art historian, patron and interpreter of the arts, whose study, *The Nude,* was published in 1956.
[15] Russian violinist (b. 1931), son of the violinist David Oistrakh.

it before our night train back to Moscow. Next week Kondrashin[16] conducts Ravel Piano Concerto (Flier)[17] and Mahler's 3rd Symphony. The Hall is ravishing, a classical Basilika-like hall, with side-aisles and galleries over, rectangular with massive circular columns down the sides with Corinthian capitals and superb vast chandeliers hanging two by two, all shining white and picked out in gold, grandly elegant. Richly furnished artists' rooms; in one, a piano in rosewood made by Diedichens Frères, St. Petersbourg; in another a gold grand, painted with pastoral scenes – Tsarist relics, but perfectly usable. We have a new Steinway for the concert.

We rehearsed for an hour on the gold grand from 12 to 1, and then at 3 tried out the Hall. It is not as sympathetic as the Moscow Conservatoire but very clear. After the rehearsal we went for a short walk along the Nevsky Prospekt, splendid street with the Admiralty towering at the end. It is very cold, and the wind seizes the throat. Streets full of people, happy, determinedly pushing into the large store under the enormous Father Christmas. Maybe the holidays are responsible, but there are no grey, unsmiling faces around today.

In the evening we had our Concert. A tall Chaliapin-like actor announced our programme. This is the custom here, to announce items, even though printed programmes are available, and off we started with *Dichterliebe*. The audience was very quiet and attentive. But at the end the applause seemed very cold to us and we thought we were a flop. Much the same after the Michelangelo Sonnets. During the Folk-Songs, announced individually, they looked a little warmer, and in fact, at the end they wouldn't let us go and we did 3 encores and could have gone on. How audiences differ! When we talked it over afterwards, we remembered it had been the same last visit. Moscow warm, Leningrad cool, but in fact equally enthusiastic. In the artists' room after, many old acquaintances, including the young people in the front row who had passed up little notes with special requests for encores. One young man had asked for *The Holy Sonnets of John Donne*!

After the concert, Ben had been specially asked to witness a performance of his *Metamorphoses* (for oboe solo) danced by a new Group, formed and organised by the Horn Player Bouyanowski, young dancers, mostly I think from the Kirov. It was done simply with a few dancers, some solo (Narcissus, Pan and Syrinx). No décor, just coloured spot-lights – on the stage where we had just performed. We were very

---

16 Kirill Kondrashin (1913–1981), Russian conductor at the Bol'shoy Theatre, Moscow (1943–56), and artistic director of the Moscow Philharmonic (1960–75). He was responsible for the premières of many works by Russian composers, most notably Shostakovich's Fourth and Thirteenth Symphonies. In the 1960s he became much admired for his interpretations of Mahler's symphonies.

17 Yakov Vladimirovich Flier (1913–1977), Russian pianist and teacher.

taken by the whole thing, and the oboe player was stunningly good. Costumes adequate if not special. Young choreographer, gifted, musical, fitting simple but subtle ideas to the single line of the music. How good to find small groups starting up here, slowly impinging on the great Monolith.

*Thursday*
One of our greatest purposes in coming to Leningrad was to see the Hermitage again. Horrified, therefore, to find that today, our only day here, it is closed! However magic words were spoken and we were welcomed there and conducted round by a gentle polyglot in French (from the Greek, poly– = *many*, from the Russian, it means *half*; both applicable here, I think). There is no gallery like the Hermitage. Not only the fabulous wealth of objects, but the richness of the setting – glamorous and glorious 18th century rooms where Renaissance bronzes look perfectly in place under a Rembrandt portrait. We were asked what we wanted to see particularly – only the jewellery and ancient Scythian gold were 'not at home'. We plumped for the Italians and Rembrandt. And wandering on our way past Greek vases and a gallery full of Falconet (it is an anniversary year for this charmer) we were tactfully and quietly taken to the Fra Angelicos, the Lippis father and son, the little early Raphael *Madonna and child*, the two Leonardos (early *M. & ch.* with the gay girl and vast baby, dark cell-like background with window full of blue sky; and late *M. & ch.* blue on blue on blue), the big Sebastiano del Piombo *Pietà* which needs cleaning, the original (?) cast of our Venetian Vittoria door-knocker of Neptune which we have in a cheap modern cast outside the Library,[18] the knock-out beauty of Giorgione's *Judith* (still calculated by magic to make it the greatest picture in the world, leaving Leonardo at the post), another Giorgione, new to us (*M. & ch.* in a broken turbulent landscape, with a face stylised like Picasso) to a big Pontormo, very fresh and brilliant in colour, full of vivid sharp pinks, with lemon shadows to the Virgin's cap, and *gamin* faces like the famous frescoes, out into the vast central Hall full of giant Tiepolos, very splendid, and Spaniards (Zurbaran, Ribera, Murillos and 2 Velasquez), the solitary El Greco of SS Peter and bald Paul, past the wonderful late-Titians of S. Sebastian and S. Magdalene, and the earlier Danae, a very fine Veronese of a *Descent from the Cross*, into a small darkish room with the unfinished Michelangelo of a *Slave* sitting on his haunches who looks as if he is trying to pull himself out of the earth by his feet, then through another room where we met by chance an excellent English-speaking Professor of Renaissance Art who told us that

---

[18]  The door-knocker can still be seen outside the Britten–Pears Library.

the curious and lively *Putto with Dolphin* in marble formerly attributed to Rosselino (?) had now been judged by an American expert to be an 18th century fake, and one could immediately see why. No-one seems to mind, and the Hermitage is not offended, since it is more interesting and special as an 18th c. fake than it was as a 15–16 c. attribution.

But as our modest guide put it, 'we are not specially strong in Italians, our Dutch section is our best', and with that we entered the big dark room with some of the greatest Rembrandts in the world in it, the *Flora* in silk so rich that you can feel the pile with your eyes, and the early *Abraham and Isaac*, the *Danae* (all ready for the shower of·gold, and her old Madame eagerly pulling back the curtain from the sumptuous bed), the portraits of the old Jews, and surely greatest of all, the *Prodigal Son* (with his broken back, shaven head, worn sole to his one foot out of its shoe, the father all loving-understanding, the three diverse characters looking on, judging, grudging, and surprised). (Of course, this is the subject for the next Church Parable.)[19]

After such things, Rubens, offered, was refused, and their other pride, the Impressionists, was brushed aside. It was our pleasant duty to meet and thank the Assistant Director, immensely-learned Prof. Levinson-Lessing,[20] an old friend of K. Clark, Philip Hendy[21] and others. Perfect English but very frail. How grateful we were to all the charming and friendly staff.

Over a late and *very* slow lunch in the Hotel, we met another sweet interpretress from previous visits, the wife of Azary,[22] who seemed to have faded out of her (and Slava's) life. Toya says: 'I did not like this man. He was always trying to arrange something.' What *can* that mean?

Lunching with us was our dear Djamal Dalghat, 1st conductor of Leningrad (Kirov) opera, furious that he had not known earlier of our visit (cf. Chulaki at the Bolshoi. Slava and Goskonzert seem to have kept our visit jealously guarded until the last possible moment!) He would of course have arranged a *Peter Grimes* for us. He has invited us to his house for tonight on the way to the station. After lunch, Ben needs sleep

---

[19] Britten's third (and final) church parable, *The Prodigal Son*, Op. 81, composed in 1968, and dedicated to Shostakovich. Britten wrote to William Plomer (librettist of *Curlew River* and *The Burning Fiery Furnace*, the previous two church parables) on his return from the USSR (6 January 1967): 'Does the idea of the prodigal Son attract you for a new Ch. Par. – inspired by a fabulous Rembrandt in the Hermitage?'

[20] Vladimir Frantzevich Levinson-Lessing (1893–1972), deputy director of the Hermitage. He compiled the first catalogue of the Hermitage's collection of paintings.

[21] Sir Philip Hendy (1900–1980), English art historian; director of the National Gallery, London, 1946–67.

[22] Azaryi Mikhailovich Plisetzkyi (b. 1937), who lived and worked in Cuba for many years.

and I want a little air. So Djamal and Toya take me out along the Nevsky Prospeckt, off past an animated Father Christmas in coloured lights to a bookshop where I try in vain to find some more Lermontov or Leskov in English translation, on to a music shop where enquiries for Tchiakovsky Songs (complete) lead to Djamal's buying two volumes for me (not the Gesamtausgabe, but a sort of Ur-text. Anyway, they will do.) Back in the Hotel, we finish packing and prepare to go across the road to the first half of the Philharmonic Concert with Rozhdestvensky[23] conducting. As one might have expected, the Mozart *Adagio and Fugue* [in C minor, K. 546] was unhappy – snail's pace *Adagio* – Contrabasses doubling the Cellos in the Fugue. Hindemith's Violin *Concertpiece* [*Kammermusik* No. 4] was much better, with very accomplished playing by Igor Oistrakh and skilful following by Rozh. We left after this, not before we had been warmly greeted by the Hornplayer and various officials as well as a chorus-member of the Peter Grimes cast. Back to the hotel to collect our baggage, and on in a car to Djamal Dalghat's flat. This was apologised for, as the decorators were in (they were indeed) but it was a nice-sized flat which house Djamal and his wife and her mother and their lovely daughter of 14 or so. Are all Russian girls so beautiful, and so exquisitely mannered as musicians' daughters? The old lady ('die alte Hexe' she calls herself and it *is* a nutcracker face but charming) and Mrs. Dj. stem from Armenia and have several ancestral portraits, striking and handsome, on the walls, as well as several by the painter we called on in Yerevan in '65, Maness Artissilian (?).[24] Djamal was born and brought up in Aza's republic, near the Caspian, but his father was Polish, hence his fine bones and that almost transparent skin on his forehead. We sit for a while in the living-room with Ben's photo in a place of pride, and many art-books (she is an art-historian, and a pupil of Prof. Levinson-Lessing) and get to know one another. A fellow-guest is the sister of Shostakovich, cheerful, chubby, warm – on top, at any rate, miles away from Dmitri. She talks French, Mrs. Dj. French and German, 'die alte Hexe' German, the little silver-birch of a daughter just looks and twinkles with beautiful eyes, too shy to air her few English words. We move to the dining-room, a table covered with varied foods and drinks, a Christmas tree dangerously alight, and spend the time until we have to go for our sleeper in happy hospitable friendliness with this sweet intelligent sensitive group who have gone to great pains to give us a memorable evening. We give them the records of Curlew River, Cantata Misericordium and Julian's and my Lute Songs, and we are loaded with Russian art-books. We hear a little of the difficulties of getting 'spiritual'

---

[23] Gennady Rozhdestvensky (b. 1931), Russian conductor. Between 1964 and 1970 he was principal conductor at the Bol'shoy. He took part in the 1963 BBC Television tribute to Britten celebrating the composer's fiftieth birthday.

[24] *Recte*: Minas Avetisjan (1928–1975), a fact confirmed by Dalghat's widow.

music performed, there seems to be a quota for the Radio, and of course Verdi's 4 Pezzi Sacri simply become 4 Choruses. He hopes to do Schubert's Masses soon. But the taxi is waiting for us, has been for an hour and we have to say Goodbye to Dmitri's sister and the ladies, and off we go with Toya and Djamal to the Moscow Station, where we bundle into our hot sleepers, surrounded with baggage. Passionate farewells, and even nice Professor Ilyitch to whom we brought a book from Belinda N B[25] has turned up to see us off. Very sad to leave Leningrad which is one of the most beautiful cities in the world. Slava and Galya meet us at the station in Moscow in their two-month old super Mercedes, and we glide silently via the flat, out to the Datchya, where we shall spend New Year and stay until we fly back to London on Monday.

*Sunday, January 1st*

Whatever anyone may say, it really *is* cold today, bright sun, dry (very) snow; we have walked each day, but today my legs were icy when I got home. There is a foot or two of snow, though none since we arrived, fog has gone and at night the moon is bright. It *must* be −20°C.

Last night was, as expected, a great occasion and many preparations were made. The idea was that we had the first course (hors d'oeuvre etc.) chez Dmitri, the next, hot, at Slava's, and the sweets at Dmitri's opposite neighbour's, Professor D. whose speciality 'ist mit Kochende Wasser zu tun' (Slava's description of an atomic scientist). The Prof. has a friendly capable wife, a pretty French-speaking daughter and perhaps a sister, anonymous.

We were summoned for 10 pm at Dmitri's, we were of course late. The surprise was a special showing of an ancient copy of *The Gold Rush* upstairs in someone's bedroom. (It is the most wonderful film and full of superb sophisticated photography – don't forget the Chaplin-into-Hen sequence). We had a quick nip of vodka before, and the film lasted exactly the right length of time (until 11.50) when with champagne bottles in hand we went out to the brightly lit Christmas Tree and toasted the New Year to the Soviet National Anthem, and went round kissing one another, the Shostakoviches, the Professor and his family, Dmitri's daughter Galya and her very odd beatnik husband, and us. Next came a meal round a long table groaning with drink and eats, and presents (indoors, needless to say). We each got some cognac or vodka, a false nose (not expected to be worn for more than a minute or two) and, later, a score of Dmitri's recent *Stepan Razin* (Yevtushenko) for

---

[25] Belinda Norman Butler, a friend of Pears's.

Ben, and a record of same for me.[26] At this point Dmitri, tired, and with a recent heart attack in mind, was packed off to bed, and we came back to 'ours', where Galya, Ben and Slava made a little music while our meal was being prepared. Boiled Soodak (fish) with an egg-sauce, simple and suitable. And then (2 am) we went over to the Prof's for tea and sweet things – jolly good, too. There was a rather amusing contrast between the houses and their owners: (i) Dmitri and the sweet, very gifted, tactful Irene, with a house varying from too much clutter to apparent discomfort. She is in her 20's, he just 60, twice a widower: his children are older than she, I fancy. (ii) Slava and Galya with tremendously expensive gadgets, chandeliers from Venice, four or five American fridges, which don't work, cupboards full of hair-dryers and electric toasters. (iii) The Prof. who is obviously a V.I.P. living like an Edwardian bourgeois with nice Persian rugs, discreet and well arranged lampshades, small dark pictures, a small grand piano. Madame Prof. is Ukrainian, and specialises in rich Ukrainian cakes. At about 3.30 am we called it a day and went back through the crisp night, snow-white to bed. Not a sound before 9.30 am, then creaks, whispers, and slow emergences towards the bathroom, followed by tea, or breakfast (untouched) upstairs at 11 or so. News came that Dmitri expected us for lunch at 2. We insisted on a walk, sunny, but very cold, among other reasons for the sake of endearing dog Jove ЖоФ, pronounced Dgoff, a young highly intelligent Alsatian, who is tied up outside even in this snow (he has a cosy little Datchya) because indoors he is too big and incontinent. He adores these walks and loves everyone except Dmitri Shostakovich's beatnik son-in-law who, by the way, is not so cretinous as he looks, speaks reasonable slow English and loves 'drizzle'. D.S. loves the winter and hates the summer – too many mosquitoes. (Remember this!) For lunch chez D.S. we had (as on our previous post-Armenian visit) exactly the same menu as the night before, and in due course tramped home to sleep, summoned to meet again at 7 pm at the Prof's for 'some tea and a little eat'. We couldn't reach the Prof's before 8.15, to find D.S. and daughter Galya + Prof. + Frau Prof. playing a card-game called KEENK (?King), a rather dull subversion, with variants, of whist. In the other half of the parlour, television was intruding senselessly, for the sole benefit of a non-speaking Chekhov character, (an aunt of Mrs. Prof.'s cousin?) who stared non-stop at it and to whom we were never introduced. After two hours (?) of KEENK, watched with growing impatience by Ben (he was horrified to see D.S.

---

[26] *The Execution of Stepan Razin*, Op. 119 (1964), cantata for bass, chorus and orchestra. The study score, with an inscription by Shostakovich dated 1 January 1967, and the recording of the cantata, with an inscription to Pears from Shostakovich on the sleeve, survive at the Britten–Pears Library (2-9401243; 3-9204682).

part with 12 roubles to the Prof,) the hint was taken and we sat down to tea, cognac, wine, brawn, ham and Ukrainian cakes. D.S. rather soon disappeared; we sat on and finally got away at 10, and in furious despair Ben called for *Winterreise*. I saw what he meant, and it was a very good cleanser for the palate and the mind; we sang the first half straight through to our dear Galya, Aza and Slava. This was as much as I could manage, without practice and with a furious tummy-ache, and in spite of Ben's sulks, refused the second half. Anyway, G. had to sing Tatiana in *Onegin* the next night, and must have some sleep. So we consulted about the morning, and agreed to breakfast at 9 and drive into Moscow at 9.30.

*Monday*

Not a sound, not a creak, nothing before 9.15 when Ben and I took our cold baths (no hot water in Datchya), a source of wonder to all. Then slowly – life. Finally we left for Moscow and shopping (our day of departure) at about 10.20. Goodbye hand shakes to Galina (cook) and kisses, hugs and embraces to Nastya, the old apple-faced, button-eyed Nana, typical Russian since time began, dressed in layers of multi-coloured aprons, felt boots, and scarfs on head; farewell pawing from Жоф and hysterical jumpings from Joy, Galya's miniature poodle, sweet kissings from Olga and Helena, beauties who will set young men's hearts fluttering soon (already set two middle-aged Englishmen's hearts melting) – Off up the icy snow – safe to the flat – Then out to the music-shop where we collect several volumes of the Tchaikovsky Edition[27] already ordered by Slava (he is ordering the rest to be sent – so blow Musica Rara!). Before this, on the way to the flat, we had looked in, at Slava's (and Irena Sh's) suggestion, at the final rehearsal of Dmitri's 13th Symphony, the one to texts by Yevtushenko (including Baby Yar – the passionate anti-antisemitic poem). The performance is tonight, Kondrashin and the Moscow Phil. Owing to our late start, we could only hear some of the last movement, to a text (Baritone Solo and Bass Chorus – 60 of them) which contrasts Galileo with a colleague who also knew the earth was round but, on account of his large family, did not allow himself to say so. 'Give me a career like Pasteur, Galileo or Tolstoi (Chorus: which Tolstoi? Solo: Leo!)' (There was a ghastly career-Soviet-novelist Alexei Tolstoi). It ended very simply, very beautifully, strings, solo string, a bell – really the work of a master – how we wish we could have heard it all. We leave the Hall for Slava's, Dmitri and Irena to come later at 4 pm to say Goodbye before we go. Lunch is to be at 1 pm and we are to shop again later. Our lunch guests are to be

---

[27]   The edition survives at the Britten–Pears Library. See also n. 10, p. 102.

(at Slava's special urgent suggestion) Tichon Khrennikov[28] and wife. This man has to our certain knowledge been the arch-enemy of liberal artistic musical thought. For 20 years, he has been President of the Union of Soviet Composers, and when we get home we must read again Alexander Werth's 'Musical Uproar in Moscow'[29] to see just how foul the things were which he said about Dmitri Sh. and Prokofiev (not to mention Ben). We have met him several times. This Gruyère-faced man is immensely dislikeable. Why then should Slava insist on us meeting him? It is too, ominously, the first time that he has ever stepped into Slava's flat. What is it all about?

1 o'clock came; Slava disappeared, Galya was asleep in her room (before Onegin). We waited: vodka: silence: more vodka: more silence. 2 pm enter Slava, from where? more vodka. Finally, Aza comes, bringing lunch with her, and we start without waiting for Khrennikov. (The marvellous Georgian chicken crushed in garlic and butter). Arrival of K. and Mrs. K. Couldn't be more affable. Much talk of avant-garde and K. expresses delight at something which Ben is reported to have said in his interview in Moscow the other day, 'especially good for the young if it comes from outside Russia'. Impossible to make out exactly what they printed, but immediate worry is perceptible that they have mis-quoted Ben. However, all goes affably and serenely enough, until, over coffee and/or tea at 3.30, the arrival of Dmitri and Irena. We have always understood that Khrennikov was loathed by Dmitri (why not?) and we felt very guilty and awkward to have these two in the same room. All Ben could do, in the few minutes that Dmitri allowed himself to stay, was to express his great admiration for the piece we had heard this morning (which at its first performance a year or two ago was slaughtered by the political critics). Then the light went out with D. and Irena, and we just passed the time until at 4 we were due to start to go, and the K.'s with much pleasantry (she is, I think, agreeable) took themselves off. The only explanation we can think up of Slava's sudden friendship for Khrennikov lies in the International Concert World. Slava plays K.'s cello concerto[30] (admittedly a rotten piece) abroad; he plays

---

[28] Tikhon Nikolayevich Khrennikov (b. 1913), Russian composer, who from the 1930s was an active spokesman for the younger generation of composers aiming at implementing socialist realism in music. He played a prominent role during the 1948 musico-politico purge which led to the condemnation of Shebalin, Prokofiev and Shostakovich, following which he emerged as the leader of the Soviet Composers' Union.

[29] Alexander Werth's Musical Uproar in Moscow (London: Turnstile Press, 1949) includes an account of the Conference of Musicians at the Central Committee of the All-Union Communist Party held in Moscow, in January 1948, at which Prokofiev and Shostakovich were both denounced.

[30] Khrennikov's Op. 16, composed in 1964.

Jolivet's concerto[31] in Moscow (he hates it); Jolivet is on very good terms with K., and conducts his work in Paris. But where does it lead? Slava says K. has done good work as Union Chairman, and there are much worse. True? We can't tell. Is Slava trying to be peace-maker? Can K.'s friendship matter to him? More musical-chairs? Not attractive but perhaps necessary? We are still in the dark, as we drove off along the glassy roads to the airport (much sliding and skidding – 'Ice-Revue', Slava calls it) and arrive nicely in time to check in our baggage with the very friendly officials – passport and customs – all smiles and 'Happy New Year's' – a few final purchases with foreign currency (we have left our roubles with Toya to put into our Bank Accounts) and out we go in the icy cold Airport Bus along with Slava and Toya right to the steps of the Comet. Warm goodbyes to Toya who has been marvellous and to Slava dearest of hosts and friends, and so to half-hour's wait owing to trouble with de-icing machine before we take off home.

*******

Rosamund Strode[32] gave me this book for Christmas, suggesting that I write another Diary in it. One should always take Rosamund's suggestions seriously (you may get into trouble if you don't) so I decided I would write a diary – and I have – and THIS IS IT!

---

[31] André Jolivet (1905–1974), French composer, whose two cello concertos were composed in 1962 and 1964.
[32] English musician§ (b. 1927), Britten's music assistant, 1964–76.

152

# 7   Nevis Fortnight (January 1967)

Less than a week after returning from their visit to the Soviet Union (see Chapter 6), Britten and Pears set out from London once again, on this occasion for the tiny island of Nevis, one of the Leeward Islands in the Caribbean, where they arrived on 8 January; they remained there until the return journey on the 22nd. While their time in Moscow and Leningrad had included professional engagements and other commitments, their stay on Nevis was happily free of any such duties: 'our first real holiday for ages', was how Britten described the trip to William Plomer (letter of 6 January 1967).

The manuscript of *Nevis Fortnight* is at the Britten–Pears Library (1-9400534). The diary remained unpublished in Pears's lifetime and, with the exception of some brief extracts included in CHPP (pp. 226–7), its inclusion in the present volume marks its first publication.

January '67

Ben & I had originally planned to go to Venice for six weeks this month, for work, primarily, at least from his point of view.[1] But he felt so badly in need of a real holiday, and rumours of Venetian flood-destruction were so depressing, that we were impelled towards a warm sun rather than cold fog, however beautiful and *Kunst-reich*! We find ourselves as a result on a small West Indian island, called Nevis, one of the lesser Antilles, on the curve of the crescent which starts from the N.E. corner of S. America and which points to Haiti, Jamaica & Cuba. A couple of Jet-hops (Bermuda Antigua) and we were here, but as Nevis possesses only a minimal air-strip one flies from Antigua in a little private 4-seater, a Piper Aztec. We spent a night at the Sugar Mill Inn in Antigua, not far from the Air-port, where 82°F seemed boiling after London's raw sleet. Next morning we were met out of the 4-seater as it bumped to a halt on Nevis at the STOP sign (we might have hit a donkey if we had not obeyed) by Isador Caplan's[2] good friends Bob & Flo Abrahams, who bought a derelict sugar-mill on Nevis seven years ago and have made a lovely place of it. They drove us up to it over monstrously bumpy roads, past groves of coconut close to miles of sandy shores and Kingfisher blue seas.

Nevis is one of the smallest of these islands. It is about a third of the size of the Isle of Wight, volcanic in origin like all these islands (there are still occasional tremors) discovered by Columbus, and colonised by the British in 1620 or so. By the end of the 17th century, it was already prosperous as a sugar-island, worked by slave labour, and remained so more or less until the abolition of slavery in the 1830s, by which time the sugar trade had slumped. It is now populated by nearly 12,000 coloured inhabitants and a few British. Good jobs are very few and there is an exodus to London. Its chief claim to historical fame is that Nelson when Captain of the Beaver met and married a Nevis lady here. The banns were read in Fig Tree Village Church down the hill, and the wedding feast took place in Montpellier House, a hundred yards away.

---

[1]   Britten and Pears had visited Venice on many occasions since their first stay in 1948. It was one of the few places, other than at home in Aldeburgh, where Britten was able to compose: for example, in the winter of 1964, much of *Curlew River* was written there, and four years later, in 1968, he returned to work on *The Prodigal Son*. For both men, it was the city's remarkable artistic and architectural treasures that drew them back time and time again.

[2]   Isador Caplan (1912–1995), Britten's and Pears's solicitor from the mid-1940s. An executor of both Britten's and Pears's estates, he was a senior Trustee of the Britten–Pears Foundation. He also acted as a legal adviser to the Aldeburgh Festival and the English Opera Group.

The Abrahams live in three buildings which were ruinous. The sugar mill, made of good local volcanic stone, cone-shaped on three diminishing stories; a store house with good stone steps which they turned into a kitchen and, over it, a dining room-cum-Nelson-museum; and a newly built bungalow (one long room with attachments). Before lunch, while we were sitting quietly acclimatising ourselves, some visitors came to see our hosts. Mr. Hunkins was the builder of the place, and Bob pointed out the excellence of his masonry, while Mr. H's black son stood listening in the elegant natural pose they all fall into so easily. Then came Mr. Byron, lawyer, brother of the Warden of Nevis, first native governor, intelligent, with a most beautiful speaking voice. There seems to be some sort of common ownership of land here, every native is entitled to a plot; and foreigners are not allowed to buy more than an acre each, though some of the old estates must still exist, I think. After a very pleasant lunch, cooked by Hyacinth and served by Wrenford, we were driven up to our hotel and said Farewell to the Abrahams who fly back to Philadelphia tomorrow. They are very much at home here; he has written a charming children's story about Nevis; their Nelson museum was shewn to the Queen on her visit last year, and he stopped the old Nelsonian grandfather clock at the moment when she signed her name in the visitor's book & he hasn't wound it up since.

Our hotel is a new one, (the gardens are still being weeded and planted by little blackamoors) sited high up the island on the corner of a hill overlooking folds of valleys falling to the sea, and behind us the Mountain (3500ft) frequently crowned with a cloud. The guests live in chalets-bungalows (2 under one roof) each having a large double bed-room, a lav-shower room, and a balcony with this glorious wide panorama of sea, with St. Kitts a little way off, larger than Nevis, and, beyond, St. Eustatius, then Eastward sometimes visible Montserrat. The hills down to the sea are spotted with coconut trees and hedges of various shrubs, some gloriously flowering frangipani and flamboyant trees, some bougainvilla and poinsettia. Cattle graze on the brown-ish hillside, very handsome mild philosophic creatures, pupils or relations of the Indian water-buffaloes quite secure that noone will illtreat them. The voice of the donkey is heard all over the island at all hours day & night; they are the prime method of transport but they do not appear so grossly overloaded as in Greece. Black legs dangle beside the twinkling feet, but not more than 2 pairs at a time usually. Flocks of sheep & goats can be met everywhere too, they all look alike to us for the most part, and I can't see why the *Dies Irae* should be so dogmatic about them (With the sheep, Lord, deign to mate me / From the he-goats separate me.)[3]

There are few things I enjoy more than sitting in the sun watching a lively landscape, particularly if it is populated from time to time. There are plenty of clouds round Nevis, the sea is always changing, and up here there is always a breeze, sometimes a strong wind. It is seldom quite quiet. The temperature throughout the year varies from 70° to 90° in the shade, very seldom more or less; at the moment it hovers around 80°, very agreeable indeed. Our room is looked after by a ravishingly pretty girl who carries herself divinely and has a beautiful slim figure, dressed in a simple blue striped frock matched with a cap tied on to her head. She does our room very thoroughly, and very quietly, and gives us an occasional smile. (Do these people ever need a dentist? Dazzling!) English is the language of Nevis, but an English which is very hard to catch. When they talk to one another, you can't understand a word. For us, they slow down and talk "scientific" but it is very obscure still.

There are 2 or 3 mainroads on the island which are asphalted and in fair condition, but off these the roads can be indescribable and only negotiable by Land-Rover or the donkey. The road up to the hotel turns off the mainroad to Gingerland into a series of rockeries, gullies, chasms, for half a mile until the spot where the hotel put down two concrete strips. We had arranged for a car to be at our disposal during our stay; one drive up was enough to discourage us, and a couple more sent us to the office to cancel the arrangement. So the Land-Rover driven by St. Clair takes us down to the beach twice a day & brings us back when we like. The beach is a great golden stretch of sand which runs in gentle curves for several miles between bright blue seas on the one hand and coconut palms on the other. There are also trees which bear deadly poisonous little apples; we are chased away even from its shade. One finds almond trees, & cotton bushes. Cotton is cultivated fairly widely on the island. Such a pretty flower, yellow or reddish, turning into a solid green fruit which splits open and displays the white cotton. They are picking some of it now.

(As I write, there is a lizard up on the edge of the wall, about a foot long or more, a brilliant green body, with a grey scaly tail, and his throat & underparts bright yellow which he blows out like a balloon. Why?)

The hotel, being very new, is nearly all ours. In the dining room and three lounges, the ping pong room with radio for the BBC news, round the swimming pool, under the old ruined Sugar-mill, we have it nearly all to ourselves. An ex-Hungarian and his ex-Irish wife from the Dept. of Agriculture at Ottawa, a Trio from Washington (professed admirers

---

3    The lines 'Inter oves locum praesta, / Et ab haedis me sequestra', which Pears quotes in an appalling English singing translation.

of Sir Benjamin) later an English couple, and a non-stop talking journalist lady of the Sunday Times, now, briefly a pair of alcoholics from up-state New York, these are all where there might be 32. I can imagine that in 2 or 3 years, it will be full up. We like it so well that we are proposing to stay on longer.

*Later* Alas! we can't get any later flights back when we want them. So we have to come back at the end of our original fortnight, only staying the extra two days here which were planned for hotter, more populated, Antigua.

Yesterday we were invited to cocktails at Government House by the Warden[4] & his British Honduran wife, both friends of Isador and delightful hosts. Our fellow guests include the victorious "Miss Nevis 1966" and her four or five runners-up. She was certainly a stunner, and we all thought the judges decision was dead right. Creamy milk-chocolate colour, she had flashing teeth and eyes which disappeared when she smiled, a lovely figure and she was wearing a closefitting red dress, just her shade. The other competitors were tending to wear shiny pink or lime silks with bows in their hair, the Sunday costume much seen on the island. "Miss Nevis" works in the Charlestown printing works. Her prizes were legion, ranging from a trip to Porto Rico & Rubinstein beauty packs to frying pans, a bed & a tin of Carnation milk, all from local firms.

After enquiry and discussion about the new National Hymn (there has been hot controversy between the local left and right press) the Warden took up his guitar and accompanied himself in a performance of it (he has a sweet voice). The 3 islands of St. Kitts, Nevis & Anguilla will become an independent group (in association with the Commonwealth) next month, and they are going to have a week of festivities, after which they hope for (but do not really expect) great developments. The general feeling is that it would have been much better if all the smaller islands had co-operated to make a confederation. As it is, Montserrat will be on its own, so will Antigua, and even Barbuda, which is, I think, largely in habited by turtles, and they will all have their national songs. The controversy on the St. K–Nevis–Anguilla anthem hinges on the word "great" in the line "peaceful, great and free". Peaceful, yes! free, certainly, but can they be called really "great"? Labour thinks so; the "Democrat" is more doubtful.[5]

---

4   Roland Spencer Byron (b. 1914), Civil Servant and Warden of Nevis 1963–9, the first Nevisian to hold the post.
5   A reference to the island's newspapers (of opposing political views), *The Democrat* and the *Labour Spokesman*.

Also at the party was a sad old clergyman from West Suffolk, guest of the Warden, & rector of Hengrave and other parishes; sad because recently widowered. There was also the head of the local chamber of commerce and one or two more, including the niece of the Warden (who cashed a cheque for Ben in the Bank this morning, – pretty flashing smile). We sat around in a circle in his large-ish drawing-room while the Warden & his wife plyed us with Rum and Ginger Ale, and prunes stuffed with peanuts & such.

*PERSONALITIES*
Our hotelier-host, ruddy faced Mr. Doyle, with a spreading moustache and large, rather bloodshot, kindly eyes was 17 years a Government Agricultural Employee in Kenya, which he & his efficient wife loved. I think this is their first shot at keeping a hotel; it runs perfectly well, if as yet without genius, and they take endless trouble to make one easy. All the other establishments on the Island (or nearly all, say 5) are American-run; we are British! Mrs. Doyle is very worried as to what will happen when Independence occurs next month:[6] the Whites will have to tread very carefully or they will be told to go. I don't believe it; the White Tourism is the only prosperous future for this island, where the casual character of the people disrupts any organisation which could use cooperation to make a go of the agriculture (cattle, cotton, sugar, coconuts). Already Nevis sees the Americans flocking to the other islands, St. Thomas, St. Croix, St. Lucia, etc. & bringing dollars: they'll come here too in time, I'm sure. But as yet it is divinely unspoilt.

The Doyles have a 17-year-old son, who, after Kenya, preferred to continue his schooling in a mixed Secondary School here than go to a public school in England. A nice chap who may study agriculture later.

The Staff here consists of quantities of local boys, ranging in colour from the "clear" as they call it to the midnight jet. They are enthusiastic, clumsy and very endearing, with grand names like Wendell Hamilton, Hugh Pemberton, Austin and Bernard. Little gardeners squat and weed, or kneel and pat. Cutlasses are used to trim the edges of the grass: we keep well out of range.

Miss Eva Wilkin is the local artist; she lives in a sugar mill which only ceased work in 1940, open to as many breezes as our hotel, with an invalid brother. We went and had a drink with her. She is a nice old bird and does some quite nice portraits of the local children, also flower pieces. In the last 2 years she has been quite successful with the American tourists. She gave us a couple of offset-prints of her drawings

---

[6]  On 27 February 1967 St Kitts–Nevis–Anguilla became an Associated State of the United Kingdom. Three months later Anguilla seceded, leaving St Kitts and Nevis as one fully self-governing state in every respect except for defence and external affairs. Full independence came in 1983.

– not wonderful but nice to have. The Anglican parson looked in for a few minutes – nice young Midlander who has been serving in the West Indies for 12 years – he is having trouble with the new organ for his Church & we offered to help when we get back. But I don't think we can do very much to hustle up a one-man firm of organ-makers near Burton-on-Trent, really!

The lady journalist who writes travel-stuff for the Sunday Times is renowned for horror all over the Caribbean. She was furious that she was not invited here "for free", criticised the climate, the island, the lack of cereal for breakfast, the size of the whiskies. For three days she could be heard talking her well-informed nonsense in a Badminton voice all over the hotel without drawing breath. Ben, particularly, was unapproachably prickly and vanished instantly on her appearance. I tried to be a little more polite and only succeeded in being silly and awkward. We all sighed with relief when she went.

The alcoholic Americans owed their wealth to Dairy Produce in New York State. She is always being turned out of hotels. Amiable but hopelessly confused, she plumped herself down at our table. I fear I was rude, but she didn't take it amiss, and was happily steered over to their table by her husband. Dark thought: is he perhaps murdering her by encouraging her to "fill up" all the time? The hotel rumours screams from their chalet at night, and whisky in her coffee at 8 a.m.! They have gone now: we shall never know. The M.P. for part of Gloucestershire, with his wife, is here. Polite, civilised, they play the British Hotel-game perfectly, that is, we bow & smile & pass the weather, and talk over our drinks *across* the lounge but do not join the same table. Again at meals they sit alone, as we do, and converse in undertones, as we do, and as the couple from Ottawa do. How shattering it was for all of us, therefore, when Madame Sunday Times thrust herself on the M.P.s and talked Roedean so piercingly all dinner. We all froze and prickled at our separate tables.

The food is English-based, plenty of eggs & bacon, soups (v. good) at all main meals, joints mostly good, sweets *weak*. The exotic is provided by Paw-Paw, a near-marrow called Christophore (I think! what an odd derivation!) and the local langouste. A good red-headed fish called Snapper; also, slightly salmon-like, King-fish. When we bathe we see flying-fish (?) doing "ducks and drakes" all over the place; crabs scuttling in and out of the sea, or digging residences in the sand and peering at us over the top with periscope eyes on stalks. Small flocks of (?) sand-pipers, at the waves' edge, scurry up the beach as the foam pursues them, and at once run round and dash down to pick their food. Ahead, the beautiful small grey-blue heron stands longing to strike at the minnows; he seldom seems to achieve one. Overhead, we have terns galore, very clever & elegant; the sensational man o'war or frigate bird, large dark gull with white head and sharply zig-zagged wings and a very long sinister forked tail. He sails mostly high up. The comedian, whom we love, is the Booby, a heavy brown Pelican-typed with a great ladle of a bill, who flies low, mostly, and then heavily splashes for his fish. Some have a white top to their heads, others brown; they grin as they float on the waves.

Outside our chalet we have a friendly grey & white bird, who perches on a bare tree-let and catches flies; he has the long strong kingfisher beak and a dangerous dark eye-line; he seems to enjoy hovering into the wind, of which we get plenty up here. Of butterflies there are quite a lot particularly sulphurish yellows, and grey-brown transparent ones. Occasionally one sees sensational great reds and blacks but they refuse to settle and get carried away at once by the wind. The wind has been – one must admit – a little too much. "We have never had so much." Of course – we all talk like that to visitors.

*Later.* The slow-moving relaxed days seemed to go on for ever, with the cup of tea at 7 am, the dip in the bright blue pool before breakfast, the eager attentions of Wendell and his colleagues, the trundle down to the beach, the lazy hours on the sand under the coconut palms, the effort to absorb Russian and to solve Perfective and Imperfective Verbs, the rum and ginger at sun-down-and-into-the-sea, the sudden showers & gusts. But two weeks are only 12 days with travel and worrying. The last day arrived, and we drove to the air-strip and gave up our Visas. Sy Green flew us in his Sea-green Plane. But just before we took off, we were entertained for an hour by one of the "characters" of Nevis who bought a plantation 20 (?) years ago, & started it as a guest house. Part early nineteenth century, it is surrounded by a verandah; she, an ex-dancer originally from Malta, has found nice period furniture & has done it casually & charmingly with real taste & invention. Lively, vigorous and fearless in the face of coloured bureaucracy, she keeps her own little plane next door at the airstrip and whizzes off the Martinique or Guadeloupe for her shopping where she can get good Camemberts and French wine ad lib. Her clientèle consists largely of Washington civil servants, and they come back every year. She is not really worried at the thought of Independence. She is so determined and independent herself that it needs a bigger island than Nevis to squash her! It was a great pleasure to meet her, and a very pleasant farewell view-point from which to leave this adorable little island.

# 8 Moscow Diary (April 1971)

On 16 April 1971 Britten and Pears flew to Leningrad where they had been invited to participate in the 'Days of British Music Festival' taking place in Leningrad and Moscow. The day after their arrival they attended a concert given by the Leningrad Philharmonic Orchestra in Britten's honour, and on the 18th Britten conducted the London Symphony Orchestra (then touring the USSR) at a concert held in the Philharmonic Hall (see p. 162) which included music by Purcell (the Chacony in G minor and the Suite of Songs from *Orpheus Britannicus*, the latter with Pears as soloist), Holst's *Hammersmith*, and Britten's Piano Concerto (with Sviatoslav Richter as soloist) and Cello Symphony (with Rostropovich as soloist). This programme was repeated in the Large Hall of the Moscow Conservatory on the 20th before an audience which included, according to Eric Walter White, Shostakovich, the British defector Kim Philby and Mme Furtseva, the Soviet Minister of Culture.

It was during this trip that Britten presented Rostropovich with the Third Cello Suite, Op. 87, which had been completed at Rostropovich's Moscow flat at Aldeburgh in March. Britten played through his new Suite on the piano before a small invited audience at comprising Shostakovich and his wife, Pears, Sue Phipps and Elizabeth Wilson, daughter of the Russian ambassador, who accompanied them as chauffeur and interpreter (see Elizabeth Wilson, *Shostakovich: A Life Remembered* (London: Faber and Faber, 1994), pp. 406–7).

On the eve of their departure, Pears and Britten gave a private recital at the British Embassy before an invited audience that included many of the most influential figures in Moscow's musical and artistic life, including Shostakovich. The programme for this occasion comprised music by Haydn (three of the English canzonets), lieder by Schubert, and Britten's *Winter Words* and folksong arrangements. Britten and Pears returned to London on 25 April; this short trip proved to be their last visit to the USSR.

Pears's handwritten diary, inscribed into a small blue-covered 'Lion Brand' notebook, survives at the Britten–Pears Library (1-9100091). His account relates only one and half days of their final visit to Moscow, and its unfinished state precluded Pears from publishing it. Its inclusion in the present collection marks its first publication.

*Воскресенье, 18 апреля 1971 года*

5-й концерт ВТОРОГО абонемента

Д И Р И Ж Е Р

**Бенджамин**

# Б Р И Т Т Е Н

С О Л И С Т Ы:

# Питер П И Р С

Народный артист СССР, лауреат Ленинской премии

# Святослав Р И Х Т Е Р

Народный артист СССР, лауреат Ленинской премии

# Мстислав РОСТРОПОВИЧ

П Р О Г Р А М М А

I ОТДЕЛЕНИЕ

**П Ё Р С Е Л Л** (1659—1695)

Чакона соль минор (1680—1683)

Четыре песни из сборника „Британский Орфей"
в аранжировке Б. Бриттена и П. Пирса

Исп. П. П И Р С

**Б Р И Т Т Е Н** (род. в 1913 г.)

Концерт для фортепиано с оркестром ре мажор (1938)

1. Токката. Allegro molto e con brio
2. Вальс. Allegretto
3. Экспромт. Andante lento } *без перерыва*
4. Марш. Allegro moderato,
   sempre alla marcia

Исп. С. Р И Х Т Е Р

Leningrad, 18 April 1971. Programme for the London Symphony Orchestra's concert in the Philharmonic Hall, conducted by Britten, with soloists Peter Pears, Sviatoslav Richter and Mstislav Rostropovich.

*Thursday* [22 April] was the day we had decided to put aside for shopping, or at least part of it. So after breakfast we sallied forth with a helpful Embassy young man plus Russian battering rain and paid a call on our Bank, the [*space left for name*]. This was a different department from that where we had deposited money in '65 but very close to it and a great deal quicker, and after only a few signatures and a short work on the abacus from the solid lady behind the grill we emerged with 500 R's each. Further, on looking at my bankbook, the balance of my account was the same as when I went in, for 500 R's or thereabouts was the interest accrued over 5 years on my 1000 odd R's deposit. So I am helping to build a dam in Siberia, perhaps, or am I rather a bloody capitalist? From the bank, we drove, always in the Embassy Rolls Royce, to the Music shop, on the first floor in a block of Tsarist appearance. It was an old friend with its walls lined with shelves piled with volumes of all sorts and manned (and womanned) by willing but tired citizens, whose job is surely made more difficult by the time wasting rule which compels the customer to buy first from the cashier a ticket to the amount of his purchase *before* he approaches the counter. When you don't know what there is to buy (and also what you *want* to buy) in a crowded shop, confusion tends to result. They are also rather cagey about letting one browse – and rouble-laden music-lovers *must* browse. After a good hour, we managed to find two more volumes for our as yet incomplete Tchaikovsky Edition, and lots of Prokofiev and some Rimsky, as well as some Russian reprints of Ben's music. We have not yet found Imogen's book on Ben in Russian;[1] it may not be out yet. From the music shop to the newly built glass and concrete book shop, in search of postcards and art-books. Not very profitable except for children's books, which had some charming illustrations. Lots of handsome books about Russian murals, ikons, but not the particular ones we were after.

Back to the Embassy, for the official lunch, with the Minister of Culture as chief guest, her assistants etc, and on our side, the LSO chiefs and Previn[2] and the Waltons. Procedure was greatly delayed by the non-appearance of Slavas Rostropovich and Richter. Will the riddle ever be solved? Did or did they not ever receive their cards of invitation? They were sent with the rest to the Ministry, the usual thing, to be distributed thence. They were not, or *were* they? Phone invitations were also made,

---

[1] The Russian edition of Imogen Holst's *Britten* (The Great Composers) (London: Faber and Faber, 1966), translated by V. Ashkenazy, with a preface by Mikhail Chulaki (Moscow: Izdatel'stvo Muzyka, 1968).

[2] André Previn (b. 1929), American conductor, pianist and composer of German birth; principal conductor of the London Symphony Orchestra, 1969–79. Previn and the LSO were making a tour of the USSR, with William Walton and his wife, Susana, as their guests. See Susana Walton, *William Walton: Behind the Façade* (Oxford: Oxford University Press, 1988), pp. 205–9.

but. Diplomacy, umbrage, tact, obedience? Anyway, no Slavas, no Nina, no Galya.[3]

I had Stuart Knussen[4] on one side, which was a great pleasure, and Mr Lumkov, cultural attaché to [space left for name] on the other – excellent English and a nice fellow. Furtseva & Ben opposite. General, easy conversation, and good speeches from host and guest.

After guests had gone, Sue & I went for a walk round the block (the Kremlin), and then I set about to do some practice while Ben went to visit Mark Lubotsky,[5] the violinist. He came back later much later having been filled with tea cakes and more spirituous stimulants, & we then went off – all of us – to visit the flat of a Greek who works in the Canadian embassy & who has a magnificent collection of the Russian artists of the first half of the century. A friend of Chagall, his walls were covered with Kandinskys, Kloons, Popovas, Tatlins, Maleviches, and other quite new names, some very good (Popova) others not so much to my taste. His pictures have been bought since the war for quite small sums and are now worth a lot. He had just given a Van Dougen to the Pushkin [Fine Art] Museum, but had refused to sell a fine early Kandinsky, as the director was proposing to put [it] in the cellar along with the other "forbidden" artists like Kandinsky. Our host preferred to keep it on his own wall. We were plied with Easter cake and pastachi? – creamy cheese, confection with candied peel in it – delicious and not heavy.

Other artists whose work we saw included Drevin and Udaltsova, one very fine landscape individual & original from 1913 of Yakuloff – and a fantastic surrealist mélange by Shibnoff.

Before we left our very kind host gave both Ben & myself a drawing early and unforced by Popova.[6] Ben was also presented by a painter with a portrait of Purcell[7] – mannered, clear, neat but not very much more.

---

[3]  Susana Walton recollects in *William Walton: Behind the Façade*, p. 208, the difficulties Rostropovich faced at this time because of his support of the writer Alexander Solzhenitsyn in open defiance of the Soviet authorities:

> Rostropovich came to the door of the hotel dining-room to say hello to the orchestra, but was not permitted to join us. Nor was he allowed to come to a lunch party in Moscow given by the British Embassy. Ben and William made an enormous fuss, and Rostropovich was finally allowed to appear, with his wife Galina Vishnevskaya, at an evening reception [held on 20 April] offered by the British Embassy for the whole orchestra.

[4]  English double-bass player (1923–1990), principal double-bass with the LSO, 1958–72. Knussen played in the première of *Curlew River* (1964). His son, Oliver Knussen, is the distinguished composer and conductor who has been an artistic director of the Aldeburgh Festival since 1984.

[5]  Russian violinist (b. 1931) with whom Britten had performed and recorded his Violin Concerto, Op. 15, with the English Chamber Orchestra in 1970.

[6]  At the Britten–Pears Library.

[7]  O. Kondaouvrov's lithographed portrait of Purcell is at the Britten–Pears Library.

Expecting Slava & Galya to appear we stayed late, only to have a message by telephone that they were already at the Embassy – and had been for a long time. We dashed off but by the time we all reached the Embassy, they were gone. This was very sad, but muddles are part of Moscow & nothing could be done. Ben rang Slava at the datchya & he quite understood but wanted an early bed on account of War & Peace the next day.[8]

*Friday* [23 April] morning was a highlight in our visit. We were invited to Dmitri's flat for a rehearsal performance in private by the Beethoven 4tet[9] of D's latest string 4tet No.13.[10] We gathered in Slava's flat & then walked across to D's & the players arrived, two young and two old men. They had given one or two performances in public, but it is still recent. A magnificent piece in one movement of great intensity and touching beauty – sad, but noble, with an extraordinary use of the bow tapped on the wood of the instruments. At our request they played it a second time, and again we were deeply moved. There is a huge part for the viola, & it was worthily played. I think Dmitri was pleased and touched by our emotion. He has not so many listeners whom he can so wholeheartedly respect as Ben.

Back to the Embassy to collect Duncan & Betty,[11] & then to the Kremlin where we and others of the British Music Days were invited by the Ministry of Culture to a reception. This turned out to be a buffet affair with a couple of speeches & not really very much more.

---

[8] Britten and Pears attended a gala performance of Prokofiev's *War and Peace* at the Bol'shoy Theatre, conducted by Rostropovich, with Vishnevskaya in the role of Natasha. On a postcard to Rosamund Strode (24 April 1971), Pears wrote, 'We saw War & Peace last nite [*sic*]. Wow!'

[9] The Beethoven String Quartet, founded as the Moscow Conservatory Quartet in 1923. From its inception, the Quartet was noted for its performances of contemporary music, especially that of Shostakovich.

[10] Shostakovich's Thirteenth String Quartet in B flat minor, Op. 138, was first performed in September 1970 in Leningrad by the Beethoven Quartet. It is dedicated to Vadim Vasilievich Borisovsky, the Quartet's viola-player. It may have been Britten's and Pears's response to this private performance that brought about the work's inclusion in the 1973 Aldeburgh Festival, when it was played by the Amadeus String Quartet.

[11] Sir Duncan Wilson (1911–1983), British Ambassador to the USSR, 1968–71, and his wife. A warm friendship was struck between the Wilsons and Britten and Pears at this time, and continued later when Wilson became Master of Corpus Christi College, Cambridge, 1971–80.

# 9   Saint Enoch (March 1972)

Pears's diary *Saint Enoch* focuses on his independent life as a concert singer without Britten, travelling to all parts of the UK to fulfil engagements. If nothing else, the diary shows unequivocally just how hard Pears was prepared to work at a time when most singers would be beginning to contemplate retirement from the concert platform: it was a pattern of life that was to continue until his forced retirement from singing in December 1980 at the age of seventy, after suffering a stroke. In the space of a little under a month (March 1972) he gave eight concerts, including three performances of Bach's *St John Passion* and one of the *St Matthew*, two of the most taxing works in his repertory. A second *St Matthew* was cancelled because of illness, and the singer's battle against throat inflammations of one kind or another becomes a further preoccupation of his text.

This diary first appeared with the subheading 'More Pages From a Diary' in the 1974 Aldeburgh Festival Programme Book as the second of a sequence of three diaries that Pears published in consecutive programme books. (*San Fortunato: From a diary* was the first, in 1973 (see Chapter 10); the last, *The New York Death in Venice*, appeared in 1975 (see Chapter 11).) Pears's original manuscript has not come to light.

167

It is Maundy Thursday, 1972. Tomorrow I must sing the *St John Passion* at the Maltings – or not?

It all started on the way to Cardiff, I think. Or perhaps as I left Cheltenham. There had been some snow there and the hills looked beautiful. The concert had gone very well;[1] it was a good little string-band with Alan Civil[2] playing the horn, and Laurence Hudson had been helpful and sympathetic and hospitable. But on the way to Cardiff there was snow and sleet and cold wet wind. I crossed the Severn and passed the time driving through the Forest of Dean, very leafy and strong. Alun[3] had drawn a sort of map, but I got lost and had to get out into the cold wind several times. Was that where it began? I knew I should be well looked after by Alun and Rhiannon – no trouble there – their *cuisine* is *haute*, all right. At the rehearsal, *On Wenlock Edge* went quite well, and the Bach.[4] No trouble with the voice – really; it always takes a little time after a long drive and a good meal. But next morning, something was wrong: the scales wouldn't run, I couldn't put any weight on the voice above E or F. I could probably manage the Bach, but I would never be able to do 'Yes, lad! I lie easy.' Lie easy, indeed! He lay very awkward.

So I had to go and see a doctor, the most helpful man you can imagine. Still I had to change the programme and apologize.[5] The press said 'No one noticed a thing', which was both comforting and insulting. I drove back to London next morning, with a wonderful present from Alun. He is a real Father Christmas of a man, and Rhiannon is just beautiful: she could start a Trojan War. The new motorway to London is straight, and I drove the [Citroën] Safari fast all the way to the Marylebone fly-over, when she coughed, deeply, just like our dog Gilda does, and stopped. I thought she was going to throw up the engine.

---

[1] Pears had driven to Cheltenham on 3 March to give a performance of Britten's *Serenade*, Op. 31, for tenor, horn and strings, with the Cheltenham Chamber Orchestra, conducted by Laurence Hudson.

[2] English horn-player (1929–1989) who worked as an orchestral player (he was principal horn with the BBC Symphony Orchestra from 1966) as well as appearing with various chamber ensembles and as a soloist.

[3] Alun Hoddinott (b. 1929), Welsh composer and teacher; Professor of Music at University College, Cardiff, 1967–87, and artistic director of the Cardiff Festival of 20th-century Music which he founded in 1967. It was at the 1971 Cardiff Festival that Pears and Britten had given the first (incomplete) performance of Britten's song-cycle *Who are these children?*, Op. 84 (words by William Soutar).

[4] Pears had been engaged to participate in the opening concert of the Cardiff Festival of 20th-century Music, performing Vaughan Williams's Housman cycle, *On Wenlock Edge,* for tenor and piano quintet (a work Pears and Britten recorded in the 1940s for Decca), Bach's Cantata 189: *Meine Seele rühmt und preist,* and miscellaneous arias by Bach.

[5] Instead of *On Wenlock Edge*, Pears sang (unaccompanied) two English carols, Pérotin's 'Beata viscera', and 'I wonder as I wander'.

Somehow she started again – and stopped and started again – all the way back to Halliford Street.[6] For two days the car stayed outside waiting to be collected. Meanwhile I rang up Harley Street for an appointment without delay.

Harley Street is vigorous, not to say rough; he sits one down, takes one between his knees, pulls one's tongue out, wraps it in lint, swishes an iodine mop round one's soft palate, clears his throat and heats up a mirror in a naked flame. A quick look up the nose, a shake of the head, and two small ram-rods soaked in antiseptic are pushed far up one's nostrils into one's brain and left there for ten minutes. Then one's left ear is hauled forward into better vision – and now the right ear – each being strongly riddled with a sort of rake, like the one our Miss Hudson[7] takes to the Esse. Ten minutes in front of a hot lamp, five minutes inhaling powdered menthol, and 'Ring me next week and tell me how you feel. The cords are slightly red – nothing much.' Indeed!

The next day [9 March] was the train journey north for two *St John Passions*, in Newcastle and Middlesbrough, with the Northern Sinfonia.[8] It was a medium-cold day, not very cold really, but of course up North, you know, there are several degrees difference in latitude and the East Coast is always blustery, so perhaps I'll wear that fifteen-year-old herringbone tweed suit which is very comfortable and smart and which I am rather proud to be able to get into still. It is heavy, of course, but never mind.

I had a first-class reserved seat in an Inter-City Express, a new coach. I got there in good time to buy something to read, found my carriage and sat down. Automatically Controlled Heating. It was icy, much colder than outside. I kept everything I had on on, wrapping my scarf over my mouth, taking no part in acid complaints from fellow-passengers. My herringbone was going to be a godsend. At Peterborough I removed my scarf and overcoat, at Newark my jacket, and by Selby I was alone and plotted taking my trousers off and covering my thighs with my overcoat. The heat was stifling, and I had only brought

---

6   8 Halliford Street, Britten's and Pears's London home from 1970 which they shared with Pears's niece, Sue Phipps and her family (see PFL, Plate 169). Britten and Pears had their own studio annexe at the house (see PFL, Plate 168). Mrs Phipps was their agent from 1958, at first at Ibbs & Tillett and then independently from 1965.

7   Elizabeth (Nellie) Hudson (1898–1982), Britten's and Pears's Aldeburgh housekeeper. A portrait of her by Mary Potter is reproduced in PFL, Plate 230.

8   Pears sang the Evangelist in two performances of Bach's *St John Passion*: in Newcastle City Hall on 10 March, and in Middlesborough Town Hall on the 11th, for which the Northern Sinfonia, conducted by Rudolf Schwarz, was joined by the Newcastle Festival Chorus; Robert Lloyd sang Christus, and the other soloists were Sheila Armstrong (soprano), Meriel Dickinson (mezzo-soprano), Gerald English (tenor) and Stafford Dean (bass).

169

sandwiches (very good) but no drink at all. I was still alive when we were reaching Newcastle, and there I was expertly met and looked after. The rehearsal was in the Town Hall, which was being redecorated, and the backstage smelt piercingly of distemper, paint and wallpaper. My pharynx began to burn. A complete sing-through was scheduled for that evening. I 'marked' the Evangelist, shamefacedly, and was very ready for bed by 9.30 pm. I was at the Turk's Head, under the roof in what must originally have been a tweenie's bedroom, into which had been squeezed a bath and loo with a ventilator which went on with the light. It was a dog-leg attic and I slept around the corner under the sloping roof.

The *St John* day was dicey as far as I was concerned, but it passed, it was all right, it was not my best, the acoustic there is unfriendly, I had given an interview in the afternoon and had said I wasn't feeling too good (very foolish to do this!) and I didn't see the press, and I couldn't care less, but perhaps he again comforted and insulted me by saying one would never know.

The drive to Middlesbrough is through some fine rolling hills and past some fine stinking mills. ICI TEESSIDE welcomes you from a vast cylinder, reminding me of the story of Lady X in Paris. The smell of Teesside soon told us what the letters meant there. Middlesbrough Town Hall is sure the *most* Victorian Gothic building extant: solider than St Pancras, more daring than anything at Oxford, it looks unbudgeable. Enormously lofty inside, the stained beams fly up, and out of sight; it is lit by neon flares which hardly affect the chivalrous gloom. But the sound is clean and clear. Singing was much easier for us all, and the performance was notably better all round. There followed a drive back to Newcastle to pick up my bags, pay my bill and catch the 1.0 am sleeper to London. Five minutes from Newcastle, the attendant told me I was on the wrong train; I was. I had not been directed to my train which came from Aberdeen; this one came only from Edinburgh. But there was, of course, Berth No. 1 vacant (there always is) and I was welcome to that; Berth No. 1 is directly over the wheels in these coaches and repose is impossible, but I am a determined sleeper, and I probably got three hours that night.

There followed four days in the bracing East Anglian air (badly needed) to recover from these doubtful fortunes.[9] I could well have done with two more days off before the Bach Choir *St Matthew* at the Festival Hall.[10] However, I was not too dissatisfied with that, and the following

---

[9]   Pears returned to Aldeburgh (via London) on 12 March, travelling to London on the 17th in time for rehearsals on the 18th.

[10]   The annual Bach Choir performance of Bach's *St Matthew Passion* (sung in English), given at the Royal Festival Hall on 19 March 1972. Pears, as was customary, sang the role of the Evangelist (accompanied by Philip Ledger (harpsichord) and Terence Weil (cello continuo)); Christopher Keyte sang the

day (Monday) rehearsed with pleasure for the Schütz *St Matthew* on Tuesday at St Bartholomew's.[11] As I get older, I become more and more besotted with old Heinrich Sagittarius Schütz, and it is marvellous in this his four hundredth year to be going through most of his major works – Christmas, the Passions, Easter, and more singing them to an intent and eager audience.[12] On this occasion at St Bart's, I had an incomparable Christus[13] to sing with, also an excellent Pilate,[14] and it was a worthy performance all round, I think. I was reminded the next day, however, that I had sung for all of an hour with very little interruption on virtually five notes in the middle of the voice, had sung with all the intensity that I was capable of, and I was tired.

There was a day and a half left before the journey up to Edinburgh. Wednesday morning was a rehearsal with Herrick[15] and the Edinburgh Christus,[16] Wednesday afternoon was spent discussing with Lucie Manen[17] her new *Manual for Singing*, at Fabers, and later with Walter Todds[18] of BBC TV. Thursday morning I promised to give a lesson; there was Lucie again in the afternoon and then the 4 o'clock train to Edinburgh. This time the Inter-City Express had been used already that day, so it was nearly at boiling point before we started. I cursed myself

---

role of Christus, with Felicity Palmer (soprano), Marjorie Thomas (contralto), Robert Tear (tenor), John Carol Case (bass), and the Thames Chamber Orchestra conducted by David Willcocks.

[11] A performance given at St Bartholomew the Great, Smithfield, on 21 March by the Heinrich Schütz Choir conducted by Roger Norrington.

[12] Apart from this concert of Passion Music, Pears was the principal artist in four other concerts held in London during 1971–2, conceived by Roger Norrington as a tercentenary tribute to Schütz. Two recordings for Decca's Argo label sprang from this cycle of concerts, the *St Matthew Passion* and *The Resurrection*, both of which show Pears's extraordinary mastery of Schütz's recitative idiom. It was the style of these recitatives, in which Schütz defined the pitches involved but omitted their rhythmic profile, that influenced Britten when searching for an appropriate means of conveying Aschenbach's interior monologues in *Death in Venice*, Op. 88 (1972). See John Evans, 'On the recitatives of "Death in Venice"', in PPT, pp. 31–3.

[13] Sung by John Shirley-Quirk§ (b. 1931), English bass-baritone.

[14] Sung by the English baritone Brian Rayner Cook (b. 1945).

[15] Herrick Bunney, English conductor and organist; Organist and Master of the Music, St Giles's Cathedral, Edinburgh, from 1946; conductor of the Edinburgh University Singers, 1952–82. Pears had been engaged to sing the role of the Evangelist in a performance of Bach's *St Matthew Passion* on 26 March, to be given by the Edinburgh University Singers in the Reid Concert Hall under Bunney's direction.

[16] Rodney Macann (b. 1950), New Zealand baritone.

[17] Lucie Manén§ (1899–1991), German soprano and teacher of singing, to whom Pears turned in 1965 (at the age of 65) for singing lessons (see CHPP, pp. 192–3).

[18] Walter Todds (1920–1983), senior music producer for BBC Television, 1965–80.

for again wearing that much-too-heavy suit; one never needs heavy suits nowadays, it's foolish, dangerous to put them on, one sweats and catches chills, and their weight bows you down. I went to the dining-room and sat in a draught to cool off. From Waverley Station I walked to the hotel (one must have *some* exercise), up those Dantesque steps where the cyclone always rages, across St Andrew's Square, side-stepping the drunks, to the hotel, with its unforgettable memories of Slava Rostropovich eating handfuls of pills in bed after a heart attack, just to show what he thought of doctors. There is a new wing now and I was almost the first to sleep in my room, a large one with no visible way to open the window, only a knob saying 'Full – Closed'. I turned it to full, whatever it was, but it made no difference. The large bathroom had not been used before and the hot water came out green and brown; I bathed in a sort of thin Vichyssoise. In the morning I found out how to open the window and regretted not having done so earlier; my mouth felt thickly carpeted. The wind down George Street was brisk, but I thought a walk would do me good, so I went searching for second-hand music which used to exist back of St Giles's Cathedral on the bridge; it had shrunk to nothing. But Edinburgh is a wonderful city to walk in, and I walked, then lunched, and was ready for a total rehearsal of the *St Matthew* with Herrick at the Reid School at 2.30. It *is* tiring (it always was, but now more so) to sing, however lightly, through that whole terrible story in either of Bach's settings. The tessitura is so extended, the line so bounding, the accents so acute that three hours of it, coupled with encouraging talk and suggestions to colleagues, are more than enough. And by 5, when we had to rush for a train without a cuppa, I was tired.

The train to Glasgow (for the Mozart *Requiem* rehearsal)[19] was boiling; the heating was turned off but still scalding air surged round my calves. I flung open the window: it merely circulated the heat. I started to strip. But Glasgow *did* arrive, kind Robert Ponsonby[20] was there, and we sped off to Paisley. The rehearsal went well enough: an excellent, typically Scottish choir, sympathetic young conductor, familiar colleagues; and Paisley is a beautiful abbey with a lovely, enhancing acoustic. The rain teemed down and the Glasgow sky was slashed with red stripes; Robert drove me to my hotel but my throat was burning. He drove me to St. Enoch's Hotel, Glasgow. Who was St Enoch? What was he that he is not in the Penguin *Dictionary of Saints*? Why was his name given to a railway station? A hermit who lived in a tunnel? A sour old

---

[19]   For a performance at Paisley Abbey on 25 March, given by the Scottish National Orchestra conducted by Julian Dawson; the other soloists were Jill Gomez (soprano), Bernadette Greevy (mezzo-soprano) and Stafford Dean (bass).

[20]   English musical administrator (b. 1926); General Administrator of the Scottish National Orchestra, 1964–72.

wizard on a heath? No royal saint, certainly, nor a holy one: just a hairy recluse, I suspect. And what had he got against me that he made every minute I spent as his guest feverish and nightmarish? According to the *Encyclopaedia Britannica*, Enoch wrote some wise holy books, and after a visit to Heaven returned home to berate his children for swearing. But I had not been swearing. At least, if so, then unwittingly. Again, supposed that the dedicatee of the hotel was not the wise Enoch, but another Enoch, also known as Kennocha of Kyle, who died in 1007, a Scottish nun from a convent in Fife – ah! this must be it – 'Formerly she was held in great veneration in Scotland, especially in the district round Glasgow'. (Thus the *Book of Saints*, compiled by the Benedictines of Ramsgate.) And – curiouser and curiouser – the date of this lady's feast-day is 25 March, none other than the very day on the eve of which I entered her fell doors. Oh, St Enoch! How had I offended? I had not questioned your Approved Cult, nor had I failed in veneration, though I fancy a great many Glaswegians may have done so over the centuries. You did not really give me a chance to pay my respects before you struck. I was chosen as a scapegoat for the whole of heathen Glasgow.

I slept fitfully; after breakfast I tested my voice in my room. The larynx itself was answering quite well; obviously the cords were not affected to any extent, but the pharynx – the top of the throat – was burning and bright red. If I had to sing that morning, it might well be much worse in the evening and the inflammation could go down into the larynx. So I asked Robert if I could be excused the morning sing-through, and I stayed in bed. The performance in fact went quite well. I was glad it was Mozart's *Requiem* and not a Bach Passion. But still, when I returned to St Enoch's that night I was a singer with a bad throat who had just had to sing and was none the better for it, and – here was the crunch – I had to rehearse next day, and sing the *St Matthew* of Bach. Was this possible? Could I really do it? I filled myself with vitamin C, Alka-Seltzer, rosehip syrup and Veganin, and sent up a prayer to St Enoch. No answer: not at home. Perhaps it was the wrong number; perhaps St Enoch had gone elsewhere, to Hell or Wolverhampton. A decision had to be made – to sing or not to sing. I rang Herrick Bunney and discussed it with him. He knew I was uneasy and – clever man – had rung up a young tenor[21] in London, who was free and was standing by. But in order to get to Edinburgh in time, he would have to catch a very early plane. I had a few hours only to decide. I tested my voice. It was still just clear but surely it seemed to be thickening, and could it possibly stand up to a performance of the most exacting music one is asked to sing? The high tessitura, the intensity of utterance, all the colours of the story, the control needed for the last

---

[21]   Martyn Hill (b. 1944), English tenor.

wonderful recitative at the end of a long sing – could one possibly do it justice? Would one get through it even? After endless phone calls and with infinite regrets, I made the decision not to sing.

Relief is followed quickly on these occasions by remorse. I had let my friends down, and was ashamed of myself: I would not be able to look Herrick in the face again, kind and understanding as he was. However, I had better forget all that and look ahead to the next job. In four days I had the *St John* at the Maltings and – *more* friends to be let down? No, no. *Not* to be let down. But how not? As is the way with infections, relaxation can let them loose and this was no different. In a few hours I was voiceless. I must get back home and go to bed. But there was no train from Glasgow that Sunday and the planes were full. So twenty-four hours more were to be spent with St Enoch. A wet Sunday – a sad hotel – a miserable throat – morale was near zero. The wind was blustery and damp down Sauchihall Street, everything was shut, one could only sit and worry, and pray. The hours passed somehow, feverish and fretful, in waiting-room and plane, taxi, train, and car, but a comfortable bed was waiting at Aldeburgh.[22]

That was two days ago, two days of inhaling and gargling, penicillin and sweating it out, and now my temperature is down, and St Enoch's virus is exorcised.

But tomorrow I have to sing the *St John* at the Maltings – or not? And I must decide – now.[23]

---

[22] Pears returned to Aldeburgh on 27 March.

[23] Pears did indeed sing the role of the Evangelist in the performance of Bach's *St John Passion* (sung in Pears's and Imogen Holst's English translation) on Good Friday (31 March) 1972, conducted by Britten. The Wandsworth School Choir and the English Chamber Orchestra were joined by Gwynne Howell (Christus), Jenny Hill (soprano), Alfreda Hodgson (contralto), Philip Langridge (tenor) and Thomas Hemsley (bass). Writing in *The Times* ('Easter at the Maltings'), Alan Blyth commented: 'One or two tentative high notes were the only indication that Peter Pears had been suffering from a throat infection during the previous week. His pacing of the Evangelist's part and the variety of timbres he employs in characterizing its expository and dramatic features were as arresting and unexaggerated as ever.'

# 10 San Fortunato (May 1972)

*San Fortunato* is Pears's partial account of an Italian holiday he and Britten took in May 1972. They left London on 7 May bound for the Italian fishing village of Camogli, down the coast from Genoa, where they stayed at the Hotel Cenobio Dei Dogi. Although they made at least one fairly far-ranging day excursion to Pisa and Lucca, most of this holiday was spent in and around Camogli, attempting to relax and recharge their batteries after a heavy schedule of concerts over Easter at Snape and in preparation for the Aldeburgh Festival in June; Britten had also been working intensively on the composition draft of *Death in Venice*. The composer described their location and daily pattern in a letter (12 May) to Myfanwy Piper, the opera's librettist:

> Well – here we are. It was all settled at the last minute – Ireland decided against, & this hotel recommended by an agent. In many ways it is what we wanted: bang on the sea, walking distance from a little fishing town, where we walk several times a day & have a Campari soda. It is rather grand, the swimming pool is heated (this is *not* a good idea!) & of course we haven't got the right kind of clothes (never could have). The problem is to relax, & if the weather would help we could do it, I'm sure – but first of all 3 days of Sirocco (shades of Aschenbach – I do see what he went through!), then one glorious day of brilliant sun, when we got burnt & felt rather ill, & now today back to clouds & wind. But we are feeling more human & I'm sure after a week more we'll be able to face rehearsals & Festivals . . .

They returned to England on 18 May, driving back to Aldeburgh on the 19th. The following day rehearsals for the forthcoming Festival began.

*San Fortunato* was first published in the 1973 Aldeburgh Festival Programme Book and reprinted in Harold Lockyear (ed.), *A Tribute to Ronald Duncan by his friends* (Hartland: The Harton Press, 1974), pp. 96–101. Pears's manuscript text is in the possession of Princess Margaret of Hesse and the Rhine; five carbon copies of a typescript are at the Britten–Pears Library (1-9400536).

We arrived the day before the Italian election. It was a little fishing village cut into the rocky face of the Ligurian coast, very sharp, and in the old Borgo the high dwelling blocks darkened the steep steps from the harbour up to the paths or roads at higher levels. The mule must once have been a very important possession. The tall houses were painted a soft yellow and decorated in the hues 'of the beetroot and the tomato'. A grey, stony, crescent-shaped beach lay to the south-east of the prominent church, which had earlier been an island a hundred yards off; but they had joined it to the mainland and built on the mole, thus providing a snug harbour to the north for the local fishing fleet and visiting yachts. Banners criss-crossed the two main streets of the village, some with slogans, others simply announcing the parties, PSI, PPSUI, the Christian Democrats, the Communists etc., etc. The election did not appear then or later to be arousing much passion, and there were no demonstrations. It was likely that most of the inhabitants would agree with our taxi-driver, who hated all extremists; I expect most of them voted for the centre, like 45 per cent of the Ligurians.

Our hotel was at the south end of the crescent beach and we had an excellent view of the village and the church and castle on their point. The church clock and bells were exceedingly audible, and every quarter-hour was announced by the full hour on one bell and the quarters on another, so that until one o'clock at night there was hardly a dull moment. In the afternoons, generally at about 4.40, a time seemed to be put aside for the young (surely) to practise bell-ringing. The peal had only five bells and the tunes were therefore limited in variation; a good time was undoubtedly had by all in the belfry for ten minutes or so each afternoon.

The day after the election the banners began to disappear, taken down or covered up, and the new large poster close to our hotel announced in red and yellow a fascinating attraction for the following Sunday 14 May – the Sagra Patronale of San Fortunato, the patron saint of the village. This was clearly something not to be missed, and by Friday, when daunted by continuous grey skies we made a trip to Lucca and Pisa (glorious both of them), there had already begun preparations, scaffolding across the quay, iron bars and planks of wood. The Festival was due to start on Saturday evening at 5.30 with a Missa con discorso, and at 9 a Manifestiazione di Folk-lore e accensione del tradizionale falo (lighting of the traditional bonfire). We went down that morning to our habitual haunt close to the far centre of the harbour, with the tall houses like tiers at the opera on three sides, and watched the illuminations, curves and sharp angles, bunches of lights, strings of bulbs, waving and curling, being strung up to the accompaniment of voices cheerful and bossy, loud with suggestions and commands. An enormous frying pan (12 feet across) with a vast handle pointing north was already in place over the edge of the water, on scaffolding in which cylinders of Agipgas were being placed, all ready to fry. Struggling men sought the best walls to hang up long bunting with the mythical Agipgas creature on it, so familiar to motorists in Italy. There were three great green advertisements for 'Olita', the oil in which the fish were to be fried: 'I pesci che abboccano frigono in Olita'.

For Sunday the poster announced masses in the church at 7, 9, 11, 12, and a general communion at 8, as well as the Messa Vesperale at 6.30 and solemn vespers 8.15. At 10.30 there was to be a Benedizione della Padella Gigante e del Pesce (the Blessing of the Giant frying Pan and the Fish) imparted by their fellow townsman Mgr Giusseppe Maccio, Archpriest of the Cathedral of Genoa, who would also utter the Panegyric of San Fortunato during the mass to follow at 11. Then centrally in the poster came in large letters within a border of its own:

FRITTURA e DISTRIBUZIONE
GRATUITO DEL PESCE
dal 10.30 alle 12 e dalle 16 alle 18.30

At 7pm multicoloured cloth fishes were to be thrown to the crowd, and after the solemn vespers, at 8.30pm, a procession with the Arc of the Saint, Panegyric (again), Eucharist Benediction 'e Scoperta'. Immediately after, the Banda della Societa Operaia Catholica di NS Guardia di Genova Pontedecimo would lead the procession round the town, the musical part of the functions being entrusted to the Cantoria Parrochiale di Camogli (the Camogli Parish Choir). At 10pm there was to be a Concerto Bandistico by the Banda della Soc. Op. Catt. di NS Guardia, and 11pm Spettacolo Pirotechnico (a fireworks display).

A long day you may say, but a delightful one.

Alas! already on Saturday evening the weather, which had only been really kind for one day in the week, turned very nasty. The cloth fishes, if they were thrown, must have been very damp, and the bonfire on the beach, which we had seen being put together the whole week, *did* blaze up very splendidly and defied the rain, but we were drier watching it from our room than the nearer observers, of whom there were probably not many. Italians don't like getting wet, and the wind and the rain were terrific.

However, the next morning things looked much better. The sun was shining, a blackcap was singing splendidly in the pine tree outside our window, and the church, decorated in outline by coloured lighted at night, seemed as gay and confident in daylight; so did the bells, which were handed over at an early hour to the juvenile ringers, obviously in high spirits.

We went down in good time for the blessing of the frying pan. All down the promenade of the little bay, stalls were being set up by the vendors, vans being unpacked, and wares laid out, jewellery of all sorts, shells great and small, sweets of all sorts (mostly sticky), nougat, truffles, chocolate slabs, a stall of nuts of all sorts, almonds being roasted and peanuts being toasted in chocolate, three different stalls of gramophone records, pop, folk, Gigli, cassettes. A book stall, a stall where you could engrave your name on glass, bunches of balloons filled from gas cylinders, spun sugar. A very dark pair, perhaps from North Africa, setting out carpets and rugs. They had not yet got their things out straight, most of them, as the real crowds had not yet started to arrive.

Down at the quay the cooks were putting on high white caps, and their assistants, twelve of them aged about 14 or 15, were collecting and stacking silver cardboard plates; the frying pan was steaming hot, waiting to be blessed. Sub-chefs had boxes of flour ready, there were a dozen or more large frying baskets; all concerned with cooking or serving had white caps and vests and aprons with STAR in large red letters. (STAR makes a good brand of consommé.) Over the front of the platform was a rope stretching from one side of the quay to the other with the flags of many nations, and in the centre, directly over the frying pan, hung a very large sheet. One side was mostly taken up by a vignette of the port of Camogli, surrounded by a wreath of laurel. On the other side a large healthy man in Roman soldier's uniform extended a welcoming hand towards heaven and pressed the other to his bosom, head well back, gazing aloft, while two rather indistinct cherubs supported him on even more indistinct clouds, one carrying a sword at rest, the other an indefinable object. This, we realized, must be the patron saint, San Fortunato. Round the border of the sheet was the Greek key motif in gold.

The Piazza Colombo, as the quay is suitably called (he sailed from Genoa), was filling up fast, and the group of choirboys in red preceding the Archpriest and his assistants had to push hard to get down the steep marble staircase from the lofty church. They reached the pan safely, and the loudspeakers which had been treating us to varied music, including the *Magic Flute* overture played a tone fast, now abruptly switched to the Benedizione of the pan. This was fine but his Panegyric went on too long, we thought. So thought the belfry boys, for a sudden burst of jingling at a solemn moment may have been intended to spur on the whole affair. Finally the Arciprete had done, and the hungry Camoglese pressed forward up the steps for their fish. The twelve efficient boys doled out, the cooks fried, the assistants floured, photographers climbed and clicked, naughty boys climbed where they shouldn't have climbed and got an extra helping for their parents, everyone was happy and good humoured, and a great cloud of fish-fry smoke floated up over the houses, until at night after the evening fry it even reached our hotel.

We didn't feel it necessary to attend the evening fry. Besides, the hotel had given us such an enormous lunch (? in honour of San

178

Fortunato) that we had to go for a long walk up through the woods to recover before eating again in the evening. But the rain, which had not been very far off earlier, began as soon as we got back, and must have damped the evening fry; however, it was not heavy, and we went down again soon after 8 to catch the procession and the concert and the fireworks. The stalls were already packing up, discouraged by the elements; they may have done quite well, for there had been large crowds there by midday, but a great deal of nougat remained unsold, and the North Africans had a lot of bracelets and rugs left. So indeed had the record shops, and the stalls with mechanical animals and engines and aeroplanes. The balloons drooped a bit but still kept up in the air.

In the Piazza the procession was waiting to form up and get moving, waiting for the saint. Standing in the centre in four separate groups, respectfully regarded by all, young men surrounded four great processional crucifixes, 12 feet high or more; two Christs were black, two were what we call white; adorned with silver plaques, at head, feet and arms, and with bunches of red roses, they were not ignoble works. They had been carried down already from the church, down the steep marble flights of stairs, and the young men were still breathing heavily, sweating. Four served each crucifix, only one at a time could carry the cross; each had a belt of leather, strapped to his waist and over his shoulders, with a pouch in front to lodge the base of the huge cross. I do not know how much it weighed, but it required every second of these strong young men's concentration to hold it upright and unwavering; it needed all their strength too; even when standing still, their heads were pressed close against the tree and they had only one thought in every muscle of their bodies.

At length the saint appeared on his tray, brilliantly lit by forty electric candles. This was the original of the picture on the sheet over the frying pan. Rosy and glowing, the picture of military fitness, he knelt on his puffy clouds supported by the two bambini with the sword and the still unidentifiable object, looking confidently towards heaven in the same comfortable posture. He needed twelve teenagers to carry his tray by its handles and some younger boys lurked underneath, ready with poles to prop up the tray in case of stoppage; but he did not look really heavy and no one sweated over much, though he must have been rather awkward to manoeuvre.

The Piazza was full of villagers, relations and friends of all taking part, old women in couples, mothers and children, braving the rain which had now let up somewhat. Now the procession was all ready: first of all, four teenage boys carrying lanterns which were propped in the same leather belts as their elder cross-bearers wore; these lanterns had a single candle in their silver cages, and were held on narrow poles 8 feet high, quite heavy and awkward; then came a flock of dark-

179

aproned little girls, shepherded by nuns with umbrellas, and they it was who set the music going with a splendid version of The Old Hundredth, of all things. Then the Banda lined up, ready to play but not yet required to. Next followed a nest of crimson-cassocked ten year-olds, and the Archpriest with some lesser clergy. Then the young men lifted their crosses and moved on, though almost immediately they had to lower their precious burdens to get them prone through the low arches: on the other side of the arches the path broadened and sloped up a long incline to the main road, the saint bringing up the rear with hangers-on like us and many more. On the main road there was a hold-up, but not for very long. The Banda had struck up the sort of tune which only Bandas know, and now for the first time there appeared in front of the Banda a small closed Volkswagen or perhaps a Fiat, with loud-speakers on top. Inside the car were visible a nun beside a bearded driver, and two girls in red (perhaps members of the Cantoria Parrochiale di Camogli) who intoned in amplified sound but erratic pitch some verses from a psalm or canticle. Did they lose heart and all sense of pitch, or did the microphone break down? For it lasted a very short time. Slowly we wended our way along and up the high street; the rain quickened and we thought to leave the procession and catch it in the last furlong below. So we ran down the steps and waited. It took longer than we expected for them to reach the village's end and to come back down the homeward slope and along the promenade. We felt guilty that we had left them and started to worry. By the time they at last reached us, it was raining quite hard, and umbrellas were up, the nuns sheltering the little girls, though the crimson choir boys had none to cover them, and they must have had a very long day. The saint's bulk to some extent covered his bearers, sweating and staggering on the slippery cobbles, went on oblivious, with that single effort of concentration still visible in their shoulders and backs and legs and knees, determined to hold straight the great crosses, black or white, their heads hugged close to the tree, as if they would never let go.

In a few minutes the heavens opened wide and we ran for our hotel. The Banda must have had to disperse concerto-less; and as we reached our room a great bang announced the beginning of the premature Spettacalo Pirotechnico which, let off as fast as possible, banged and crackled and popped and dropped and, dropping, coloured the sky for a brief while with stars red and green and white and blue and yellow, banging bravely and defiantly until the real thunder and lightning and wind and rain took over for the night.

# 11  *The New York* Death in Venice *(1974)*

In the autumn of 1974, at the age of sixty-four, Pears made his début at the Metropolitan Opera, New York, recreating the role of Gustav von Aschenbach in Britten's final operatic masterpiece, *Death in Venice*. The libretto, after Thomas Mann, was by Myfanwy Piper, whose husband, John, had designed the sets; Colin Graham re-staged his English Opera Group production, first seen at the Snape Maltings during the 1973 Aldeburgh Festival, and Steuart Bedford, who had conducted the opera's première and the subsequent Decca recording, conducted the Met performances also. The other member of the cast from the original EOG production was John Shirley-Quirk, like Pears also making his Met début.

Pears's New York diary covers the rehearsal period and the first performance (18 October), concluding a few days later. There were, in fact, eight further performances of *Death in Venice* that autumn, the last on 20 December after which Pears was able to return to Aldeburgh and be reunited with Britten. Pears had originally intended to make a return to England during a break in the run of performances to see Britten, but his own poor state of health (see pp. 186–93) mitigated against such a journey. He wrote to Princess Margaret of Hesse and the Rhine on 1 November:

> [Ben] hasn't mentioned lately my coming back for a visit and he seems to have accepted my being away until Christmas. I must say that the thought of such a visit appals me. I have been on the same sort of pills as Ben, still am. My heartbeat is much too irregular (always was!) and my blood pressure much too high. But actually I do feel rather better from the treatment.

The three-month period of separation was undoubtedly a trial for the composer, still in a delicate state of health and convalescing after the only partially successful major heart surgery of some eighteen months earlier. As a consolation for not being able to travel to New York to witness the première of *Death in Venice*, he spent part of that autumn at Princess Margaret's home at Wolfsgarten, in West Germany (accompanied by his nurse and companion Rita Thomson), where he completed the *Suite on English Folk Tunes*, Op. 90. Nevertheless, it was a difficult, keenly felt separation, but one which engendered a marvellous exchange of correspondence between the two men (see DMPR, pp. 60–61) showing unequivocally that their love for one another was wonderfully intact after over thirty-five years together.

The original handwritten diary can be found in a pink, soft-bound exercise book at the Britten–Pears Library (1-9400529). The text differs significantly in a number of respects from the published (shorter) version which appeared in the 1975 Aldeburgh Festival Programme

Book, pp. 9–14. It is Pears's original that is reproduced here. Neither manuscript nor published version is complete in the sense of covering the entire stay in New York (the original manuscript stops in mid-sentence!), but a letter from Britten to Pears (probably dating from 1976) suggests that Pears might have intended to finish the diary at a later date. Pears had been taken ill while staying with Osian and Irene Ellis (see CHPP, p. 266) when Britten writes:

> I am so sorry that your temp. is up again – but you must try to be very patient. Can you read? I am sure there'll be nice books around you. Or what about going on with that diary? – don't be shy about saying what happened in N.Y. at the Met! It is lovely that you are with the Ellis' – how glad I am you arn't stuck in a hotel – St Enoch's! [a reference to Chapter 9].

In the event, Pears never continued his account.

*29 September 1974 – En route to New York*

I do not really think that there is anything more to be said about Airports. They are a deplorable necessity, and while Ben's attitude to long flights always was 'Fill yourself up to the top and get poured onto the plane', I thought that this time I would exercise a little restraint. So after bidding farewell to Sue, Jack and Martin[1] at Passport Control, JSQ [John Shirley-Quirk], who was travelling in the same plane (but not the same floor – to my shame, he was travelling *my* class, I was travelling *Ben's*, at B's especial insistence and expense) and I boarded our Jumbo, for such it was, with 327 passengers out of a possible 351, having previously raided the Tax-Free Shop (Horrors! One is permitted 6 bottles of spirits into U.S. So, obeying this implicit convention, I burdened myself with six more heavy objects). I was right in front, inside and no view. Next to me was a well-preserved and carefully groomed lady of my age(?). We chatted a little. Then we taxied and finally took off. She had the window and the view. What was my horror when, after the indecipherable lap-strap sign was turned off, she lit a cigarette. Above her head was a clear 'no smoking' sign, and I had booked my seat there specially for obvious reasons. After only five minutes' nervous fidgets I took all my courage in my hands, cleared my throat, and said 'Er – Er, excuse me, I am terribly sorry to be a bore, but this side is in fact "no smoking".' She was stung and agitated – 'I am an inveterate smoker' – but was not cross with me, only with BA [British Airways]. 'I reserved this seat, the best in the plane, in June, and nobody said it was no smoking.' Mercifully, all the stewards great and small gathered to cope with this outrage. And she disappeared. My relief was huge – 7 hours with an inveterate smoker six inches to port. Unthinkable.

The aeroplane was quite quiet, but there was a rather strong smell of ODORONO (or was it MUMM) which finally evaporated. Florid menu and good food. But after food came a movie – a French 'crime' – impossible to disregard as the screen was a foot above and ahead of my forehead. So of course I squinted up at it, on and off, but didn't hire a head-phone. Fitful dozing. The man who took the stung lady's place discussed business ethics with me, and much later the man on the other side of the gangway, nice-looking, amiable, turned out to be a subscriber to the Met., is coming to the 2nd perf. of 'D.in V' [on 24 October], a friend of Ray Leppard.[2] Gave me his card, he is an architect; I might ring him.

Hans Bruyus of Decca, assistant to Terry McEwen, met me with enormous Cadillac and Italian driver. At the customs I had been let

---

[1]   Sue Phipps, her husband (who was later to become General Administrator of the Aldeburgh Festival, 1981–2), and their son.

[2]   Raymond Leppard[§] (b. 1927), English conductor, harpsichordist and musicologist, who had occasionally worked at Aldeburgh in the 1950s.

through by an interested young viola-player. No troubles.[3] Tip seems to be a dollar, where twenty years ago it was a quarter. All New York out Sunday driving, in spite of a warm fog (74° plus). At last we reached the Hotel Mayflower, and I have a pleasant room on the 14th floor looking on to Central Park. I have just got through to Ben at Aldeburgh in about four minutes. Now I have unpacked and am going to have a gin. Harold Shaw[4] has rung me and will call again in the morning, to tell me my rehearsal time.

The New York Marathon has just finished. It consists of running four times round Central Park – about 26 miles. There were flags and enthusiastic followers, but now the rain has started much harder.

I must stay up at least until 7 pm N.Y.time, otherwise I shall wake up much too early.

Suddenly the rain stops, and the sun shines all over the trees in Central Park. Ravishing – the air begins to cool.


*Monday 30*
I woke at 3 am, fully slept, then dozed until 5 with some effort. My window shows me a perfect dawn, rosy and golden-fingered, through the high white houses on Central Park East. The trees look very splendid, with some turning of the green. There is a bird with high shrill squeaks which sounds almost Indian. The car-hooters and tyre screams destroy the dawn pretty soon however, and we go back to heat and humidity. A call to the coffee-shop at 7 is answered 'Not until eight'. After 8 I order coffee and bacon and eggs, which is brought in two bags, with knife, fork, plate, cup – all disposable (and some re-cyclable). Good coffee. All costing $2.32 plus tip, about £1.

---

3    The 'troubles' to which Pears refers concerned difficulties that both he and Britten experienced when applying for visas to gain entry to the United States. In 1949, while in New York, Pears and Britten had signed an open letter for a church concert given in aid of pacifist causes; because of their support of the Fellowship of Reconciliation and the War Resisters League they were both viewed with some suspicion by the US immigration authorities. It was not until the 1980s that Pears was finally freed from these difficulties once and for all, after a compulsory interview with an embarrassed but sympathetic embassy official in London. As Christopher Headington notes in his biography of the singer, 'characteristically, Pears had never bothered to complain and it was Donald Mitchell who insisted that something should be done about what struck him as a shameful and unwarranted treatment of a celebrated artist, who had no intention of subverting the American state' (CHPP, p. 322).

4    The American artist manager (b. 1923) and Pears's US agent. In 1974 the Shaw firm was the largest individually owned concert management organization in the United States.

I am very blocked up and sore, too heavily under the jet flight influence. My first rehearsal is put off from 10 to 11 and then again 2.30, when we do the first scenes and later, the last 'He saw me' labyrinth.[5] They are a very nice set of young singers, belonging to the Met Opera Studio, which backs them, to what extent I have not found out. They are very well rehearsed and know their music well, and do their good best for Colin,[6] who quickly gets on to good terms with them. I meet my Tadzio (Bryan [Pitts]), a straw-blond, tall, beautiful in a way, and a very good dancer (Faith[7] says). He comes from Balanchine's company,[8] and arrived at the last moment, just as they thought they would have to put a blond wig on the Jaschiu who is dark – Italian. Thank God.

My pianist Richard Forster is good, but I shall have to find some time to work with him, he doesn't yet have the right feeling for the pedalling of it.

In the evening Faith Worth (Fred's assistant, in charge of choreography) and I go shopping. Prices not outrageously high. Then meet Colin, Bryan (Colin's assistant) and a friend for a meal. Too much. Madly thirsty, I drink far too much ice-water, and long for bed. It is, after all, 3 a.m. Aldeburgh time.

Calls from Betty Bean[9] and Clytie Mundy.[10]

*Tuesday 1 October*
A good start at 8.0 am with a call from Ben! Marvellous to hear him so clear and near, and seems cheerful. Ian[11] had been to see him and was 'fairly' satisfied. But *my* voice was not so clear as Ben's. The jet flight plus humid heat and the air-conditioning (and perhaps iced water) have

---

5    A reference to scene 16 (Act II), 'The last visit to Venice', when Aschenbach sings, 'He saw me, he saw me, and did not betray me.'

6    Colin Graham$ (b. 1931), English opera director.

7    Faith Worth, assistant to Sir Frederick Ashton (1904–1988) who choreographed the dance element for the original EOG production of *Death in Venice* at Snape in 1973.

8    The New York City Ballet, founded by the dancer and choreographer George Balanchine (1904–1983).

9    American music administrator and publisher.

10   Clytie Hine Mundy (1887–1983), Australian-born soprano and singing teacher who emigrated to New York in 1920. Pears studied with her during 1941 in New York: '[Peter's] changed his teacher much for the better I think, & is already showing signs of improvement' (Britten to Peggy Brosa, 24 February 1941). In his obituary notice of Mrs Mundy (*The Times*, 12 August 1983), Pears wrote: 'I had the pleasure of studying with her for some time and was much helped by her straightforward direct teaching.'

11   Ian Tait, Britten's doctor in Aldeburgh.

taken their toll, and I am voiceless. However don't despair. Stayed in till late this morning, then went and walked a bit, fine and warm in the 60F. Bought something for lunch and future eating. Calls from Michael Burt & Laton Holgrun[12] and Betty; agreed to postpone meetings for a few days until I can freely utter. Went over to Met (10 minutes' walk) for 3.30 rehearsal and marked the Pursuit scene [Scene 9] and others. Terrible underground studio – everyone smokes – awful air. What little voice I had vanished. Back to my room, and hot whisky–lemon–honey, a *very* good drink, healthy, cheering, nourishing. Some gorgeous flowers – purple asters, orange and yellow African marigolds, light scarlet carnations, and long-haired yellow chrysanthemums – have arrived from Donald and Kath.[13] Marvellously kind and cheering.

7.0 pm. When I looked out last there was a great golden full moon over the East Side. Now at 7.15 it has already gone down. 7.35. The moon has come back: colossal, circular, smiling. Have I gone mad?

A notice in a bar: KEEP YOUR CITY CLEAN. EAT A PIGEON.


*Wednesday 2*
Woke with no voice. Rang Harold Shaw, who arranged an appointment for 10.45 with Dr Wilbur Gould. (E77th St.) Got there v. early in a taxi. (Drivers don't change anything higher than $5 bills, now.) Waited for 40 minutes in the usual waiting room with long grey faces. Had to fill up a huge form saying what my mother's maiden name was and who was paying for the bill. Tried to look through the *N.Y. Times*, 64 pages, dropped it all over everyone else's feet. The doctor is efficient and brisk, and occupies part of a floor made up of small cubicles. A charming 40 year old lady received me, a girl summoned me, a large black man in a white coat escorted me to a small hutch with the usual doctor's chair. He left me for a minute or two, then returned and said "'re you Rush'n?' I said, 'No, I'm English.' He almost died laughing. He meant 'was I in a hurry?' The doctor gives one 10 minutes of his time for $60 the first visit, $30 the second. A quick look and 'yes, an infection – cords very swollen. Antibiotics – nasal syringe and spray and lacti-something for the stomach.' Also took some blood. Oh, dear!

He turned out to be a friend of Norman Punt, my London ENT [Ear, Nose and Throat] man.

Walked back gloomily and ate in the coffee shop. Slept, read, walked out for some air. Weather rather lovely now – not quite so warm. Bought two paperbacks to read in my room, and some juices. Colin

---

12  Michael Burt: English bass. Laton Holmgren [*recte*], General Secretary of the American Bible Society.
13  Donald Mitchell§ (b. 1925), English musicologist, critic and publisher, and his wife, Kathleen (b. 1916), both of whom were close friends of Britten and Pears.

rang, v. sweetly; I shall take tomorrow off, and see doctor again on Friday morning.

New York goes on the same as ever; lively, noisy. There's a new police car noise like DOING DOING etc., very syrenish quick up and down. Awful. And then comes a terrible roar and finally what sounds like pistol shots – but perhaps that is only on certain occasions. Negro with bare feet outside the hotel last night – choice or necessity? A rather well-dressed man on Madison Ave. asked me for a 'couple of dimes' for a bowl of soup. I gave him a quarter. If he had had a knife, I suppose I would have given him $10.

*Thursday 3*

Another beautiful dawn. Pink smoke curling up and slowly turning grey. Central Park quite tropical, like Madras. Last night I tried turning off the air-conditioning, previously kept on at night in spite of its awful noise. I think I liked it better, and the air seemed somehow to come in through the wide-open window, which it had never succeeded in doing before, and even tasted fresh. There appears daily in the *New York Times* a brief report on the condition of New York's air the previous day; four days out of five it is reported as 'Unacceptable'.

In order to avoid the fuss of ordering breakfast from the coffee-shop, I have bought Nescafé, milk, honey, butter and bread, and make myself coffee with the exceedingly hot water which in time comes from the tap. This, with fruit juice, is really more agreeable than that hot noisy coffee-shop, where those very old ladies congregate, brittle and haggard, with good shoes and many beads, who daily and painfully stroll the sidewalk with their slightly younger companions and often a small dog, miniature poodles or such. (Peg,[14] there was a beautiful Mops crossing to Central Park South yesterday.)

I went out for two walks; the weather is fine, although the wind is treacherous. On one walk I went to my new bank Chase National opposite the Met and took my passport and a cheque from the Met, and was formally given a cheque book & pay-in book by a very sad character, with some physical deficiency of speech, whom I found very difficult to understand. Mercifully he didn't try to talk too much. Communication can be v. difficult.

On the other walk, I bought books, one by a Jewish writer, Weiseler,[15] recommended by Murray P.[16] and *Slaughterhouse Five*, by

---

[14] Princess Margaret of Hesse and the Rhine.

[15] Unidentified.

[16] Murray Perahia$ (b. 1947), American pianist. During the run of performances of *Death in Venice* in New York, Pears gave a recital at the Alice Tully Hall with Perahia on 11 November. The programme included music by Haydn (five English

Kurt Vonnegut Jr,[17] which I had heard of. The latter *very* good, alarming, ghastly and exceedingly funny and sad. I am also reading Milton. After *Samson Agonistes*, now *Paradise Lost.* What extraordinary language! So many words I have to puzzle over – and the syntax!

I gave 2 quarters to a redheaded negro who said he would pray for me. I hope he will.

*Friday 4*
Today has been frustrating – a waste. Voice definitely improving. But I had an appointment at 10 with Dr Gould and having waited the mandatory half hour, I was told by him that he was not pleased with my biopsy (blood test) and wanted me to see Dr Eisenmenger (shades of Thurber!).[18] So – made appointment for 4.30; and meantime walked the city. (Met Harold Rosenthal[19] in the street.) Beautiful weather with a

---

canzonets), Schumann's *Liederkreis*, Op. 39, and Britten's *The Poet's Echo*, Op. 76, and folksong arrangements. Pears wrote to Britten about this concert, on the 13th:

> The concert with Murray on Monday seems to have been well received – yes of course it was – dear youngish audience, v. enthusiastic, and after Beate & Brigitte Steiner & Murray & his Sophie & Vlado Habunek came back to Betty's for a very nice cosy eat & drink! V. nice occasion . . . I know if no one else does & I think Murray does, how many hundred miles away it was from the music-making of you and me. However Poet's Echo went well, perhaps better – yes certainly better – than the Haydn or Schumann. We make the 1st Song very free – pause after each crunchy chord before I take off – and a strong long dim. to ppp. Also No. 2 (My heart) much better now. The last also goes very well now I think. How difficult the Schumann are. And I was really full of frogs and cracks all the time. However the enclosed tells you what a press man thought, and another. I am not sure that I should send you them, in case they make you cry.

[17] American writer (b. 1925). Vonnegut's 1969 novel *Slaughterhouse-five* was a futuristic treatment of his experiences as a POW during the Second World War in Dresden.

[18] James Thurber (1894–1961), American humourist and comic artist who exerted a decisive influence on the tone of the *New Yorker* with his satirical drawings, anecdotes, and stories. Pears was fond of Thurber's writings, which he first got to know when visiting the United States in the mid-1930s: for example, he selected two extracts from *Fables for Our Time* when making his choice for BBC Radio 4's *With Great Pleasure*, broadcast in January 1986. Pears's connection of the name of Dr Eisenmenger with Thurber is probably related to Thurber's well known scepticism of psychoanalysis which he cruelly ridiculed in his book (with E.B. White) *Is Sex Necessary?* (1925).

[19] English critic and writer on opera (1917–1987), editor of *Opera*, 1953–86.

sharpish wind round corners; went to a blue movie, dreary. Back to late lunch from fridge, and walked off to Dr. E. on E68 St.

Waited three-quarters of an hour, too late to go to Colin's rehearsal at Met., which finished at 6, and then was examined by nice Dr E. I have Bilirumen (! can this be right?) in my blood, too much. Also blood-pressure is up and needs treating. Oh, dear. I can see this is going to cost money, but still worth it if I can get right. Left him at 6.15 and walked home. Supper out of fridge, but tomorrow I *will* go to the rehearsal and also have a hot meal somewhere!

Next doctor's appointment at 9 a.m. Monday, then two later in the week! Oh dear, oh dear!

*Saturday 5*
Ben called early, very clear to hear.

I *did* go to the rehearsal at 10.30 of Act I, and I started very well and got most of it right. Then suddenly at about 11.45, I lost memory, courage and all, and left the rehearsal in despair. However before doing so I made a date with Richard Voitach,[20] the understudy for Steuart Bedford[21] and a junior conductor on the Met staff, to work with him on *D in V* at 4 o'clock. We spent a MOST VALUABLE 1¾ hours on the opera, which restored my confidence and made me feel much BETTER. A nice helpful man. The Met's acoustics are so good that a small voice like mine well-projected will sound perfectly clear and good! Let's hope so . . .'.

Was stopped by a boy with beard as I left Met who had heard *D. in V.* at Aldeburgh. Madly enthusiastic. Had just seen *Don Giovanni* matinée.[22] 'How was it?' 'Well, it was well conducted.'

6.30. Home to a gin and my view over Central Park. The trees darken, the lights go on, the other side (East) looks like a chalk cliff, with a pale glow above. Reminded me of the olive trees below Delphi!!

Still taking ANTIBIOTICS. Back to Milton. *Paradise Lost*: splendid scene of Lucifer massing his forces, who move 'in perfect phalanx to the Dorian mood of flutes and soft recorders'. Poor instruments! Do they belong to the Devil?

---

[20]  Richard Woitach (b. 1935), American conductor and pianist; assistant conductor at the Metropolitan Opera, 1959–68; resident associate conductor since 1973. Woitach coached all the young singers from the Met Studio in the small roles for *Death in Venice*.

[21]  English conductor and pianist⁵ (b. 1939).

[22]  Performances of Mozart's *Don Giovanni* were being given at the Met, conducted by Max Rudolf, with Sherrill Milnes in the title role.

*Sunday 6*
Another glorious day. Very warm, nearer 80° than 70°, I would think.
A very quiet time, with hard work at *D in V* in morning; a late and
excellent salad lunch downstairs, and a stroll in the Park. A pleasant
custom is that most or all Sunday, the Park is only usable by bicycles or
the old horse-cabs. Crowds of cyclists, also baseball players, footballers,
dogs, etc. One can notice the trees slowly turning. Bought the *N.Y.
Times* Sunday edition; nearly *all* advertisements, practically nothing to
read. There is a great deal of music made in N.Y.

I finished the day with a very pleasant quiet meal with Harold Shaw
at his apartment up on Broadway. A fascinating walk there and back;
many blacks and browns, and oh how many unhappy bewildered drunk
dotty people.


*Monday 7*
Again fine, but cooler.

To Dr Eisenmenger at 9 (thus missing a call from Ben) for a
cardiograph and chest X-ray. What is it all about? Rehearsal at the Met
ON THE STAGE for the first time, and the acoustic obviously is good &
nice to sing in. Relief!! The auditorium is really very splendid, gold and
red, both very good colours too. It holds 3,684 people (I think).

Was approached and kindly and warmly spoken to by the great
Placido Domingo,[23] the ruling Met. tenor. Sweet man. Wants to give up
singing and take to conducting!

The Tadzio is quite disappointing (Oh! for Bob!)[24] and his mum is
*very* balletic. Indeed, they all are and one misses the natural movements
of our London cast. (Does that sound rather odd?)

A very pleasant hour between rehearsals was spent by me sitting in
the Plaza, outside the Met–Library–Theatre–Phil Hall, looking at the

---

[23] Spanish tenor (b. 1941) who was appearing at the Met in Verdi's *Les Vêpres
Siciliennes*, and is widely regarded as the supreme lyrical-dramatic tenor of the
late twentieth century. His singing was much admired by Pears. Domingo has
occasionally appeared as a conductor of opera.

[24] Robert Huguenin, a member of the Royal Ballet who played the role of Tadzio
in the EOG production. Pears wrote to Britten on 12 October:

> I miss Bob Huguenin *very* much. This boy Bryan is a much better
> dancer; he is from Balanchine's Co. & as light as air, very fine
> movements, & the new dance is v. elegant & fine. But he has *not* got
> IT at all!! Oh dear! I wouldn't dream of looking at him for more
> than 5 seconds. A sweet chap and all that, 19 or 20 year old, blond
> from N. Carolina, but no Bob. I have written to Bob to tell him so,
> it might cheer him up a bit! Tadzio's mum is no Deanne [Bergsma]!!

Henry Moore[25] which should have been bottom-deep in water, but there's a leak. Anyway it was lovely, with the leaves falling off and rustling 'over the Piazza'. As I left a slim black object approached me to help him find the way to an address which I knew (I think). The object was perhaps 14 and dressed (reading upwards) in gym shoes, the regular pale blue jeans, a wide pink-scarlet sash round the waist, an orange blouse shirt with v. full sleeves, and on top of his head a huge hat shaped like a straw hat (wide brim) made of brown knitted wool. Perfect manners and great elegance.

Betty Bean came at 7.30 for a gin on the rocks before taking me to *Wozzeck*, first night.[26] Betty is enormous and was dressed right royally in long purple gold and silver. I sported my new black velvet jacket, rather disappointing. So also was *Wozzeck*. The orchestra terribly heavy throughout, and oh that German Expressionist Period. It is like watching and listening to an unhappy simpleton being dissected alive and eaten by mad human beings. Give me *Albert Herring* every time. We left after the second act. Met Sam Barber there.

*Tuesday 8*
The day started marvellously with a call from Ben, just arrived in Wolfsgarten. Such a great and joyful relief, and such a firm gay voice, too. Lovely!!

And then on my way to the Met for a 10.30 call, who should I run into getting out of a small car but Aaron![27]

Rehearsals are going through a tricky time, with stage rehearsals in danger of going stale, the chorus catching colds and coughs, forgetting and being unsure. The Players' scene [Scene 10] not good enough, the laughter weak, and the labyrinth scene [Scene 13] getting less and less good, in spite of changes. The Tadzio has not yet come out as a character at all. Very disappointing, and Mum feeble. None of the dancers have any feeling for acting, mime or character, and compare very unfavourably with our little ones.

---

[25] English sculptor (1898–1986). The figure to which Pears refers is Moore's work, *Two Piece Reclining Figure*, a half-size model of which Moore lent to Britten and Pears in 1967 to stand outside the newly opened Snape Maltings Concert Hall.

[26] Berg's operatic version of Büchner's play was conducted by James Levine, with Peter Glossop in the title role. The producer was Patrick Libby and the design was by Caspar Neher. Although Pears goes on to reveal his distaste for the work on this occasion, *Wozzeck* was an opera that Britten had admired since its UK première in 1934. Moreover, and of some interest in the context of *Death in Venice*, the composer made a point of attending a performance of *Wozzeck* in 1972, while working on *Death in Venice*. See also DMPR, pp. 391–5.

[27] American composer (1900–1990), whom Britten first met in London in 1938; Pears was not to encounter Copland until the following year in the United States.

*Wednesday 9*
Routine rehearsals, rather in pieces. Lighting in part. The sets look well. Everyone stale and insecure. Neither JSQ or I like these rehearsal times. 10.30–11 through to 3, and again 4 on. The day is mis-shapen. Early bed.

*Thursday 10*
*New York Post* journalist came at 9.30. A pleasant knowledgeable, keen fellow, and I chatted away about Ben and opera for a half hour.[28] Why do Americans always want to know where one was born? What can Farnham, Surrey, mean to them? Or is it in some way to do with one's stars and the horoscope?

Rehearsals of Act I on stage with orchestra. A good deal of stopping but none unnecessary, and Steuart did a very good job with the orchestra, which is a good one. The percussion are improving and there are some ravishing sounds; strings also sound very well. The lighting is getting set, and the 'Leaves' Projection (Scene 1)[29] looked good, I thought. There is talk of the boy's head being projected in beginning of Act II, which I don't approve of.

I have as my dresser John, who I think must have been one of the original dressers in the old Met. Rather deaf, frail-looking and very slow-moving, I speak to him as if he were a much-loved backward child and he understands and appreciates it. But he was there at the side of the stage for the quick change and it worked perfectly well.

I am made up by Victor,[30] much younger, more vigorous, efficient, quick. My grey-white wings of hair are causing some trouble. We shall see.

In the afternoon I had two doctor's appointments. The first was 3.30 at Dr. Eisenmenger's. (E 68 St.), an urbane slow but sure talking grey haired internist, with a charming smile. I had hurried to get there, especial permission, quick washing etc., and then of course had forty minutes to wait. He has come to the conclusion that my Billy Roomin' is not important enough to treat and he told me why (taking 15 minutes). But my heart is a-rhythmic; it beats irregularly; he doesn't like it (nor do I particularly) especially as my blood pressure is up,

28 Speight Jenkins's article, 'Peter Pears Bows at the Met', appeared in the 'entertainment section' of the *New York Post* (2 November 1974).
29 A reference to one of John Piper's designs which was projected onto the backcloth.
30 Victor Parker, a photographer whom Pears met in New York in 1974 and invited to Aldeburgh the following year. One of Parker's portraits of Britten appears as a frontispiece in PFL.

200/128 (is that right?) – too high, he says. *So* I am joining Ben in the Digoxin club *and* the Diuretic Association.

From Dr. Eisenmenger I went on to Throat Doctor Gould, where I waited for 50 minutes. When he finally looked at my throat for two-and-a-half minutes, he was lyrical! He had never seen such a pure spotless beautiful pair of vocal cords. I told him I had been singing all day. Absolutely astounded and full of congratulations. So goodbye to Dr Gould until the next crisis. Meanwhile I await the bill! Dr Eisenmenger I shall visit again in a fortnight.

On the way home asked for money by a boring half-drunk Irishman who would have liked a fight, but I eluded his grasp.


*Friday 11*

Another journalist came at 9.30 and we covered much the same ground as yesterday.

Rehearsal of Act II on stage with orchestra. Ups and downs, but many good things. Chorus improving in Players' Scene; JSQ having trouble with the machines, not properly charged. Lighting *is* very dark, too dark? I *must* work at Phaedrus Song;[31] making appalling mistakes. Saw something of Ted Uppman, delightful chap, civilised, looking very much as he did as the original Billy Budd in 1951.

In the evening took Betty Bean to Julian [Bream]'s concert at Town Hall.[32] Packed audience, mad enthusiasm. J played some Laurencini (1580), v. interesting, and the marvellous Dowland arrangement of 'Walsingham', also a dotty Giuliani show-piece of a potpourri of Rossini arias – a bit much. Betty and I wandered up Sixth Avenue. It was 64°F at midnight, and we ate salads and drank beer.

---

[31]  'Does beauty lead to wisdom, Phaedrus?', Scene 16 (Act II), 'The last visit to Venice'.

[32]  In a letter to Britten (12 October 1974), Pears writes:

> Last night . . . I went with Betty Bean to Julian's concert at Town Hall packed with mostly young or youngish people. He played a new (to me) Dowland arr. of Walsingham – beautiful. He was in medium to good form. Bach Chaconne a bit too much for him in places. Looks rather plump & bald but still so much charm and dear artistry. They adore him. Saw him briefly after.

On 31 October at the McCarter Theatre, Princeton University, Pears and Bream together gave a recital which included music by Morley, Dowland, Lennox Berkeley (*Three Songs of the Half-light*) and Britten's *Six Songs from the Chinese*, Op. 58.

*Saturday 12*
I was rung at 7.30 by Kath. She and Donald *had* arrived last night and *were* in the hotel, in spite of what the Hallporter had insisted – not expected, cancelled room, etc. Had breakfast with them and Myf,[33] who came with them. Lovely to have them.

A day off from the Met. Went shopping after lunch, at Bloomingdales. Bought a few basic necessities: one spoon, two knives, one fork, one cup, one saucer, and *12* glasses. (Drink parties anyway! if not much eating) Steuart has found and given me one of those little electric infusers, with which at the risk of your life you can make a cup of tea. They are not allowed in England, it seems, as being too dangerous. However I shall try to be careful.

Lunch at a v. good and reasonable Japanese restaurant. Delicious little frittered prawns and asparagus, exquisitely served.

Evening visit to a Jewish 'Deli' on 7th Ave. Toasted cheese on rye, and yet I slept well.

*Sunday 13*
Have I really been here two weeks already?

A free day from the Met. So Donald, Kath and I walked across to the Met. Museum, quite a walk through the Park. Saw some lovely Italian drawings from the Louvre, superb Michelangelo; the whole collection is full of beauties, two adorable Boningtons, Salisbury Cathedral, wonderful Turners, Gainsborough portrait of Dr Burney, quite stunning; a lot of postcards but still not everything is available. A very nicely arranged Restaurant & good food. Then a cab back. Drinks at Laton's newish apartment, wonderful view up the Park. Nobuo's successor is charming & most successful. Delicious eats. Then walking up Broadway with Colin to Bryan Pitts (Tadzio) for a party, several from the dancing world. John Taras,[34] critic & Balanchine's No. 2.

*Monday 14*
Rehearsal of music in C Level Room, three floors underground. Terrible air. Exhausting. Chorus sang very well; v. useful rehearsal finishing at 2. Lunch at the Balloon; deep sleep. Up to meet at 5 in Schuyler Chapin's[35] room to discuss Talk to Met. Op. Assoc. Members about *D in V* with

---

[33] Myfanwy Piper$ (b. 1911), English librettist and wife of the artist and stage designer John Piper (1903–1992).

[34] *Recte*: John Taris, American dancer, choreographer and ballet director with the New York City Ballet.

[35] American music administrator (b. 1923), general manager of the Metropolitan Opera, 1972–5.

Colin and Steuart. All very friendly and welcoming. Talk took place to full little auditorium. Questions after. Finish at 7.30, and drinks with Donald & Kath. Modest eats from fridge, and early to bed. Contacted Norman S.,[36] who rang later to say Sue's plane was cancelled & she would be on the 1 o'clock plane from London tomorrow. This weather is confusing and really *too* warm.

## Tuesday 15

Acts I and II rehearsal on stage with piano. Usual long arduous repeats and notes. It is an enormously long and exhausting part for me. I have been singing out a great deal in order to get the measure of the Met, but it tires me greatly and by 3 o'clock after five hours in the theatre and very little break and no food, I am exhausted.

Tonight went to Norman Singer's receipt of a decoration from the French Cultural Attaché at the French Centre, met various old friends and acquaintances: Alice Tully,[37] Claire Reis,[38] Thea Dispeker[39] (my first 'agent' in New York in 1940). Sue was there, just arrived 19 hours late! Didn't stay long, and came home and went to bed.

## Wednesday 16

General Dress Rehearsal. Large audience. Seemed to go well. The chorus is improving all the time, and they are sweet dear young singers, paying me such dear bouquets of compliments and admiration. The dancers are also coming alive; Tadzio much more alert, and the games are charming, really much better with slightly older boys 18–19–20 year olds, not too big, and there is one quite a bit younger – *c.* 14. The girls are waking up too.

The audience was keen by all accounts. Then after notes, changing, & more notes we had a Press Conference. They had been waiting & drinking for an hour or so; bored and frustrated, silly, tiresome people, but three of them intelligent and sympathetic. One man from Ottawa, sensitive & intelligent.'

---

[36] Norman Singer, an American friend of Pears's who lived in New York.

[37] American soprano and patron of the arts (1902–1992), after whom the Alice Tully Hall at the Lincoln Center for the Performing Arts is named.

[38] Claire R. Reis, a prominent figure in New York musical life. She was a founder of the League of Composers and a director of the American Friends of the Aldeburgh Festival.

[39] Thea Dispeker came from Berlin to New York in 1938 where, after working in a variety of musical positions, she opened her own office in 1947. Today she is one of New York's most prestigious agents. See F. Paul Driscoll, 'Leading Ladies', *Opera News* (July 1992), pp. 20–24.

After a cheeseburger at the Balloon, back here with Sue, and before long I was tired enough to decide to stay in and go to bed early.

*Thursday 17*

The day of relaxation before the Great Day! Very quiet morning. Now that Jean Uppman[40] (bless her!) has provided me with a minimal equipment – frying pan, saucepan, spoon, mugs – I can make quite an elaborate breakfast. So I start at 7 with a cup of tea; at 8 I take orange juice with one Digoxin and one Hygroton; and at 9.15 I eat egg and bacon, and toast (toasted on an electric ring) and honey, and a cup of Nescafé. What more can I want, especially with the sun shining on Central Park and the air freshening?

Lunch with Norman Singer at his home on W. 78th, which involves an easy walk up Central Park West to the Natural History Museum with its memorial to Theodore Roosevelt who, from this, would appear to have been the most universal man since Leonardo da Vinci. Delicious lunch, the principal feature being Chinese Honey Duck ready prepared at the Deli in foil, waiting only to be warmed through, indescribably delicious. The American Deli has evolved into something superlative.

Walked homeward and found some nice prints in the Ballet Shop for first-night presents.

At 4.30 pm gave interview to a lady from the New Yorker who seemed intelligent and sympathetic.[41]

A short rest, then over to Betty Bean's for drinks and, indeed, eats. Her sister Nan, the Heinsheimers[42] (memories of piano duet performances of Mahler 6th Symphony 25 years ago) Mario di Bonaventura,[43] Schirmer's new Music Director (late of Dartmouth) who may prove helpful in getting American composers to write for harp and voice. Then home & to my really rather *un*comfortable bed and a rather broken night. Nerves?

Rung by young singer–guitarist with questions about repertoire.

---

40   Ted Uppman's wife.
41   Jane Boutwell, whose piece on *Death in Venice*, for which she interviewed Pears and Shirley-Quirk, appeared in the 'Talk of the Town' section of the *New Yorker* (4 November 1974).
42   Hans W. Heinsheimer$ (1900–1993), German-born publisher and writer on music. It was probably during Pears's and Britten's trip to the United States in 1949 that the piano duet performances of Mahler's Sixth Symphony took place. (Britten and Heinsheimer were both passionate devotees of Mahler's music.)
43   American conductor (b. 1924), vice president of G. Schirmer, 1974–80. He was professor of music at Dartmouth College, 1963–72.

# METROPOLITAN OPERA

Wednesday Evening, December 4, 1974, at 8:00 O'Clock
*Subscription Performance (Wednesday 3)*
New Production

*The 7th Metropolitan Opera performance of*

BENJAMIN BRITTEN'S

# Death in Venice

*Opera in two acts*

*Words by* Myfanwy Piper *after the story by* Thomas Mann

*Conductor:* Steuart Bedford
*Directed by* Colin Graham
*Choreography by* Sir Frederick Ashton
*Sets designed by* John Piper
*Costumes designed by* Charles Knode
*Lighting by* John B. Read
*Choreography recreated by* Faith Worth
*Associate Designer:* David Reppa

| | |
|---|---|
| *Gustav von Aschenbach* | Peter Pears |
| *The Traveller and* | |
| *The Elderly Fop* | |
| *The Old Gondolier* | |
| *The Hotel Manager* | John Shirley-Quirk |
| *The Hotel Barber* | |
| *The Leader of the Players* | |
| *Dionysus* | |
| *The Voice of Apollo* | Andrea Velis |
| *The Polish Mother* | Vicki Fisera |
| *Tadzio, her son* | Bryan Pitts |
| *Her Two Daughters* | Alison Woodard / Claudia Shell |
| *Their Governess* | Diana Levy |
| *Jaschiu, Tadzio's friend* | Anthony Ferro |

*Cast continues*

*Latecomers will not be admitted during the performance    Knabe Piano used exclusively*

The taking of photographs and the use of recording equipment are not allowed in this auditorium

*Death in Venice*, Metropolitan Opera, New York, 1974.

197

*Friday 18*

Glorious morning. Temperature today in the 40s. Very quiet day indoors. Wrote letters and worked at *D in V*, trying to get every word into my head and every note too. Julian called from Wisconsin. Had a late lunch at 2.45 at the Beef and Brew with Donald and Kath, and filled myself with first-class protein. Then back to the Hotel for further rest, until I was called for by Tony, Decca's Cadillac driver, a great opera-'buff', and taken to the Met, at about 7 o'clock. Many many lovely telegrams of good wishes from friends both here and at home. Presents, often a single red rose, from the cast, a splendid tie from Harold, and many messages. I could not have been more warmly greeted. Sweet people. I was very nervous, and the voice felt terribly dry, my uvula seemed 'to cleave to the roof of my mouth', and I had been warned that the audience habitually greet a new Visitor with applause on their first appearance in any context, so I was ready for the opera never to get started at all, what with me *and* JSQ! However . . . it started and they didn't burst into applause. Indeed they seemed to listen very quietly indeed. I made several silly mistakes right up to the end of the First Act. But after the Interval I definitely improved, and the Second Act went well. The orchestra was nervous too, but Steuart was a tower of strength. All the lighting cues were correct and Colin was very pleased. So, it would appear, was the audience, who received us at the end really splendidly, with tremendous cheering and applause. I would call it a big success. Schuyler Chapin and the Met are all delighted, so was Heinsheimer and the Schirmer boys, and of course Donald and Kath, and the English contingent, Lettie and Charles, Joan and Isador [Caplan], Caroline L., Bill and Pat,[44] Keith Grant[45] (over from Philadelphia) and our American Friends, Aaron, Claire Reis, Betty Bean and many more. All these were at the party given by Schirmer's after in the Belmont Room. We had a couple of drinks & then across the road to eat some good beef before home at 1.30 am to bed and a medium night.

---

[44] Lettie and Charles = Laetitia and Charles Gifford; Charles Gifford (1909–1994) was for many years Treasurer of the Aldeburgh Festival. Caroline L. = Caroline Lippincott. Bill and Pat = William and Pat Servaes; William Servaes was General Manager of the Aldeburgh Festival, 1971–80.

[45] English administrator (b. 1934), General Manager of the EOG, 1962–73. Grant left the EOG to become Secretary to the Royal Society of Arts, for whom he was on a business trip to Philadelphia in 1974 and chanced to be able to see the first night of *Death in Venice* at the Met.

*Saturday 19*

I rang Ben at 8 to tell him, but the line died after a few minutes, and so I called again. He was only concerned to know how they had liked *me* – dear Ben – I am not sure that I satisfied him! But they did *seem* to like me. He was still not quite over his cold. I wish we could give him more resistance, more power to fight them away. I do hope that the first night being over may relax him a bit and he can get quietly on with his work.

At 10 I had to say Goodbye to Kath and Donald, she going to Wolfsgarten, he to San Francisco and Australia, tomorrow. But I'm going up into Massachusetts with Norman Singer, in his car, also Sue and a Dutch friend, Gosse Gorter.

We drove 2+ hours through the Parkways. The most beautiful autumn colours you can imagine: wonderful brilliant reds yellows orange purples browns, and sometimes a group of pale grey leaves, also a leaf with olive green one side and silver the other, and some palm. Geoffrey greeted us at their charming blue white wooden house with 64 acres of wild woods, which they try to keep clear-ish. The cleared part of about 5 acres is still rough but they have dug some beds and made Alpine gardens, rock gardens, heather gardens, and planted quantities of shrubs, rhododendrons, and vegetables which get eaten by every known named animal, porcupines which eat the wooden floors of the outhouses; racoons which eat the corn; voles moles and mice which try to get at their favourite diet, deer which overprune the apple trees; beavers which simply flood the roads by building dams; squirrels which take the bulbs, woodchucks which don't seem to chuck wood, and a possible bear looking for honey and conceivably a lynx. The battle against nature is constant. But it is a beautiful spot, much colder than New York.

I slept in the afternoon, while the others went for a walk. Later an excellent dinner and early to bed.

*Sunday 20*

Cold, beautiful sunny morning with small dumpling clouds being blown across the sky. The leaves are off the silver birches, and the silver skeleton stands up glittering in front of firs and larches and the maples which have not yet shed their leaves. The ground is covered with leaves and the prevailing colours are lemon and silver. One has seen coloured photographs of this very often and it remains extremely beautiful. The quiet is intense. The beavers have rebuilt their broken dam, which will be broken again by the farmer who wants to persuade them to go further downstream. There is ice on the pond.

We were driven to close friends of Norman & Geoffrey who had marched with them anti-Vietnam War, extremely nice & sympathetic pair Jim and Ros Becker, who live in a lovely old house which they are doing up themselves. We were given a delicious lunch, and went back to Norman's to collect our things before driving back again to New York along those beautiful parkways splendidly looked after and as lovely as they are reported to be. Excellent Chinese meal at Broadway and 94th. Spoke to Dick Vogt[46] and Clytie & then to bed. Donald and Kath gone off in different directions, he to Aus., she to Ben.

## Monday 21

A very pleasant midday meal with Ted & Jean Uppman at theirs. They are the most kind hospitable people you can imagine. Jean has provided me with a few more pots and pans so that I can cook a breakfast for myself.

## Tuesday 22

A visit to the Museum of Modern Art with Sue. Good to see those rooms full of Picassos and Matisses, Rousseaus and all the rest. They provide an excellent lunch at the pleasantly laid-out, airy restaurant, in or out of doors. Some interesting younger American painters. The big Beckmann[47] triptych of Perseus (?) A big Ma[48]

---

[46] An American friend of Pears who was director of the Greenwich Choral Society of Connecticut and 'minister of music' at the First Congregational Church, Old Greenwich. While Pears was in the United States, he participated in a concert at Greenwich under Vogt's direction on 1 October.

[47] Max Beckmann (1884–1950), German artist who emigrated to the United States in 1947. His series of triptychs represents the most authentic comment of German culture on the disorientation of the modern world.

[48] Pears's text stops in mid-sentence.

# 12   *The New York* Billy Budd *(1978)*

The success of Pears's début at the Metropolitan Opera, New York, in 1974 led to his being invited to sing Captain Vere in the Met's first staging of *Billy Budd* in the 1978–9 season. He participated in all eight performances, given in two runs: five performances were held in September and October 1978 (first night: 19 September); and a second group of three followed in March 1979. He flew to New York on 22 August 1978 in readiness for the stage rehearsals, returning to England on 5 October the day after the last performance of the first group. The second run of performances formed only part of a substantial number of commitments undertaken by Pears in the United States and Canada that spring which included some teaching on the West Coast.

These performances at the Met marked the first occasion Pears had sung Vere on stage since the original Covent Garden production in 1951–2, although he had taken part in the première of the revised, two-act version (a BBC Third Programme transmission) in 1960, Basil Coleman's 1966 BBC-TV film, and in Britten's Decca recording of 1967. While his performance was, as ever, an inspired interpretation in more introspective and intimate moments, his lack of a powerful delivery (itself a cause for concern at Covent Garden in 1951) was marked when compared with the declamation of a whole generation of younger Veres. Nevertheless, his presence undoubtedly lent authority to John Dexter's production which was widely praised for its imaginative and eloquent touches. Its initial success led to several equally acclaimed revivals, most recently in 1993.

Pears was sixty-eight when he appeared in *Budd* at the Met. Perhaps not surprisingly, it proved to be his last major appearance in a new opera production; indeed, these *Budd* performances were among his final stage appearances anywhere, bringing to a close an operatic career that spanned over thirty-five years. Only cameo appearances were to come: at Aldeburgh in June 1979 as Monsieur Triquet (*Eugene Onegin*), and at the Edinburgh Festival in August that same year as The Prologue (*The Turn of the Screw*).

Like his account of the Met *Death in Venice* production, Pears may have intended the *Billy Budd* diary for publication in an Aldeburgh Festival Programme Book. It remained, however, unfinished and therefore unpublished (it relates only his first six days in New York in August 1978). Pears's original, inscribed on an A4 pad using one of those idiosyncratic pink felt-pens he seemed to favour at that time, survives at the Britten–Pears Library (1-9400535).

[*Tuesday, 22 August 1978*]

The Concorde is a very decent air-ship. It is small and doesn't give me agoraphobia (if that is right here) which the Jumbo does. One's cubic atmosphere is much the same as in other planes & there are no luxuries in that direction, but the service is unceasing, the food & drink excellent, and one only takes 3½ hours to fly 3½ *thousand* miles (average 1000 miles an hour) and at the moment I am totally unaware of jet-lag (1 am by my & your time). One big advantage on reaching Kennedy Airport is that being a small airplane (c. 70 people) it takes no time to get through passport & customs. There can't be many people who immigrate into the U.S. by Concorde! All our visas (including mine) are in order!

New York was its characteristic self right from the word "go". My taxi driver concluding from my Copenhagen cap that I was a musician, played me a cassette of "Fiddler on the Roof"[1] non-stop into Manhattan, & went a long way round to avoid a traffic block somewhere which made the journey cost $30 instead of $20. However he was amiable & drove as all N. Yorkers do, bump bump over the appalling surface.

I arrived in my hotel to find an encouraging cable from Neil,[2] and a Zabar bag full of goodies from Dick Vogt and v. soon Ted Uppman appeared with a basket of further useful things and a bottle of gin. Typical American kindness, they are the most hospitable. After I had

---

[1]  Jerry Bock's and Sheldon Harwick's immensely successful 1964 musical.
[2]  Neil Mackie (b. 1946), Scottish tenor and a pupil of Pears with whom the singer had a close and abiding friendship from the early 1970s, but particularly towards the end of his life. See CHPP, p. 262.
Pears wrote to Mackie on 4 September 1978:

> *Thank* you for your telegram. I was very encouraging to receive it on arrival and sweet of you to think of it. It hardly seems that I have been here over a week – in some ways it seems like a month. The weather is my least favourite one for singing – the throat feels like wet cotton wool. Just too hot, 80° and 90° and over, and high humidity – you leave your air-conditioned room and plunge out into an oven, and then after ten minutes walk into a subterannean ice-box.
>
> My friends here have been very kind and helpful, but I am homesick! And now I am staying in bed for a day with a violent tummy upset and a fever! The rehearsals have been going alright, John Dexter producing & Ray Leppard conducting, nice & easy to work with, some good voices, & a fine chorus, but I always feel out of place at the Met. I don't belong here. However, enough grumbling!

settled myself into my room where I shall be for six weeks,[3] and had a brief nap, I thought I would go for a walk and shop.

So out I went. It is warm here, probably about 80°, and humid too, but pleasant. I wandered downtown and as I crossed 59th St at Columbus Circle, I saw a chap the other side of the street, waving with both hands about his ears in my direction. I presumed of course that there was someone behind me at whom he was waving, and I put on a face of stone. He was smiling or just being New Yorkish & gesticulating against Fate. As I got up to him, & I heard he was saying Peter Pears, Peter Pears, isn't it? (I had to admit that it was.) He was a 50-or so old man who needed a shave, who had been carrying two small but heavy parcels by the string, and was excited. A lot of words came out "For Billy Budd? Of course, I shall be there. I love your "Schöne Müllerin", so tender, and "Peter Grimes", they like Vickers[4] here, but you are much better. My mother was English. Look at me, the greatest tenor in the world, having to carry these parcels. Your Dichterliebe, too . Verdi was four-quarters. Caruso[5] 2, Gigli 3. Wonderful your début at the Met at .64."

We parted and went on our ways. A sweet enthusiastic man supported in his life by music & singing, and 100% New York. After half an hour's walk, I found a shop where I bought an electric cooking-ring (my room has a kitchen but no cooker) and then I bought some tea-bags, some butter and a French loaf so I am all ready for breakfast!

Later Dick Vogt rang and then came in with one of his sopranos to have a drink on the way to the Philharmonic concert in Central Park – free – Mehta[6] conducting Rienzi, La Valse and Tsch. IV. I to an early bed, but 3 a.m. by my English time. It really is quite hot, but pleasant.

---

[3] As in 1974, Pears stayed initially at the Mayflower Hotel.

[4] Jon Vickers (b. 1926), Canadian tenor, whose interpretation of the title role in *Peter Grimes* was widely admired at this time on both sides of the Atlantic. (Vickers sang the role at the Met and at Covent Garden.) It was not, however, much to the taste of the composer (who saw Vickers as Grimes in 1975) or Pears. Vickers recorded *Grimes* (both audio and video formats) with Colin Davis and Royal Opera House forces in 1979.

[5] Enrico Caruso (1873–1921), Italian tenor.

[6] Zubin Mehta (b. 1936), Indian conductor, who was principal conductor of the New York Philharmonic Orchestra, 1976–91.

*Wednesday* [23 August]

I rang Ray[7] & am to dine at his tonight. Tomorrow rehearsals, 10 a.m. with my officers. Ray is very excited by the set and the production. I had a first rehearsal after all in the afternoon, met the very nice staff, familiar faces, very welcoming and most civil. I felt back at home. John Dexter[8] was there, lively, highly strung, full of ideas but not all pressing. The set is cunningly made with minimum of big-scale change. It should be impressive. Dinner with Ray (and Peter Schaffer)[9] drinks at his large pleasant flat, typically New York, non-modish & then to 'Bailiwick' for excellent food, muscles [*sic*], lamb.

---

[7] This production of *Billy Budd* marked Leppard's début at the Met. *Raymond Leppard on Music*, edited by Thomas P. Lewis (New York: Pro/Am Music Resources Inc., 1993), pp. 174–6, includes a short memoir of his experience of conducting *Budd* at the Met and working with Pears. Leppard recollects:

> It was during the rehearsals and performances of *Budd* that, for the first time, I got to know Peter very well; Ben had died and he was terribly alone . . . for all his fastidious ways, he evidently preferred eating large hamburgers with me at Marell's, an old speak-easy on Lexington Avenue to fois-gras at the Four Seasons. He came often to my apartment on Park Avenue at 86th Street where we had long long, quiet talks which I remember with real affection . . . Peter's portrayal of Captain Vere seemed to reflect the restraint he and Ben used to live their lives. He made it clear that it was containment of emotion in public that led Vere to make his appallingly wrong decision.

In a later chapter ('Images and Impressions', p. 435), Leppard recalls:

> Peter was an unsurpassable Vere but there was one place, after Billy has struck Claggart and caused his death, which he never could get right, a complicated little two-four section beginning 'God o' mercy'. He came to my dressing room before the last performance and we went through it, he determined to sing it correctly at least once in the run.
>
> Come the moment, of course, he got out again and was so cross with himself he came down to the footlights and instead of singing: 'Fated boy, what have you done? Go in there, Go! God help us every one,' he looked down at me and sang 'Fated boy, what have you done? Bloody fool. Damn. God help us every one.' I was the only one who laughed.

[8] English director of *Billy Budd* (1925–1990), director of productions (a post especially created for him) at the Met, 1974–81. His production of *Budd* was widely praised and typical of his directing style, being tightly organized and schematic in conception, with effects derived mainly from a clever manipulation of soloists and chorus within the context of a highly structured set design.

[9] Peter Shaffer (b. 1926), English playwright.

*Thursday* [24 August]

Rehearsal at 11. Lunch at 'Gingerlma' salad (much too big), more rehearsal on cabin scenes [Act I scene 2, Act II scene 2], going well, David Ward[10] (Sailing Master), Peter Glossop[11] (1st Lieut.). Met Richard Stilwell[12] (Billy) – very nice singer and nice chap. Quiet evening, early to bed.


*Friday* [25 August]

Not quite so hot today, yesterday was well up in the 80° & getting more humid. Today there is a breeze, tho' overcast & grey.

Claggart is played & sung by James Morris,[13] a nice young singer with a very splendid strong bass voice of great consistency – not much subtlety as yet, but no ham at all. Most promising.

I spoke to Betty Bean, who is, poor dear, very unwell indeed, in hospital, undergoing all sorts of tests, enduring great pain. The doctors can't find the problem or the solution, but it may be an abscess on the spine. She has been in hospital for 10 days and is expected to be there for another two or more weeks. She is really suffering.

Spent a very happy evening with the Uppmans and their daughter & son-in-law, and 2 ravishing grand-children, (Jenni) Furry and Jonathan. Furry is simply stunning, aged ?5.


*Saturday & Sunday* [26–27 August]

Two lovely days with sun, but too hot for me really. I strolled in the park and was fascinated by hundreds of runners round the park in a marathon (23 or 26 miles). Each Sunday this happens – no cars, no trucks – only bykes and horse-carts. Every sort of runner from the dazzling athelete to the ancient of both sexes. I can't believe the old things go all the way, but they certainly start. Indeed every morning from my window I watch the joggers doing their half hours or whatever.

---

[10]   Scottish bass (1922–1983).
[11]   English baritone (b. 1928) who sang with the EOG in the 1960s. Glossop recorded Billy Budd in Britten's Decca recording and in the 1966 BBC Television production of the opera.
[12]   American baritone (b. 1942) who made his Met début in 1975. See Plate 23.
[13]   American bass-baritone (b. 1947) who joined the Met in 1970. Although during the early part of his career he concentrated on the lyric Italian repertoire, he is most well known today for his authorative interpretations of Wagner's bass-baritone roles, most notably Wotan/The Wanderer in the *Ring* cycle.

The noise in the streets of N.Y. is more extreme than ever. A favourite device is to be black, & with your family & friends roam through the streets playing a large transistor at the top of its voice.

Opposite my window there are some benches, mostly occupied by ?tramps, one black man & a white woman, particularly at night. They often sleep there & leave a large litter of paper bags & old food. It gets cleared up & no one minds.

# Appendix

The following is a transcription of the original German text of Pears's diary of the 1959 Ansbach Bach Festival (see Chapter 3). Pears's German is left unedited as his idiosyncratic vocabulary and style adds much to the flavour of the piece.

*Juli.23*

*Donnerstag*: Im München um 8 uhr morgens pünktlich zu Sixt's Auto Hire-Service; nach ein ¾ stunde wartung (warum? frag' mich nicht) bin fort am weg in einer Opel "Olympia" (etwas Non-U, ich glaube). Es geht ziemlich gut, am rechten Seite der Autobahn, und ohne weitere incident bin ich in Neuendettelsau angekommen. Schöne wetter, schöne Landschaft, schöne Leute, und jetzt natürlich hier besonden gute Leute. Erste probe mit Richter; O.K; Ich finde dass ich habe eine von der Arien nich beobachtet, so muss ich es sicht-lesen (sight-read!) aber es ist nicht schwer und furchtbar schön; gut so! Am abend bin ich im Auto eine kleine spaziergang zu machen, zu Schwabach (sehr schön spät Gotisch Pfarrkirche, mit sieben Mädchen und 2 Junger Männer ein Gottes dienst singend – in die Plakate "Glaubet ihr nicht, Kommt ihr nicht". Ich zögerte.)

Wir essen zusammen, alle Musiker, in eine sehr warme Saal, voll mit Pflanzen & Bäume, und unsere Speisekarte ist etwas Schulweise, das heisst:

Dicke griessuppe,
Schweins cotelette mit Knödel
Birnen mit Schokolade Sauce.

Gut für wachsenden Tenöre!

*Freitag.* Noch zwei Proben für diesen furchtbar schwere Arien. Hoffentlich es wird gut gehen. Meine Collegen sind:

1. *Ursula Buckel* (Deutsch aber aus Gent) Sopran, mit seinem Mann. Bürgerlich reiz. Ihre wohnzimmer ist beige und spinat-grün, ich meine. Ich habe sie noch nicht gehört – singend.

207

2. *Hertha Töpper*, schöne altistin, nette Mensch, mit seinem Mann, sehr böse angesicht, ohne charm. (viellicht Isländer?)

3. *Keith Engen* bass, Amerikaner, mit seiner Frau (ist sie Deutsch oder Amerikanish?) nett aber langweilig.

Mit dieser ausgezeidnete Menschen muss ich noch um dreissig Mahlzeiten passieren! Du lieber Gott!

Heute abend's Menu:

Gefüllte Pfannkuchen mit Salat.
Käsebrot & Fleischbrot.
Punkt.

Am abend wird's Kühler. Man hört junge Protestanterinnen Mozart und Dussek übend. Eine leichte ferne Lachen. Zwei fünfzehnjahrige laufen herum die Gebaüde mit einen Kollegen auf eine Bicycle – sechsmal – siebenmal – jetzt zehnmal. Es ist nicht wie in Jokmotik, es wird dunkel. Die Schwestern sind schon in Bett – nur eine bleibt die ganze Nacht im Toalett, wahrscheinlich – weil sie ist immer da, wenn ich möcht' es.

*Samstag.* Um 6 uhr jeden morgen einer Last – Kraftwagen herumfahrt um die Ecke meiner Zimmer und weckt mich auf von Traümen. Um ½ 7 die Bauern folgen mit Ochsen; um 7 die Schwestern wässern die Blumen, und überall kommt ein ruhige Fleissigkeit. Um 7 uhr auch heute hat M. Nicolet zu üben angefangen. Er schläft in No. 8. Ich bin in No. 10. Aber er hat nicht gespielt in seinem zimmer. Er war weit, im Augustana Saal, 100 metre weit, aber ich konnte jeden Ton hören. So auf! ich nehme meine Frühstück 8 uhr und geh' im Aug. Saal nach M. Nicolet und übe von 8.30 bis 9.30. Dann probe. Gott wie schwer ist Bach, aber immer schön. Heute abend, die Hauptprobe in Gumbertuskirche. Ziemlich gut. Ich habe ein schöne Arie mit cello obbligato, und er spielt es sehr schön. "Sehr elegant" sagte ein Herr So-und-so Bachwochefreund, klein und schmall und etwas Englisch Typ, gesicht bekammt vom vorige Jahre. Nach abendessen (Spaghetti mit Fleisch, Käsebrot, dazu ¼ Wein nötlich) zu Bett.

Ein gesegnete Packete von der heilige Peg kommt heute mit zwei Horrors, Mozart-Briefe und Knut Hamsun; ein gut ausgeglichenes Menu!

APPENDIX

*Sonntag*

[Drawing by Pears: see p. 78]

Alles ruhig! Kein ochsenwagen! Nur glocken um 7 uhr – & Schwestern
zu Kirche – auch keiner Nicolet. Sehr faule Tag. Enorm mittagessen.

Dicke Suppe
Schwein mit Hundert Knödel
Weincrème

Schlaf. Um 5, eine halbe Stunde. übung – und dann umziehn fur den
ersten Cantaten Abend. Furchtbar heiss – habe wahnsinnig geschwitzt.
Wunderschöne musik – habe teilweise gut gesungen – gewohnte gesichte
– Frau Klarwein – Klaus Hoesch. Alte Pferdgesichte – grosse Damen.
    Nach dem Konzert hab ich mit Hans Ludwig und freundin gegessen
im Schwarzen Bock. Was fur erinnerungen an Lupeg, Mrs Clewes,
Yehudi etc.! Habe nicht Mrs C. gesehen. Nette abend.
    Richter etwas besser als eher, vielleicht er kennt die Cantaten nicht
so gut wie die Passionen. Auch man kann kaum diese übertreiben. Er
ist etwas böse mit mir dass ich bin fur Karfreitag in Hamburg engagiert,
statt München.


*Montag.* ½ 6 uhr ochsenwagen.
    Freies Tag. Bachlos – für mich. Nach eine stunde Übung (8.30 am
– 9.30) bin ich nach Nürnberg; zum ersten mal im Auto langsam
gefahren. Sehr heiss. Stadt furchtbar zerstört noch. Aber hab 3 sehr
schöne Kirche besucht.

1. Frauenkirche, schöne form, nichts besonders hinein, aber
lebendig west front.

2. Sebalduskirche. stark romanisch und hoch Gotisch zusammen.
schöne plastik, und eine sehr seltsam "Sebaldusgrab" vom 16te
jahrhundert Figuren von Classische Helden & Götter mit Heilige,
Putten & Barbarossa, tieren und engeln, Joshua und "Simson".
Es geht alles etwas zu weit, ich finde.

3. Lorenzkirche. glänzend weit stoss verkundigen und auch
ausdrucksvolle Crucifix.

Alle drei Kirche schön restauriert, (Gute Fische & Wein zu Mittagessen)

*Germanisches Museum:* sehr schöne Sache; fruh gotik Plastik, & diese fabelhaft Goldene Evangelienbuch von Echternach. Das ist etwas Keltische einfluss. Farbe noch wunderschön hell.

Um 4 uhr, todmüde, zurück nach Neuendettelsau.

8 uhr *Richter orgel Konzert* – in Heilsbronn Münster. Ganz neues Orgel, das ist halb caput im ersten stück. Ich habe mit Bischof Lilje gesessen. Reizender Mann, ausgezeichnete Englisch, sehr nett & complimentvoll zu mir. Hatte die Cantaten gehört. Habe nur zehn worten mit ihm wechselt, aber er hat eine grosser eindruck gemacht.

Nach ein kurze kleine Landduft-volle spaziergang mit den Altistin (und mann) zu Bett.

Die Frau von Keith Engen ist aus Wien! & wie!


*Dienstag* Lange morgen probe; es sollte Hauptprobe in Gumbertuskirche, aber er was besetzt von einen Bach gespräcer. Nachtmittags ruhe. noch ½ st. probe. Abends II Cantaten Konzert. Gewitter als ich nach Ansbach fahrte: etwas nervös, habe nicht sehr gut gesungen; schade! schöne arien; meine nette spinat & beige Sopran hat sehr schön ein wunderwolle Arie gesungen.

Furchtbar heiss.


*Mittwoch.* Freie Tag!

Das Wetter hat gebrochen. Grau überall. Es wird regen. Bonjour, M. Nicolet. Aber ich folge. ¾ Stunde übung. Nach dem Frühstück fort nach *Bamberg* über kleine strassen und Pommersfelden. Aber da waren so viel Umleitungen & die Strassen waren so oft gesperrt dass ich hatte niemals Pommersfelden erreicht. Immer müsste ich nach Bamberg fahren; und genau als ich haltete in Bamberg hab' ich gesehen dass meine vorne links Reime war flach! Gott sei dank dass es war nicht eine halb stunde früher in der mitte des Oberfränkischen Wald, auf schreckliche Strassen, in der Wüste! So während ich mittagessen nahm, meine Wagen war gepflegt – alles in ordnung. Aber ich war etwas nervös darüber, und verlass Pommersfelden. Zurück über Heilsbronn, wo war ein gutes kaltes helles!

Nicht zum Konzert. Zu bett früh nach ein sehr dumm & entäuschend Übung.


*Donnerstag.* Auch frei. Nicht zu machen, sonst BACH! Aber dass . . .

Ganze morgen übung. (Nicht im Prunksaal für Richter's Goldberg-Variationen.) Etwas weiter mit diesen schweren Arien.

Am abend ins Konzert im Orangerie. (Die Wienerin hat für mich einen Knopf angenähet (?) sehr reizend – sehr charmante.) Keilberth dirigiert Bach wie ein richtiger Bayerischer biertrinkend Bauer. Wenn Richter ist nicht unser "Tasse de Thé", was kann mann über Keilberth sagen? Ich zittere vor meinem "Matthäus" in Hamburg mit ihm.

Sehr begabte Geiger – Szeryng – auch Nicolet hat wie immer gespielt. In der Pause, hab' ich zeitlang zu Frau Rosenkrantz aus Wuppertal gehört. Sie plapperte, und schwatzte, und zwitscherte, und zirpte, und murmuelte und quickte. Ich glaube dass ich habe versprochen die Rosenkräntzen zu besuchen in November nach unsere Wuppertalscher Konzert. Was wird Ben sagen?

Nach dem Konzert, ein Empfang im Prunksaal. Sehr schön. Viel zu essen. Viel zu trinken. Mit enorme Frau Klarwein (zoll dame) gesprochen. Schwer zu verstehen. Mein Deutsh [sic] wird jedem tag schlechter & Frau K. hat wenig Englisch. Viele Leute schwarz angezogen. Wir sängern zusammen waren vielleicht ein kleines bisschen beschwipst. Ich habe sehr schnell zu hause gefahren. Ssst!

*Freitag.* Wetter bleibt kalt – regen – Gewitter. Lange Morgen proben und üben. Der Wein letzte nacht war nicht wirklich gut. Noch etwas probe nach schlaf nach mittagessen. Abends - III Cantaten Konzert. Noch einmal wunderschöne Musik. Ich dachte dass ich sang schlecht. Sopran hat sehr schön "Mein Gläubiges Herz" gesungen; es gibt ein entzükkendes nachspiel, so lustig, & leicht und klar. Wunderschöne J.S.B.

Nach dem Konzert, etwas zu essen & trinken mit Hans Ludwig. Sehr gemütlich und freundlich.

*Samstag.* Kalt, grau, hesslich. ½ 10 Probe, schwere Arien. Dann zu Ansbach in der renovierte Johannes Kirche. Gut gemacht, obwohl nicht genial. Schrecklich Moderne Tapisserie an der Wand. Gute Akoustik. Konzert von Thomaner Chor, aus Leipzig. Schönen stimmen, reizende Klang, aber Kurt Thomas zu langweilig als dirigent. Richter treibt immer, ist zu subjectiv, und hat mittelbar ohren. Thomas ist kühl & klar, objective, ohne musikalische empfindung. Welcher ist der beste? oder der schlechste?

Viel regen ganzen morgen. Ich war sehr nass. Dann mit Hans und nichte zu Rotenburg fur mittagessen & Creglingen und D.?–gen Riemenschneider Altaren zu sehen. Sehr schön, aber tausend scheussliche touristen überall, in autobusen etc. und regen, regen, regen. Etwas erkältet, zu bett, früh.

211

*Sonntag.* Der letzte Tag. Schade.
Ich verlange nach Aldeburgh zurück zu fliegen (etwas Bachtexte einfluss!) aber die Bachwoche ist immer ein Erlebnis, wahrlich. Dieser alte Protestant, so tief gegründet, so treu, auch so lieb, ist einer eigenartige kamerad – obwohl verdammter schwer zu singen!
    Nach dem Konzert, zurück nach Neuendettelsau. Aufwiedersehen, Schwestern, Diakonissen, Novizen, Alte, Jünge, Glocken, Blumen,
        zwei gläser Nackt-Arsch,
            ein letzte Käsebrot.
        Adiö
            Ursula
                Hertha
                    Keith
                        Adiö!
        Beide Karl –
            und beide Frauen.
        Bye-bye Bach

                    *******

    WELT ADE! ICH BIN DEIN MÜDE,
        ICH WILL NACH DEM HIMMEL ZU
    DA WIRD SEIN DER RECHTE FRIEDE
        UND DIE EW'GE, STOLZE RUH'.
    WELT! BEI DIR IST KRIEG UND STREIT
    NICHTS, DENN LAUTER EITELKEIT;
        IN DEM HIMMEL ALLEZEIT
        FRIEDE, FREUND' UND SELIGKEIT.

            Schluss choral: Kantate 27.
            "Wer weiss, wie nahe mein Ende"
                J.S. Bach

                    *******

GEDICHT

    Nonne? warum sind sie nicht
    Eva und Elsa und Elisabeth
    Unter diesen Bayreuthischen Sonne?
    Es war –ja? – ein Himmlisches G'schrei
    Nachklingend in diesen Sonntags Glocken
    Das hat ihrer so – blonden Seelen
    Einen Tag zu schwarz-weiss gefärbt.
    Tugendhaft, fromm, doch nicht kalt,

Tauft Ihr uns – so – in ihren Schatten
Eh'unsre Abendssonne wird plötzlich getrübt.

*Auch Diakonisse Thusnelde Schmid,
Leiterin des Kindergärtnerinnen seminar

# Personalia

The notes here supplement the information to be found in the footnotes to the main text. The page number at the end of each entry indicates the location of the main reference to the person concerned.

**Barbirolli, John** (1899–1970), English conductor, who was principal conductor of the New York Philharmonic Orchestra, 1936–42. In 1943 he returned to the UK to take up the post of conductor of the Hallé Orchestra in Manchester, a position he retained until his death. Barbirolli and the New York Philharmonic gave the premières of two of Britten's most important works from his years in the United States, the Violin Concerto, Op. 15, in 1940 (with Antonio Brosa as soloist) and the *Sinfonia da Requiem*, Op. 20, in 1941. [p. 13]

**Bean, Betty**, American music administrator and publisher. For many years Ms Bean worked in the New York office of Boosey & Hawkes, beginning as director of promotion, press and public relations. In 1949 she accompanied Pears and Britten on their coast-to-coast recital tour of the USA (see PFL, Plate 242) and subsequently remained in touch with both men. In the early 1970s she was director of press and public relations for the New York Philharmonic Orchestra. [p. 185]

**Bedford, Steuart** (b. 1939), English conductor and pianist closely associated with Britten's music, who joined the English Opera Group in 1967 making his conducting début with them in Britten's version of *The Beggar's Opera*. Bedford conducted the stage première of *Owen Wingrave* (Covent Garden, 1973), and the first performances of *Death in Venice* (1973), the *Suite on English Folk Tunes*, Op. 90 (1974), *Phaedra*, Op. 93 (with Janet Baker, 1976), and the revised version of *Paul Bunyan* (1976). He has been an artistic director of the Aldeburgh Festival since 1974. [p. 189]

**Bream, Julian** (b. 1933), English guitarist and lutenist. During the early 1950s he formed a distinguished recital partnership with Pears, exploring Elizabethan lute-song repertoire that led to a revival of interest in this music. Their partnership also influenced Berkeley, Britten, Henze, Tippett and Walton (among others) to write for voice and guitar. See also Tony Palmer, *Julian Bream: a Life on the Road* (London: Macdonald, 1982), pp. 167–9, and CHPP, pp. 173–4. [p. 19]

**Burra, Peter** (1909–1937), English writer on art, music and literature. He was a close friend of Pears and a key figure in his life from their schooldays (they were at Lancing College together, and at Oxford), and during 1936 Pears lived for a time in Burra's cottage, Foxhold, at Bucklebury Common, near Reading, from where he would commute to London as required. It was Burra's tragic death, the result of an aeroplane accident, that brought Pears and Britten into a closer relationship. Britten too had known Burra well and visited him at his cottage. (DMPR, pp. 479–81, and CHPP, pp. 17–66 passim.) [p. 14]

**Carson, Nellie**, second soprano of the New English Singers, and second wife of Cuthbert Kelly, the Singers' founder. In the early 1950s, after her husband's death, Carson revived the Singers for a brief time. She was the sister of the actress Violet Carson, well known to television audiences for her portrayal of Ena Sharples in Granada Television's long-running soap-opera, *Coronation Street*. Nellie Carson occasionally accompanied members of the New English Singers on the lute, Pears included. A review of a Wigmore Hall concert given by the New English Singers in February 1937, after their return from their 1936 North American tour (Chapter 1), noted that, 'She and Mr Peter Pears fascinated their hearers with John Bartlet's "Whither runneth my Sweetheart", and to Ford's "Fair, sweet, cruel", her solo song to her own accompaniment, she was forced to add another . . . Miss Carson seems to have caught something of the "heavenly touch" ascribed to John Dowland' (*The Times*, 20 February 1937). [p. 8]

**Coleman, Basil** (b. 1916), English opera producer who worked extensively with the English Opera Group in the 1940s and 1950s, and was responsible for the first stagings of Britten's *The Little Sweep*, *Billy Budd*, *Gloriana* and *The Turn of the Screw*. During the 1980s he worked alongside Pears in student productions of several Britten operas at the Britten–Pears School for Advanced Musical Studies. See also Coleman's 'Staging first productions 2', in David Herbert (ed.), *The Operas of Benjamin Britten* (London: Hamish Hamilton, 1979), pp. 34–43. [p. 100]

**Copland, Aaron** (1900–1990), American composer, whom Britten first met in London in 1938; Pears was not to encounter Copland until the following year in the United States. Britten's and Pears's friendship with Copland lasted until the end of their lives although it was, quite naturally, at its warmest during their years together in the United States (1939–42). In 1950 Copland 'newly arranged' his *Old American Songs* for Pears and Britten, the first performance of which they gave at that year's Aldeburgh Festival and subsequently recorded for HMV (DA7038–9). See Philip Reed, 'Copland and Britten: a Composing

215

Friendship', Aldeburgh Festival Programme Book 1990, pp. 28–9, and DMPR. [p. 191]

**Dalgat, Djemal** (1920–1992), Russian conductor, who did much to promote Britten's music in the Soviet Union. He conducted the first Russian (concert) performance of *Peter Grimes* in 1963 and two years later the first stage performances at the Kirov Theatre, Leningrad, and at the Bol'shoy Theatre, Moscow. In the early 1970s he conducted highly successful performances of *The Prince of the Pagodas*. In addition to his work as a conductor, Dalgat translated many of the texts of Britten's works into Russian, including *War Requiem* (published in the Soviet Union in 1968). [p. 125]

**Douglas, Basil** (1914–1992), English musical administrator. It was at the Charlotte Street flat shared by Trevor Harvey (q.v.), Douglas and Pears that the first documented meeting between Pears and Benjamin Britten took place in March 1936 (CHPP, p. 424, and DMPR, p. 519). The two-storeyed apartment was close to Broadcasting House where Pears and his flatmates were working at that time. Harvey was assistant chorus master of the BBC Chorus, and Douglas a tenor in the same chorus as well as being chorus librarian. Douglas was later involved in the English Opera Group (founded by Britten et al in 1947), as General Manager (1952–7). [p. 3]

**Fischer-Dieskau, Dietrich** (b. 1925), German baritone, with whom Pears first sang at Ansbach in the mid-1950s, and with whom he recorded Bach's *St Matthew Passion* in 1962. The solo baritone parts in *War Requiem*, Op. 66 (1962), and *Cantata Misericordium*, Op. 69 (1963), were written for Fischer-Dieskau, as was the Blake cycle *Songs and Proverbs of William Blake*, Op. 74 (1965), and he occasionally appeared at the Aldeburgh Festival in the 1960s and 1970s. [p. 107]

**Graham, Colin** (b. 1931), English opera director who joined the English Opera Group in 1953 as an assistant stage manager for *The Beggar's Opera*, and undertook his first production of Britten's setting of the Chester Miracle Play, *Noye's Fludde* five years later. This marked the beginning of a close professional relationship with Britten and Pears that resulted in collaborations on the first performances of the church parables, *Owen Wingrave* and *Death in Venice*. His association with the Sadler's Wells (later English National) Opera was to bring forth an important revival of *Gloriana*. In recent years he has lived in the USA, where he has directed the first revival since the 1950s of the original four-act version of *Billy Budd* (St Louis, 1992). See Graham's 'Staging first productions 3', in David Herbert (ed.) *The Operas of Benjamin Britten* (London: Hamish Hamilton, 1979), pp. 44–58. [p. 185]

**Habunek, Vlado** (1906–1994), Croatian theatre and opera director, who produced Britten's *The Rape of Lucretia* in 1952 and whose association with Britten's music was to continue when he directed *A Midsummer Night's Dream* at Zagreb in 1962, and *Curlew River* in the USA in the late 1960s. [p. 24]

**Harvey, Trevor** (1911–1989), English conductor. It was at the Charlotte Street flat shared by Harvey, Basil Douglas (q.v.) and Pears that the first documented meeting between Pears and Benjamin Britten took place in March 1936 (CHPP, p. 424, and DMPR, p. 519). Harvey was assistant chorus master of the BBC Chorus. Pre-war Harvey collaborated with Britten on two important radio features, *The Company of Heaven* (1937), in which Pears participated as soloist (Britten's incidental music included the first song specifically written with Pears's voice in mind), and *The World of the Spirit* (1938). Harvey was later involved in the English Opera Group (founded by Britten *et al* in 1947), as a conductor of *The Little Sweep*. [p. 3]

**Heinsheimer, Hans W.** (1900–1993), German-born publisher and writer on music. He was head of the opera department of Universal Edition in Vienna before his emigration to the United States in 1938. In America he was first employed by Boosey, Hawkes, Belwin, Inc., and then later by G. Schirmer, Inc., where he became director of the symphonic and operatic repertory. Britten had first met Heinsheimer in Vienna in 1934, and their paths again crossed during the composer's stay in the United States between 1939 and 1942 (see DMPR, pp. 355–6), and again in 1949 when Britten and Pears made a coast-to-coast tour of the United States and Canada. [p. 196]

**Hesse and the Rhine, Prince Ludwig of** (1908–1968) and his Scottish-born wife **Princess Margaret** (b. 1913). Pears and Britten were introduced to the Hesses by Lord Harewood (the Hesses' cousin) in the early 1950s. They became close friends and were in future years to undertake several overseas trips together (see, for example, Chapters 2 and 4), as well as becoming devoted supporters of the Aldeburgh Festival. Britten dedicated his *Sechs Hölderlin-Fragmente*, Op. 61, to Prince Ludwig on the occasion of his fiftieth birthday in 1958. Under his pen name – Ludwig Landgraf – Prince Ludwig made German translations of many of Britten's vocal works. [p. 39]

**Horder, Mervyn** (b. 1910), English 'gentleman composer', whose father was Physician in Ordinary to Edward VIII and George VI. Horder was a friend of Pears's from the 1930s and was one of a group with whom the singer holidayed abroad in the summer of 1937 (CHPP, p. 70). Horder later sat on the board of directors of the EOG. [p. 9]

**Hürlimann, Martin** and **Bettina**, directors of Atlantis Verlag, Zürich, who had commissioned, translated and published the first book on Britten's life and music, Eric Walter White's *Benjamin Britten: eine Skizze von Leben und Werk* (1948) which was subsequently published in English by Boosey & Hawkes. Bettina Hürlimann was a pioneering editor and publisher of children's books, and made a German translation of Britten's *Let's Make an Opera*. In 1957 she invited Britten to make a setting of a poem from *Des Knaben Wunderhorn* for her husband's sixtieth birthday: he responded the following year with his *Einladung zur Martinsgans*, an eight-part canon, for voices and piano (unpublished). See Bettina Hürlimann, *Seven Houses: My Life with Books*, trans. by Anthea Bell (London: The Bodley Head, 1976). In 1973, when Britten was awarded the Ernst von Siemens Prize, it was Martin Hürlimann who made the speech in honour of the composer (published in 1976 as 'Laudatio auf Benjamin Britten'). [p. 20]

**Jones, Parry** (1891–1963), Welsh tenor. Jones sang for the British National Opera Company and Covent Garden, as well as for the BBC for whom he took part in the UK premières (all concert performances) of Berg's *Wozzeck* (1934), Busoni's *Doktor Faust* (1937) and Hindemith's *Mathis der Maler* (1939). As a member of the post-war Covent Garden Opera, he sang Bob Boles in the 1947 production of *Peter Grimes* at the Royal Opera House (Pears sang the title role). [p. 5]

**Leppard, Raymond** (b. 1927), English conductor, harpsichordist and musicologist, who had occasionally worked at Aldeburgh in the 1950s. Although a coolness persisted for a number of years after Leppard became involved with Glyndebourne, this gradually faded and both Britten and Pears often visited him in Cambridge where he was a Fellow at Trinity College in the 1960s. After he left Cambridge, Leppard pursued a freelance conducting career: between 1973 and 1980 he was principal conductor of the BBC Northern Symphony Orchestra. He subsequently settled in the USA and took American citizenship. [p. 183]

**Ludwig, Professor Johannes** (b. 1904), German architect and friend of Princess Margaret, who taught at Munich University and with whom Pears occasionally stayed when in Munich. Ludwig and his wife, Belke, were for many years annual visitors to the Aldeburgh Festival, when they were often among the party of friends and colleagues staying at the Red House with Britten and Pears. [p. 79]

**McInnes, (James) Campbell** (1873/4–1945), English-born baritone who settled in Canada in 1919. McInnes sang the solo baritone roles at the premières of Vaughan Williams's *Sea Symphony* (1910) and *Five Mystical Songs* (1911), and was associated with Butterworth's *A*

218

*Shropshire Lad.* In Canada he founded several choral groups and continued his solo singing career where he was well known for his performance of the role of Christus in Bach's *St Matthew Passion.* On his death Vaughan Williams wrote, 'The death of Campbell McInnes recalls wonderful memories . . . of a lovely baritone voice, a fine sense of words and above all the power which few singers possess to make a tune live.'

McInnes' first wife was the novelist Angela Thirkell; their younger son was the writer, Colin MacInnes (the 'Mac' spelling was Colin's own later adaptation). See also Tony Gould, *Insider Outsider: The Life and Times of Colin MacInnes* (Harmondsworth: Penguin, 1986), pp. 14–21 and 59–64.

In June 1939, when he was in Canada with Britten, Pears sought out Campbell McInnes and had some lessons with him. Later that year Pears described McInnes and the lessons in a letter to Ursula Nettleship: 'Interesting and he is a very charming old man and wanted to be remembered to you and all his other English friends. I'm not sure that the lessons were enough to be of much use but I think he helped to loosen me up a bit. You will be pleased to hear that I am not frowning so much as I used to!' (DMPR, p. 731). In the same letter Pears mentions working with William Shakespeare's treatise *The Art of Singing* (1898–9), the use of which may well have been encouraged by McInnes as he himself had been a pupil of Shakespeare's. [p. 11]

**Manén, Lucie** (1899–1991), German soprano and teacher of singing. Manén's *The Art of Singing: a Manual* was published by Faber Music in 1974, accompanied by an illustrative disc specially for recorded for the publication by Pears and two of her other pupils, Elizabeth Harwood and Thomas Hemsley; Pears also contributed a preface to the volume. Manén participated in the founding weekend of the Britten–Pears School at Snape, in September 1972. [p. 171]

After the Venetian première of *Death in Venice* in 1973, Pears wrote to his teacher full of gratitude:

How incredibly lucky I was to 'find' you just at the time when I most needed you, and how wonderfully understanding you have been to me for how many years? It was all part of my 'destiny–fate–good fortune' that I should go to far-and-away the most intelligent teacher I had met just at the time when I was ripe enough to profit from her (and stand up to her!) And just as I thank my stars for so many things, so I thank you, dear Lucie, for all your help, your kindness, your courage, your warmth, your generosity, the example that you set us all. *Death in Venice* is obviously the peak of my career, and it is marvellous to have you there with me ... [Quoted in Manén's contribution to PPT, p. 60.]

**Mann, Thomas** (1875–1955), German novelist. The Manns were friends of Elizabeth Mayer (q.v.) both in Germany and in the United States where Thomas Mann had settled, like Mrs Mayer, in 1936. When Pears and Britten lived with the Mayers on Long Island in the early part of the war, they came into contact with the Mann family. Moreover, Mann's son, Golo, was for a time one of the extraordinary procession of residents at 7 Middagh Street, Brooklyn Heights, New York, the Brooklyn brownstone house where Pears and Britten lived in 1940–41 (DMPR, pp. 863–6). In 1973 Britten and Myfanwy Piper (q.v.) set Mann's novella *Death in Venice* (see Chapter 11). [p. 11]

**Mayer, Elizabeth** (1884–1970), who with her husband, the doctor and psychiatrist William Mayer, and their family – two sons (Michael and Christopher) and two daughters (Beata and Ulrica) – were to become the most important figures in Pears's and Britten's lives during their period in the United States between 1939 and 1942. For a full account of Mrs Mayer's friendship with Pears and (later) Britten, see DMPR, pp. 679–83. [p. 6]

Pears's flatmate, Basil Douglas, had studied German with Mrs Mayer in Munich, and her son Michael had visited the Charlotte Street flat when studying in England. In 1936 Mrs Mayer, accompanied by her youngest children, was emigrating to the United States where she was to join her husband; the half-Jewish Dr Mayer was already in the States having been banned from practising in Nazi Germany. Mrs Mayer left Hamburg on 5 November; the ship docked briefly in Southampton, where Michael Mayer, then in England, took the opportunity to go on board and spend a few hours with his mother. Basil Douglas had already written during the previous month to inform her of the extraordinary coincidence that his friend, Peter Pears, would be sailing to America on the same boat and entreated her to seek him out.

When Pears returned to the States the following year, again on tour with the New English Singers, he evidently renewed the friendship with Elizabeth Mayer when in New York. His pocket engagement diary for that year contains three entries of her name during the month of December, including New Year's Eve, and her address 'Amityville 2, New York' is hastily scribbled.

**Menon, Narayana** (b. 1911), Indian music administrator, writer and composer. As music adviser and producer of the BBC Eastern Service (1942–7) he became known for his understanding (rare at that time) of both Indian and Western art music. He was subsequently director of staff training (1948–63) and director general (1965–8) of All-India Radio, and was also the Secretary of the National Academy of Music, Dance and Drama, New Delhi (1963–5). Menon visited the Aldeburgh Festival in 1960. [p. 71]

**Mitchell, Donald** (b. 1925), English musicologist, critic and publisher, and his wife, **Kathleen** (b. 1916); both were close friends of Britten and Pears. From the outset Mitchell has been one of the most consistent champions of Britten's music, and his enthusiasm for the composer has been evident in a succession of books, articles, lectures and documentaries. He founded *Music Survey* in 1947, which he edited with Hans Keller from 1949 until its demise in 1952, the year in which he and Keller edited and contributed to an important early symposium on Britten, *Benjamin Britten: A Commentary on His Works from a Group of Specialists* (London: Rockcliff). Mitchell continued his critical writings in a number of journals, notably in *Tempo*, which he edited from 1958 until 1962, and the *Daily Telegraph* (1959–64), and after a spell as head of the music department of Faber and Faber, he was instrumental in the founding of Faber Music in 1964, the year in which they became Britten's publishers. He remained with Faber Music (managing director, 1965–77; chairman, 1977–87) until his retirement. In addition to his activities as a publisher, Mitchell was professor of music at the University of Sussex, 1971–6, and has pursued his scholarly interest in the music of Mahler in a significant sequence of analytical and critical studies. Mitchell was one of Britten's and Pears's executors, and is a Trustee of the Britten–Pears Foundation. *The Burning Fiery Furnace* is dedicated to him and his wife. [p. 186]

**Nash, Heddle** (1896–1961), English tenor. Apart from his work at Covent Garden and with the British National Opera Company, Nash was the mainstay of the early seasons at Glyndebourne where he was particularly noted for his interpretation of Mozart. In 1938, while a member of the Glyndebourne Chorus, Pears occasionally played the piano for Nash, an experience which he described in a letter to Britten as 'rather funny' (DMPR, p. 559). [p. 5]

**Perahia, Murray** (b. 1947), American pianist. After winning the 1972 Leeds International Piano Competition, Perahia was brought to Aldeburgh by Marion Thorpe (q.v.) where he attended what proved to be the last Pears–Britten recital at the Snape Maltings. When Perahia was appearing at the Edinburgh Festival the following year, Pears, who was singing Aschenbach at the same Festival, invited the pianist to accompany him in place of Britten (Britten's heart surgery in the spring of 1973 and the stroke he suffered at that time prevented his playing in public after that date). Until Pears's enforced retirement from the platform in 1981, Perahia often acted as his accompanist in repertoire that included lieder by Schumann and song-cycles by Britten. They recorded together a disc of Schumann lieder in 1979 (CBS 36668). Perahia was an artistic director of the Aldeburgh Festival, 1982–9. See also Perahia's contribution to Alan Blyth (ed.), *Remembering Britten* (London: Hutchinson, 1981), pp. 167–72, and PPT, pp. 70–71. [p. 187]

**Piper, Myfanwy** (b. 1911), English librettist and wife of the artist and stage designer John Piper (1903–1992). Mrs Piper wrote the librettos for three of Britten's operas, the adaptations from Henry James, *The Turn of the Screw* and *Owen Wingrave*, and *Death in Venice*. She has written perceptively about her association with the composer: see 'Writing for Britten', in David Herbert (ed.), *The Operas of Benjamin Britten* (London: Hamish Hamilton, 1979), pp. 8–21. [p. 194]

**Richter, Karl** (1926–1981), German organist, harpsichordist and conductor, who was appointed organist of the Thomaskirche, Leipzig (Bach's own church), in 1947. In the early 1950s he founded the Munich Bach Orchestra and Choir with whom he made recordings of the major works of Bach, including a cycle of church cantatas. See Nicholas Anderson, 'Karl Richter's Bach', sleeve note to CD recording of Bach Cantatas, Vol. 1 (Archiv 439 3692, 1993). In 1958 Pears was one of the soloists in a recording of three Bach cantatas conducted by Richter (Teldec 9031776142). [p. 75]

**Richter, Sviatoslav** (b. 1915), Russian pianist, who regularly appeared at Aldeburgh Festivals during the mid-1960s, when he would often be partnered by Britten (either as a second pianist, or as a conductor) and occasionally accompany Pears. In 1970, he recorded Britten's Piano Concerto, Op. 13, with the English Chamber Orchestra conducted by the composer. [p. 140]

**Rogers, Iris Holland** (d. 1982), a friend of Pears who shared a flat with Anne Wood (q.v.) during the 1930s. She was among a group of friends with whom Pears went on holiday in Europe on two occasions, in 1937 and 1938. A talented linguist, she lived and worked in Prague during the first part of 1938, where Pears visited her in March. Later, she made translations of Britten's French folksong arrangements and, for the English Opera Group in 1958, she and Pears collaborated on a translation of Monteverdi's *Il ballo delle ingrate*. Her verse translation of *Die schöne Müllerin* was used by Pears and Britten in programmes for their performances when sung in German. A photograph of her with Pears and Anne Wood in the Charlotte Street flat appears in CHPP, Plate 4. [p. 14]

**Rostropovich, Mstislav** ('Slava') (b. 1927), Russian cellist, pianist and conductor, who first met Britten in 1960. Britten was much taken with the warmth of Rostropovich's personality as well as with his remarkable cello-playing. The two men became close friends, with Britten

222

composing several works for Rostropovich: a Cello Sonata, Op. 65 (1961); the Cello Symphony, Op. 68 (1963); three solo Suites (1964; 1967; 1971); the Pushkin cycle, *The Poet's Echo*, Op. 76 (1965), for Galina Vishnevskaya (q.v.) and Rostropovich (as pianist); and, unfinished at the time of Britten's death, the Sitwell setting *Praise We Great Men* (1976). See also Rostropovich's 'Dear Ben . . .', in TBB, pp. 14–19, and his and Vishnevskaya's contribution to PPT, pp. 79–81. An account of Rostropovich's connections with Aldeburgh, Britten and Pears by Rosamund Strode, 'Britten and Rostropovich: an Aldeburgh perspective', appeared in the programme book for Rostropovich's and the London Symphony Orchestra's *Festival of Britten*, (London: Barbican Centre, 1993). [p. 100]

**Seefehlner, Egon** (b. 1912), Austrian musical administrator, deputy director of the Vienna Staatsoper under Böhm and Karajan, 1954–61. He was subsequently deputy, later director general, at the Deutsches Oper, Berlin, 1961–72, and returned to Vienna as general administrator of the Opera, 1976–86. Seehfelner played a significant role in securing the German première of *Death in Venice* for the Deutsches Oper, who first gave the work in September 1974. [p. 21]

**Sheppard,** the Very Revd **Hugh Richard** ('Dick') (1880–1937), English clergyman and peace-campaigner, who was among the founders of the Peace Pledge Union in 1936. Both Pears and Britten were members of the PPU, Britten as a sponsor from 1945. In 1947 Britten composed his *Canticle I: My Beloved is Mine*, Op. 40, a setting of a text by Francis Quarles based on the Song of Solomon, which received its first performance, given by Pears and the composer, at the Dick Sheppard Memorial Concert held on 1 November that year. [p. 10]

**Shirley-Quirk, John** (b. 1931), English bass-baritone. Shirley-Quirk joined the English Opera Group in 1964 to create the role of The Ferryman in Britten's *Curlew River*, going on to create roles in the other church parables, Spencer Coyle in *Owen Wingrave*, and the multiple bass-baritone role in *Death in Venice*. He also gave the first performance of Britten's de la Mare settings, *Tit for Tat* (1968), with the composer, and in 1971 was one of the dedicatees of *Canticle IV: Journey of the Magi*, Op. 86. He was a much-valued colleague of both Pears's and Britten's, with whom he also performed and recorded music by Bach, Elgar and Schumann, and has maintained his links with Aldeburgh and the Britten–Pears School at Snape. [p. 171]

**Silk, Dorothy** (1883–1942; killed in the Blitz), English soprano, who gained her reputation during the 1920s in London and at the leading provincial festivals, particularly as a sympathetic interpreter of Bach.

Between 1921 and 1926 she sang in a pioneering series of chamber concerts that included cantatas by Schütz and Tunder, repertoire that was unfamiliar at that time. Although Silk rarely appeared in opera, she sang with success in the first public performance of Holst's *Savitri* and thereafter became Holst's preferred soprano, taking part in the first performances of his *First Choral Symphony* (1925), the *Humbert Wolfe Songs* (1929) and the *Choral Fantasia* (1930). [p. 4]

**Stone, Janet** (b. 1912), Pears's distant cousin (they are both descendants of the prison-reformer Elizabeth Fry), wife of the artist and engraver Reynolds Stone (1909–1979). Although she originally trained as a singer, Janet Stone later became a photographer. A volume of her portraits, including photographs of Britten and Pears, was published by Chatto & Windus in 1988 under the title *Thinking Faces: Photographs 1953–1979*. [p. 18]

**Strode, Rosamund** (b. 1927), English musician, Britten's music assistant, 1964–76, and Secretary and Archivist to the Britten Estate/Britten–Pears Foundation until 1992. She was a key member of Britten's staff and has written several articles about her association with the composer and Pears, including 'Working for Britten (II)', in Christopher Palmer (ed.), *The Britten Companion* (London: Faber and Faber, 1984), pp. 51–61; and 'Reverberations', in PPT, pp. 89–90. She contributed an obituary of Pears to the *RCM Magazine*, 82/2 (1986), pp. 39–42. [p. 152]

**Thorpe, Marion** (b. 1926). The only child of Erwin Stein, Britten's publisher and adviser, she first met the composer in 1939; from the mid-1940s, when for a time the Stein family shared Britten's and Pears's London home, she became and remained an intimate friend of both Britten and Pears. She is Chairman of the Britten–Pears Foundation and one of Pears's executors. [p. 100]

**Uppman, Theodor** ('Ted') (b. 1920), American baritone, who took the title role in the première of Britten's *Billy Budd* at Covent Garden in December 1951. (Pears created the role of Captain Vere.) Uppman and his wife, Jean, maintained their friendship with Britten and Pears (see Chapters 11 and 12), and in the years since Pears's death in 1986 Uppman has taught occasionally at the Britten–Pears School for Advanced Musical Studies, Snape. [p. 86]

**Vishnevskaya, Galina** ('Galya') (b. 1926), Russian soprano, married to Rostropovich (q.v.). She first met Britten and Pears at the 1961 Aldeburgh Festival when she gave a recital at which she was accompanied by her husband. (At the 1963 Festival, Pears and the baritone Peter Glossop joined her in an operatic recital, with Britten accompanying.) Britten wrote the solo soprano part in *War Requiem* for her, although she was prevented from taking part in the première by the Soviet authorities (she later recorded it with Britten), and she was the first singer and joint dedicatee (with Rostropovich) of Britten's Pushkin settings, *The Poet's Echo*, Op. 76. In 1984 she published her auto-biography, *Galina: a Russian Story*. Like her husband, she made many appearances at Aldeburgh during the 1960s and 1970s, and was an annual visitor to the Britten–Pears School when Pears was Director of Singing Studies, where she has remained a much-valued teacher of the Russian repertoire. [p. 100]

**Warner, Sylvia Townsend** (1893–1978), English writer. In her later years she came into Pears's and Britten's circle via their mutual friends Reynolds Stone, the artist and engraver, and his wife Janet (q.v.), and a warm friendship with Pears ensued. *A Tribute to Sylvia Townsend Warner* was presented at the Jubilee Hall, Aldeburgh, as part of the 1977 Aldeburgh Festival, on which occasion Pears read from her stories and poems, and Kenneth Bowen (tenor) and Alan Bush (piano) performed settings of her poems, including Bush's song-cycle *The Freight of Harvest*, Op. 69. [p. 4]

**Wilson, Steuart** (1889–1966), English tenor and administrator, and a distant relative of Pears (he was the son of Pears's father's first cousin). He had been a founder member of the English Singers and was a distinguished Evangelist in Bach's *St Matthew Passion* and Gerontius in Elgar's oratorio, as well as singing in opera. After retiring from singing he taught at the Curtis Institute, Philadelphia (1939–42), returning to England to become music director for the BBC Overseas Service. He was music director of the Arts Council of Great Britain (1945–8) and then Head of Music at the BBC (1948–9). He was knighted in 1948. [p. 5]

In her biography of her husband, Margaret Stewart published an extract from a letter Pears had written to her about Wilson:

I didn't meet Steuart until about 1937–8, but I always heard his Evangelist before that whenever I could. He made a great impression on me and I owe a lot to him; indeed his Evangelist was what started me off . . . He gave me a lesson on the *St Matthew* in 1938, I think, very kindly. It was my ambition to follow in his footsteps in the Bach Passions. If I have done something in them, a large part of it is due to Steuart . . . When I started singing lessons in 1933 and professionally in 1934, he was the one English tenor who inspired me (I never heard Elwes or Coates) and I shall always be grateful to him.

[Margaret Stewart, *English Singer: The Life of Steuart Wilson* (London: Duckworth, 1970), p. 142.]

**Wood, Anne** (b. 1907), English contralto and a friend and colleague of Pears's in the BBC Singers during the 1930s. She was the other soloist in Pears's earliest commercial recording, a performance dating from 1936 of Warlock's *Corpus Christi Carol*, with the BBC Chorus conducted by Leslie Woodgate (Decca K. 827) (CHPP, pp. 53–4). She was one of a small, close circle of Pears's friends who all holidayed together in the summer of 1937 (CHPP, pp. 70–74). Post-war she was active in the formation of the English Opera Group of which she was General Manager (1947–51). In 1949 she founded, with Joan Cross, an 'Opera Studio' under the aegis of the EOG from which the National Opera School subsequently emerged. An accomplished singer of oratorio and frequent broadcaster, she took part in a number of important first performances, including the UK première of Britten's *Spring Symphony* in 1950. [p. 3]

# Index

Figures in italics refer to illustrations

227

# INDEX

INDEX

# INDEX

# Corrigenda

The original diaries, sometimes written in difficult conditions, are often a problem to read; the following emendations have come to light since the first printing. Instances where the sense has not been changed have not been noted, but a full list is held on file at The Britten–Pears Library.

All changes are shown in bold.

| | |
|---|---|
| Page 2, line 16 | Winnipeg **(23rd and 24th)** |
| Page 2, line 24 | At Carnegie Hall on the **18th** |
| Page 11, line 22 | Frau **M.** knew D.H. Lawrence |
| Page 24, line 2 | French **prov.** hotel |
| Page 24, line 21 | **Jugo Slavia** was absolutely **heavenly** |
| Page 26, line 32 | green trees, white clothes, **bright** saris |
| Page 32, line 8 | Malcolm Sargent **offered** to drape |
| Page 36, line 29 | some sort of **old** |
| Page 38, fn 60, line 1 | Robert (Robin) Woods **(1914–1997)** |
| Page 43, line 4 | bangs-**squeals**-tinkles-screeches |
| Page 52, line 14 | Lunch **Tang** Club |
| Page 54, line 15 | Britten told Roger Duncan (**21 February 1956**) |
| Page 54, line 17 | Peter **&** I had every **movement** photographed |
| Page 54, line 19 | *Next day* to NHK. **Furukaki** |
| Page 56, line 21 | Chanting solo: then 5 **dances** |
| Page 62, line 10 | Home **Kumagai** |
| Page 63, line 15 | **Furakuki** – Japanese meal |
| Page 66, line 22 | Excursion to **Negumbo**, bathing |
| Page 66, line 28 | the Colombo edition of the *Ceylon **Daily News*** |
| Page 67, line 10 | Buddha & **Ananda** |
| Page 67, line 32 | there & then drove back through the jungle to **Sigirya** |
| Page 67, line 44 | in this village **Sigirya, &** then |
| Page 68, line 3-4 | the cool of the **early** morning |
| Page 68, line 9 | (boy, tea, late, **thrown** over) |
| Page 68, line 36 | Tea with Suya **Senya** |
| Page 68, line 37 | Cake. Young men. **Senya's** own songs. (work) |

| | |
|---|---|
| Page 68, fn 98, line 2 | a bewildering **Indian** trick |
| Page 68, fn 98, line 3 | cards spread out in any **old** order |
| Page 71, line 9 | Sculpture. **Descent of Ganges**. Bathing. |
| Page 71, line 26 | Pictures of **Khano**. Lunch |
| Page 73, line 34 | young & a bit silly, violin a **very** adequate |
| Page 75, line 14 | all the musicians in a **very** warm hall |
| Page 78, line 14 | – old horsefaces – **grand** ladies |
| Page 78, fn 10, line 10 | "Meinen Jesum **lass** ich nicht" 124 we did at Bideford **years** ago |
| Page 79, line 15 | Sebalduskirche: **pure** Romanesque |
| Page 80, line 1 | Lorenzkirche: splendid **Veit** Stoss Annunciation |
| Page 80, fn 18, line 7 | Lovely arias for me – fair, not **fizzing** |
| Page 81, line 19 | sewed on a button for me, very **sweet** – very charming |
| Page 81, line 30 | (**[illegible word]** lady). |
| Page 82, line 8 | something to eat **and drink** with Hans Ludwig |
| Page 84, line 1 | Under this **Bayreuth** sun? |
| Page 86, line 25 | to regard [us] as some **guides** to a wider world |
| Page 86, line 27 | came & we ate again in the restaurant, delightful **pair**, intelligent |
| Page 87, line 14 | Jamini Roy of Tagore & Ghandi. **Could not** |
| Page 88, line 6 | nice company, **Mrs** Norman Butler |
| Page 88, line 7 | Mrs Cazalet **Keir** |
| Page 88, line 9 | K. **Kanna** |
| Page 88, fn 7, line 4 | **Naryana** Menon |
| Page 90, line 2 | early plane to Udaipur via **Jaipur** – Dakota. Picked up T. Cazalet **Keir** |
| Page 90, line 9 | well preserved statuary, **series** of lakes |
| Page 90, line 19 | we stayed 9 years ago: met $D^y$ H. Comm. |
| Page 92, line 19 | not *so* bad here. **Our** car ride |
| Page 94, line 23 | oleanders & **bougainvillas** |
| Page 94, line 37 | glorious view I have **ever** seen anywhere |
| Page 95, line 12 | eat meat, but **we** European |
| Page 96, line 6 | Indian wife, and **then later** they drove us |
| Page 96, line 22 | DOLCE **FARNIENTE Aranyia** Nivas |
| Page 97, line 12 | contralto practising in **her** |

| | |
|---|---|
| Page 106, fn 18, line 6 | the **pair of gentleman's** shoes |
| Page 106, fn 18, line 8 | his slippers **and** writing |
| Page 106, fn 18, line 18 | Slava **when** they could go to buy shoes, |
| Page 110, fn 26, line 7 | But it was nice to find that I **seem** to have **got the emphasis right, and have** caught something of the |
| Page 129, fn 58, line 3 | **Rostropovich's Aldeburgh** Festival recital, in 1961, a concert … |
| Page 130, line 2 | **they** played it superbly |
| Page 130, fn 60 | **It was Sar'yan's *Sunny Day* that was given to Britten and Pears. A photograph of Sar'yan presenting his painting to a grateful composer can be found in Edgar Oganesjan, 'Britten Days in Armenia', *Sovietskaya Musika*, 12 (1965), p. 110 (information from Professor Lyudmila Kovnatskaya, St Petersburg).** |
| Page 134, line 8 | 'Babyar' **text**, which had had |
| Page 143, fn 14, line 1 | Sir Kenneth (later, Lord) **Clark** |
| Page 144, line 23 | the applause seemed very **cool** to us |
| Page 148, line 38 | Dmitri's recent *Stapan Razin* |
| Page 151, fn 28, line 4 | the 1948 **musico-political** purge |
| Page 160, line 30 | next door at the **air-strip** and whizzes off **to** Martinique |
| Page 163, line 3 | Russian battering **ram** and paid |
| Page 164, line 21 | Creamy **cheesy confection** with |
| Page 168, fn 1, line 1 | to give a performance **the next day** of Britten's |
| Page 170, line 11 | The *St John* **next** day was dicey |
| Page 170, line 19 | The smell **on** |
| Page 170, line 21 | Hall is **surely** the *most* Victorian |
| Page 171, line 16 | Thursday morning I **had** promised to give a lesson; |
| Page 171, fn 17, line 2 | (at the age of **55**) |
| Page 173, line 7 | **suppose** that the dedicatee |
| Page 173, line 36 | had **rung a** young tenor[21] in London |
| Page 176, line 37 | and at 9 a **Manifestazione** di Folk-lore |
| Page 177, line 38 | outline by coloured **lights** |
| Page 180, line 28 | bulk to some extent covered his bearers **and proppers and his lights still blazed; the cross-bearers,** sweating and staggering on the |

| | |
|---|---|
| Page 182, line 4-5 | (probably dating from February **1975**) |
| Page 184, after line 15 (add missing line) | **I have a wretched sandwich in the coffee-shop.** |
| Page 184, fn 3, line 3–4 | Pears and Britten had **published an open letter in a programme for a** concert given in aid of pacifist causes; |
| Page 187, line 37 | Murray P. and **another,** *Slaughterhouse-Five,* by |
| Page 189, line 19 | *D in V* at 4 o'clock. **After a fair lunch in the Coffee shop, I rang him at 3.30 and confirmed our appointment. Went along and** spent a MOST VALUABLE 1¾ hours on *D. in V.,* |
| Page 191, line 14 | that German Expressionist Period – **somehow I have had.** It…. |
| Page 191, line 23 | Aaron! **So good to see him looking fine and as always. A dear sweet man.** |
| Page 191, line 31 | our little ones. **In the evening Terry McEwen rang & asked me to join him for dinner, & we had a v. pleasant dinner, with two of his friends Alan Davis who designs for Decca and Jim Pettit a Texan music-lover.** |
| Page 191, fn 26, line 7 | See also DMPR, pp. **394**–5. |
| Page 192, line 26 | **Everyone here is welcoming and kind and helpful; so nice.** In the afternoon |
| Page 193, fn 32, line 10 | And **Britten's** *Songs from the Chinese,* |
| Page 194, line 6 | Went shopping **with Myf, K & D** after lunch,… |
| Page 196, fn 41, line 1 | for which she interviewed **Myfanwy Piper,** Pears |
| Page 200, line 11 | pans so that **I cook** a |
| Page 200, line 17 | Some **uninteresting** younger |
| Page 202, fn 2, line 5 | **It** was very encouraging |
| Page 202, fn 2, line 7 | in some ways it seems **more** like a |
| Page 204, line 8 | (and Peter **Shaffer**) |
| Page 207, line 7 | **In** München um |
| Page 207, line 13 | hier **besonders** gute |
| Page 207, line 14 | Arien **nicht** beobachtet |
| Page 207, line 18-19 | dienst singend – **& eine** Plakate |
| Page 208, line 5 | Mit dieser **ausgezeichnete** Menschen |
| Page 208, line 18 | morgen einer **Lastkraftwagen** herumfahrt |
| Page 208, line 27 | die Hauptprobe **im** |